I'LL MEET YOU THERE

Other Books by Heather Demetrios

Something Real

I'LL MEET YOU THERE

Heather Demetrios

Henry Holt and Company
New York

Henry Holt and Company, LLC
Publishers since 1866
175 Fifth Avenue
New York, New York 10010
macteenbooks.com

Library of Congress Cataloging-in-Publication Data
Demetrios, Heather.
   I'll meet you there / Heather Demetrios. — First edition.
        pages   cm
   Summary: Skylar Evans, seventeen, yearns to escape Creek View by attending art school, but
after her mother's job loss puts her dream at risk, a rekindled friendship with Josh, who joined the
Marines to get away then lost a leg in Afghanistan, and her job at the Paradise motel lead her to
appreciate her home town.
   ISBN 978-0-8050-9795-5 (hardback) — ISBN 978-1-62779-292-9 (e-book)
[1. Coming of age—Fiction.   2. Family problems—Fiction.   3. Love—Fiction.
4. Friendship—Fiction.   5. Amputees—Fiction.   6. People with disabilities—Fiction.
7. Hotels, motels, etc.—Fiction.]   I. Title.   II. Title: I will meet you there.
   PZ7.D3923Ill 2015   [Fic]—dc23   2014035851

Henry Holt books may be purchased for business or promotional use. For information
on bulk purchases, please contact the Macmillan Corporate and Premium Sales Department
at (800) 221-7945 x5442 or by e-mail at specialmarkets@macmillan.com.

First Edition—2015 / Designed by Ashley Halsey
Printed in the United States of America by R. R. Donnelley & Sons Company, Harrisonburg, Virginia

10 9 8 7 6 5 4 3

For Mom, Dad, and Papa

Out beyond ideas of wrongdoing and rightdoing,
there is a field. I'll meet you there.

When the soul lies down in that grass,
the world is too full to talk about.
Ideas, language, even the phrase each other
doesn't make any sense.

—*Rumi*

JUNE

chapter one

The Mitchells' backyard was packed, full of recent and not-so-recent grads in various stages of party decay. The girls leaned against one another, wilted flowers that looked on while the guys got louder, sweatier.

I craned my neck and scanned the crowd for Chris, but my wingman had disappeared.

"Shit," I muttered.

Like I needed any more confirmation of my loner status. I moved purposefully through the crowd, on a mission. The last thing I wanted was to have some drunk dude notice I was alone and try to hit on me.

A girl to my right stumbled, spilling her beer on my All Stars. I had to reach out an arm to steady her before she stabbed me in the toe with her stilettos. I sighed and shook my foot.

"Thanks!" she said, more to the air than me, as she turned back to the knot of girls beside her.

"Skylar!"

I turned around—Chris was over by the keg. When I raised

my arms like, *WTF*, he turned over his empty cup, then made a sad face and pointed to the line of red-faced guys in front of him. Obviously he hadn't taken me very seriously when I'd said, *Let's get out of here as quickly as possible.*

I pulled out my phone and started texting Dylan while I made my way to Chris. Knowing her, she was probably in the back seat of her boyfriend's beat-up Chevy Malibu, but I wanted Brownie points for coming out at all. Really, I was only here to see Josh Mitchell, this Marine I used to work with who had just come home from Afghanistan. I could have waited to see him some other time, but it seemed like a dick move; someone comes back from fighting a war, you go to their homecoming party.

U still here? Looking for Josh.

No answer.

People stumbled through the Mitchells' back door, probably looking for the bathroom or somewhere to hook up. Every now and then, someone would wander out grinning stupidly from Reggie Vasquez's hastily rolled joints. Linkin Park blared inside the house, and I wondered what the night would feel like if someone switched the soundtrack from angry kick-the-shit-out-of-stuff to Ben Harper or the Chili Peppers.

I stopped by the doorway when I saw a flash of long blond hair, but it wasn't Dylan so I backed away, ignoring the *what's she doing here* looks people were shooting at me. They weren't mean-girl looks—I just didn't belong. Didn't want to.

Drunken laughter erupted from groups of partiers at regular intervals, but not because anything was funny. It was like laughter was just something you were supposed to *do*. I scanned the faces around me: the usual crew of locals from my high school. There were also a lot of slightly older faces—Josh Mitchell's friends, partying with the teenagers, doing the same thing they had done every Saturday night since they were in junior high: Drink. Smoke. Screw. Repeat.

Chris walked toward me, sipping on his frothy beer as he picked his way across the lawn. He was wearing the shirt I'd given him for graduation, the words *mathematician* and *ninja* under the heading CAREER GOALS. He held out a can of Coke like a peace offering.

"Dude, *you never, never leave your wingman*," I said. "Didn't you learn anything from *Top Gun*?"

I had this thing about *Top Gun*—it was my dad's favorite movie, and I'd been obsessed with it since I was six.

"I told you I was getting a beer! I thought you were behind me when I made the turnoff at the kitchen." He gave me the puppy-dog eyes that always got me laughing, and I grabbed the Coke, trying to keep my lips from turning up.

"Well, thanks for this." I hit the can against his plastic cup. "To graduating," I said.

"Hell, yeah, to graduating!"

It had only been three hours since the ceremony ended, but it looked like any normal Creek View night. I shouldn't have expected it to feel different. I knocked the Coke back like it was eighty proof, keeping my eyes peeled for Josh Mitchell.

It'd been no surprise when Josh joined the Marines two years ago. Like most of the guys in Creek View, his choices had been limited: the military, truck driving, or crappy part-time jobs along the highway. We lived in a blink town—blink and you'll miss it—off California's Highway 99. It was just a trailer park, a few run-down houses, a couple of businesses that barely made enough to keep their doors open, and the Paradise Motel (aka my part-time job).

Though we'd worked together at the Paradise and I'd grown up around him, I'd been weirdly shy when Josh came up to me in his uniform, his head all shaved, calling me ma'am. I'd asked if he was scared, and he said no, that this was as good as it would get for him. He couldn't wait. For a minute we'd just looked at each other and then I kissed his cheek—which surprised both of us—and told him good luck. Then he was gone.

"Have you seen Josh yet?" I asked.

Chris shook his head. "No, but I wasn't going out of my way to hang out with a jarhead the night of my graduation."

"Insensitive much?"

Chris snorted. "Josh Mitchell is a dick. I'm only here for the free booze."

"That's pretty much why everyone's here," I said.

"True that. Listen, since we're stuck in this backyard until the American hero graces us with his presence," Chris said, "I vote we get shit-faced and freak out the squares. We can tell our grandkids how we got all crazy when we were youngsters."

This was our little joke, calling the Creek View kids *squares* when I'd never had a sip of alcohol in my life and we were probably the only virgins over the age of sixteen in our zip code.

"I bet you'll look good with bifocals and a walker," I said. "Grandpa Chris." A smile sneaked onto my face.

"You having a moment?" he asked.

"Yeah, I'm having a moment."

"Nice."

I'd been like this all night; we'd be doing whatever and then

I'd remember we were finally getting out of Creek View. Hopefully for good. And I'd get these mini joygasms, like, *yes.* Even the girl throwing up into an overflowing trash can a few feet away couldn't really kill the buzz of satisfaction that had been humming inside me all day.

I took another sip of my Coke, then set it on a broken lawn chair. "But me getting sentimental doesn't mean I want to waste any more of my life at this party. Josh has gotta be here somewhere."

"Mitchell!" a voice yelled over the crowd. "Hook me up!"

Wrong Mitchell.

Blake, Josh's brother and my sort-of ex, was walking through the back gate, a twelve-pack of Bud on his shoulder and another one dangling from his hand.

Why, why, *why* had it seemed like such a good idea to hook up with Blake after an entire adolescence of pretty much zero boy action? And *Blake,* of all freakin' people!

As if reading my thoughts, Chris patted me on the back. "Hey, you could have done worse. Imagine if you'd spent spring break making out with *Josh* instead of Blake? You chose the better brother by far."

I glared at him. "*Not* comforting."

It was still hot, but a cool breeze swept through the party, and I rubbed my arms to erase the goose bumps that scattered across my skin. California tricks you like that—a scorching hot day, and you still need a sweater once the sun goes down.

"This is the most anticlimactic graduation night in the history of graduation nights," I said.

"Agreed."

"What's up, bitches?"

I turned around: Dylan was dancing her way toward us, shaking her hips to the music. Whoever was playing DJ had switched from Linkin Park to hip-hop.

"Hey, Mama." Chris whistled, and Dylan did a little pirouette as she got closer.

"Hey, hey," she said.

"Where's Seanie?" I asked, my eyes automatically straying to Dylan's left hip.

Sean was Dylan's six-month-old. I'd been helping take care of him, insisting on Dylan doing her homework so that we could graduate together, on time.

"The little man is with his grams—probably watching so much *CSI* he's gonna become the youngest serial killer in the history of murder, but whatever. This mama had to get out."

A stab of sadness shot through me at the thought of saying good-bye to Dylan at the end of the summer. Dylan had been my neighbor since we were little, but she became family after she punched someone in the face for calling my daddy a drunk. That someone had been our Sunday school teacher. I'll never forget how nine-year-old Dylan had rolled her eyes at the blood spewing from our teacher's nose, then turned to me and said, "She puts the *trash* in white trash, huh?" It was a favorite saying of her mother's.

I didn't want to think about days without Dylan's brassy commentary on everything from tamales to tampons. I had the urge to grab her in a bear hug, but I didn't know how to explain missing her while she was standing right next to me.

Dylan looked over her shoulder, then leaned forward. "Did you hear about Lisa?"

I shook my head, but Chris just stared fixedly at Dylan's

forehead, avoiding looking at her chest with the same concentration he'd applied to his AP Calculus homework.

"Dylan, you are super boobalicious. You should cover those things up—they've got to be illegal in all fifty states," I said.

Dylan laughed and shook her chest. "Hey, I'm enjoying the perks of motherhood. Besides, it's just Chris."

"Thanks," he muttered.

Just Chris.

If she knew he'd been in love with her since the days we played with Power Rangers and Barbies, she might not say shit like that.

"Okay, so check it out." Dylan lowered her voice even though someone had just turned the music up even higher—some dude rapping about how I needed to bend over. *God.*

"Lisa eloped with Raul right after graduation, and her dad is, like, freaking out. He's all, 'If I see that wetback, I'm going to cut off his—'"

"Yo," said Chris. "Brown boy standing *right here.*"

"Christopher, I'm *quoting* the racist bastard," Dylan snapped. "Hello? My son's half Latino."

"Just call it the W-word," Chris said. "How hard is that?"

"*Anyway,*" said Dylan, rolling her eyes, "you guys are lucky to see me alive. Her dad was at Ray's, literally waving around a butcher knife. I refused to take his order. I was like, I'm too young to die, you know?"

"Dylan!" someone shouted.

She looked across the yard: Jesse Hernandez, aka Dylan's baby daddy, was waving her over. "Gotta go get some," she said.

Chris's hand tightened around his red cup. "One baby's not enough?"

Dylan patted the pocket of her skirt. "Oh, we learned our lesson. I came prepared." She looked back over her shoulder and began edging away. "You guys hanging around?"

"Do we ever?" I asked.

"There's a first time for everything." She fluttered her eyes at me. "Remember what we talked about."

"*Dylan!*" I swatted at her, but she was already too far away. She was currently making it her life's mission to get me to third base before I went off to San Francisco State.

Chris stared after her until she was lost in the crowd.

I socked him in the arm. "Eyes on me, *amigo.*"

"What?"

"You know what. Why do you torture yourself like that?"

A thick pair of arms came from behind me, and I started as they wound around my waist.

"Hey, you," whispered a low voice, lips against my ear. I knew who it was—I'd spent a week drenched in that smell. I swear to God, Blake must have poured on half a bottle of Curve just before the party.

"Blake," I said, "go hug your girlfriend if you're feeling sentimental."

I tried to maneuver out of his grip, but he had the strength of a man who'd already downed a six-pack. There's nothing worse than getting affection from drunk people. It's almost as bad as if someone had paid them to be nice to you.

"But I want to hug *you*," he said.

Chris snorted, and I gave him a look loaded with dire promises. He just rolled his eyes and took a long drink of his beer.

"Blake, I'm, like, two seconds away from using self-defense on you," I said.

He laughed, soft, and loosened his hold just a little. "I miss you."

I gripped his arms and pulled them off me. "That's your Budweiser talking. We lasted a week—you can't miss me after seven days. Besides, I'm sure Alexis loves when you're all up on other girls."

Out of the corner of my eye, I noticed his girlfriend staring at us, her glossy lips turned into a frown.

"*Sky*," he said, as if I were being unreasonable. Then he grinned, like we had a secret, which we didn't.

He caught sight of Chris and raised his hand for his half of the obligatory fist bump. "What up, dude?"

Chris hesitated, then hit his knuckles against Blake's. "Hey, man."

"Fuckin' graduation, huh? I'm glad that shit's over." Chug, chug, chug: half his beer down his throat in seconds.

Chris and I proceeded to have an eye conversation that went something like this:

What the hell did you see in him?

Nothing, I don't know, shut up.

I pled temporary insanity to Dylan and Chris after that week of ill-advised hooking up, even though I knew better. It'd had nothing to do with Blake.

"Hey, is your brother around?" I asked. "We wanted to say hi, see what's up with him."

Blake wiped the back of his hand across his mouth and looked around the yard. "Yeah, somewhere. Probably inside or something."

"When does he have to go back?" I asked.

Blake shrugged and started peeling the label off his bottle. He wouldn't meet my eyes. "Not sure."

Chris elbowed me, and I elbowed him back. I thought we were having another secret conversation about Blake, but then he elbowed me again and whispered, "Sky."

I looked in the direction Chris was staring.

"Hey, Skylar. Long time no see."

The voice was familiar, but I barely recognized the person in front of me. In the dark, all I could make out was a shaved head and gaunt face, but then I saw the eyes. Those were what tipped me off. They were Van Gogh eyes—swirls of dark and light blue. All the Mitchells had them.

"*Josh?*"

He smiled, but there was nothing behind it. His eyes were glazed over, two bottomless wells that reflected the kitchen lights but held none of their own.

"Yeah, if you can believe it."

I looked at Blake, almost for confirmation, but he'd gone back to peeling the label off his bottle, his shoulders hunched and lips set in a hard line. The place between expectation and reality had instantly become so wide that I couldn't see to the other side of it. There weren't any words I could build a bridge with. Words didn't mean shit.

"Welcome home," I whispered. At least, I think I did. I felt my lips move.

Josh opened his arms for a hug, but as he moved forward,

his body jerked to the side in an awkward limp. I looked down and choked on the air.

His leg. He'd lost his leg.

———————

Fuck. God, God, fuck.

"Like it? It's my souvenir from the Taliban," Josh said, giving a slight kick with the metal cylinder that used to be his left leg.

All I could think was: Josh squatting by the Paradise pool, his bare feet leaving wet footprints on the concrete; Josh on the roof of the motel, looking out over the orchard and saying, *Dare me to jump?*; Josh walking toward me, tall and proud in his uniform but trying to be cool, like it was no big deal.

"Now I can be a goddamn pirate or something, right?" he said. "Got the peg leg and everything."

"Shit." Chris breathed.

Josh shrugged. "Shit happens."

I had to tear my eyes away from the metal pole that began somewhere under Josh's khaki shorts and ended inside a tennis shoe. I was like those drivers out on Highway 99 who felt compelled to slow down and stare when there was an accident. *Lookie-Loos.* The more gruesome the wreck was, the slower the Lookie-Loos drove, their eyes drawn to the thick pools of blood and shimmering shards of glass that spread across the asphalt like a Jackson Pollock painting.

I lurched forward and hugged him, holding my breath as his arms went around me. He reeked of whiskey, weed, and rank sweat. It was a stiff, graceless hug—me trying not to accidentally kick his leg, him trying to stay balanced. I wanted to kill someone. Whoever had done this to him, his parents for telling him he should go, the president. It was the sickest thing I'd ever seen, this man-boy whose whole life was screwed.

"This is so fucked up," I whispered.

Words.

His breath caught, and he let out a raspy "yeah."

A bridge.

We stayed like that for a few more seconds, then I pulled away. Chris was staring at Josh's leg, and I hoped I didn't look like him, so shell-shocked. Blake was still pulling at the label on his empty bottle, letting the torn pieces flutter to the dead grass at his feet.

"So you're home now? I mean, for good?" I asked.

"Don't know." Josh frowned. "What about you? How's the motel?"

"Same, same," I said.

It seemed like those long days working together at the Paradise were a million years ago.

"I believe it." He turned to Chris, as if he'd noticed him for the first time. "What about you, faggot? You still playing with computers and shit?"

Chris's eyes flashed, and he opened his mouth to reply, but then Josh clapped him on the back.

"I'm just fucking with you, man. You're all right."

I could almost see the debate in Chris's head: is it, in fact, morally reprehensible to deck a one-legged dude who's been fighting for his country?

It got quiet then, the air oozing awkwardness. All I could think about was that leg, blown to bits.

"You need a drink," said Josh, pointing to my empty hand.

He called out to a girl in super short shorts and a crop top—it took me a minute to realize it was Josh's thirteen-year-old sister, Tara.

"Baby girl, hook us up with some beers, will you? And put on some goddamn clothes."

Tara rolled her eyes and headed over to the coolers.

I shook my head. "I'm okay."

Josh gave his brother a knowing glance. "Ah, still a good girl, I see."

"*Dude*," growled Blake.

Our town was so small that even a guy who'd been in *Afghanistan* knew about our stupid fling.

"Get your head out of the gutter, Josh," I said.

"Um, that's impossible." Blake's lips turned up just a little. Josh snorted in response—for a second, we forgot about the leg. Seemed to, anyway.

"Josh! Get over here, soldier!"

He turned around and gave a thumbs-up to a bong raised high in the air. A group lay sprawled on the grass a few feet away, staring at the sky. Josh turned to us and shrugged.

"Duty calls. See you later."

He gave us a lazy salute and then limped away, his fingers groping the darkness, as though he were trying to take hold of the night's hand.

Blake cleared his throat and looked away, toward the garage that was filled with guys playing beer pong. I stole a glance at him. For the first time I noticed his tense shoulders and how his clenched teeth made the lines of his jaw sharp and pointed.

"I'm sorry about your brother," I said. Josh was nineteen years old. *Nineteen years old.* I reached for Blake, because right then he looked like a little boy trying not to cry, but Alexis was still staring jealous-girlfriend daggers. My hand dropped against my thigh, slapping the skin.

"He'll be okay. He's tough." Blake threw his beer in the general direction of the trash cans lined up along the fence. "You gonna be around for a while?" he asked, scanning the packed yard. "I gotta resupply the coolers."

"I don't think so. I'm pretty wiped out from the ceremony."

Strange. It was only a few hours ago that Mom had given me a bouquet of wilted carnations dyed a bright, unnatural blue to match our school colors. Seeing Josh had turned it into a distant memory. The war had come home, and it was ugly and senseless, and I just wanted to be in my bed, to be anywhere but here, really.

Blake grunted, and I risked putting my hand on his arm. "When did you guys find out about . . . you know?"

"January." He shoved his hands deep in his pockets and looked up at the starless sky. "He was in some hospital in Maryland for like six months, doing rehab or whatever, but he didn't want any of us to visit him. Then he was in San Diego, doing whatever guys like him do on a military base. He made my mom promise not to tell anyone."

"Shit," Chris said again. It seemed to be his only response.

"Blake, I—"

But I didn't know what to say. It seemed like I should have guessed. How could you kiss someone every day for a week and not know his family was going through hell?

"S'okay. He's a Mitchell. He can take it."

Tara waved him over from one of the empty coolers. "I've gotta motor, but, you know, thanks for coming. I know this isn't your scene."

I nodded, surprised he realized that, and he went toward the house. I glanced at Josh again; I didn't know if it was because it was so sad—all of it, all of *us*—but my vision started to blur.

"Let's get the hell out of here," I said.

Chris's face was all kinds of relieved. "Lead the way."

People were starting to pass out on the grass, and couples were peeling away, leaning into each other as they stumbled to their cars. For a second, I was jealous. I wished I had someone I could lose myself in. I watched Blake maneuver through the crowd, saw Alexis slip her arm around his waist. Pot and cigarette smoke hovered above the party, covering the wasted youth of Creek View with a thick, pungent haze. It was like the whole town was swimming in failure, but no one realized they were drowning. I turned my back on everything I never, ever wanted to be and headed toward the chain-link gate near the driveway.

"Hell," Chris muttered. He stopped for a moment and looked back.

I followed his eyes. "Yeah," I said, my voice soft.

I could just make out Josh, leaning on his real leg, surrounded by the bodies of whole people. All I could think about were those words he'd said, just before he left for Afghanistan: *This is as good as it gets for me.*

JOSH

I get that Vonnegut line now, got it after that sniper wasted Sharpe but *really* get it now—broken kite. *This isn't a man. It's a broken kite.* Flew all the way from Afghanistan and crashed in the middle of fucking nowhere, right back where I started except minus a goddamn leg. Major combat stress. But this is my welcome home party, so I gotta look happy and fuckin' mingle. This dude I knew in high school comes up to me, and he's all *Hey, man, what's up* and shit, and then we sort of shake hands and drink beer and watch the party.

So what's it like over there? You get to kill some Iraqis?

Afghanis.

Yeah, yeah, whatever. So . . . what's it like, man?

What's it like? It's seeing your friend die and then trying to scrub his blood off your boots except it won't come out. The water turns pink and your hands are shaking and you've got what's left of someone you were just standing next to under your fingernails and you need these boots for inspection so they gotta get clean, they gotta get clean, and suddenly you're angry, so fucking angry, *stupid bastard had to die all over me,* and then you're crying like a fucking baby and the boots are red and there's nothing you can do.

But I just say, *Crazy, man. Crazy.* Then I belch and hold up my empty beer bottle and say, *Gotta refuel. I'll catch you later. Good seeing you, bro.*

Fist bump.

Clap on the back.

Exit.

chapter two

I only saw Josh once during that first week after graduation. I was at Ray's Diner, picking Dylan up. I'd just gotten off from the motel and was groggy because Amy had called in sick so I'd been there for eighteen hours and had to deal with one pissed-off trucker who'd gotten a flat, two hippies who I'd caught smoking weed by the pool, and a woman from LA who spent most of the morning complaining about her room. The diner was oppressively hot, and from the fans set up on the counter, I could tell that the air-conditioning had broken again. The blinds were half closed, and flies buzzed around the pastry case, which only had two questionable-looking cinnamon rolls in it. It was just after the lunch rush, so most of the booths were empty. Because Dylan was the only waitress on, everything was clean and organized—you wouldn't have known it by looking at her, but she was an absolute neat freak. As soon as Dylan saw me, she started taking off her apron and pointed to the back, and I nodded, getting ready to sit at the counter and wait while she sorted out her receipts and tips.

Then I saw Josh.

He was sitting at one of the cracked vinyl booths by himself, pushing steak and eggs around on a plate, staring out the grimy window. I remembered he used to come in with his friends, taking up two or three booths, so loud that you either had to join them or find another place to eat. Josh was always between two girls—different ones each time—who he pretty much ignored in order to do the male-bonding thing. The status of guys in our town rose and fell on those nights, and it all came down to who Josh laughed with and who he laughed at. He was never cruel, not the kind of bully they warn you about in school assemblies. He was just the final answer in whether or not you belonged.

Josh and I had never been what you'd call friends, but I'd worked with him at the Paradise since I was fourteen, and that counted for something. Besides, while Dylan was in the back, I couldn't just pretend I hadn't seen him. Creek View's not that sort of town—it's what my dad called a "shoot-the-shit" kind of place. I went up to the booth and leaned against the side opposite him.

"Hey."

He looked up, blinking, like he'd been somewhere else and had forgotten where *here* was.

"Skylar," he said, after a moment. "What's up?" His smile slid all over his face, like it couldn't make itself comfortable.

"Not much. How's it going?" Dumb, dumb, *dumb* question to ask someone who'd just lost his leg.

He took a long sip of his Coke. "I'm hot as hell. You?"

"Same." I was wearing my usual summer attire of cutoffs, tank, and flip-flops, but I would have joined a nudist colony just to peel them off.

"You look good," he said.

His eyes traveled down the length of me—typical Josh Mitchell move—and when I caught him and raised my eyebrows, his lips twitched and he took a bite of his eggs.

I swear, the Mitchell boys were raised on *Playboy* while the rest of us normal kids were reading Dr. Seuss.

"I look like crap," I said. "You've just spent the past two years with a bunch of dudes. I bet you'd hit on Marge if you had the chance."

Marge, our boss at the Paradise, was in her fifties and what you'd call a "large" woman.

Josh laughed, sort of. "I don't know about that."

"Okay, I take that back." I grimaced a little. "I really don't want that picture in my head anymore. Actually, when you think about it—which maybe you shouldn't—"

"No, I really don't want to." He shook his head.

"Okay, but if you *did* want to think about it—like maybe on a particularly lonely night—it's kind of kinky. You and Marge would make quite an interesting pair."

"I've been home for, like, two seconds, and you're already cracking one-legged sex jokes?"

"It wouldn't be a joke to Marge."

"That's nasty, Sky."

"Although maybe you should wait to hit on her until you get a tan or something. You're looking kinda pasty right now."

Finally, a real laugh. I felt my body relax: shoulders going down, hands unclenching. I hadn't even realized I'd been tensing every muscle in my body until I suddenly wasn't.

He shook his head again, then looked down at his plate and

focused on cutting his steak. "Trust me, I look amazing com-
pared to a few months ago."

What could I say to that? What were the lines you weren't
supposed to cross in these sorts of conversations? It seemed like
there needed to be a whole other language for what had happened to Josh, one that didn't need words to clog up what you
were trying to say. *I'm sorry. This sucks. Hang in there.* None of
it was right. I sat down across from him, folding my legs under
me. I couldn't stand seeing that booth swallow him up.

"So, what are you up to today?" I asked.

I grabbed the container that held all the sugar packets and
organized them so that all the Sweet'n Lows were together. Then
I decided to alternate each packet: sugar, Sweet'n Low, sugar,
Sweet'n Low. I kept my eyes on my hands.

"I was helping out my dad at the shop for a bit." His father
owned the sometimes-open garage just off the highway, a few
miles past the Paradise. "I'll probably go home and . . . do something, I don't know. Maybe head to the creek when the sun goes
down. What about you?"

"Pretty much the usual," I said. "Dylan and I are going into
Bakersfield to get stuff at Walmart for her baby. Then we're
meeting up with Chris later."

Chris's mom had taken to cooking massive meals full of his
favorite foods because, as she said, "Boston is full of *gringos*
with *gringo* food."

Josh's eyes widened. "Dylan has a kid?" I nodded, and he
shook his head. "Damn. I mean, I'm not surprised, but—"

My hands stopped organizing packets. "What's that supposed
to mean?"

"Skylar, don't get all . . . I'm just saying, you know, Dylan's always liked to have a good time."

If Chris were here, he'd be giving me shit because I could literally feel my nostrils flare. Sometimes Chris or Dylan would say stuff to piss me off just to see The Flare.

"Is that your way of calling her a slut?"

Josh, I could tell, was seeing The Flare.

"Jesus, Sky." He threw up his hands. "I'm sorry. You know I've always liked Dylan."

I grunted in response, because Josh "liking" a girl was reason enough for her dad to buy a shotgun.

The radio was too loud, so the air was filled with never-ending commercials with lines like "Buy now!" and "Don't miss it!" The Fresno Tire Center was insisting I go in there right away to take advantage of their fabulous summer savings. A huge Evangelical church was announcing its summer Bible studies, and McDonald's wanted me to try their new summer shakes. I pushed the sugars against the wall and looked down at the Formica tabletop, tracing my hand along the lines of fake marble.

Sometimes it was hard to breathe, knowing how small my world could be. Maybe in San Francisco it wouldn't feel like the universe was conspiring to keep me in a bubble. I looked up, caught Josh's Van Gogh eyes for a second. God, they were intense. Was it rude to stare when you were staring *back* at someone? As soon as I tried to hold them, his eyes dimmed, like he'd shuttered them somehow. It was silly feeling disappointed, but I was.

Josh cleared his throat. "Hey. Uh. Sorry about the other night. At my house. I was pretty wasted."

"It's fine. Seriously. Everyone was off their ass that night."

"Not you," he said.

I shrugged. "Never me. But I'm, you know, weird like that."

"I was being a dick to Chris, and . . . shit, I don't even remember most of the night."

He let out a slow breath and rubbed his hand over his shaved head. He looked thinner, more vulnerable, with just that brown stubble covering his skull. Why do they make guys shave their heads when they become soldiers? It makes them look like lost kids.

"I didn't think it was all that memorable. No offense," I added, because it was sort of his welcome home bash.

He shrugged. "It's cool."

"Besides, it was your brother who was being the dick, not you."

Josh laughed. "You're the one who dated him."

"*Dated* is a very strong word."

He leaned back in the booth and crossed his arms. "Well, I'll tell him to stop trying to get in your pants then."

"That sounds scary, coming from a Marine and all."

"Yeah, I'm terrifying, aren't I?"

He tried to make a joke of it, but he spit the words out, like food gone bad. His eyes shifted to the window, and he pointed to the faded snowmen painted on it.

"Fuckin' Ray ever gonna clean off this Christmas shit?"

"I think that's been there since I was a sophomore."

He snorted. "This town."

I grabbed the napkin wound around the silverware in front of me because paper was my lifeline and I needed to touch it, to know that maybe when I went home later, I could collage him and then it would all make sense, *he* would make sense. I hoped my fingers would remember the exact quality of the sunlight on his forehead, the shadows under his eyes.

"Marge said you're coming back to the Paradise?"

I spread the napkin out and began folding it. It'd be easier if it were made of actual paper, but I'd done napkin origami before.

He nodded. "Yeah. Guess I'll be a handyman again until I figure out . . ." He waved his hand in the air. "Stuff."

"Good. I'll have someone to play checkers with."

"Oh, I'm a chess man now," he said. The ghost of a smile played on his face.

I raised my eyebrows. Josh Mitchell—chess? He was the kind of guy who would have called a "chess man" a fag. "So that's what's really going on in the Marines, huh? Bunch of guys just sitting around playing chess?"

His eyes went dark for a second, and I worried that my teasing had hit a nerve, but then he sort of laughed.

"Half the time, yeah. Basically, when we weren't patrolling, we were stuck on base. And by base I mean this shitty-ass camp we set up in the middle of nowhere. The military is, like, ninety-six percent boredom, four percent action. All hurry up and wait. So, it was chess or trying to get online or, you know, jerking off to—" He saw the look on my face and stopped himself. "Anyway, I can kick your ass on the board, Evans, so watch out."

I handed him the napkin I'd folded into a crane. He held it up, looking at the wings, the beak.

"A bird?"

"Crane. It means peace. It's better with paper, but this was the best I could do."

He looked at it for a long moment. "Peace, huh?"

"Josh. Eat that before it tastes worse than it already is," Dylan said, sidling up to our table. Her face was still flushed from her shift, and I could tell how exhausted she was by the fact that she hadn't even bothered to fix her hair or reapply her makeup.

He pushed the plate away. "I think it's reached that point already."

"Well, next time, take my advice." She turned to me. "I told him the cheeseburger was the way to go."

"Should have listened to you," he said. "I thought the stuff in the corps was bad, but Ray can't cook for shit."

Dylan agreed with him about her boss's inability to make edible food, then told us her Worst Customer of the Day story. Josh asked to see a picture of Sean, and he looked at me like *what?* when I glared at him. A few minutes later, we were waving good-bye, leaving Josh to stare out the window and crunch on the ice in his glass. As we got in the car and headed down the highway, I couldn't concentrate on whatever Dylan was talking about. I just kept seeing Josh by that dirty window. Looking out, but not seeing anything. And then I thought of how the first thing he'd said to me was that I looked good.

"—and I was all, *no*, Jesse, you can't give a baby gum. Right?"

"Huh?" I looked over at Dylan.

"You weren't listening, were you?" She was practically shouting above the funky sounds my car was making, and I gripped the steering wheel, praying we wouldn't break down.

I shook my head. "Sorry. It's just . . . Josh. You know?"

"Yeah." She rolled down the window and spit out her gum. "It's weird. I mean, Josh has always been kind of a bastard, but now I feel, like, so bad for him. I mean, he *lost his leg*. Like, *his leg*. Plus, he saw some serious craziness. It might have been all *Saving Private Ryan* over there, you know?" Dylan looked at me. "Maybe he's different now—like the war changed him or something."

I wasn't naïve. It was obvious Josh could never be the same kid who used to spend his nights driving around in his souped-up truck, throwing beer bottles at abandoned buildings on the highway—way too much had happened for that to be enough for him.

"He's still a sexist pig," I muttered. "He, like, talks to my boobs more than me."

Dylan pulled down the visor and looked in the mirror as she dabbed lip gloss on her lips. "Yeah, but he's probably extra horny right now, with all of us walking around in shorts and tanks. I mean, the women in Afghanistan are covered up in, like, sheets and stuff. Don't they wear those things where you can't even see their faces?"

I rolled my eyes. "*Dylan*. They do not wear sheets. *Jesus*."

"Anyway, he's still hot. I wonder what it would be like to . . . you know. I mean, he's still got what matters."

"Oh my God, Dylan, shut up. I don't need that image in my head."

"It's totally in your head, isn't it?"

"*No*." Except, *yes*.

Dylan laughed and turned up the music. We had an hour of driving just to get to the nearest Walmart, but it wasn't too bad if you had some company and a working radio.

I stared out the window, at the unbearable flatness of the Central Valley with its endless fields where workers bobbed up and down over the plants, their straw hats and bandannas sway-ing like dancing flowers. Somewhere, in one of those fields, Chris's dad was supervising the picking, reminding himself that the crappy wage was worth it because his son was going to col-lege. And miles behind us, my mother was just getting to Taco Bell, ready to spend another day in fast-food hell. And Josh was sitting alone in a diner, thinking about whatever horrible stuff was going down thousands of miles away.

I pressed my foot against the accelerator.

I'd splurged on new bedding for my dorm, and I couldn't wait to show it to my mom. It was the first thing I'd bought for school—having it made college feel more real than my accep-tance letter. I'd also bought a bunch of paper for a collage I was making as a going-away present for Marge: thin-as-tissue Japa-nese rice paper, thick construction paper, Canford papers to sculpt objects that burst from the collage, and the shimmery, expensive sanded pastel paper that I hadn't been able to resist. I hugged the bags to my chest, thinking about roommates and being an art major. I hoped the stuff for my dorm looked appro-priately arty. It was hard to know, being in a town like Creek View.

The birch trees planted around our little lot stood like friendly sentinels that welcomed me home, and I could hear the distant shrieks of the neighborhood kids as they ran through sprinklers and gunned each other down with water hoses. I looked at the forlorn trailers and beat-up cars. The sky was still a bright corn-flower blue, and the sun shoved against everything it touched.

The heat, the dust, the disrepair—it didn't bother me so much, knowing that I'd be leaving soon. Even our sea-green trailer wasn't too bad, though it could definitely use a paint job and a couple of the shutters were about to fall off. I almost felt nostalgic.

I put the key in the lock, but at my touch, the door swung open and bright shafts of light streamed into our darkened living room. For a second, I just stood on our tiny front porch, my key still raised, heart beating fast. Mom was supposed to be at Taco Bell until late tonight, and she was just as paranoid as I was about locking the door. It wasn't uncommon to have burglaries in the trailer park, so my mom and I were borderline obsessive-compulsive about locking up, especially since my dad had died. Not having a man in the house was something I didn't think Mom would ever get used to. Which was why she put up with skeezy Billy Easton, who came around to "help" with repairs but really just wanted to ask my mom out for the thousandth time. Five years, and he still didn't understand the word *no*.

I stood on the front porch, paralyzed, until I heard my mother's familiar cough coming from her bedroom. I stepped inside and wrinkled my nose against the stench of cigarette smoke that hung in the stale air.

"Mom?" I called, setting my things down on the floor and shutting the door behind me.

No answer.

The trailer was dark, all the blinds closed and curtains drawn. I opened the kitchen window to kill the sour smell. The darkness, the smoke, the heaviness that blanketed everything—I knew what it meant.

Mom was having one of her bad days.

At her room, I took a breath before I pushed open the door, cheap plywood that made it easy to hear her when she cried at night. She was lying in the middle of her bed, wrapped in my dad's bathrobe, and the room was thick with smoke. *Judge Judy* was on the tiny TV on top of her dresser, but it was muted, its light the only color in the room.

"Hi, baby," she whispered.

I moved close to her, then gently took the cigarette from between her fingers and put it in the Coke can she was using as an ashtray. Stray pieces of ash from her cigarettes dusted her nightstand and covered the collage I'd recently made for her of the Golden Gate Bridge, a little reminder of me when I was away at school.

"Hey." I smoothed back her hair, then planted a kiss on her forehead. "Wanna take a shower?"

She shook her head.

"You sure? It always makes you feel better."

"No." Her voice was far away.

I pushed down the fear that I wouldn't be able to bring her back this time, that she'd never leave that dark place she went to on her bad days. Her eyes slid back to the TV, and I concentrated on picking up her room. Work clothes were piled on the floor, and crumpled packages of Little Debbie snacks littered the carpet beside her bed. The shade on her lamp was cockeyed, as though she'd stumbled into it.

"You need me to give the Bell a call? Tell them you can't go in tomorrow?"

Mom cackled, and I turned away to throw the clothes in her

overflowing hamper so I wouldn't have to see the bitterness stamped on her face. I'd have to go to the Laundromat soon—it looked like half her wardrobe was in there.

"Oh, sure," she said. "Call them. I'd love to hear what Brian has to say."

Brian was her manager, a smarmy zit-faced kid just a year or two older than me.

"What are you—"

"They fired me," she said. Her voice had turned dull, flat.

"*What?*"

She stared at the TV, as if she couldn't bear to miss one second of Judge Judy's court proceedings. "Yep," she said. "After eighteen years, it was like, *Fuck you, Denise!*" She reached for her pack of cigarettes, and I leaned in close, grabbing her arms.

"Mom. Look at me. Are you serious right now?"

Her eyes filled with tears, and she nodded. "I screwed up. I screwed up bad."

My stomach turned, like I'd put bad milk in my coffee. "Okay. What happened?"

She looked down, playing with a loose thread on her robe. "I was closing and . . . I . . . I left one of the tills on the front counter. I was tired . . . just forgot it was there. Some punks broke in after I closed up. I came in this morning, and Brian showed me the tape. Little bastard. I could tell how happy it made him."

"But it was an accident!" I said. How could some teenage manager fire her, after all those years?

"Doesn't matter—that kid hates me, always has. If it wasn't this, it'd be something else. Says he has 'cause' to fire me. Can you believe it? He says I left the cash drawer out *on purpose.*"

"That's insane. Why would he say that?"

She grabbed the cigarettes and fished one out of the pack. "Because I was upset that he wrote me up at the beginning of my shift last night. I was late—just a couple minutes, but you know how he always rides my ass. I called him a prick."

"He can't fire you for calling him a prick." Besides, it was true.

The flame from the lighter flickered, then caught the cigarette. She sucked in the smoke. "He's saying I left the till out to get back at him. Says he has witnesses."

"Mom, we can totally fight this."

"No one's gonna be on my side. Whatever. I'm out."

She started chewing on her lip like she always did when she got anxious, and I knew she'd be bleeding in a minute.

I squeezed her hand, but she pulled away and took another shaky drag of her cigarette. "What are we gonna do?" she whispered.

Mom started crying for real now, big sobs that seemed to grate against her insides. I pulled her to me and let her cry, her tiny body shuddering in my arms. I hadn't seen her like this since Dad had died. Her bad days could usually be taken care of with a shower, some good food, a night in watching movies. After a day or so, she'd come back to herself. But without a job to return to, how could I pull her out of this?

"Sky." Her voice broke, and I patted her hair, her back.

"Shhh," I whispered. "It's okay, Mom. It's gonna be okay."

"No it's not," she said.

She cried for a long time, and I held her while I watched the cold shadows that the TV cast on the walls of her room lengthen and bleed across the bed. As I sat there trying to hold my mother together, I realized that the thing I'd been fearing for most of my life was finally happening: that I'd be so close to getting out, then just at the last moment, something would happen that would keep me in Creek View indefinitely. I always thought it would be a freakish thing, like a natural disaster or getting a brain tumor. Not this.

JOSH

I'm walking across the field. Everything's brown: brown huts, brown mountains, brown dirt. Harrison is handing out soccer balls and candy to the kids. He's laughing because they keep screaming "I LOVE AMERICA I WANNA CANDY," and Sharpe is lighting up another Marlboro and my gun's in my hand and my gear is fucking heavy and I'm so hot. Davis is leaning against the Humvee, talking to Abdul. You're shooting the shit with the village elders. *As-salaam alaikum. As-salaam alaikum.* You call me over when you're done and I say, *Let's go to that wall, man. I need to take a fuckin' knee.* The sky is blue blue and all I can smell is dust and the smoke from Sharpe's cigarette, and we're going toward the wall but then I say, *Hold up, I'm gonna check behind that hut.* I raise my gun. Five steps to the hut. Four. Three. Two. Then I wake up. Sweating, fucking sobbing like a little bitch. Just like every night. Looking for my rifle, but it's not there—*shit, where is it?*—and then I remember I don't have one anymore. And my leg that isn't there is burning—I can feel it but it's not there—and I look at the clock and fuckshitfuck it's only one in the morning and it won't be light for hours. So I lie back down and stare at the ceiling and run through every cadence my drill instructor taught me at Camp Pendleton and then I repeat the Rules of Engagement and I think of all my favorite quotes from *Three Kings* and I play imaginary games of chess with you in my head and you always win because I forget about the queen again. I'm so tired, so goddamn tired, but sleep isn't happening. It's just me, the ceiling, and the night becoming morning.

chapter three

There were only two reasons the Paradise Motel stayed in business: we rented rooms by the hour, and there wasn't any competition for seventy miles in either direction. All you could see from the highway were a bunch of scraggly trees and our old-school sign at the beginning of a long dirt drive. Once the sun went down, the freaky-looking angel sitting on top of the sign became neon pink and green, winking at drivers as they passed on the highway. The motel itself squatted behind the trees—it was one story with an inner courtyard in typical Cali style, with ten rooms and a pool, bordered on three sides by Gil Portman's orchard.

The Paradise needed a paint job bad—Marge said it looked like a kid had vomited an orange Slurpee all over her walls—and the TVs didn't have cable. But it wasn't creepy in that *Psycho* kind of way. In fact, we'd recently been featured on a blog called *Quirky California* because of our themed rooms. You'd be surprised how many people were into the unicorn room.

Everything was falling apart at home and school was out, so I was happy to spend more time than usual at the Paradise. There was something kind of cozy about the broken stool I sat on behind the front desk and the way people would pop in at all hours of the day and night. And I didn't know how I would have gotten through Creek View summers without the pool.

Working at the Paradise was fine when it was an after-school job, but I couldn't imagine myself sitting behind the counter in September, when I should be in San Francisco feeling all chic and intellectual. But as the days rolled by, Mom got worse, not better. It wasn't just that she wasn't applying for jobs—she wouldn't leave the house. Whenever I got home, she was always sitting on the couch, staring at nothing. For the first time, I realized that maybe my mom wasn't just depressed about Dad. Maybe she was like me and felt the hopelessness of Creek View in her bones, but unlike me, she didn't have a ticket out. There had to be a way to help my mom and still move to San Fran. I had eight weeks. At the beginning of the summer, I'd thought the days couldn't go by fast enough, but now all I wanted was time.

It was a Friday afternoon, and my shift was almost over. I tipped my stool back, leaning my damp head against the wall behind me. There was a heat advisory, and the air settled over me like a lead blanket, sapping all my energy. The only sound in the Paradise lobby was the distant roar of cars and the whiny creaking of the overhead fan. Every now and then, a big rig would sound its horn out on the highway, jolting me awake. I swatted at the fly that kept tiptoeing down my neck and put the can of Coke I'd just gotten out of the vending machine against my cheeks. I was in that dazed limbo of overcaffeinated drowsiness, coming off another graveyard shift and trying to stay awake until Amy showed up. I set my Coke down and let my head fall forward, not even caring that I was lying on one of my collages. It was a crappy one, anyway.

"I need a room."

My eyes snapped open. I didn't know how long I'd been out. A woman about my mom's age was standing at the counter, drumming her long fingernails on the scratched wood surface. I sat up, tried to look welcoming.

"Sure. We have a few vacancies." A *lot*, but who was counting? I peeled myself off the stool, the back of my legs sticking painfully to the leather seat.

"Single or double?" I asked. I used my professional voice, the one that the girls who worked at the Hilton had. I knew because sometimes I would call the fancy LA or San Francisco hotels, just to listen to the way they answered. Marge said my talents were wasted here, and honestly, I had to agree.

"Single."

The woman frowned as she looked around at the decorations. The lamps and artwork were straight out of 1970—all creams and bright orange and brown. My favorite thing was the tangerine-colored vase with yellow ceramic bees attached to it. It used to be in the David Bowie room, but I'd found a vase shaped like an electric guitar at Goodwill, so the bee one ended up in the lobby. Marge had owned the place for two years by the time I came on, but the rooms didn't turn into themed extravaganzas until my love of art and her worship of all things kitsch came together.

I opened the registry to see what we had available. "One night or—"

"God, just one, I hope." The woman pulled a wallet out of her designer purse.

I gave a pointed look at the framed article from *Quirky California* that we kept on the wall next to the room keys.

"So . . . ," I said, flipping through the registry. "We have the *Grease* room, the Tom Cruise room, the *Viva México* room, and the *Gilligan's Island* room available."

"Are you serious?" she asked.

"As a heart attack." That was a Marge phrase that I had to use surprisingly often around there.

The woman wrinkled up her nose. *"Gilligan's."*

Gilligan's Island was this show from the sixties that Marge loved.

"Great," I said. "Just don't light the tiki torch—"

"Tiki torch?"

"Tiki torch." The woman nodded, and I turned the registry around for her signature. "That'll be thirty-nine dollars."

I ran her card, then turned around to the row of tiny hooks behind me and grabbed the key for *Gilligan's Island*. I slid it across the counter, forcing my lips to go up. "Here you go."

She held the keychain between two fingers, like the plastic etched with a number five (written in Sharpie, because we were classy like that) carried multiple diseases. I wanted to tell her that poverty wasn't catching, but I just leaned across the counter and pointed to my left.

"If you just go to the sliding glass door to your right and cross the patio, it's the room directly in front of us. There's an ice machine and a couple of vending machines down this hallway." I motioned to the left of the reception desk, where the light was dim to hide how bad the stains in the carpet were. "And the pool is open until ten."

"Thanks," she muttered. I kept smiling until we had two

inches of sliding glass door between us, then I leaned back in my chair and groaned.

Out of the corner of my eye, I saw the screen door open. "What a bitch," a voice said.

Josh stood in the doorway, looking thoroughly entertained. The sun behind him was bright, outlining him like a woodcut, all sharp, jagged lines and invisible details.

"Hey," I said. He stepped inside and let the door swing shut behind him. "Who's the bitch—her or me?"

He laughed. "Her, of course."

He was wearing a pair of aviator sunglasses, so I couldn't tell if he still had that haunted look in his eyes from Saturday night or just the dazed one from the diner. He seemed better, though. As he walked toward me, my brain kept chanting, *Don't look down, don't look down.*

"You were way too nice to her," he said, nodding toward *Gilligan's.*

I shrugged. "I wouldn't want to be stuck in Creek View, either."

Josh sighed. "Yep."

Central California was a veritable no-man's-land: this was not the California of people's dreams. We didn't have a music-video world of palm trees and sandy beaches that we frolicked on under the sun. I mean, there were more items on the McDonald's Value Menu than there were things to do in Creek View.

"How's the Sky today?" he asked. It was this old thing we used to do, him asking me how I was, me answering with a corresponding weather condition.

I tilted my head to the side, thinking. "Hazy," I decided.

"Why so?"

"Um . . ." Was I seriously thinking about telling this guy *my* problems? "Well, I think my brain's gone all fuzzy from the lack of air-conditioning in here."

"So . . ." Josh's eyes swept over the walls. "Nothing's changed since I've been gone, then."

"Well, more stuff's broken. And the pool has suffered greatly. It missed you," I said.

"Glad something did."

His words hung in the air, their weight an almost tangible thing. I wanted to say, *No, Josh, everyone missed you. We talked about you all the time.* But I'd have been lying. When people left Creek View, everyone who stayed took it as a personal offense. Like you'd gotten all bougie or something just because you wanted to live in the kind of place where you could get a Frappuccino without driving fifty miles. But in his case, it wasn't like that, not exactly. He hadn't left a void so much as taken a break. There was no doubt he'd be back someday.

Thankfully, Marge saved me, so I didn't have to figure out a way to lie well.

"Josh? Is that you?" she called. Her room-slash-office was down the hall, and if she wasn't there, she was either by the pool or lying on the couch in the lobby, filling me in on the latest celebrity news.

"Yeah, it's me," he said.

Marge shuffled in, wearing one of her muumuus and patting at her burgundy hair. It was supposed to be red, but every time she dyed it, the color ended up more purple than anything else. She was a few years older than my mom, a Midwest transplant who couldn't get enough of the California sun, even when it was punishing. She'd said opening this motel had been her dream. I thought Ohio must have been pretty bad if opening up a motel in the armpit of California was your dream.

"Look at you," she whispered. She was beaming, her eyes suddenly glassy. "Come here, hon."

Josh limped over, and she threw her arms around him, pressing him to her thick body. She reminded me of a mama bear, all hulking and protective. It was how she was with all her employees. I couldn't even count how many times she'd helped me with college applications and schoolwork. This was different, though. Marge's son had been in the Army, gone to Iraq. He'd died—in Fallujah, I think. Ever since Josh joined the Marines, she'd been obsessed with getting him back home.

"I prayed for you every single night," she said, her voice thick with tears. "Every single night."

I busied myself with the guest register so that I could look away from Josh's balled-up fists against Marge's back and the way he'd squeezed his eyes shut.

When my cell rang a second later, I grabbed it and slipped outside, grateful for the excuse.

"Hey, Chris."

"Hey, hey. What's up, *chica*? You sound all depressed."

I kicked at the weeds pushing up through the brick walkway, stomping on them as if they'd committed some terrible offense. "It's been a crappy morning."

"Just remember: you're getting the eff out of here in T minus sixty days!"

When we were freshman, Chris and I had promised each other that we'd be the ones to get out—we called it our Sacred Pact. We nagged each other all throughout high school, when one of us wanted to be lazy or give in to giving up. Whenever I liked a boy, Chris had been all, *The pact! The pact!* Because, of course, romance was bad for GPAs. I didn't think it was a coincidence that Chris started the pact once it became clear Dylan was never going to fall for him.

"Yeah, but, you know. Creek View still sucks," I said. Each day felt like I was walking on a sidewalk full of cracks and I had to keep jumping around so that everything wouldn't collapse.

"Which is why we're going to Leo's," Chris said. "Tonight. Get ready to get down, know what I'm sayin'?"

Leonardo's was this Mexican restaurant about a half hour away that turned into a local dance hall every Friday and Saturday night. It was mostly reggaeton and hip-hop, and everyone went because the drinks were cheap and they didn't card. I went because Chris's cousins were the DJs, and they always played stuff you couldn't help but dance to.

"I don't know, Chris. I'm wiped out. Amy is late as hell, and I gotta help my mom with some stuff."

"You say that every time. And then I practically have to pull you off the dance floor to go home. Besides, Ricardo said he wanted to say hey since he couldn't come to graduation."

"Chris, I'm not—I repeat, *I'm not*—going on a date with your twenty-eight-year-old cousin."

"Dude. It's not like that. He just—"

"I'm tired. Like, I-want-to-sleep-forever tired."

"I'll buy you as many virgin strawberry margaritas as you want."

"You can't buy something that's free," I said. Chris helped the restaurant with its accounting in exchange for free food and booze. He had all kinds of little deals like that around town.

"Don't hate because of my mad math skills. Come on. You'll wish you'd said yes when you're in San Fran and I'm in Boston."

And, really, you couldn't say no to that. "Fine. My car's not working great, so we have to take your dad's truck or I'm staying home and watching *Friends* with my mother."

"That's pathetic, Sky. *Pathetic.* I'll pick you up at eight."

We hung up, and I waited to go inside until I heard the glass door open, then I went back into the lobby, watching as Josh and Marge walked toward the pool. Every few seconds, she would look up at him, shake her head, and beam. They'd gotten really close after he joined the Marines, and I'd seen letters from him come to the Paradise every now and then. Once I'd even heard her on the phone in the middle of the night—I'd known it was him because of the questions she was asking. She cried for a long time after they'd hung up. Now I was wondering if that had been after he lost his leg.

A car pulled up in the driveway, and I checked the customer into the *Grease* room (a road tripper who wanted to stay at our place because it was so "random"), and then went outside to where Josh was sitting by the pool in the shade of a stand of tired-looking palms. His prosthesis was stretched out, the sunlight glinting off the thin metal, and he was absently rubbing his thigh. I didn't know how much of his leg he'd lost—he was wearing long board shorts—but I wondered if he was in pain or if touching the stump was compulsive. I steeled myself against feeling horrified or grossed out, but those feelings never came. It was just so . . . it gave me the same feeling as looking at a Dalí painting, where everything is upside down and inside out. Surreal.

"Where's Marge?" I asked, pulling one of the creaky lawn chairs over.

"Bitching to Gil that he has to cut down those branches." He pointed to where the orchard trees were beginning to slither over our wall.

"Never a dull day at the Paradise," I said.

He smiled, his eyes on the water. Seeing and not seeing it. "I'm gonna clean the pool when the sun goes down a bit. You still swim every day?"

I nodded. "Yeah. I try to keep the leaves out, and sometimes Chris comes over and does the thing with your pool tools, but he's not as good as you." I bumped my shoulder against his. "Glad you're back."

"Yeah." His eyes were far away again, and he was fiddling with his fingers, pressing against each nail.

I didn't know what made me do this, but I turned to him and said, "Do you want to go dancing with me tonight?"

His jaw kind of dropped, and I stumbled over my words, trying to explain. "I mean, with me and Dylan and Jesse—that's her boyfriend—and Chris. At Leonardo's."

I suddenly remembered about his leg, and my whole body broke out in this embarrassed sweat. "I mean, we don't have to dance. It's just, I thought maybe you were bored as hell and . . . never mind. It was a dumb idea. I mean, I don't even know if I'm gonna go."

I took off my sunglasses and wiped the lenses with the bottom of my tank top, just to give my hands something to do. What was I thinking, inviting Josh to go *dancing*? He probably thought I was an idiot.

"That'd be cool." He looked down at his leg. "I don't know about dancing, though."

I laughed, more from relief than anything else. "Okay. Do you want us to pick you up?"

"How about I pick *you* up?" He pointed to his leg. "I need a little room when I'm in the car."

"Oh. Duh. Okay. Um." Someone rapped on the glass door, and I jumped up, thankful for an out. A middle-aged couple waved me inside. "It's one of the hourlies."

Josh shaded his eyes and looked toward the door. "Is that dude a sheriff?"

I raised my hand and waved. "Yep. The woman sells real estate up near Hanford—they're here every Wednesday and Friday."

"I wonder if he takes her out to lunch after," he said.

"Yeah, I don't think so. He doesn't strike me as the romantic type. Anyway, I better go in."

He stood up, wincing a little. "Dude looks like he's in a hurry."

I laughed as I went back to the lobby. A half hour later, after I'd told Chris I was hitching a ride with Josh, Dylan was texting me, asking if one-legged men turned me on. I looked out the window at Josh. He was shirtless, his dog tags glimmering in the sun, and there was a tattoo on his back—the words *Semper Fidelis* in dark, Gothic letters that moved up and down with his muscles as he worked.

I texted her back: Shut up.

JOSH

Why did I say I'd go? I'm gonna look like an idiot. This isn't the kind of stuff they help you with in rehab. There aren't fuckin' dance lessons for gimp Marines. I couldn't even dance when I had *two* legs. Remember when Gomez decided that he wanted to make his wife a video of our squad doing Beyoncé's "Single Ladies" routine for Christmas and so we all had to learn it like a bunch of homos? (*Don't say homo, Josh,* you tell me. *That's fucking bigoted.*) Still, you have to admit, we looked like a bunch of homos. You asked a medevac to film it with the crappy camera you bought off one of the translators in Kandahar and somehow the video ended up on YouTube, so we were kinda famous for a week or two. When I get home from the Paradise, I decide to watch it, don't know why. Just need to. Guess Sky asking me to go dancing made me think of it—this shitty video was the last time I danced on two legs. Last time I danced, period. I find it on my computer and even though the video's all wobbly, it's like I'm right back there. I'm off to the side, fucking up the dance and laughing so hard and Sharpe is getting way too into it and Harrison is wearing the bra his girlfriend sent him to help him

get off on thinking about her. At the end we all just start dancing like idiots. I'm doing some cowboy rodeo thing and you're
pretending to slap my ass and Gomez is humping the floor like
it's his wife or something. And here I am sitting alone in my room
in the States, cracking up and it feels so good to laugh, man, but
then the laughing turns to something else and before I know it
I'm on my feet and punching the wall, which hurts like a bitch,
but I do it again and again until my mom opens the door and
says, *Jesus Christ, Josh*, and then slams it closed. My knuckles are
bleeding and the video is finished. We're frozen on the screen.
And now I'm looking at Sharpe and you, posing like trannie
models, and at me with my two beautiful goddamn legs and it
doesn't make sense, doesn't make any fucking sense that you're
both gone. How can you do some dumb dance like that and then
not exist anymore?

chapter four

"Mom, *please*. You can't sit here all night. Come on. I made you the pasta you like—the squiggly kind. And a salad."

She didn't even look at me, just kept her eyes glued to the TV. *CSI* was on, and they were cutting up a body while calmly discussing the atrocious rape-slash-dismemberment of the victim.

"My ride's gonna be here any minute, and I really need you to eat something before I go."

She reached for her cigarettes, but I darted out and grabbed them. In our house, cigarettes meant a day when Mom couldn't stop thinking about Dad and how he'd gotten into his truck that night when he should have let someone drive him home. They didn't help her forget. They helped her remember.

"You'll get wrinkly. Then George Clooney will never have sex with you."

Her mouth twitched, but she beckoned for me to give the cigs back. "Don't you have to finish getting ready for your date?"

"It's not a date."

It wasn't. It was . . . a thing. An outing. Whatever. What was

I thinking, going dancing? It was wrong to leave her, but just being inside there for too long made my chest feel like someone was pressing against it as hard as they could.

I heard Josh's truck roar into the little patch of dirt in front of the trailer that served as our driveway, Kid Rock blaring. My face reddened as I imagined myself in Josh's truck, looking like some girl he'd picked up for the night.

Mom looked at the door, as if she could see through it. "That Chris?"

She knew it wasn't. Chris didn't listen to loud music, and his dad's old Chevy sounded nothing like Josh's flashy truck.

"Josh. Did you want bread or—"

"Josh *Mitchell*?" she asked.

"Uh-huh."

I put some ranch on her salad and threw the bottle back in the fridge, then dished out her pasta.

Mom frowned. "Maybe you should stay home tonight."

I heard the door of Josh's truck slam shut. There was no way I was canceling on him, even if these past few hours with my mom had worn me out more than my whole shift at the Paradise.

I reached over to squeeze her shoulder. "Why don't you give Crystal a call? I bet she's babysitting Seanie for Dylan tonight. You could go over there for a bit."

Crystal was Dylan's mom. Their trailer was practically across the street from ours, and other than a few of the women at work, she was my mom's only friend.

Josh knocked on the door.

"I won't stay long," I said. "And I'll have my cell if you need anything."

Mom pursed her lips, and her eyes slid to the TV. She

grabbed the remote and turned it back on. When I opened the door, Josh was leaning against our rickety railing, his hands in his pockets. Only a few tiny beads of sweat near his temples gave away his difficulty getting up the steps. Even so, I had to admit he looked good. He wore long cargo shorts and a plaid button-up shirt with the sleeves rolled, his sunglasses in his front pocket, and a Marines baseball cap. I was sort of angry at him for looking so good. Because this wasn't a date, and I was suddenly wishing—against all my better judgment—that it was.

He smiled. "Hey."

The sun had just gone down, so the sky was purple and the first stars were coming out. It was a warm twilight, an exhalation after the intense heat of the day. Creek View almost seemed pretty.

"You found me." I frowned. What a stupid thing to say. Of course he'd know where the trailer park was, and it wasn't like it was a particularly complicated neighborhood to navigate. Was it the leg thing that made me so dumb or was it that he was standing on my doorstep, which was strange enough in and of itself?

"Yeah," he said.

We sort of stood there for a moment, my palms getting sweaty, and then I motioned inside. "I'm just gonna grab my purse, okay? I'll meet you in the truck?"

"Cool."

When I shut the door behind me, Mom was still staring at the TV. I grabbed my purse. "Love you."

She nodded. "Have fun."

I blew her a kiss the way we always do, pressing my lips to my fingers then raising my hand in a wave as I shut the door behind me.

Josh's truck was a thing I'd only seen from afar, except for the one time Blake drove me home in it. It was a red Ford F-150 with extra-big wheels and two annoying stickers in the back window of naked female silhouettes looking in opposite directions. There was also a Marine Corps decal and an American flag sticker.

"Josh, on behalf of women everywhere, I demand that you remove those skanky stickers from your back window."

He turned around and fixed me with a look of mock horror. "How dare you call the flag of the greatest country on earth *skanky*!"

I punched him on the arm. "You know which ones I'm talking about."

He rolled his eyes and handed me his MP3 player. "You can pick the music."

I scrolled through his albums. "Gee, how's a girl to decide between Fifty Cent and Metallica?"

He grabbed it out of my hands. "Never mind."

We went back and forth like that all the way to Leo's, me feeling surprised that he was so easy to talk to, him trying not to make it obvious that he was checking me out.

On top of his dashboard was a black, leather-bound journal. It would have been number one on my Things Josh Would Never Own list. I was about to ask him why he had it when he beat me to an uncomfortable question.

"So, what's with you and my brother?" he asked, as we turned into the packed parking lot.

"Nothing."

"At the party you two seemed kinda . . . you know." He wiggled his eyebrows.

Ugh.

"Blake needs to remember that he has a girlfriend, and last I checked, that girlfriend isn't me. You know how he is when he gets drunk."

"You mean he acts like any dude in the world?" he said.

"Eww."

Josh snorted. "When Blake e-mailed me about you, I was seriously like, what? *Skylar?*"

I laughed, but not in a ha-ha way—more in a bitter what-the-hell-was-I-thinking way. "I don't know, Josh. It was only a week—just spring break. And I guess I was feeling like, why not? We weren't a couple or anything. We were just . . . it was dumb."

I didn't tell him how that had been one of the worst weeks of my life or that I'd never done anything with a boy, not really, and that, after each afternoon with Blake, I'd go home and cry in the shower and wonder what was wrong with me. And then I'd meet him by the creek the next day and it would happen all over again. It wasn't like we even went that far—it just felt far to *me.*

"Wow. That's romantic."

"Oh, I'm sorry. Would you prefer *your* version of relationships?" I asked.

"You mean the ones where the girl actually wants to be with me? Um, *yeah.*"

He parked the truck, and I sighed, wondering if we were still joking or not.

"What?" he asked.

"Nothing. You ready?"

"Oh, no. You're pissed. I said something wrong." He shook his head. "This buddy of mine always tells me—" He stopped for a second and tapped his key against the steering wheel. I waited for him to finish his thought, but it was like he'd already gotten out of the truck. Like Mom, he wasn't there.

"Josh?" I reached out to touch his arm, but he jerked away.

"I'm fine," he snapped.

"Okay," I said, my voice soft.

We sat there for a minute, sharing air, the music from Leo's slipping through our slightly opened windows.

I cleared my throat. "I know we're not, like, best friends or whatever, but if you need someone to talk to . . ." His whole body seemed to tense up, so I stopped and opened the door. "C'mon. I'll buy you a beer."

He gave me a sideways glance. "You don't drink."

"Yeah, but I bet the only way I'll get you on the dance floor is if *you* drink. Besides, Leo's doesn't card." Leg or no leg, the dude needed to have some fun.

He shook his head. "I'm not dancing."

I shrugged. "Okay."

"Seriously."

I gave him a we'll-see smile, then jumped out of the truck and came around to his side.

"Do you need any he—"

"No." He shifted his good leg around to jump down from the truck, which was way too high up because of the extra-huge wheels. He slammed the door and grabbed my hand. "Let's go."

I didn't know how that happened—my hand in his—so

quickly, and why wasn't I pulling away? He opened the door, and that's how we walked into Leo's, looking like a couple, but he let go as soon as we got past the dark entryway. It was like this little secret that I knew would hang over my head all night. And Dylan would see it right away; I knew she would. It was probably written all over my face, this feeling in my chest that was tight and loose at the same time. I let Josh walk ahead of me and I put the hand he'd held against a pillar just inside the entryway, letting the cold seep through my skin and up my arm. I told myself I wouldn't stay long.

And I'd get a ride home from Chris.

———————

The restaurant-turned-dance-hall was packed, as usual. The walls were covered in sombreros and black-and-white photographs of people in traditional Mexican dress. Colorful piñatas in all shapes and sizes hung from the ceiling, their thin paper blowing in the breeze from the air-conditioning vents. The wooden tables that covered the floor during the day were pushed against the walls, stacked on top of each other. In the far corner, Chris's cousin Carlos was spinning. One of my favorite reggaeton songs was playing, that familiar *buh-buh-bump-bump, buh-buh-bump-bump* thumping, and I focused on the music, letting it massage my brain until all I could think of was getting that beat inside me for the rest of the night.

"Dance?" I asked Josh. I'd decided he needed to, bum leg and all.

"Beer," he said.

We went over to the bar, but before we'd even made it,

Ricardo, Chris's incurably flirtatious older cousin, was catching me up in his arms.

"*Mi hija!* Congratulations!"

I let him twirl me around for a minute and then I was back on my feet, dizzy but laughing.

"It's just high school graduation, Ricky."

"Yeah, but around here, that's a big thing." He looked over at Josh, and I started the whole Josh-Ricky-Ricky-Josh introductions and then we were at the bar. Josh wouldn't let me buy him a beer, and he handed me a Coke before I could say anything.

"Ohmygod, *Josh?*" A gorgeous girl I didn't know pushed between us, and in seconds, he was all up on her, which was so par for the Mitchell course.

"So, is this, like . . . a date?" Ricky whispered.

The girl had her hands on his waist and was leaning into him, laughing at something he'd said.

"No! *God.*"

How did girls do that? I mean, how did they manage to have a guy's full attention in less than a minute?

Ricky raised his eyebrows. "Well, in that case—"

"Aren't you supposed to be spinning?" I pointed to the DJ. "You just left Carlos up there all by himself. That's cold."

He laughed and started toward the turntables just as Dylan shimmied up to me. I wouldn't have to be Josh Mitchell's third wheel all night, after all. Awesome.

"Hi!" Dylan said, already a bit tipsy.

"Hey, Mama."

"When did you guys get here?" She kissed my cheek and leaned across me to give Josh a thumbs-up. "You clean up good, soldier."

"Hey, Dylan," Josh said, turning away from the clingy goddess. "You want a beer?"

"I won't say no." She threw an arm around me. "Um, Chris needs a dance partner *pronto*. You know I can't salsa for shit."

I was pretty sure Chris didn't care about that, but I needed an excuse to get on the floor. "You don't need to tell me twice," I said.

I took another sip of my Coke, and Josh took it out of my hand. "Get out of here," he said.

It was like we were together, but not. So weird. Out of the corner of my eye, I could tell Dylan was already psychoanalyzing us. I turned on my heel and booked it to the dance floor. I could feel eyes on me, but I didn't turn around. I didn't want to know whose they were.

I saw Chris's curly head in the middle of the floor, a few inches above everyone else. I danced my way to the center, spinning out of the random hands that reached for me. I loved to dance, but I never danced with strangers—the last time I tried that, some dude tried to grab my boob.

"Sky!" Chris's hair was damp with sweat, and he took my hand and started twirling me around before I had a chance to say anything. We swayed our hips in perfect rhythm, our days of boredom in his backyard paying off in our snazzy salsa performance.

For a while, I just let the music have its way with me. The beats soaked into my skin and filled me up. I tilted my head back and laughed into the rainbow-colored lights, my body slick with sweat. A couple of girls threw me envious glances as Chris pulled me closer. This was an oft-discussed phenomenon among

Chris, Dylan, and me, because girls never gave Chris a second glance until he was on the floor at Leo's.

"Don't look now, but you are seriously ruining your chances of getting laid tonight," I told him. If only they knew how *not* sexy Chris was to me. Or noticed how often his eyes shifted to where Dylan stood by the bar.

"Hey, I'm not the one who walked in with Josh Mitchell," he said. "That's like wearing a T-shirt that says DON'T TOUCH ME UNLESS YOU WANT YOUR ASS KICKED."

I swatted at his arm. "Not you too! He's a Mitchell. *Hello?* I've learned my lesson."

"I know. I'm just giving you a hard time. It's cool that you brought him out. I mean, he's a total douchebag, but it sucks to be him right now."

Did I ask Josh out of pity? I wasn't so sure. You don't pity someone that your fingers itch to touch.

"He's not a douchebag," I said.

Chris leaned in close so I could hear him over the music. "He called me a faggot. That officially classifies him as a douchebag."

"Well, okay, that wasn't cool. Douchebaggery was involved there."

"And I'm still pissed at him about my dad's truck."

Once, Josh was so drunk he crashed into Mr. Garcia's parked truck, then left a note that said *Oops.*

"Chris, that happened, like, three years ago."

"Yeah, yeah."

Carlos switched up the music, and Chris and I both shouted as one of our favorite Ozomatli songs came on, the momentary seriousness of our conversation forgotten. The floor was packed, and the energy was crazy hot, everyone getting lost in the music.

"Hey, wanna see how low we can go?" Chris yelled.

I nodded and followed his lead, twisting my body lower and lower as I held on to his waist for support. Our knees were almost to the ground, my dress hiked up in a seriously indecent way, but I didn't care because I was having fun for the first time since I graduated.

"Up, up!" I gasped, my thighs burning.

We managed to stand again, laughing at the expressions on his cousins' faces.

"Oh, man, I'm gonna hear about that for the next few days," Chris said.

His family was convinced we were madly in love, even though we'd told them over and over that it was so not happening. It wasn't just the Dylan thing. We'd made out once—in seventh grade—but it had felt too incestuous, so after five minutes of sweating all over each other, we gave up. You either feel it or you don't, and we just didn't, much to his mother's disappointment.

"Those moves are gonna kill in Boston," I said.

"Don't I know it. I'm gonna get me a hot little math major, just you wait."

"As long as you don't use any of your math pickup lines on her."

"I'm totally using my math pickup lines. Works every time."

"On who?"

"A gentleman never tells." He got close to me and did his best impression of this telenovela star that his mother loves. "*Hola, señorita*. I just want you to know that I've been watching you all night, and I can tell that you're as sweet as 3.14."

"Oh my God!" I pushed him away, cracking up. "That is the *worst*."

He pumped a fist in the air. "Yes! My Latino charm strikes again!"

"Sweet as pi? *Ugh*."

"You laughed," he said, pointing at me. "You know what all my female cousins say? They want a man who can make them laugh."

"A man they can laugh *with*, not *at*."

"My mathematical suaveness is irresistible, and you know it."

He grabbed my hand and proceeded to drag me around in a tango. For the next few songs, it was just Chris and me being our usual goofy selves. Chris sang along in his terrible, warbly voice and my crappy week evaporated. When I was out there dancing, it was like anything was possible. The thought that we wouldn't be doing this come September threatened to crush me; Chris was my *other*, my kindred spirit, and he was moving thousands of miles away. I pushed the thought back to where I'd put my worries about going to school and taking care of my mom. I just wanted to dance it all away.

I only looked over at the bar once, but Josh was still talking to that girl. As if he sensed me, his eyes found mine, and I gave him a quick wave and then looked away, my face burning. Dylan and Jesse joined Chris and me, and the four of us busted out our best moves, Dylan hanging on me like she does when she's had a few.

My heart was hurting from all this love for her and Chris, and I pressed my lips against her cheek and held tight to Chris's hand, just to let some of it seep out so I didn't drown in it.

Dylan grinned. "I know someone who might want in

on some of that lip action," she said, with a nod in Josh's direction.

"*So* not interested." I pulled away from her and reached up to throw my hair into a ponytail. "I'm saving myself for Art Boy."

After I got into SFU, we created the perfect boyfriend for me. I'd meet Art Boy in the Intro to Russian Art class I was taking, and he'd be from some fancy East Coast family, and he'd draw portraits of me like Leo did of Kate, except we wouldn't be on the *Titanic*, and I'd keep (most of) my clothes on.

Dylan stared me down with her psychoanalyzing X-ray vision. "Art Boy isn't here, and yet you look extra hot tonight." She glanced at Josh, then back at me. "Are you *sure* this isn't a date?"

I was wearing my slightly faded black sundress that went to my knees and a pair of dirty All Stars. "Dyl, I hardly think this qualifies as sexy." I gestured to her dress, a skintight number verging on lingerie status. "But I see you thought this was a pajama party."

"Hilarious," she said.

She pinched my ass, and I yelped, slapping at her. "Stop it!"

Jesse pulled her in for the slow dance, and for a second, Chris and I stood there awkwardly. I could feel his good mood seep out, like one of those shiny balloons that start to sag as they lose air.

He leaned in. "Dude, I need a drink. And maybe some taquitos. Wanna take a break?"

I nodded and followed Chris as he pushed his way through the writhing, sweating bodies around us.

"Remember," I said, "there's a hot little math major in your future."

Chris wiped the sweat off his forehead. "Yeah, yeah."

I patted his arm, but there was nothing more I could say. Dylan and Jesse had a kid together and were crazy in love. It was just never gonna happen.

When we got to the bar, Josh was still there, now trading high school football stories with one of the guys he'd graduated with. Their voices were loud, the conversation peppered with *fuckin'-A*'s and other choice phrases from the locker-room phrasebook.

"Hey," he said, when we came up. The other guy turned back to his date, a non–Creek View girl I'd never seen before.

"Hey, yourself," I said.

He handed me my Coke, his eyes glassy from however many beers he'd managed to down, and I took a long sip while Chris ordered a beer for himself from the bar. Chris was so obviously not twenty-one—he had one of those baby faces that ensured he'd be carded until he was forty—but the bartender was a distant cousin or something, so Chris always got whatever he wanted. Josh was only nineteen, but he was just one of those people you didn't say no to.

"You guys come here a lot?" Josh asked, his eyes taking me in with one quick glance. I was keenly aware of the sheen of sweat that coated my skin and made my dress cling to me.

"Yeah," I said. "Like, twice a month?"

He shook his head. "I didn't think you were into, you know, going out or whatever."

"Just because I don't hang around Creek View parties doesn't mean I don't go out, Josh." True, other than Leo's, "going out" for me usually meant seeing a movie in Bakersfield with Dylan and Chris or going for a post-midnight dinner at the Denny's an hour up the highway.

He shook his head. "*Skylar*." He said my name in a singsong way. "Don't get upset. I was just . . ." He put a fist up to his lips to block a silent burp. "Joking around."

Yep, he'd definitely gotten through a few beers.

I wanted to be angry with him, or grossed out by his sober-to-drunk ratio, but it was hard. Maybe he'd wanted to get out of Creek View just as badly as I had and then he'd gotten out and some asshole in Afghanistan had sent him back. If I were him, I'd be drunk too.

Another slow song came on, and I set my drink down and held out my hand. "I didn't invite you so you could be an ass. Come on."

Josh's eyes widened. "No way."

"Yes way. Or do you want to wait until something really fast comes on?"

He frowned and, when he could tell I wasn't taking no for an answer, stood up, setting his empty beer bottle on the bar with a long sigh. "I'm not drunk enough for this."

I rolled my eyes and tried not to shiver when he put his hand into mine. What the hell was I doing?

Chris was still talking to his bartender cousin, but his eyes followed me as I walked onto the floor with Josh. I gave him a look like, *What?* and he responded by swirling his index finger next to his temple in the international sign for *loco*.

"Let's go in the middle," I said, pulling Josh after me. "It's better there."

In the crush of bodies, you could dive into the music and forget yourself. I felt like Josh and I both needed that right then. I expected it to be awkward, like we'd have to come up with a game plan for dancing with prosthetics, but he just pulled me against him, one arm slipping around my waist while the other rested between my shoulder blades, his hand on the base of my neck. I reached up and draped my arms over his shoulders, and he looked down at me as we swayed in a little circle. Part of me was terrified of stepping on his fake foot or something, but it was fine. More than fine.

"This song sucks," he said. The lights painted his skin blue and pink.

"You're just saying that because you don't speak Spanish."

"No, I'm saying that because it sounds like some Mexican cowboy lost his dog and is drowning his sorrows in a bottle of Cuervo."

"Oh my God, you are so annoying."

"C'mon, you have to admit this shit's cheesy as hell."

"What, do you prefer to slow dance to Metallica?"

"Hell, yeah."

"Remind me never to ask you to dance again."

"Mission accomplished."

But he pulled me closer so that my cheek naturally rested against his chest, and I let him do it because there is nothing more, I don't know, *naked* than dancing with someone while looking into their eyes. Josh's heart was beating out a quick rhythm, and I wondered how much of his casual bravado was for show. Had it always been that way, even before his accident?

When the song ended, I pulled away, twirling out of his arms. I couldn't breathe so well, and my bones felt like Silly Putty, like you could twist me into all kinds of crazy shapes and it wouldn't even hurt.

We stood there in the middle of the dance floor, staring at each other, my hand still in his. His blue eyes were shining and clear, all that glassiness gone, and a slow smile spread across his face.

"You wanna get out of here?" he asked. "Go swimming?"

My mouth opened; I didn't think. "Yes."

This time he didn't let go of my hand. We slipped out of Leo's, leaving the loud music and laughter behind.

chapter five

Josh took me to the Paradise pool (or, rather, I took him, since he wasn't totally sober yet), which was perfectly clean after his afternoon with it. It shone like a new toy, and I grinned.

"Look at you," he said, shaking his head. "You really got a thing for pools."

"They're my first love." Pools didn't get you pregnant, and they didn't die on you. Who needed anything more?

The moon was crazy full that night, its milky light spilling across the surface of the water. The motel was quiet, just a few lights peeking out of closed curtains. Amy was at the desk behind the glass door, her headphones on. She had no idea we were there.

Josh unbuttoned his shirt and threw it onto the lounge chair behind him, but he left his dog tags on. Even though it was dark, I could see dozens of scars crisscrossing his chest, like ridges in a sand dune. What else had that place done to him?

"From the bomb," he said, his voice tight.

"They got you good, huh?" I wanted to ask him about the scars, but it seemed like shaky territory. Just being around him shirtless felt like shaky territory. There was too much skin, and my body still hummed from our dance at Leo's.

"Oh, yeah," he said. Then he gestured to the water with his trademark sneaky smile. "Ladies first."

There was no way I was undressing in front of him. "Yeah, I don't know about that," I said.

He folded his arms across his chest, the left side of his mouth inching up at my hesitation. "I won't look."

I raised my eyebrows. "Promise? You're not gonna get all pervy on me after a perfectly nice evening?"

He threw back his head and laughed. "Skylar Evans, where the hell did you come from?"

I kicked off my tennis shoes. "Same place you did. Don't tell me your mom never explained the birds and the bees."

I held up my finger and twirled it around, once, and Josh sighed and faced away from me. I slipped off my dress, thankful I'd decided to wear the underwear without holes. I wasn't trying to be a prude—I knew my bra and panties covered just as much as my bathing suit. But you don't take off your clothes in front of Josh Mitchell and expect to be a virgin by the end of the night.

I dove into the water, swimming until I touched the bottom of the deep end. The pool lights cast trembling reflections onto the peeling baby-blue paint. It was ghostly down there, as if I'd somehow pushed through to another world. I stayed under for a while, letting the cold water devour every bit of heat in me. Like I was a drunk trying to get sober.

When I broke through the water's still surface and turned around, Josh was sitting on the edge of one of the lounge chairs.

"Hey, Skylar?"

"Yeah?"

"Can you, like, not pay attention to me for a minute while I get in?"

"Sure. I'll be over there." I pointed to the diving board, and he nodded.

When I got to the board, I reached up and hung off the end, going underwater every now and then when I heard him grunt or sigh. I wanted to help, to let him know that it was totally okay, but I was afraid he'd snap at me like he did when I offered to help him out of the truck.

When I pulled myself up, I heard a splash and whipped around, worried that he would drown or something, which didn't make sense, but that was the first thought that went through my head. He was fine, a dark shadow swimming underwater. My eye caught a glint of metal; his prosthesis lay across the lounge chair. It was so strange, this limb, separate from a body, abandoned on the patio. Not human. Where there should have been blood and bones, there was only metal and plastic. Seeing the leg sitting by itself—that was the moment when I really understood what had happened to Josh. Here I was, treading water like it was nothing when for him it would be everything. I reached down and touched my leg. I ran my hand over my foot, past my ankle, along my shin, my calf, my knee, my thigh. Still there. I flexed my foot, turned my ankle round and round. It was a miracle, this leg.

Josh's metal calf ended at a plastic joint that acted as a knee—it was how he was able to bend the leg when he sat. Above the joint was a hollow plastic tube, like a soda bottle, but not transparent: dark blue and thick. I realized it made up for the part of his thigh that he'd lost. What did it feel like, to have that under your hand when you touched your leg? To scratch at an itch that couldn't possibly be there?

"Crazy, isn't it?"

I jumped at Josh's voice, my face reddening. I didn't know how long he'd been watching me. Had he seen me touching my leg? I felt like a Peeping Tom.

"I'm—I'm sorry. It's just . . ." I bit my lip, searching for an answer.

"It's okay," he said, after a minute. "I'd be curious too."

I wanted our laughter and joking around to come back, but it was too late. I'd screwed everything up.

He flipped onto his back so that he was floating in the water, staring up at the sky. His dog tags glistened on his chest, and the pool lights hit him from below so that he had a sort of halo all around him, like those pictures of saints in Chris's house. He'd put on a pair of long silky basketball shorts, so I couldn't see his stump—the extra fabric swayed in the water like a jellyfish, and I swam over to him, careful not to invade his space.

I hoped he hadn't put on the shorts because he thought it would bother me, seeing his stump. But I wasn't honestly sure how I would feel if I saw what was left of his leg. Grossed out? Scared? I thought about how everyone at Leo's had avoided it, as if nothing had changed. The pretty girl, the high school friend, Ricky. Even Dylan and Chris. Their eyes never left his face, and they were always smiling, smiling, smiling. You don't talk about lost limbs and smile. You don't talk about war and sacrifice when you're wearing your Friday-night clothes. And I wondered if that was what Josh really wanted—that pretending. I didn't think I would. I'd want to talk about it or at least be honest about the fact that it had happened.

"Does it hurt?" I asked.

He let out a sigh and his body seemed to relax and sink a little more into the water. I decided that I'd made the right choice.

"Yeah," he said. "Always. But it feels good to be in the water. At Walter Reed they had these pools we could swim in every day, for rehab and stuff. I miss that."

I stopped treading water and lay on my back to float beside him. The stars were never very bright in Creek View—it was in a valley and there was too much pollution blowing down from San Francisco. But they were still pretty, so far above us.

"You've changed," I said.

He snorted. "No shit."

I gently pushed him on the shoulder. "Shut up. You know what I mean."

"Yeah."

His voice was soft, and it made me think of that moment when he was in his uniform and I kissed him on the cheek. Maybe he'd started changing even before he'd lost his leg. Maybe I hadn't bothered to notice.

I don't know how long we floated on the water, the only sounds our breath and the pool water gushing in and out of its drains. I wondered what he was thinking about and why I cared so much. I wondered if I pitied him and if that was why I'd said yes to swimming in creamy moonlight.

But I didn't want to be anywhere else.

"Blake said you're moving to San Francisco," he said.

"Hmm" was all I said.

My throat had suddenly closed up, like San Francisco was Mom, like the two had become so attached that I didn't know how to break them apart. All I could think was, *Please don't let me be stuck here forever*, and I didn't know if I was praying or just talking to myself.

"Was that a yes or a no?" he asked.

"It's an I-don't-feel-like-talking-about-it."

"Not even to a one-legged dude? I promise I'll keep your secret."

"Not even to a one-legged dude. Maybe to an armless one." I turned my head a little, let my lips turn up. "You have too many limbs. Sorry."

Josh laughed and pushed his body down, standing in the water by moving his arms in slow circles as he looked at me. I put my eyes back on the sky.

"I think it's cool," he said, after a little while. "You know, that you want to go to college and stuff. Full scholarship, right?"

I nodded.

"What do you want to study?"

"Art. I want to . . ."

"What?" He was looking at me like he really wanted to know.

I shifted so that we were eye to eye. "I was thinking that I could work in an art museum someday. Or teach art, like a class about Impressionism at a college or something? But at night I could work on my collages. I'm also thinking about paper sculpture." I tilted my head back, stared down the stars. "It's stupid."

He kept looking at me. "That's not stupid." When I didn't answer, he moved a little closer. "It's not a crime to get out. Even if . . . even if it doesn't go the way you thought it would."

"Maybe," I whispered. I took a breath, cleared my throat. "I'm turning into a prune."

I showed him my wrinkled fingertips, then slipped under-water, swimming to the shallow end. When my hands collided with the stairs, I broke the surface and climbed out.

"Shit," I said. Water pooled at my feet and I looked at the glass door to the lobby, wondering if a towel was worth Amy talking my ear off for the next hour.

"What?" he asked.

"No towels."

"You can use my shirt."

Too late, I realized that I was standing there dripping wet in nothing but my bra and underwear. I instinctively covered my chest and backed away from the pool.

"Nice panties," he said.

"Turn around," I snapped.

He raised his hands in the air and flipped onto his back. "You need to learn how to take a compliment. Besides," he added, "I've seen a lot less on a girl, believe me."

"Yes, Josh, everyone in Creek View is well aware of your sexcapades."

He snickered. "*Sexcapades.* I like it."

I stomped over to the chair where he'd thrown his shirt and dried off as best I could. I slipped on my dress and pulled off my soaked undergarments, balling them up in my hand so Josh wouldn't make another comment about my lack of clothing. The wind gusted through the palms and the fronds rubbed together like crumpled tissue paper. It carried the scent of manure and gasoline and the orchard behind the fence. It blew under the thin material of my dress, and I shivered when it slipped over my skin. I envied its reckless abandon, the way it touched without fear.

A train was going by in the distance, and I closed my eyes and listened to its slow, clunking progress through the fields surrounding Creek View. I wanted to be on it, flying away from Mom and the trailer park and these strange feelings that were taking root in the pit of my stomach. I wanted to get out of there, under cover of darkness, hiding in a metal boxcar.

"I used to jump them," Josh said.

I opened my eyes and turned around. He was sitting on the edge of the pool, his good leg dangling in the water.

"Jump what?"

"The trains," he said. "It's a fuckin' amazing rush."

This was what country boys did, the Industrial Revolution's answer to cow tipping.

"Can't you, like, *die* doing that?"

"You can die doing a lot of things."

I hugged my arms, the wind suddenly too cold. I'd seen some pretty real stuff in my life—my mom, before she got sober, sitting in a pile of her own vomit the day my dad died, missing him too much to care about anything but dulling the pain; my best friend giving birth to a baby she was terrified to have. But what Josh saw in the war . . . I wasn't sure how to touch on that. Or if he wanted me to.

I'd heard the stories about Afghanistan. Guys coming home all screwed up with PTSD, lots of them killing themselves. I thought of the pictures in the paper, with the coffins being unloaded on airfields and the American flags folded into neat triangles at funerals for guys who weren't even old enough to legally drink. But it had never been real to me. Now I could see the flesh and blood of it.

I forced my feet forward and crouched behind him, then raised my hand, my skin inches from his, hesitating. Then I traced the letters on Josh's back: *Semper Fidelis*. He sighed as I silently trailed my finger along the intricate letters.

"Always faithful," I whispered. "To what?"

"The guys," he said, his voice low. "I should be out there with them. I'm a fucking waste of space here, Skylar."

I swept my palm across the words. "No, you're not."

He snorted.

"You're an excellent dance partner. A badass pool cleaner. Probably the best mechanic in town, but nobody will ever know that because—"

I stopped myself, afraid of going too far.

"You can say it," he said, keeping his eyes on the water. "I know my dad's a total screwup."

"Well. My mom has spent the past few weeks sitting in her bedroom, feeling sorry for herself and eating enough Little Debbie snacks to keep them in business. So, you know, it is what it is."

He turned to look at me. "Why's that?"

I shook my head. "She lost her job. Long story." I stood up and started putting my shoes on. "Speaking of . . . I should get going. She's probably mildly freaking out right now."

It was only eleven, but the longer I stayed out there with Josh, the more our night got hold of me.

His eyebrows drew together. "What are you gonna do?"

I swallowed the lump in my throat and made myself look him in the eye. "Work, like always. And try to . . . I don't know—" My voice caught, and I turned away.

"Hey," he said. Gentle—very un-Josh-like.

He reached out a hand and grabbed my wrist so I couldn't run off like I wanted to. I almost missed the devil-may-care Josh who made stupid jokes and was sober for about three hours a day. He was so much easier to deal with.

For a minute we stayed there, looking at each other. The wind rustled the orchard trees and whispered secrets to us.

"I'm fine, seriously." I shrugged him off and headed toward the back gate. "I'll wait out front, okay?"

When I got to his truck, I leaned against it, drinking the night air in great, heaving gulps. My hands were shaking, and my lips tingled, and the skin around my wrist—the part that Josh had touched—the skin was singing.

chapter six

"What the hell?" I muttered as Josh pulled into my driveway.

A rusted truck sat behind the Prizm my mom and I shared, the bed sticking out into the narrow road between the trailers. All the tension I'd pushed down threatened to boil over as I looked at the truck in front of me.

It shouldn't have been there this late at night.

"I think that's Bill Easton's truck," Josh said. He turned to look at me, his eyebrows drawn together in a V. "He a family friend or something?"

"No," I said, my voice flat.

Billy Easton was a good-for-nothing loser, one of my dad's old drinking buddies. He was the kind of guy that women tried not to make eye contact with, a tall, wiry snake with a loud, mean mouth. I'd be lying if I said he didn't scare me. Even when Dad was alive, I never thought Billy was all right. But after Dad died, he'd latched on to us, coming over every week to fix the sink or take a look at the stove. Anything to flirt with my mom a little.

Josh put the truck in park, and I opened the door—I could hear my mother's laughter coming out the open window and Billy's voice smacking the night air. I didn't know what was pissing me off more—the fact that *Billy Freaking Easton* had gotten my mom to come out of her cave when I couldn't, or that he was probably wasted and I'd have to give him a ride home.

"I gotta go," I said, sliding out of the truck. "Thanks for . . ." *The skin on my wrist, singing.* "Tonight. I'll see you."

"Skylar, let me walk you—"

"I'm fine. Thanks, though."

I slammed the door behind me and hurried up the steps. Josh's truck was still there when I looked back, and I could see him peering out the window, worried. I waved and opened the door, gagging as a wall of cigarette smoke hit me.

"Baby!" shrieked Mom. She was standing in the middle of the living room, wearing a pair of my jeans, which were way too tight on her. One of the sleeves of her tank top had slipped down, and her body glistened with sweat. She was wearing lipstick, and her mouth was stretched in this huge, manic smile. "Billy's here!"

A cold, hard knowing settled in my chest and spilled down into my stomach. Of course. *Of course* everything would go to hell just when I was about to get the fuck out of Creek View.

"Hey, honey," he said.

Honey, he'd called me. *Honey.*

He stood behind her, close, like they'd been in the middle of—I couldn't even think about what they might have been in the middle of.

"Hi," I said. The word sounded like a dropped book, thudding into the center of the trailer.

"You want a wine cooler? Got some in the fridge," he said.

I blinked, wanting to think I'd heard wrong, waiting for my brain to process what *wine cooler* meant for me. For my mom. We hadn't had alcohol in our house since the day Mom quit cold turkey. I'd promised her I wouldn't drink either. Not ever. Not one little sip. I looked around, spotted a wineglass on the table with lipstick on the rim.

I brushed past them and headed toward my room. "I don't drink."

"She's my good girl," Mom said.

The words stuck together, accented with a slight slur. Tears gathered in the corners of my eyes, but I kept walking. I'd talk to her about it tomorrow, when Billy was gone and she had the hangover she deserved. I pictured myself taking whatever he'd brought over and making her watch me dump it down the drain. I'd bring Dad into it if I had to.

I paused at the door to my room and turned around. "I have to get up early for work tomorrow," I said. "Would you guys mind keeping it down?"

Billy smiled, his yellow teeth wolflike in the dim lighting. "Sure, honey."

I slammed my bedroom door behind me, trying to ignore my mom's giggles. I thought about going over to Dylan's, but I knew she'd still be out with Jesse, probably parked in a field somewhere, since they both still lived with their parents. My eyes roved over the walls covered with my collages and prints of famous paintings. Magritte, Kandinsky, Kahlo. My origami shapes hung from fishing wire, dangling above my bed. They shivered in the slight breeze blowing through my open window. It was my own little escape pod, but none of it was enough tonight. Not after Josh and definitely not after Mom.

I shoved my earbuds in, but the music wasn't taking over everything I was feeling, as it had at Leo's earlier in the night. I heard glass breaking and then more laughter. I sat up and threw open the door.

"Seriously!" I yelled. "I have to work in, like, five hours."

Mom gave me an exasperated look. "Oh, Sky, don't be such a wet blanket."

Anger, black and cold, swept through me. I turned around and grabbed my backpack, shoving clothes, a book, and my MP3 player into it. I hooked my keys around my index finger, then swept past them.

"You're blocking me in," I said to Billy.

"Where are you—" my mom started, but I held up my hand.

"I'm going to the motel. I'll just sleep in one of the rooms, okay?"

I wanted my mom to say, *No, of course not, Billy was just leaving*, and give him a meaningful look, but she didn't. She shrugged and pushed Billy toward the door. I hated how her hand lingered on his arm. I suddenly wondered if she'd been doing more than watching *Judge Judy* for the past week.

Billy lumbered past me, going outside in his bare feet. He didn't say a word, just got in his truck and backed out. I threw my stuff into the front seat of the Prizm and was so angry I stalled twice before I could get the car in reverse. I wouldn't look at him as I pulled out, but I could feel his watery eyes on me, goading, amused, a little triumphant. I tried not to think of his hands, his lips, all over my mom.

"Sorry, Daddy," I whispered. Dad was rolling in his grave—he had to be.

I sped out of the trailer park, and when I got to the Paradise,

I pulled under one of the oak trees at the far end of the dirt parking lot and just stared into the darkness for a long time, my mind numb. Then I leaned my seat back, covered my eyes with the extra tank top in my bag, and cracked the windows. Exhausted, I fell asleep to the sound of crickets and the hum of the highway.

JOSH

It's hard driving away from her. I don't know, man, I just want to, to take care of the situation. Like, she had this look on her face when we pulled up—it was just for a second, but she was panicked and I could feel myself go into battle mode, that rush of *let's do this* and for a second I remembered what it felt like to have a purpose, a mission. To wake up and know *this is who I am, this is what I do, this is where I belong.* To have tasks and accomplish them. To have some goddamn pride. And she needed backup, I could tell, and I wanted to, I don't know, be her fuckin' knight in shining armor, I guess, but I couldn't get out of the truck fast enough. She was running to the trailer and I threw off my seat belt but before I could even open the door I jammed my fake knee against the steering wheel and it hurt like a bitch and then—*snap*—I'm ready to kill someone. That combat switch flipped and I was on, ready to go, a registered lethal weapon. This anger just pouring through me and I was shaking and everything turned red then black and so I tried to focus on that Marine Corps mantra my physical therapist is always shoving down my throat: *Improvise. Adapt. Overcome.* I gripped the steering wheel and tried to breathe. *Improvise. Adapt. Overcome.* He tells me, *You can't roll like you used to, Josh. Gotta find a new way of doing things.* Sky turns around and waves and she has this little smile on her face and suddenly I'm okay, like she broke through the mess of me. I remember I don't need to be at that razor's edge anymore, so I drive home. I don't realize I'm smiling until I see my reflection in the side mirror. Didn't even recognize myself.

chapter seven

After a night of sleeping in the car, I wasn't in the best of moods. All I could think about was that wineglass with lipstick on it. The problem was so much worse than I'd thought. Getting my mom a job: I could handle that. Getting her back on the wagon . . . no way. I'd already done it once, just after Dad died. It had taken almost a year—I had less than two months.

I'd been short with guests all day and had even given Marge some attitude when she'd asked me to run to the bank for her. I'd apologized, of course, and it was fine, but I didn't want to be one of those girls who brought her personal drama to work. Amy, the other receptionist, was like that. Nearly every second she was going off about her boyfriend or her crappy stepmother or how broke she was. I'd asked Marge to cover the desk so that I wouldn't have to deal with people, and I'd started cleaning the rooms, even though we had a lady who came in to do that once a day.

I took my frustration out on the dirty towels and the dust on the nightstands, on picture frames that weren't perfectly aligned and on flat pillows that my fist could punch and shove into their proper place. Seeing my mom like this was pressing Rewind on my life, taking me right back to those bleak months after Dad died, when the world turned gray. Not that I needed reminding. I thought about him all the time. But now it was like I was suddenly twelve again, holding her hair as she puked over the toilet bowl, trying to keep my tears in so she wouldn't feel worse than she already did.

I was starting to see each day before August 29th—the day I was moving to San Francisco—like a hurdle. Run. Jump. Run. Jump. Run.

There was a soft knock on the open door of the room I was cleaning (unicorn theme), then, "How's the Sky today?"

Josh.

I turned around, shading my eyes against the bright rectangle of light. He leaned in the doorway, watching me.

"Hey." I looked down at the industrial sheets in my hands. I could almost smell the chlorine from the pool. The feel of his skin under mine as I traced the *Semper Fidelis* on his back.

"A little cloudy?" I finally said.

It was so much easier to turn the past twelve hours into a metaphor.

He nodded. "Thought so. Marge said you were begging her to do manual labor instead of sit at the desk."

"The desk gets old after a while."

"Need some help?"

He walked into the room, limping slightly. I wondered if he would ever be able to walk with those long, confident strides he'd had before he left.

"Sure." I handed him one corner of a bottom sheet and scooted around to the other side of the bed.

He'd left the door open, and sunlight streamed into the stuffy room. We worked quietly for a few minutes, but it was an easy silence. A couple of kids ran by the door, shooting at each other with water guns. Their shrieks scattered the silence as though it were a flock of startled birds. Josh stopped what he was doing and watched them for a second, a faint smile on his face.

"Kids are the same wherever you go," he said, turning back to me. "Afghani, American—they're all the same."

"Do the kids in Afghanistan have toy guns? I mean, they see enough real ones, right?"

Josh laughed. "Oh, they have them. Scared the shit out of me the first time I saw one. I remember one day we were in this village, passing out school supplies to the kids, and this little guy lifts up what looks like an assault rifle, and I remember thinking, *fuck, I can't kill a kid*, you know?" His jaw tightened for a second, but then he shrugged. "It was cool, though. His mom started going off on him—I mean, I don't know what she said, but she sounded like a mom, right? Hit him upside the head and everything. And then he throws the gun down and kind of waves at me. Swear to God, before his mom said something, I almost pissed my pants."

"Wow." I let that sink in, tried to wrap my head around his reality, but I couldn't. It was too big, way beyond anything I had experienced. "I'm sort of not able to imagine you there. Like, it's weird, you know? A totally different world."

"Yeah. Totally different." He cleared his throat as he balled up the dirty sheets from the bed. "I had fun last night. Thanks for taking me out."

I leaned down and started putting a clean top sheet on the

bed, letting my hair fall across my face so he couldn't see how it betrayed me, all blushing maiden like.

"Yeah, well, Leo's, you know? It's always a good time." I pointed to the sheets, which he'd tucked super tight and straight on his side. "You're, like, a master bed maker."

"Military training," he said. "You should see how organized my closet is."

"Were you messy before?"

"Oh, yeah."

We put new pillowcases on the pillows, and Josh would smile whenever I caught his eye. I felt clumsy, like I couldn't figure out how to use my hands anymore.

"I got it," Josh said, as I reached for the comforter. I let him deal with it while I busied myself by restocking the bathroom with hard, thin towels and soap that smelled like plastic.

"Everything okay at home?" he asked when I came out of the bathroom.

"Why?" The word came out sharp, bladelike.

He shrugged. "You seemed upset about Bill Easton being at your place."

"Oh." I wanted to tell him about the wineglass and how my mom had borrowed my jeans. "Um. It's fine. It's . . . whatever."

"Well, now I understand the situation perfectly." The side of his mouth snaked up, and I couldn't help but laugh a little.

"Okay, that was the world's vaguest answer. Can I plead the Fifth?"

"Free country."

He followed me outside, and I shut and locked the door. The sun was pounding on me, and I gave the pool a longing glance.

"Marge was telling me she wanted to do a lot of renovations this summer," he said. "You think I should repaint the rooms?"

Renovations? This was news to me. I wondered if Marge was trying to keep Josh busy.

"Anything would be a vast improvement on what can only be called Dung Brown," I said. It was the standard wall paint under the paraphernalia in all the rooms.

"Thought so."

He followed me to the next room (Tom Cruise), helping me with the bed again. I didn't ask why. It was nice having company—I'd been spending way too many hours alone with my own thoughts.

"I can't believe these are still here." Josh pointed to the model fighter jets hanging from the ceiling. He'd put them together to add to the *Top Gun* theme. "Thought they'd have fallen apart by now."

"*I feel the need*—" I began.

And together: "*The need for speed. Ow!*" We high-fived, just like Goose and Maverick in the movie. We were sort of nerdy like that when it came to *Top Gun*.

"Good times," I said, remembering how we'd decorated the room together. "You played that 'Danger Zone' song so much. Marge wanted to kill us."

He nodded. "Yeah. I can't believe you had the sound track. Like, who has that?"

"Cool people like me, obviously."

"Obviously."

Josh was the only person I knew who indulged my *Top Gun* obsession. Chris had tried, but he couldn't get through watching it without snarky commentary. Now I realized that Josh must have loved it because it was all about the military.

"You know, I never told you, but *Top Gun* was my dad's favorite movie."

"Yeah?"

"Uh-huh. That's why I started watching it so much. But now I just love it. I guess that's kinda weird."

"No," he said. "It lets you feel closer to him. Makes sense."

There was more quiet bed making and bathroom stocking and nightstand dusting.

"That's why I hooked up with your brother," I blurted out.

He looked up at me, his head cocked to the side. "Because of *Top Gun*?"

"No. It was . . . God, I don't know why I'm telling you this." I looked down at the rag I was using to dust, but I knew he was watching me, waiting. "It was the anniversary of my dad's death and, I don't know. Maybe it was because of graduation coming up without him, but I just . . . I needed a body. That sounds so slutty. But it's the truth. I just had to forget, for a while."

I hadn't told anyone that before. Not even Dylan. I didn't know why I needed to tell Josh, but it felt like I did.

He was quiet for a minute, and I wished I could take the words back, but then he said, "I understand, Sky. That's not slutty at all. Or, if it is, then I'm the world's biggest slut."

I laughed and finally looked up. He was smiling at me, a funny smile. Kind. "I can see the headlines now," I said. "'Wounded Warrior Says He's World's Biggest Slut.'"

"Oh, man. The guys in my old unit would love that."

I wondered if he could hear the longing in his voice when he mentioned the guys he used to fight with.

"You miss them," I said. Not a question.

His eyes widened, like no one had ever made the connection before. "They were my family," he said simply.

I got that—it was what Chris and Dylan were to me. "You need people like that," I said. "Sometimes they're the only ones who have your back."

"True that."

"You ever see any of them?"

"Nah. Everyone's all spread out, and the unit's back in Afghanistan for another tour. Mix of old and new guys. A couple girls too, actually. Lady Marines are badass."

I'd never thought about that, how women would be over there too. I wondered what it was like for them, being around so many guys, fighting in a country where it was a victory for girls just to go to school.

"I had a few visitors when I was in the hospital, but it was just too . . ." He ran a hand over his shaved head. "It wasn't the same."

"Gotcha," I said. Through with dusting, I leaned against the TV stand while he finished the bed. "So after the renovations, what are you gonna do?" I asked.

He'd only ever worked at the Paradise part-time, and unless he took my job when I left, I couldn't imagine that there'd be enough for him to do. We never had more than five rooms booked a night.

Something passed over his face—a shadow or a memory. He looked out the window for a second, suddenly far away. Maybe back in Afghanistan.

"It's none of my business," I said. Didn't know why I wanted it to be. Shit, why'd I have to be so nosy?

He threw pillows on the bed as he spoke. "No, it's cool. I don't know what I'm gonna do. Blake's helping my dad out in the shop, and he doesn't really need more than one of us. I mean, we thought I'd be in the Marines forever, so—yeah. My mom thinks I should try truck driving, but I don't even know if they'd take me with . . . I was also thinking maybe I'd go to school."

"Like . . . *college*?"

He smirked. "Yeah, us jarheads can read *and* write. Pretty crazy, huh?"

I hugged a pillow to my chest. "Sorry. I didn't mean . . . I just thought you weren't into school. Like, at all."

Honestly? I'd been a little surprised he graduated.

He shrugged. "I read more than *Maxim*, if that's what you're asking."

"I'm a dick, sorry."

He laughed. "Chicks can't be dicks."

I waved my hand. "Semantics." I threw him a pillowcase, and he put it on the last pillow. "Okay, so if you *did* go to school, what would you study?" I asked.

He shrugged. "No idea. The government will pay for it, though, if I ever think of something. So, yeah, I don't know. I'm not out yet, so nothing's decided."

"Wait." Something in me twisted, but I ignored it. "You're still in the Marines?"

He nodded. "I'm on leave right now. I've got six weeks of convalescence, six weeks of regular. I have to decide by the end of the summer if I'm gonna stay in and take the desk job they've offered me or get out. They said in the future there might be a training position."

"But you wouldn't have to, like, fight again, right?"

"I want to. If I can up my PT—uh, my physical training—and get one of those badass robotic legs, hell, yeah, I'd want to go back. Be useful."

"To *Afghanistan?*" I wanted to say, *Haven't they done enough? Haven't you done enough?*

"Without a doubt. I'm supposed to be there. You know, there're guys who lost way more than me who are still in. Their eyes, all their limbs. I used to think they were crazy. Thing is, being a Marine is the only thing I'm good at. Well, until the bomb anyway." He sighed and shook his head as he turned toward the door. "I'm starving. You want anything from McDonald's?"

It was the nicest way to say *conversation closed.*

"Oh. Sure, that'd be great."

I gave him my order and then scooped my heart out of my stomach while he walked away toward his truck. After a second, I ran to the door.

"Josh!"

He turned around. "Yeah?"

"Being a Marine isn't the only thing you're good at. Maybe you just don't know what your thing is yet, you know? I think . . ." I took a breath. "I just think you're selling yourself short."

He smiled, but it didn't reach his eyes. "I'll be back soon."

Hanging out with Josh was like learning how to drive stick. It was hard enough just to start and then it was one stall after another. But somehow I always managed to crawl forward, just a little bit.

chapter eight

It'd been a long day at the Paradise, and after the intense conversation with Josh, I wasn't ready to deal with Billy Easton. I breathed a sigh of relief when his truck wasn't in our driveway, but the trailer had evidence of Billy everywhere. It smelled like a bar—sour and a little bit sad. The cigarette smoke from last night clung to the couch, the curtains, the towels. I opened all the windows and doused the place with air freshener that smelled only marginally better. I could hear the shower running, which was good because it meant Mom was at least awake. An empty pizza box lay on top of the stove, and the trash can was full of bottles. I took the trash out, then started on the dishes that were piled in the sink. I knew the sight of me cleaning up wouldn't mean a whole lot—my mom was used to that. But I was hoping that she'd be more willing to talk if I wasn't sitting on the couch with my arms crossed, glaring at her. Which was what I wanted to do.

The neighborhood was pretty quiet for a summer night. There was the slow clatter of a train heading north, maybe up to San Francisco, and the screech of some kids as they rode by on their bikes. I thought of the story Josh had told me of the kid in

Afghanistan and wondered what it would be like if there were soldiers in our neighborhood, peeking into our houses and passing out candy to the kids. Pointing their guns. I couldn't imagine it.

I reached my hand up and trailed my fingers through the wind chimes that I'd hung over the kitchen sink. There wasn't a breeze, but I wanted to hear their cheerful, tinkling sound. I closed my eyes as my fingertips brushed the metal tubes, and for a moment the bright notes took me away. It was a flying, dancing, falling sort of sound, and I decided there was hope in the world when you could make a sound like that.

I set to work, scrubbing at dried melted cheese and cups rimmed with old coffee stains. The water was hot, maybe too hot, but it kept my mind off of what was coming.

"You're back," Mom said.

I turned around and there she was, leaning against the door frame, her hair wrapped up in a towel. I hadn't turned on any lights, and the twilight shadows spilled across her face. I flipped a switch, and the dull kitchen light nuzzled the darker corners of the room, brought out the circles under her eyes.

"How you feeling?" I asked. She looked about ten years older.

Mom sighed and walked over to the fridge. She must have seen me stiffen because she pulled out a bottle of Nestea and shook it at me. "Just tea," she said.

Like I was some kind of narc.

Last night was hanging in the air between us, a heavy, ugly thing that leered as it waited to be called onstage. I wished she would bring it up, but that wasn't her style. She was a sweep-things-under-the-rug kind of person.

I turned off the water and slowly wiped my hands with the dish towel. It smelled bad, and I threw it on the floor where my mother had begun an impromptu laundry pile. Then I turned around and leaned against the kitchen sink.

"Mom, what's going on?"

She sipped at her tea. "I just had a little fun last night, Sky. When's the last time I did that?"

I didn't say anything, and she rolled her eyes and sat down in a huff. "Jesus, you'd think I'd shot up or something."

I thought about Josh and what he was up against. This was nothing.

"I just don't understand why you're drinking again. Or why you were hanging out with Billy. I mean, how many times did you tell me he was scummy?"

Mom reached into her bathrobe pocket and pulled out a pack of cigarettes. I didn't even bother saying anything about her smoking—what was the point?

I looked down at my bare feet. I hadn't painted my nails in weeks, and the light blue polish that Dylan had put on them for graduation night was chipping. Graduation. About a million years ago.

When I looked up at my mom, she was watching me, five different emotions and none of them anger flashing across her face. She put down the cigarettes and crossed to the sink, pulling me into one of her viselike hugs. It had been days and days since she'd hugged me like that, and I could feel my stiffness and anger melting away.

"I know I'm such a disappointment to you, Sky," she whispered.

"No," I lied. "I just . . ." I swallowed the tears that were threatening to come out and hugged her even tighter. "We can get through this. Together."

Mom let go and backed away a bit. She lifted up one of her callused hands and tucked a stray strand of hair behind my ear.

"Baby, what I need you to be thinking about right now is college."

"I *am* thinking about college," I said. "But I'm not leaving you like this. We have to get you a job. I just found out the gas station's hiring, so you could work there, and if we get Billy away from here—"

"Sky, I've spent the past eighteen years making tacos. I don't think a couple of weeks off is such a crazy idea."

"I know, but—"

"And who's gonna hire me?" Her voice started to rise. "Taco Bell's the only job experience I have. If I apply somewhere else, they'll call the Bell and find out about the robbery and how it was all my fault. You think someone's gonna want to hire me after that?"

"I mean, can't you try?"

"Waste of time. Plus I'd have to apply online."

We didn't have Internet at home, and the chance of getting my mom over to the Paradise to use Marge's was slim to none.

"What about unemployment?"

"I'm not eligible. Since it's my fault I got fired, the state's gonna leave me high and dry."

Shit. I hadn't realized that.

A truck rumbled into the driveway, and I looked out the kitchen window, a silly part of me hoping it was Josh. Not that there was any reason it would be. Then I spotted the faded red truck: Billy was pulling up, a cigarette dangling from his lips.

I turned back to my mom. "Seriously?"

"I deserve to have a little fun, don't you think?"

"So let me take you to the beach. We could go to Pismo, or, I don't know, one of those Indian casinos. Or camping in Yellowstone . . ."

I could hear the note of desperation in my voice, not to mention that we had never once gone camping. Even when my dad was around, the closest I'd ever gotten to the great outdoors was spending a day by the creek with our old portable Weber grill.

"Baby, cut me some slack, okay?"

This thing was building in me, so big, so much. I couldn't do it anymore—be her cheerleader and therapist and parent and daughter all in one. And screw her for making me.

"Why?" I said, the words spilling out. "So you can get drunk off your ass and drive into an eighteen-wheeler like Dad did?"

It was like knocking over a glass and watching it fall to the floor, knowing you won't be able to catch it before it shatters. She stared at me, her mouth open in a perfect O. The words had felt poisonous sliding off my tongue, but it felt a little good too, that burst of pissed-off adrenaline. Her eyes dimmed, and I saw her actually leave for a minute and go somewhere else while her body stood there rigid, shocked. That wasn't what I'd wanted. Not that. Not ever.

"Mom," I whispered.

God, how could I be so stupid? I'd pushed her too far. Guilt prickled my skin and whispered that it was my fault if she drank too much tonight.

There was a hard knock on the cheap metal door.

"Mom."

She blinked, then moved past me to let Billy Easton in.

JOSH

I line my pills up in formation, like they're about to be inspected. It's time for roll call, motherfuckers: Zoloft for depression (Here!), Abilify for depression (Here!), Klonopin for anxiety (Here!), Oleptro and Lunesta for sleep (Here! Here!), Neurontin for phantom limb pain (Here!), ibuprofen for TBI headaches (Here!). If I stare at the pills long enough, they start floating like tiny stars in the sky. Creek View fades away and now I'm on post, sitting near a canal, eyes peeled. The stars cover the sky, thousands of them. Never seen stars like that before. Made me wish I knew the constellations. *When you wish upon a star,* I joke-sing. I can't sing for shit, and we all know it. You laugh and say, *Dude, stars are for pussies. I wish on the moon.* Gomez shakes his head. *You can't wish on the moon.* You raise your eyebrows. *Why not?* Gomez shrugs. *Ask fuckin' Disney why not. They wrote the song.* I laugh and say, *You can't wish on anything.* You look over at me: *If you could wish on the moon for something, what would it be?* I think about everything that's gone down since we deployed—Sharpe dying, Panelli losing his arms, that IED blowing up in Harrison's face so now he looks like Freddy

Krueger. The Afghanis that got wiped out by that drone strike the week before and the ones I see on the side of the road sometimes, Taliban roadkill. Before we shipped out, I thought it was so cool that I was going to war. Felt like a bad motherfucker. Then I saw our first guy go down and it wasn't so cool anymore. *I'd wish them back, man,* I say. You nod as you pack some more chew. *I'd wish all of them back.* Now I look at the pills lined up on my desk and my empty room and my metal leg. The moon's not big enough to wish on. Nothing is.

chapter nine

I looked at the clipboard in my hand, making sure that I'd written down everything we needed to order: prepackaged soaps, mini bottles of shampoo, more industrial towels, thin plastic cups. Satisfied, I closed the storage closet door and walked over to the window beside the lobby couch. The sickly sweet scent of cat pee hovered in the air above the cushions, a present from a guest's feline companion. My stomach turned a little—the combination of urine and stifling heat was too much.

Josh's truck still wasn't in the driveway, but I told myself that wasn't what I'd been looking for. I'd wanted to see . . . No, I couldn't pretend. I wanted to see Josh. It didn't make any sense, but I kept finding myself thinking about him, hoping we'd run into each other. I'd spent the past few nights lying awake in bed, listening to the sound of Mom's TV through the thin walls, unable to sleep. Worrying, yes, but what bothered me almost as much as our dire straits was Josh and how I couldn't escape him in the dark. At night I'd lie awake with these crazy fantasies of him showing up at my window, and I'd wonder if he was awake too, and if he was, was he thinking about me? Then I'd tell myself he probably wasn't alone. Josh Mitchell wasn't known for sleeping by himself, and I was an idiot, imagining doing things with him that made me blush when he was probably doing those things to some other girl with absolutely no thought of me whatsoever. Then I'd get jealous and feel stupid and punch my pillow and try to push him out of my mind. What was happening to me? I'd become tidal, the current of my want pushing me toward him, pulling me away from him. Toward him, away from him.

A crush. I had a silly crush because he'd suddenly become exotic, an enigmatic hero. He'd been in a land full of mysteriously clothed women and men in long tunics and turbans. He'd seen the kind of stuff Picasso painted *Guernica* for. He had stories to tell, unlike anyone else in this town.

But I'd had crushes before, and this . . . this was no crush. *The pact,* I reminded myself. I was convinced that the reason Chris and I were the only ones from our graduating class to get out of Creek View was because of our self-imposed celibacy. Something about falling in love (or lust) seemed to anchor people to this place.

I turned my back on the window and stood in front of the box fan to let the cool air dry some of the sweat that was dripping down my neck. All I wanted to do was sit in a refrigerator. After a few minutes, I gave up on the fan and went back to the counter. I ran my hands over the part of Marge's collage I'd been working on for most of the morning. The plan was to connect these smaller collages by collaging them into one big piece. Right now, I was trying to get the angel on the Paradise sign just right. I'd taken to going out and studying her at night, to make sure I was capturing all the details, like the way the neon wasn't working on all the feathers on her wings. I'd chosen some pretty metallic paper to create the neon glow of the sign. I'd already fashioned 3-D wings for the angel—pipe cleaners covered with papier-mâché, so now I grabbed a sheet of shimmering gold sanded pastel paper and began slicing it into tiny strips with my razor blade—the angel's hair.

As I worked, the lobby fell away, my world whittled down to the feel of the paper under my fingers and the creature straining to burst from the collage. My sound track: the whir of the fan and the soft sounds of cutting and arranging. I wasn't in Creek View anymore—or, rather, I was in a Creek View of my own making, where all that mattered were angles and colors and the steady beat of my heart as the angel slowly came to life. Nothing—and no one—could touch me here.

The sliding glass door opened, and Marge walked in, fanning her thick face and startling me from my cocoon. I looked up, dazed. I'd forgotten the heat, the time—everything.

She crushed the can of Diet Dr Pepper in her hand and frowned. "Hey, sweet pea. Still no Josh?"

I shook my head. "Want me to try calling him again?"

"I think his cell's off. He was supposed to be here an hour ago."

She threw the can in the wastebasket next to the candy dispenser and looked over my notes on the clipboard, muttering to herself. As she got closer to the counter, I shooed her away.

She narrowed her eyes. "What are you doing over there—snorting cocaine?"

"Very funny," I said. "It's your collage, and you know it. Don't think I can't tell when you're trying to be sneaky!"

She huffed in mock offense. "I'll believe it when I see it."

"Weren't you the one telling me patience is a virtue?"

"I hate when my own wisdom bites me in the ass."

I laughed and gathered up the scraps of paper I wasn't using, then dumped them into a plastic bag for later, in this collage or another. Nothing ever goes to waste with collaging. It was the perfect medium for a broke-ass person like myself. Besides, if it was good enough for Picasso, it was good enough for me. It was his collages that had made me want to work with paper in the first place. In my essay for San Fran, I'd written about how I'd always felt like there was something magical about taking bits and pieces of the world around me and creating something whole. It gave me hope: if you could make a beautiful piece of art from discarded newspapers and old matchbooks, then it meant that everything had potential. And maybe people were like collages—no matter how broken or useless we felt, we were an essential part of the whole. We mattered.

I gave my collage one last, loving glance, then put it in the large portfolio folder I'd bought for myself when I got into San Fran. Marge still stood near the window, frowning. I glanced at the clock. It wasn't like Josh to blow off a shift like this.

"The electrician's here, and Josh has my keys," Marge said. "The guy needs to get into that back room where the generator and electrical panels are. Would you mind running over to Josh's house and seeing if he's there? If he's not home, you can check the garage."

I got that fluttery feeling that seemed to attack me every time Josh was around: in my chest and the pit of my stomach and in a place it's not polite to mention in mixed company. What was I supposed to tell her? *No, Marge, I'm sorry, but I can't go to Josh's house. You see, I'm experiencing a fluttering sensation.*

I leaned over the counter and grabbed my keys and wallet. "I think I'm gonna need a raise for this."

She handed me twenty bucks from her pocket. "Subway. You fly, I'll buy."

I pushed her hand away. "Kidding, Marge. Of course I'll go over there."

She stuffed the bill into the front pocket of my jean shorts. "Get out of here, and don't come back without a six-inch roast beef, no—"

"—mayo and extra pickles. I know, I know."

It only took me six minutes to drive to Josh's house. I hadn't been there since the night of the party. It seemed different in the daylight—smaller. Josh's truck was in the driveway, but the house seemed deserted. Maybe it was just the malaise of Creek View at noon, when the sun was at its most sadistic.

I got out of my car and headed up the concrete front walkway. The grass was brown, and the house sort of sagged in on itself, like a toothless old man. I knocked on the screen door, the sound echoing in the silence that had wrapped around me. I shaded my eyes and looked around the neighborhood, eerie in its emptiness. I half expected a tumbleweed to roll by. I pictured Afghanistan like this, but scarier and with mosques sounding out the call to prayer five times a day. Moon dust. A film over everything. Desolate.

I knocked again, and this time the door opened into a darkened living room. The girl standing in the doorway looked at me without saying anything, and I tried to smile, but she didn't smile back. Her dirty blond hair hung in limp strands around her shoulders, and her skin was pale, like she never went outside. But there was a certain Mitchellness about her—those Van Gogh eyes and thin lips twisted into a smirk.

"Hey, Tara."

She looked back at the living room for a second, probably checking the TV, bored with me already. It was annoying that a thirteen-year-old had the power to make me feel like an intruder. You'd think I was one of those people from the Evangelical church fifty miles away that came to Creek View a couple of times a year to save our miserable souls.

She turned back to me. "Blake's not here."

I could feel the blush smearing my cheeks. Damn. I wished I'd never said yes to Blake's offer to give me a ride home that Friday before spring break. That *yes* was going to haunt me for the rest of my life.

"Actually, um, I'm looking for Josh. Is he home?"

She crossed her arms over the little halter top she was wearing and jutted her hip out to the side in an almost comical mean-girl pose. "Why?"

The sun was burning the back of my calves, where it shot across the covered front porch. I shifted my feet, wiped the sweat pooling on my upper lip. She still hadn't opened the door to invite me in, but the cool air sneaked past her and teased me. Farther in, it sounded like there was a soap opera on TV, and I thought I could hear faint music—the heavy bass and reggae beats of Sublime—coming from deeper inside the house.

My eyes started to adjust to the dark room in front of me. Tara's face was pinched, and her eyes were already jaded. Another Creek View kid bites the dust.

"Marge needs her keys, and Josh took them home by accident."

Tara finally nodded and pushed open the screen door. "J's in his room. End of the hall."

I stepped inside. She was already on her way back to the TV.

"Thanks," I called. She did a backward wave and then plopped onto a sunken couch.

I shut the door behind me and let my skin soak up the cool air while I looked around. The house was a mess: old newspapers piled on a battered sofa, cans of beer and soda on the tables. It smelled like old dinners and too-strong air freshener that didn't do much to cover up the scent of pot. I passed a low bookshelf that had a cheap frame with a picture of Josh in his dress blues sitting next to a few chipped curios. There was just something about people in uniform: a quiet dignity about them that made you feel proud, even though it had nothing to do with you. Josh's eyes were serious, and he wasn't smiling, though there was a faint hint of one in the corners of his mouth. He looked so much older now. Josh must have gotten this taken right after he enlisted. He'd only been seventeen then. I wondered what he'd been thinking when they took that photo. It was the one the military would use if he died. He had to know how many guys were going home in coffins or wheelchairs. But he didn't look afraid. Not one bit.

I felt that tidal pull again, dragging me closer and closer to the shore that was Josh. I wanted to know more. About him. The war. I had to make sense of this need that was pulsing through me.

I passed the bookshelf and went down the hallway, the music getting louder as I got to the end. Definitely Sublime. The door was ajar, but I knocked instead of just walking in, suddenly nervous.

"Mom, I said twenty minutes!" he yelled. "*Jesus.*"

"Um. *Not* Mom. Or Jesus."

"What?" he said. Annoyed, strained.

I pushed open the door. Josh was doing push-ups in the middle of the room, shirtless, and his prosthesis was leaning against the bed. He was wearing the long athletic shorts he'd swum in that covered his stump completely. The muscles in his one calf were taut with the movement, and sweat dripped down his face. Push-ups with one leg looked about as much fun as push-ups with two legs. He glanced up as I walked in, his eyes widening. He stayed in the upward position for a second, just looking at me.

It was dumb, us staring at each other like this. I wanted to tell this tongue-tied, mush-of-a-girl Skylar to take a hike. So he had some muscles. Big freakin' deal.

"Sorry. I'll . . . Marge needs the keys," I blurted out. "To the . . . I don't know. The closet with the generator? So that's why I'm here."

Wow. Awesome, Sky. Way to go.

Josh lowered his knee and kind of sat back so that his leg was bent beneath him, the extra fabric from his stump pooling on the carpet. "Keys?"

"I guess she gave them to you yesterday?"

"Oh. Shit. I totally forgot about those. Uh . . . would you mind turning around for a sec, so I can deal with my gimpy leg?"

"Yeah, sure. Right." I turned to face the half-closed door, feeling a little bit like I'd gotten put in the corner.

"Sorry about yelling at you," he said. "My mom's been on my case all morning about some crap she needs cleaned out of the garage."

"It's not like you were expecting me."

"Yeah, well . . ." There was the sound of some shuffling, then, "Oh, hey, you know what I ran across last night?"

"Do you mean *ran* literally or figuratively?"

"Ha-ha," he said.

"Sorry, I couldn't resist."

"Guess you're keeping me on my toes," he said.

"All five of them."

Josh laughed. "I walked right into that one—er, limped."

I kept my eyes on the wall, smiling to myself. I heard the sound of a spray bottle, shuffling of fabric, then a kind of vacuumized click.

"Found some old letters from you. The ones you sent when I was over there."

The music suddenly turned off.

"Yeah?"

I'd only sent a few. Mostly when Marge suggested I should. It wasn't that I didn't care. It was just that Josh and I hadn't been super close. And I'd had no idea what to talk about, so I'd ended up sending him clips of the Sunday comics or a collage. He'd always write back, short little messages about the weather and the food and stuff like that. I kept every letter. Why?

"You can turn around now."

He was standing by the desk, and he held a paper out to me. "This was my favorite."

I took it, smiling a little at the familiar collage. I'd cut all these cool street art photos from different art magazines and glued them onto one thick piece of paper, then I'd folded it up and written *The Skylar Evans Gallery—Admission: Free.*

"Got it the day we came back from a long-ass patrol. It had been like extreme camping. We'd been away from the FOB for, like, five days or something. Following these crazy hajjis—er, Afghanis—all around this one little area, runnin' and gunnin'. And I was in such a bad mood 'cause we'd lost a couple guys, and I was just tired and had all this gear that needed to be cleaned for inspection. And then I opened your letter. Made my day."

I handed it back to him, my face hot. "The other Marines must have been like, who is this freak that sends art projects?"

He shook his head. "You'd be surprised at the kinds of mail some of the guys got." He chuckled to himself, like he was remembering something.

"What?"

"Let's just say some of the wives and girlfriends got creative."

My stomach flipped a little. "Oh."

He pointed to a tiny hole at the top of the paper. "I had it up near my bed for a while."

I brushed my fingers across the collage, touching Away. Touching the not-Creek-View-ness of it. "I hoped you'd be into it. I was thinking, like, if I were there, what would I want to see? Chris told me you'd probably prefer *Penthouse*, but I took a chance."

"Blake had that covered." Josh laughed at the face I made. "I'm glad you sent me your art. Gonna be worth a lot of money someday."

I rolled my eyes. Blushed. "We'll see."

He walked over to the bed and pulled a shirt over his head that said MARINES in big red and gold letters, standard Josh attire.

"What's up with you and that Chris dude, anyway?"

"What do you mean?"

"Like, are you together or . . . ?"

"*Chris?* God, no."

He raised his eyebrows.

"What?" I said.

"Just hard to believe you guys didn't hook up or whatever."

"Josh, contrary to what you might think, two people of the opposite sex can be friends without wanting to jump each other's bones."

He grunted.

I didn't want to think about why he was so curious. Didn't want to acknowledge the fizzy feeling buzzing through me.

"What's an FOB?" I asked.

"Huh? Oh. Forward operating base. It's like a remote outpost. Not the easiest assignment, but you see a lot of action."

"That's a good thing?"

He shrugged. "At least you know there's a point to you."

My eyes caught the crane I'd made out of a napkin that day at the diner. It was sitting on his nightstand.

"You kept it," I said. Goofy happy.

He looked over at the crane. Smiled at me. "Yeah."

I pointed to the photos tacked to the wall above his desk. "These your guys?"

"Yep. This one's of us around this time last year," he said, pointing to a photograph of himself with three other guys, all of them decked out in body armor and helmets. They held their guns so casually by their sides, as if they were shopping bags.

Behind them was a dusty field with huge mountains towering beyond it. Afghanistan. So weird, thinking about Josh living in another country. My heart beat a little faster as I got closer to the thing that had changed him. If I could figure out what made him tick, maybe the allure would wear off. Then I could go back to thinking he was an attractive dumbass who would never in a million years keep me up at night.

"Who's that?" I asked, pointing to the guy Josh was standing next to. Their arms were around each other, and they looked like they were both mid-laugh.

"My buddy Nick."

He picked up a keychain lying on his nightstand and held it up for me. I opened my hand, and he dropped Marge's keys into it.

"So why didn't you come in today?" I asked.

He put on his watch, keeping his eyes lowered. "Wasn't up for it."

There were dark circles under his eyes and a couple of empty beer bottles on the floor by his bed, but I decided it wasn't my business. He'd have to come up with something better for Marge next time he saw her, though.

I needed a safe topic. Felt like everything I said just brought up the reason he had those bottles by his bed in the first place. I picked up the dog-eared paperback beside his alarm clock. *Slaughterhouse-Five*.

"This any good? I keep meaning to read it, but it seems like such a boy book."

"Yeah. It's amazing."

I handed it to him, and he hesitated for a second, like he wanted to take it back, but then he shook his head. "Read it. Just—don't lose it. It . . . belonged to a friend of mine."

He looked at the book like it was precious, the kind of thing you keep in a glass case. *Belonged*. Past tense. I wanted to know why he'd give something like that to *me*.

"You sure? 'Cause I never lend books. I'm sort of a Nazi about it if someone gets even a smudge on the cover."

"Well, this one's been to war and back, so I think it can handle you."

I held the book against my chest. "Thanks."

"Yeah, sure."

The dude was a total mystery. I couldn't picture him sitting anywhere and just reading a book, yet here I was, borrowing one from him. I looked around the room, searching for clues. There wasn't much to see. It was practically empty. It looked totally different than it had just before he got home, when I was hanging out with Blake over spring break. I remember he'd wanted to grab a couple of Josh's CDs, so we'd gone into the room. Then, there had been posters on the walls of cars and girls—typical Mitchell fare. Now the walls were bare, except for a few postcards and photos tacked to the wall and a pile of neatly folded clothes in one corner, a stack of weights in another.

"So you planning on decorating anytime soon?"

"Maybe." He gestured to the door. "You want a beer or something?"

"Or something," I said.

"Right—you're good like that." He brushed the air with quotes on *good*, and I narrowed my eyes, hackles up. I was getting sick of everyone pointing out that I was "good."

"What's that supposed to mean?"

"Just . . . you never screw up, do you?"

"Like how? You mean I don't get arrested for egging people's houses?"

That was a Josh Mitchell stunt, circa his sophomore year.

He snorted. "Don't get pissy."

"I'm not getting pissy."

Except that I was totally getting pissy.

"Sky. All I'm saying is, you know, you're wound a bit tight."

"Is that a euphemism for *virgin*?"

He held up his hands. "Whoa. I wasn't going there." He arched an eyebrow. "But if you're up for it—"

"*Ugh*. Thank you," I snapped.

"For what?"

"Reminding me why you're such a dumbass."

It annoyed me that I felt so disappointed. No. I wasn't feeling disappointment. That new emptiness in me was relief. Because maybe, if he'd kept surprising me, I would have made a huge mistake. I mean, there were times in the middle of the night when . . . it was just good to have a reminder. I'd figured it out: the Mitchell boys, they brought out the desperate in me.

chapter ten

Josh grinned, like me calling him a dumbass was some kind of compliment.

"Hey, that's progress," he said.

"What?"

"That you need *reminding* that I'm a dumbass."

I grunted and glanced at the door. "Whatever. I'm on the clock, so . . ."

He gestured toward the hall. "After you."

I rolled my eyes at his attempt to be a gentleman, and he sort of sighed-laughed. I started out just as the door across the hall opened. His mother stood in the doorway, frowning. Her hair was in a long braid, and she wore a tiny, faded cotton sundress and a pair of flip-flops. She was super thin and had a slightly distracted air; rumor had it she was addicted to pain pills. Seeing her in front of me now, I didn't doubt it. I wasn't surprised that she was home in the middle of the afternoon. Blake had told me she helped their dad with paperwork for his business, but that she spent most of her time in her room, complaining about her back.

"Oh. Hi, Mrs. Mitchell. I don't know if you remember me, but I'm—"

"Skylar." She nodded. "I know."

I'd only talked to her a few times, when Josh was still in high school and she'd come by the motel, looking for him. She leaned against the doorway, and her eyes strayed down to Josh's leg. She sighed, staring at the metal. I felt Josh stiffen.

"You going to rehab today?" she asked.

He shook his head.

"Then why aren't you at the Paradise?"

"He's off today," I said, surprised at the lie. Josh looked at me out of the corner of his eye, but I ignored him. "I just came by to pick up Marge's keys."

"Huh." She looked at Josh. "Don't screw up that job," she said. "It'll be damn hard to find another one."

Her words felt like a punch to the stomach, and it wasn't even *me* she was belittling. Josh brushed past her and motioned for me to follow him.

"You gonna clean out that stuff?" she called after him.

"Yes." Josh didn't look back at her, but I didn't need to see his face to know how pissed he was. He'd practically spit out the word.

Tara was gone and the TV off, but I could hear Katy Perry's "California Gurls" playing from inside a room to my right.

Josh's mom pounded on Tara's door. "Tara. I'm going over to the garage. Don't let your pothead friends burn down my house."

A muffled "whatever" and then the front door slammed. As soon as his mother was gone, it felt a bit easier to breathe.

I followed Josh into the kitchen, trying to picture him living in this dismal house. With all the shut doors and dark corners, I got the sense that the Mitchells didn't spend a lot of quality family time together. Maybe all those years when Josh was running around town, acting like an idiot, he was just trying to find a way to escape. Maybe that was what all of us were doing, in our different ways.

"Why'd you tell my mom I was off?" he asked.

"She seemed like she was sort of, I don't know—"

"Riding my ass?"

"Well. Yeah, that's one way of putting it."

I leaned against the kitchen counter. Dirty dishes were piled in the sink and an empty box of Entenmann's doughnuts sat in the middle of the kitchen table. The stove was splattered with stains—old pasta sauce and who knew what else. The whole kitchen smelled like grease and burned toast. After two years in the military, Josh must have been going crazy, stuck in that house. As if he'd read my mind, he looked at the box of doughnuts and threw it into a nearly overflowing trash can, cursing under his breath.

"Your little sister's better than a guard dog," I said, as another Katy Perry song filtered through her door and into the kitchen. "I thought I was gonna have to show her some ID before she let me inside."

Josh chuckled and grabbed a Coke for me and a can of Bud for himself. "Yeah, she's cool like that." He took a long sip, then looked off toward the front door. "When I first got home, there were some reporters. Wanted to know about the war."

"You didn't want to talk to them?" I asked.

He played with the can's tab, twisting it around until it finally broke off. "Some guys are cool with reporters, talking to them all the time and stuff. We had a couple embedded ones for a while, and they were okay, I guess. I mean, it's weird having someone take pictures of you right after some shit goes down, but I started to forget they were even there. Just part of the land-scape. But I don't want to talk about . . . I just don't want to get into all of it. Especially with reporters who were never there."

I took a sip of my drink, watching him as he finished off his beer in one long gulp. Somewhere between walking down the hall and drinking the Coke in my hand, the annoyance I'd felt in his room had slipped away. I was starting to notice things again. Like how he had great hands—tan and strong looking. Or how he'd rub his stubble when he was thinking and the way he'd tilt his head down, then look up at me and smile.

Dammit.

"I love the Marines," he said. "Don't get me wrong. I was a punk-ass kid when I went in, and now I've had the chance to serve my country. I miss the hell out of it, if you want to know the truth."

"Really? Even after—"

"Yeah," he said. "Even after."

I thought of the picture tacked to his wall. The laugh I could almost hear.

"You ever felt like you belonged somewhere?" he asked.

I knew I didn't belong in Creek View—it had always felt wrong, like a too-small shirt or seeing Christmas decorations in June. But then where did I belong? It was a hard question to answer. I only knew how to live my life in negatives; it seemed like everything I *was* could only be seen in relation to what I *wasn't*. Like Josh said, I was "good," but only because I didn't screw up.

He started whistling the *Jeopardy* theme song, signaling I'd zoned out for way too long, and I blushed. "Don't rush me," I snapped. "That's a deep question."

"You're totally stalling."

"Okay." I drank the last sip of my Coke and pushed the sides in. The crunch of metal was oddly satisfying. "I've never been somewhere I belonged, but there are places where I think I could be happy. Like San Francisco. Well, do art museums count? Because I feel like I belong in them."

Josh nodded. "Art museums count." He threw his can in the trash bin by the door. "I hear the Skylar Evans Gallery is pretty cool. And it's free."

Did he realize how he was sometimes able to say the perfect thing? Because if he was trying to get in my pants, it was working.

I gestured to the front of the house. "I'm getting Subway for Marge and—wanna come with?"

Here I went again, asking him out. But it felt like I didn't have any control. With him, I never knew what the hell I was gonna say or do.

He smiled. "Yeah, sure. How 'bout I drive and we'll get your car when your shift is over?"

"You're gracing us with your presence this afternoon?"

"Get your ass to the truck, Evans."

I saluted him. "Yes, sir."

He shook his head. "We're gonna have to work on that salute."

———

The Subway closest to us was part of a truck stop ten miles up the road, in the same area as the Taco Bell, McDonald's, and the gas station Chris worked at. It was always pretty busy, full of people stopping during their long treks up or down the highway.

I sighed as the automatic doors slid open and I walked into a wall of cold air.

"I bet there's air-conditioning in heaven," I said.

"Maybe it's just the perfect temperature—low seventies with a breeze?" Josh said.

"Look at you, getting all philosophical."

"It's been known to happen."

We were halfway to the counter when a woman with two little boys stopped us.

"I'm sorry," she said to Josh. "I don't mean to bother you. But I just wanted to thank you for your service."

The Marines shirt he was wearing plus the prosthetic leg sort of screamed war hero, but from the look on Josh's face, it was obvious he thought he was anything but.

He cleared his throat a little and stuffed his hands into his pockets. "Thanks, ma'am," he said. "I appreciate it."

She put her hand on the boys' shoulders. They were both staring at his prosthesis, and I couldn't tell if they were freaked out or just fascinated. "You see this young man?" she said to them. "He's a real American hero." She looked up at Josh, smiling, while the boys leaned into her side, suddenly shy. "Our church is keeping all of you in our prayers. It's just so amazing, what you're doing over there."

Josh nodded and put his hand on the small of my back, gently pushing me toward the back of the truck stop, where the Subway counter was. He was just trying to get away, but at that moment, the only thing I knew or understood in the world was the heat of his hand.

"Thanks," he said to her. "Thanks a lot. It's our job, but we appreciate the support."

She gave his shoulder a squeeze. "You take care of yourself now, okay?"

He nodded. "Yes, ma'am. Thank you."

She walked away, but there were others smiling at Josh now, and when we got to the Subway counter, the girl insisted on giving him a discount. Josh wasn't beaming with pride—he'd grown quiet and distant, like he couldn't wait to get back into the safety of his truck. Two more people stopped to shake his hand on his way out, and he thanked them. They'd all smile at me, like I was somehow deserving of praise too—one woman even hugged me and said she appreciated what "our military families" were doing. By the time I found my voice to try to explain, she'd already gone off to the convenience store part of the truck stop.

"I wonder if she thought you were my sister or my wife," Josh said.

I blushed and kept my eyes anywhere but near his. "I don't know how you do it."

"I usually use the drive-thru is how I do it," he said as we walked back into the heat of the day. We got into the truck, and he started blasting his air-conditioning.

"You don't like it," I said.

I could see that he'd wanted to melt into the ground every time someone stopped him.

He sighed. "It's . . . it's just kinda weird when people thank me. Happened at the airport too, because I was in uniform. This old lady came up to me and said, 'Thank you for your sacrifice,' and it was really, like, sweet of her, but . . . I mean, I want to say, 'Don't thank me. Just don't pity me either.' I can't stand people's pity." He ran his hand over his head and looked over at me. "It's nice, and I know they mean well. It just feels weird, being thanked for something you wanted to do in the first place. Does that make any sense?"

I nodded. "Yeah. Yeah, it does." I curled up on my side and looked at him. "But it's okay to be proud of yourself, Josh. You did good. You know?"

He stared out the window, at the endless highway. "I tried to. But some of the stuff that went down . . ." He shook his head. "Yeah. I don't know."

"Subject change," I said. "If you could go on vacation anywhere in the world, where would it be?"

"Hawaii."

I made a face. "Really? But it's technically in the U.S. You could go *anywhere*—Thailand, India—"

"Nope. All I want to do is lie on a beach and drink more than I should. Plus, they speak English in Hawaii." He looked over at me. "You?"

"St. Petersburg," I said immediately.

"Russia?"

"No, St. Petersburg, Florida. *Yes*, Russia! I want to go to the Hermitage. It's one of the biggest art museums in the world, plus it's in the czar's Winter Palace, which is so freakin' cool. But, actually, if I could have two places—"

"No dice. You said *one*."

"Okay, but it's too hard to choose between the Hermitage and the Louvre."

"Which is . . . ?"

"The museum of museums. It's in Paris."

"Nope. You gotta choose."

"You're evil."

"I've been called worse."

I sighed. "Well, Paris is more practical. It has the *Mona Lisa*."

He smirked. "That painting sucks."

"*Josh!*"

"Oh, come on. That chick is ugly as hell. I don't see what the big deal is about."

"You're impossible."

The Paradise came into view, and he looked over at me. "Hey. Your mom find a job yet?"

I leaned my head back against the seat, my good mood instantly gone. "No. It's . . . no."

"Anything I can do to help?"

It occurred to me that we were the same, in a way. Both of us treading water, pushing against forces we couldn't control.

"Yeah," I said. "Help me eat these chips?"

I held up the little bag of Lay's I'd gotten at Subway. We put our hands in at the same time, and I jumped back with a nervous laugh.

I wondered if he'd felt the same charge I had when our fingers touched. I snuck a look out of the corner of my eye. He threw a chip into his mouth, a little smile playing on his face.

Yeah. He'd felt it.

JOSH

Marge comes up to me after work today with a bottle of Jack and two glasses and she says we've gotta talk. So we go outside and sit in the back of my truck and she pours us both a double and she drinks hers all at once. Then she tells me some really fucked-up shit. About her Army son and how he didn't die in Fallujah like we all thought. Like she told us. He offed himself. Came home to Ohio all messed up in the head and fuckin' slit his wrists in the bathtub. *Jesus, Marge,* I say. Like an angry prayer. *Jesus Christ.* And I don't know what else to say, because there's no magic word to bring him back, so I just hold her hand while she cries and I'm so angry at him. This dude I never met I just want to drag him up from hell and beat his ass. Because it's guys like him that make everyone freak out over guys like me. And now Marge is worried I'll do the same, like I'm some fuckin' coward who can't handle his shit. I can handle it. I can. I tell her that, too: *Marge, I'll be okay.* And she says, *I hope so, sweet pea. I really hope so.* Which is not what I needed to hear. She goes back inside, and I get in my truck and drive. Don't know where I'm going, I just keep driving and driving. For some reason I end up at Walmart and I go inside—why I don't know—but I go inside and I'm walking up these aisles full of shit nobody needs, just looking for the chip aisle because I have to eat. I mean I'm here I have to do something and the lights are so bright and "Single Ladies" comes on and I'm in the middle of an aisle full of bath towels but I see us all dancing and smiling and fuck this place and suddenly I know why her son did what he did and I just stand there in the towel aisle and close my eyes and breathe. *Improvise. Adapt. Overcome.* The song ends and a Walmart ad comes on: *Don't forget the Fourth! Celebrate our nation's freedom in style with a new GrillMaster . . .* I lean my head against a towel and laugh because that is the only thing you can really do. That or what Marge's son did. I gotta get out of here. I walk back through the store and out the door, past the greeter with the Support Our Troops button. Go back to my truck, get in, roll down all the windows, and gun it. I hate the part of me that understands Marge's son. I don't know what went down for that dude in Fallujah, what he saw, who he killed, but I have some pretty good guesses. I imagine him sitting at home by himself and seeing shit that isn't really there and just wondering what the point of things is. I can picture him trying to mow the lawn or fill his gas tank or buy more milk because the milk in the fridge is expired and him thinking, *Why the hell am I doing this?* He's tired and the nightmares won't stop and nobody understands, they just want him to be like he was before he left but he can't be, he can't ever go back because you can't unsee what you saw. Maybe he wasn't a coward—maybe he knew that the war was never going to stop and all he was doing was bringing down the people around him. Maybe he thought it would be a relief and not just for him: for everyone.

chapter eleven

A day off.

For once, it felt good to have the sun beating down on me. Its red light pulsed behind my closed eyes and my mind collaged strange amoebalike sculptures out of it. Fire creatures. I was lying on a thick beach towel next to Dylan, the air heavy with the scent of her suntan lotion—a tropical vacation in a bottle. An old boom box she'd had since she was a kid was softly playing Jack Johnson. According to Dylan, it wasn't summer without his guitar and that low voice mixed in with the sound of the creek tumbling by us.

"This feels so good," I said.

"Mm-hmm."

I wondered if I could put this sensation in Marge's collage. The heat, the delicious drowsiness of it. The way sparks of light were going off like fireworks behind my eyes, and how my skin was melting into the sand and my problems were like a distant itch I couldn't be bothered to scratch.

"Sky." Dylan's voice was hesitant, and I lifted up my hand to shade my eyes, then looked over at her.

"Yeah?"

She sat up, this perfectly tanned blond goddess in a flowered bikini. With her bug-eye sunglasses and sparkling lip gloss, she looked like a model for *Seventeen*. You'd never know she'd had a baby in January.

"Your mom was hanging out at our place yesterday for a little while—when you were working."

I sat up. "That's good! I've been telling her for weeks to go visit your mom." Maybe this was a sign that things would go back to normal. "Did your mom give her advice about jobs? Or . . . about anything else?"

Dylan took a swig of her Diet Coke. "You mean about Billy."

I nodded. He'd started sleeping over every night. It had gotten to the point where I was mostly working graveyards, just so I didn't have to hear them.

Dylan wrinkled up her nose. "Are they still . . . you know?"

I stood up and looked out at the creek. The sun was bouncing off the water, sending shards of glass our way. Scrubby trees lined the bank, their boughs heavy with dust from the nearby fields. There wasn't much of a beach—just a strip of dirt and rocks, but it was ours.

"It's so disturbing, Dyl. I can't even . . . I know my dad's gone, but it's just so *wrong*."

"I guess your mom probably hasn't gotten laid since—I mean, you know, for a long time. Are they loud?"

My stomach turned. "Yeah."

I walked over to the creek and waded in, gasping as the water numbed my legs. Pebbles cut into my feet, but I kept going. Even though it was over a hundred degrees, the creek got most of its water from melted snow that came down from the high mountains surrounding the valley. Even in the summer, they had snow on their peaks.

I looked back at Dylan. "So, what did The Moms talk about?"

Our moms became The Moms a long time ago. Like us, they were best friends. A unit. Or at least they were until my mom dropped off the deep end. Again.

"Well, that's what I sort of wanted to ask you. I don't think your mom's planning on going back to work, Sky. Like, ever. Or for a super long time."

I sank deeper into the water, tried to focus on the sting of it. "What'd she say?"

"I mean, it was more the way she was talking. Like, well, like Billy was maybe helping her out."

Fuck Billy.

"How? All he does is buy beer."

Maybe that was why she was with him—because he was promising to help her somehow. We'd covered all the bills last month, but just barely. I knew this month there'd be no Taco Bell checks, and I still wasn't sure how we were going to scrape by. *If* we were going to scrape by.

Dylan shrugged. "All I can say is that this is the first time I've actually been *happy* that you're leaving."

I stared down at the water, letting the sunlight on the surface blind me a little. Part of me felt sick, like I wanted to throw up the bag of Ruffles I'd just eaten. The other part of me was outside my body, seeing a girl in a black bikini standing in a slow-moving creek. Observing. Waiting.

"You *are* leaving, aren't you?"

I wondered what my dad was thinking right now. If dead people could think. It always felt like he was close by when I was at the creek. Not just because we'd scattered his ashes here. Some of my best memories were of him teaching me how to swim in this water. Watching him fish. Or eating soggy peanut butter and jelly sandwiches with him and my mom, all of us squeezed onto our ratty picnic blanket. Sometimes, if I remembered hard enough, the creek still had that old magic.

Dylan sat on her knees, her lips pulled into a frown. "You're not thinking about staying here, right? Because that would be ten kinds of insane."

Maybe Billy was saying he'd take care of her when I was gone. Maybe all of this—Billy, the drinking—was because she didn't want to be alone.

"She's scared," I said.

"Huh?"

I waded farther into the water.

Hi, Daddy, I thought. I trailed my fingertips along the surface. I pushed the *if only*'s out of my mind. He was gone, and I was alone, and there was nothing I could do to change that.

"I haven't been thinking about this whole thing the right way," I said. "I thought she was depressed about the job. But she's not freaking out just because we're broke. Not working at the Bell means that her whole life is going to change when I leave. Nothing will be the same, except for the trailer."

After Dad died, I'd thought that was it, that there was no way I could leave Creek View. Mom had been in a bad place and it seemed like she'd never be okay on her own. But then she got better, and I started to believe that it was possible. By the time sophomore year rolled around, I knew I was getting out. I'd pushed away thoughts of my mom spending her nights alone, with nobody to keep her company. I'd told myself she could go hang out with Dylan's mom. When I felt guilty, I'd reminded myself that going to college was what my parents had always wanted for me—and that when I graduated and got a good job, I'd be able to take better care of her.

But working all day at a shit job, then coming home to an empty trailer and a TV dinner—what kind of life was that? Now she didn't even have the shit job.

Dylan shook her head. "*Not* your problem. Your mom's an adult. So are you."

I didn't say anything, just kept looking at the water. Feeling numb.

"*Sky.*"

I sank down, let the water cover my head. Gave my whole body a brain freeze. I stayed under the surface, felt the gentle current swirl around me, grabbed rocks with my hands, held on to them like they were gold nuggets.

I waited until the sob that was building in me drowned. Waited until the water felt good. Then I swam up to the bank and walked back to my towel.

"I don't know what I'm gonna do," I told Dylan. "If I just leave, I don't think she'll be okay."

"Sky, look at me." Dylan grabbed my hands, turned me around so that I faced her. "Staying here is not going to help your mom at all. The only thing that will do is make her feel even worse."

"But—"

"No. Shut up and listen."

I closed my mouth.

"What you need to do is find her another job. ASAP. I guarantee you that once she has a routine again, she'll be fine. And

San Fran is only a few hours away. You can visit her every weekend if you want to. But I swear to God that if you give up that full scholarship so you can stay here and take care of your—no offense—drunk-ass mom, I will personally kill you. With a nail file. Or something equally creepy. Got it?"

I closed my eyes and listened to the creek, the birds, the distant hum of an airplane. I knew she was right. I just wished there could be another way for Mom and me to both get what we needed.

"This sucks," I said.

"It's life."

I bit my lip, guilty that I felt so much relief. I could still go. All I had to do was find my mom a job. Not beg her to look for one herself, like I had been, but physically go out and get her job interviews myself. I had to start taking control of the situation.

I reached over and hugged Dylan, hard. She was greasy from the tanning lotion, and her skin was hot against my cold, creek-drenched body. "Thanks," I whispered.

"Hey, you did it for me when I got knocked up. I owe you one."

She settled back onto her towel and turned up the Jack Johnson. I sat down in the sun and looked out at the creek, watching the water slide by and roll over rocks and fallen tree branches that were in its way, steadily eroding whatever wouldn't budge until, finally, it made a path for itself to where it wanted to be.

chapter twelve

I'd never been so broke in my life.

No matter how many times I did the math, there wasn't enough. Rent. Car insurance. Gas. Electric. The maxed-out credit card. Food. Without Mom's checks from the Bell, it was all on me now. Even if she got a job right away, it'd be two weeks, maybe more, until we saw any money. Forget basics like toilet paper and deodorant. I only had a few days to figure out how to keep the lights on.

I threw the calculator on the ground and watched it slide across the cracked linoleum.

"Crap." Like I could just go out and buy a new one—*Look at me, I'm so rich I can throw calculators around!* I stood and picked it up, shook it. Still worked.

I looked out the window; Mom was sitting in one of the lawn chairs underneath the birch trees, the smoke from her cigarette wafting around her so that she looked like an old photograph, sepia tinted and out of focus. She'd been out there for over an hour, staring into nothing, moving only to bring another cigarette to her lips.

Usually when I did the bills, she would sit with me and tell funny stories about the people she worked with or make Rice Krispies treats. But today she'd just shuffled by the stack of bills and walked outside, her slippers and my dad's robe still on. When Billy wasn't around, it was like she went into hiding. I missed hanging out with her. Now she was a roommate I never saw.

I felt like my life had turned into a Magritte painting, where nothing made sense anymore. *Ceci n'est pas une pipe*, it said, under his painting of a pipe. I wanted to take a picture of my mom right now, then surround it with a halo of cigarette boxes and pages from her *TV Guide*, like those icons of saints. Underneath, it would say *Ceci n'est pas ma mere*: This is not my mother.

It was close to dinnertime, and my stomach was starting to grumble. I hadn't realized just how much free Taco Bell we'd been eating until Mom stopped coming home with it. I could kill for a Mexican pizza and a Pepsi. Instead, this was what I had to choose from: a box of saltine crackers and a can of Chef Boyardee. A bottle of sprinkles sat alone on the top shelf, where I'd put them after Dylan and I made Christmas cookies last winter. The fridge wasn't much better—expired milk, a few slices of bologna, a stick of butter, and a twelve-pack of Billy's Coors beer.

I had to leave for the Paradise evening shift, so I grabbed the box of saltines. They were stale and sat like a lump in my stomach, but I ate the last pack and pretended I was full. I put the Chef Boyardee on the counter, next to a bowl and spoon. I hoped she'd remember to eat. I headed outside, thankful the heat had subsided to a dull, uncomfortable pulse.

"Hey, Mom."

She squinted, like she was trying to figure out who I was. "You off to work already?"

"It's almost six."

She blew out a puff of smoke. "Really. That late?"

"Uh-huh."

"You doing a graveyard?"

"No, I'm off at midnight. I switched shifts with Amy because she had a thing to go to."

"Huh."

I had one of those headaches that live right behind your eyes, like some evil little elves had gotten in there with sharp tools. All I wanted to do was lie down in a cool, dark room. Give up. But Mom was doing enough of that for the both of us.

She sat there, queen of the trailer park. Getting Dad's robe dirty. The elves went *pound, pound, pound,* and I hated that cigarette between her fingers and the fact that the *TV Guide* in her hand was three weeks old.

"I'm calling Aunt Celia," I said.

The last resort. We'd reached it weeks ago, but I'd kept hoping she would do it herself. I didn't want to go behind her back and call the sister-in-law she hadn't spoken to since my dad died. What Aunt Celia had said at Dad's funeral was pretty unforgivable. But I didn't want us to be homeless, either.

"It's bad," I said, when she didn't say anything. "And I know she'll be able to help us out—lend us some money. I can pay her back."

She stood up, the *TV Guide* falling to the dust at her feet. "No."

"Look," I began, "I just ate crackers for dinner. We have to call her."

She started toward the house. "Just lay off, okay? I'll find the money."

"How?" The word flew out of my mouth like a smack in the face, but I was past caring. "The money isn't just going to fall from the sky!"

"Fuck you," she yelled.

Ceci n'est pas ma mere.

She touched her lips with the tips of her nicotine-stained fingers, her eyes wide.

Somewhere on the highway, a big rig sped by. A kid up the street shrieked. Then a gust of dusty wind swept between us, carrying something important away, but I didn't know what it was.

I turned around and practically sprinted to the car. *Away*—I had to get away.

"Tomorrow," I said, pulling open the door. "If you don't call her, I will."

Mom shouted my name, like she was crying out in her sleep, but for once I ignored her. I jammed my key into the ignition and backed out, driving way too fast. Reckless.

Away: that was the only command my body could respond to. *Away Away Away.*

———————

By midnight I was ravenous. I resisted the Paradise vending machine—I couldn't afford to waste seventy-five cents on a handful of candy. I was in a dilemma; the stuff at our local bodega was way overpriced, but it would cost me a lot of gas to drive to the nearest grocery store, which was an hour away. And fast food was too expensive. I decided that as soon as Amy came in, I'd buy a box of pasta at the bodega and cook it up at home. It would be at least two, maybe three meals.

"Skylar, you rock!" Amy said as she pushed through the screen door. She was still wearing a skimpy sheath from her date. "Thank you so much for switching."

"No problem. I wasn't doing anything better, trust me. Have fun?"

"Oh, yeah. We went to Red Lobster and then we spent, like, three hours at Starbucks. God, I can't wait to move to Bakersfield. You're *so* lucky you're going to San Fran."

Away Away Away.

I slid off the stool and grabbed my bag and the part of Marge's collage I'd just finished, Mom's *fuck you* a whisper in my ear. "I'm definitely looking forward to living near some civilization."

Every time someone mentioned school, my answers sounded like rote memorizations for a part I no longer had, in a play I'd always wanted to be in.

"Lucky, lucky," she said.

Amy sauntered over to the counter and proceeded to settle in. For her this meant wearing slippers, painting her nails, and eating copious amounts of junk food.

"Night," I said.

She gave me a wave. "See ya."

I got into my car, dreading going home. Dylan was probably up, but I didn't want to risk waking the baby. I called Chris, and as usual, he answered on the first ring.

"What's up?" he asked.

I could hear one of his video games and the shouts of several males in the background—his cousins were over for another one of their all-nighters.

"Nothing," I said. "I just wanted to see what you were up to, but I can already tell you're deep in some violent alternative reality."

"Oh, yeah. And kicking some major ass in it. Wanna come over?"

The last thing I wanted to do was sit around and watch a bunch of guys play video games. Why did they always think girls *liked* doing that?

"Nah. I better get to sleep. Long day."

"Just think about it this way: in a couple of months, we'll be having this conversation, only you'll be complaining about your nymphomaniac roommate."

I laughed because it was what he was expecting from me. "I would much prefer that."

"Oh—gotta go. My turn to kill some zombies."

"Get one for me."

"Will do."

I stared at the phone for a minute after Chris hung up. I could picture him in his living room, surrounded by family. Laughing. Shoveling chips or his mother's homemade tamales into his mouth. Caring about nothing but killing zombies.

Must be nice.

That wasn't fair, I knew. I'd seen his family go through some seriously lean times. No one deserved to be happy more than Chris. I scrolled through the few numbers I had in my phone, pausing at Josh's. But how desperate was that?

I threw the phone into my bag, sick of myself, of everything, and started up the car. A couple minutes later, I parked outside

Market, our local twenty-four-hour bodega. I didn't even know if that was its actual name, but we all called it that because it was the only word on the sign painted above the door.

I put the car in park and rested my head against the steering wheel for a few minutes. The thought of going home made me literally sick to my stomach. I didn't know if Billy would be there. Couldn't handle it if Mom pretended everything was okay or, worse, was drunk again. Screwing him. I gripped the steering wheel and squeezed my eyes shut.

God, I'm hungry.

A sob broke out of me, loud and ugly. I rolled up my window, fast, and covered my mouth with my hand. *Stop crying, Skylar. Stop fucking crying.*

I needed to collage, get my hands dirty with glue and scissors and paper that melted under my skin. I'd take all our bills and receipts and tear them up into tiny pieces. Then I'd turn the pieces into a kite, flying up into the sky. Or I could collage a cheeseburger with a thick, creamy shake. Maybe a train, heading out of Creek View.

I stayed in the car until I was certain the tears were gone, then I wiped my eyes, took a breath, and got out. Javier, the owner, nodded at me as I came in, the bell on the door jangling, before he went back to watching his soccer game.

It wasn't very big inside—more a convenience store than anything else—but since Creek View was in the boonies, it also had stuff like big bags of rice and ground beef. I headed over to the dry goods and candy aisle and stopped in front of the tiny shelf with pasta.

"Two seventy-nine?" I said, picking up the box of spaghetti. Javier looked over at me. I waved it in the air. "Seriously?"

He just grunted and went back to watching the TV.

"I wouldn't pay that if I were you."

I turned around. Josh was standing behind me, a Red Bull in one hand and a bag of Doritos in the other. I hadn't noticed his truck in the parking lot. Which pretty much illustrated how messed up I was feeling, since it wasn't exactly a subtle vehicle. I tried not to read anything into his being there; things like this weren't serendipitous when you lived in the smallest town ever.

He smiled, and I was suddenly awake.

I looked at the stuff in his hands. "That's a seriously disgusting combination."

He laughed. "I still can't get over being able to just walk into a store and buy whatever I feel like."

"I'm guessing there wasn't an ample supply of junk food in Afghanistan."

His eyes skimmed the rows of candy behind me. "Oh, there was. Just not where I was posted. Now, if I'd been in the Army . . . those dudes were hooked up." He reached down to grab a Snickers and a pack of M&M's.

I set the pasta down, picked it back up. Set it down. Would it look weird to come all the way out here, then leave empty-handed? But if I bought it, I'd be down to less than seven bucks.

For two weeks.

And two people.

"Sky?"

"Huh?"

"You okay?"

"What? Yeah, totally." I kept my eyes anywhere but on his—I wondered if they looked red or if my face was all blotchy. "I'm just out of it."

He nodded, but the way he looked at me said *bullshit*. I should never have told him about my mom. It was like the whole me-inviting-him-to-Leo's thing had started us on this weird path of knowing too much about each other.

"So what are you up to?" he asked. "Other than having trouble picking out your pasta."

I grabbed the box and headed toward the counter. "Nothing. I'm on my way home. I didn't get a chance to eat dinner, so . . ." I held up the spaghetti.

He took the box out of my hand and put it back on the shelf. "Come with me."

chapter thirteen

I pointed to my watch. "It's almost twelve thirty."

"So? McDonald's is open twenty-four hours."

I frowned, thinking. They did have a dollar menu. Just the thought of chicken nuggets made my stomach growl.

Josh laughed. "I'm taking that as a yes."

"Yeah, I guess that sounds pretty good," I said.

"Cool." He paid for his snacks, then opened the door. "We'll come back for your car after."

I nodded and followed him outside.

"So what's your excuse for raiding Market at this hour?" I asked as I climbed into the truck.

"Honestly?"

"Sure." A rock station blared as soon as he turned the truck on, and I jumped.

"Sorry." He turned it down and pulled onto the highway. "Blake and Tara had friends over. And everyone was laughing, just laughing nonstop. About *nothing*. And the whole house smelled like pot. I mean, right now, my unit's out there trying to—" He stopped himself, then just shook his head, looking . . . old. Definitely not nineteen. "I just had to bolt."

"It must be weird, having to live with your family again."

"Yeah. It was nice being on my own. Of course, people were trying to shoot my ass." He snorted. "Still beats sleeping in my sixth-grade bed."

"That must be one uncomfortable mattress."

He laughed. "Yep."

I thought about the day I'd been in his room, the bareness of the walls. Just a few pictures above his desk, like he hadn't really unpacked.

"You still thinking of staying in?" I asked.

He looked over at me and I met his eyes, but I wasn't sure what I was seeing there. It was like he wanted something from me, but I had no idea what.

"Not sure yet," he finally said.

We were quiet for a bit, but it didn't feel weird not talking. Actually, it was nice. Chris and Dylan weren't people I could be quiet with. Chris was always spouting sci-fi trivia or going on about BU's science department, and Dylan could talk your ear off in her sleep. I didn't realize I needed companionable silence until I was speeding down the highway in Josh's truck.

At this time of night, the empty fields felt mysterious, like as soon as the sun went down, they became the dominion of mythical creatures, fairy kings that ruled grapevine realms. The headlights of passing cars twinkled as they sped by, one long strand of oversized Christmas lights stretched between San Francisco and Los Angeles. It was almost pretty.

"So what's up with you?" he asked.

"What do you mean?"

"I saw you in the parking lot at Market. Something's wrong."

I leaned my head against the window. The glass was cool against my cheek.

"You don't have to tell me if you don't want to," he said softly.

My reflection in the side-view mirror had dark circles under her eyes. Hair slipping out of her loose bun. I beat her to the sigh. "I'm so tired."

Josh nodded. He knew I wasn't talking about my shift at the Paradise. He got what it meant to be tired of life. So tired you felt it in your bones.

"I thought when I graduated, everything would be okay," I said. "Like getting through Dad dying and making it out of high school was the hard part. It's not."

"Nope."

I turned my head toward him, studied the shadows the dashboard lights were painting on his face. "Why did you come back?"

"Besides the obvious?"

I looked over at his leg, then rolled my eyes. "Doesn't mean you have to spend the rest of your life in Creek View."

"What would you do?"

"If I were you?"

"Yeah."

"I wouldn't stay in. I'd use my GI Bill and pick a school as far away from here as possible. I wouldn't look back."

The yellow arches came into view. He slowed down. "Like you, huh?"

I just shrugged.

We pulled into the drive-thru, and when I only ordered one

thing off the dollar menu, he shook his head and changed my Chicken McNuggets to a Super Size Value Meal. He wouldn't let me pay.

My throat clenched, and I knew I was about to start freaking crying again, which was so stupid, but I hated not knowing if he felt sorry for me or if he was my friend or if he wanted more, and what did it mean that he was buying me food? I stared out the passenger window and tried to keep the tears in, frustrated that the five-dollar meal he'd just bought me was half my net worth.

"See that plastic bag behind you?" he said as he passed me the food and pulled back onto the highway.

I looked in the truck's tiny back seat. "Yeah."

"Take a couple bottles out of there."

"Why?"

"You'll see."

I reached into the back and grabbed two empty bottles at random. One Bud, one Heineken.

He pressed the button for his window to go down. "Ready?" he said.

"For what?"

He held out his hand, and I gave him the bottles.

"Hold the wheel."

"What? No—dammit, Josh!" My hands flew out to the wheel as Josh wiggled his fingers in the air like, *Look! No hands!* The truck swerved, and Josh laughed when I shrieked and pulled it back into our lane. The highway was mostly empty, but still.

"Hold it steady, Sky!"

"You are such an asshole, you know that?"

"I've been called worse." He slowed the truck down, then put it on cruise control.

In seconds he was half out the window, his knees facing me—even with his prosthesis, he was crazy fast, like he'd done this a million times.

"Joshua Mitchell, I swear to God—"

"Steady, Sky," he shouted over the wind.

With the windows down, the cab filled with the smell of manure and dew and grass and car exhaust. The wind stung my eyes and pounded against my eardrums. I was too scared to look away from the highway, but out of the corner of my eye, I saw the dark shape of the station. The broken sign loomed above it, the faded red of the Texaco star just visible in the moonlight. Josh grunted, and I could imagine the empty beer bottles flying over the top of the truck and smashing against the gas station. He slid in and grabbed the wheel as I sat back in the passenger seat.

"That was awesome," he said. His eyes were bright, and he was grinning, his breath coming out in heavy spurts.

"I'm never driving with you again."

"Your turn," he said. He pushed a button, and my window went down. "C'mon."

"No way."

"I'd suggest getting wasted, but that's not your thing. So throw."

"One: I'm not a low-life hooligan. Two—"

Josh snickered. "I can't believe you just said hooligan."

"Shut up or I'm eating all the fries."

"You wouldn't."

I leaned closer to him. "I would."

His eyes snagged on mine, just for a second, and then he slowed way down and waited for a big rig to pass before he did a U-turn in the middle of the highway. He passed the Texaco, then did one more U-turn, so that it would be on my side of the road.

"I can do this all night, Evans."

"What if someone's there and I, like, kill them?"

"No one's there—that place has been closed for ten years. Can you give me a fry?"

"Don't try to distract me."

I stuck my hand into the bag and pulled out a fry. He opened his mouth, and I popped it in—the whole thing felt strangely intimate, as if we'd kissed.

I leaned away from him. Too close. Too comfortable. Too wired from the Joshness of him.

"Thank you," he mumbled. He pointed out my window. "Any day now."

I shook my head. "Josh—this is insane. Like, super-redneck status."

"Do it. I promise you'll feel better."

I cursed under my breath and grabbed a bottle. The smell of beer hit me, and I wrinkled my nose.

"There's still beer in this!"

"Well, then you better get it out of here before a cop pulls me over, huh?"

"You hick bastard."

"I love it when you talk dirty."

I punched him on the arm, which was about as effective as smacking a rock, then I leaned the upper half of my body out of the truck, so that my chest was parallel to the road. The wind was pushing against me, and I closed my eyes for a second, gripping the handhold inside the door. I could hear the tires speeding along the road, the slap of rubber against asphalt. This was so stupid, so dumb, but it felt amazing. Feeling the wind grab at my hair, being five fingers away from death—all I had to do was let go.

I opened my eyes and shouted into the truck as I clutched the bottle. "Don't stare at my ass."

"I'm not making any promises."

I gave him a look, but he pointed up the road. "Just throw as hard as you can."

Every muscle in my body was tense, ready to spring. The asphalt beneath sparkled as we sped by, like a river of black diamonds. We came up to the gas station, and I let the bottle go, throwing it with all my might toward the building. As we drove by, I thought I heard it crash against the wall. I screamed at the night and laughed at the stars. I heard Josh's "Hell, yeah!" from inside, and it made me laugh harder, which hurt my empty stomach, but I didn't care.

I slid back inside. My blood was carbonated, and I was awake and young and alive, and screw everything because this moment was *mine*.

"I'm warning you, it's addictive," Josh said. "You're gonna be begging me to take you out again, just you wait."

I covered my face with my hands and shook my head. "You're right. This is the dumbest thing ever, but *damn*." I wanted to throw another one, but this time at Billy Easton's truck. Or Aunt Celia's house . . . wherever it was.

"I kinda get why you were such a hell-raiser before you left," I said. It was silly, but throwing that bottle made me feel a little more in control of my life. I couldn't sit around and wait for Mom to magically get better. I had to take everything into my own hands.

"Yeah?"

"Yeah. Thank you for kicking my ass into gear. I've felt like a total wimp these past few weeks."

"You are anything but wimpy, Sky." His lips turned up. "But if you *really* want to get your ass kicked, you could always join the Marines. You'd look good in uniform."

"*Oorah!*" I pumped my fist in the air, and he laughed. "I saw a movie where the Marines were always saying that. What does it mean?"

"It can be loosely translated as *fuck, yeah*. One of my buddies says it's Jarhead for *let's do this*." He smiled. "You used it right."

Oorah. I needed some of that in my life.

Josh did another U-turn, then went down the dirt road beside the gas station.

"Are we the kind of delinquents who pick up after ourselves?" I asked.

"Hell, no. Takes the fun out of it." He slowed down as we drove past the station. "I'm taking you to my favorite restaurant in town."

The gas pumps were eerie in the moonlight, like forgotten toys. Graffiti covered the boards on the windows, and the ground was littered with beer cans and probably cigarette butts. I couldn't see them from the truck, but it seemed like that kind of place.

Josh parked behind the station and turned off the ignition. The instant silence was almost loud. Other than the occasional car on the highway, the only sound was the breeze and a few crickets.

"If I didn't know you, I'd be pretty freaked out right now," I said. It felt like we were the only people in the world. There weren't any houses or buildings around for miles. Just fields and the jagged outline of the mountains in the distance.

"Well, at least you know that if I try anything, you can out-run me."

"True. That's comforting."

He laughed and we got out of the truck.

"Wow," I said. The moon hung low in the sky like an over-ripe fruit, rusty orange with swirls of yellow. *Starry Night* come to life.

"Kinda creepy, huh?" Josh said as he pulled down the tailgate.

"No. I like it. I feel like I'm watching a movie right now, you know?"

I gazed at the vineyard in front of me, the vines dark tendrils in the moonlight. I longed to slip off my shoes and run through them. I wanted cool earth under my feet. I wanted to pull grapes off the vines and taste their sweetness and let the juice drip down my chin and onto my shirt. Didn't matter if they were ripe or not. I wanted to feed one to Josh and feel his lips against my fingertips. The echo of the bottle throwing pulsed in my skin. If I had the guts, I would howl at the moon.

"Can you grab the blankets in the back seat?" he asked.

I handed him the bags of food, grateful to step away from his side for a second. When I came back, we spread the blankets on the tailgate, then hopped up. He grunted a little, rubbing his stump while he leaned over to adjust his shorts over his prosthesis.

"You okay?"

"Just a little sore today. It's nothing."

I doubted it was nothing, but in Creek View, it seemed like

there were two schools of thought on expressing how shitty life could be. Some people bitched and moaned all the time—that was almost everyone. But a few tried to be stoic, to play off their personal tragedies as though they were minor inconveniences. I liked that he was the latter. I supposed you'd have to be that kind of person to be a Marine.

We both put our hands in the bag, searching for fries, and this time we laughed when our fingers touched. There was lightning in our skin. God, what was happening to me?

"Ladies first," he said.

I pulled out my fries and let him take the bag. I ate with my head bent over the carton, my hair hiding my face. Boiled, over-priced pasta felt so much safer than this.

"Thanks for dinner."

Josh took a bite of his burger and nodded. "Thanks for giving me something to do."

"Like you couldn't make a few phone calls and have twenty people begging you to hang out with them."

"Maybe." Then his lips curled up in a smile, and he looked at me out of the corner of his eye. "I like this better, though."

"Don't even think about hitting on me," I said. I dunked a chicken nugget in barbecue sauce and shoved it into my mouth, glad it was nighttime and he couldn't see how pink my cheeks had gotten.

He gave me a mock salute. "Yes, ma'am."

We ate in silence for a couple of minutes. I hadn't realized the depth of my hunger until the ache in my stomach disappeared. Josh stared at the rows and rows of grapes. He chewed his burger slowly, then brought his soda to his lips and took a long sip.

"One night, I was out with my squad, and there was a moon just like this," he said, his voice quiet. "Our commander had gotten a tip from some village elder that there were dudes building IEDs in a factory out in the middle of nowhere. Which is saying a lot, because everywhere you go in Afghanistan feels like the middle of nowhere. Anyway, we get to this factory, and there's nothing around. Just some broken shit and trash. Like this place. But we had orders to secure the location, so we had to spend the night there, see if any Taliban came poking around. We couldn't really check the place out until daylight, so we just shot the shit all night, playing cards, talking. Smoking. One of the guys—Sharpe—he died a few days later. Firefight on a patrol. Sniper wasted him. Good guy."

I had a sudden urge to throw my arms around him and say, *You made it. You made it back.* But I kept my hands in my lap.

"How old was he?"

"Twenty-one."

"Damn."

Josh crushed his empty carton of fries, twisting the cardboard until it fell apart. "Shit happens."

"Yeah, but it still sucks. It's okay to think it sucks. I mean, I think about my dad every day. I always will. And sure, he was gonna die somehow, some way, but it's still shitty that he's gone and that he died the way he did."

"Your dad was good people."

I hadn't realized Josh would even remember him. "Yeah. He was."

We stared at the crazy moon for a while.

"Do you ever . . . *talk* to your dad?" he asked. "You know, like, in your head?"

"You mean like a prayer?"

"Kind of. Just—we don't know what happens when we die, right? I mean, maybe we go up to some perfect place in the sky, or maybe we turn to dust, or we're spirits and can still think and hear and go places. So talking to the person that's dead isn't crazy. They could be listening to you. Right?"

I nodded. "Sometimes I think I'm talking to myself—in my head, I mean—and then I realize I'm actually talking to my dad. About my problems or my day or whatever."

I ate the last of my fries and took a sip of my soda. It felt so good to be full, but there were parts of me that still felt empty and hungry, and I could tell it was the same with Josh. Sometimes I wondered if I'd ever find something to fill those places inside me that never stopped wanting.

"You lost a lot of friends in the war?"

He balled up his hamburger wrapper and threw it in the bag. Then he lay down on the blankets, staring up at the sky. "Yeah."

I lay down next to him. "I'm glad you're home," I whispered.

His hand found mine and held it. Not in a romantic way. He was just telling me he understood.

We stayed like that, hand in hand, our faces pointed to the stars. It wasn't until the sun came up and the sky had turned the color of a peach that we folded up the blankets and went home.

JOSH

I'm out here watching the pickup football game I used to play in every week and it straight-up sucks. Instead of being out there, I'm sitting on the back of my truck, a fuckin' spectator, while all these dudes I've never been jealous of before in my life screw around on the field. Watching them and feeling fuckin' helpless. This black thing inside me wants to kick some ass so bad. These are guys whose girlfriends used to climb in my window in the middle of the night and no one would ever know. Guys who've never had to kill, haven't seen their best friend— Haven't seen any of it. These dudes are running, just . . . running. Like it's nothing. Not even thinking about it, like in those dreams where I'm running or walking and it feels so good, so real, to be moving like that again and I wake up and for the tiniest second think maybe all this—being Stateside, the bomb, the fake leg—was the dream. Then I look down and there's nothing there. *Nothing.* And now I'm sitting here, watching a shitty-ass football game and feeling a leg that doesn't exist anymore, a leg that burns like someone just put a hot poker against it. "Phantom pain," Darren calls it. My physical therapist has a name for fuckin' everything.

And I'm feeling so goddamn tired because I couldn't sleep again, couldn't stop seeing that day or thinking about Marge's son. Sitting here like some fuckin' mascot or something, wondering how the hell did I get back here? After everything I saw, the places I went . . . how did I end up right back here, drinking cheap beer in a field that smells like cow shit?

And why don't I leave?

chapter fourteen

I carried the memory of that night with me all through the next day and clutched it in my pocket like a child with a coin or some small treasure they'd discovered on the ground. I turned it over and over until it shone, and when I'd catch myself thinking of him, I'd shake my head, blushing, my body straining to wherever I imagined Josh to be at that precise moment.

"It's four," Chris said. "Just in case you haven't looked at the clock in the last three minutes." He gave me a weird look, as if he knew who I'd been thinking about.

My eyes slid away. "I know. I was just sort of hoping the clock would stop at three fifty-nine."

"That'd be very *Twilight Zone*. I'm not sure which is worse— possible creepiness from a stopped clock or your aunt Celia."

"My aunt Celia."

We were sitting on my couch, flipping through one of Mom's old *People* magazines until I could bring myself to pick up the phone. I'd promised myself I would do it at four if she didn't make the call herself. I'd waited all morning and most of the afternoon, but Mom only left her bedroom to go to the bathroom or stare into the empty fridge.

I tried to summon up the feeling of throwing that beer bottle at the gas station the night before. *Oorah.*

"I'm just worried she won't pick up. She won't recognize my number," I murmured. Mom's bedroom door was shut and the TV on, but I didn't want her to hear us plotting.

"Then leave a voice mail and tell her you'll keep calling until she picks up."

"That simple, huh?" I asked.

He tugged on my ponytail. "That simple."

I took a breath and grabbed my cell phone. "Okay."

"Dude, it's gonna be crazy tonight. Check it out." Chris pointed to the TV, which had footage of a reporter by the coast with huge waves behind her. It was on mute, but you didn't need sound to see we were in for a serious storm. "It might even hail!"

The afternoon had gone gray, and wind was battering the trailer, the gusts sending thick, dark clouds that promised rain. Usually I loved the few rainy days we had in Creek View, but it felt like a bad omen.

"Great. I'll probably be getting soaked all night helping stranded travelers into their rooms," I muttered.

"And I'll have a bunch of *gringos* with car problems," he said. "Just wait until you, too, wear the honorable orange tunic."

"Don't remind me," I said.

Chris was wearing the offensively bright orange Pump and Go shirt that I'd be putting on for the first time in just a few days.

I'd gone into the gas station that morning, telling myself that getting a second job meant I was taking control of the situation at home. I filled out the application, chatted with the manager, and became a weekend clerk ten minutes later.

"So I'm guessing I shouldn't mention that I thought the whole reason you went into P&G was to get your *madre* a job."

I sighed. "That was the plan, but we need cash *now*, you know? And she's . . . I just thought it would be better to get more work for me, then I'll find something for her."

"Sky."

I looked over at him, and he made the wash-your-hands-of-her motion. I shook my head.

"Not possible," I said. "C'mon, you know that."

I stood up and grabbed the address book with the faded daisies on it that we'd had pretty much all my life and turned to the E's for Celia Evans. The address book was mostly empty—neither of my parents had had many friends, and we were out of touch with all of our family, so the numbers were mostly for coworkers and neighbors.

I pushed through the pages. Looked again. One more time.

"It's gone," I said, staring at the book. I could feel the panic spreading from my gut up to my chest. Choking me.

"What's gone?"

"My aunt Celia."

I held up the address book, open to where the entry had been: an empty page with the torn remnants of another page beside it.

"Hell," he said.

I threw the address book against the wall, and it slid under the couch, where it would probably stay forever. Chris took off his glasses and rubbed his eyes.

"Okay," he said. "It's officially bad."

"It's been officially bad for *weeks*," I snapped.

Seriously, Chris could be such an idiot sometimes. It was like the closer he got to leaving Creek View, the more clueless he became. A few months ago, he would have been freaking out on my behalf.

"Sorry," I muttered.

"It's cool." He sat there for an awkward few seconds, then stood up and pulled me close for a hug. But I didn't want that. Didn't want *him*. When had Chris and Dylan stopped being enough?

But I knew. I could pinpoint the exact moment. *Damn bottles.*

I stepped back, out of Chris's arms. "I don't care if she's sleeping. I gotta talk to her about this."

"Talk to me about what?"

Mom.

I turned around. "Where's Aunt Celia's number?"

She flinched a little, but then shook her head. "We don't need her."

"What are you gonna do when I go to school?" My voice rose, and I could almost feel the weeks of frustration stacking up inside me, waiting for me to shove them all onto her.

She pulled her robe closer, like it could shield her from reality. "I'm figuring it out. Don't worry about me."

"I do. I worry about you. A lot. I mean, God, look at you! When's the last time you took a shower?"

Chris coughed quietly behind me. "Um. Sky, I'm gonna . . ." He gestured toward the door, and I nodded.

Neither of us looked at him as he left, but when I heard the door shut, I stepped closer to my mom.

"Give me her number. Please. I'll call her. I'll set everything up. You don't even have to see her if you don't want to—"

"Can't." She turned back to her room. "I threw it away."

I opened and closed my mouth, suffocating on those three words: *threw it away.* I hadn't realized how much I'd been holding on to that one name written in our address book until it was gone.

"That's the only family I have!"

The words rushed up from somewhere inside me that I'd never wanted to look, an ugly abyss where I'd stuffed Dad's death and Mom's bad days and those afternoons with Blake when I'd just wanted to lose myself.

"Did you think about me at all?" I was screaming, spit flying out of my mouth, all the stuff I'd tried to forget pushing up, up.

"You don't need family like that!" Her voice came out in a half-articulate screech. "That woman walked away from *us.* Don't you remember how she left you standing out front with your dad's ashes? Just drove off, even though you started running after her. *That's* the kind of family you want?"

And I was right back there. The cold February wind. Dad reduced to a cardboard box with a death certificate taped on top.

"You were drunk," I whispered.

"What?"

I'd hated that Mrs. Garcia or Dylan's mom would see us like

that, when they came to pay their respects. You gotta have some pride left. Some dignity.

"That was the worst part. Dad was dead, and you were drunk, and there was no one to help."

"That's not fair," Mom said. "Anyone in my place would have—"

"No." I shook my head. It was like I could finally see that day—and all the years after it. "I was *twelve years old*. Cleaning up after you, night after night, when you'd had too much to drink. Taking care of the house, doing the laundry, the bills. Calling in sick for you. Making you get out of bed and trying not to take it personally when you kept saying you wanted to die. And now here we are again."

She leaned against one of the chairs at the kitchen table. "I know you had it pretty bad, okay?" she said. "I *know*."

"But you don't. You have no idea what it's like to grow up without any family and then have the only person left in your life fall apart. At least you had grandparents and aunts and uncles and brothers and sisters—"

"And I *ran away from them*, Skylar!"

Her eyes were deer-in-headlights wide, her voice raw from too many cigarettes and too little talking.

"Okay, but why? Can't you just—"

She shook her head, her eyes dark. "No."

There was no point in pushing her. I'd never know anything about that side of my family. Even before Dad died, that had been an off-limits topic.

I had to get us back on track. Aunt Celia—our only hope.

"But Dad's family . . . maybe they're just waiting for us to, I don't know, *try*. Like, maybe they think *we* don't want to see *them*."

Mom snorted. "Trust me. They don't want anything to do with us."

"We don't know that—not for sure."

She wouldn't look at me. She seemed so frail and broken, like she'd given up long ago.

"Mom, I've got nobody but you."

"I'm not going anywhere," she said, her voice low.

I was dry kindling, and all I needed was that tiny spark to set me off.

"That's the problem!" She flinched as though my words were a whip, and I took a step back. "I'm sorry," I said. "I'm . . . this is just . . ."

Why is it that some people in the world get to wake up in beautiful houses with fairly normal parents and enough food in the fridge while the rest of us have to get by on the scraps the universe throws at us? And we gobble them up, so grateful. What the hell are we grateful for?

I kicked the couch, understanding why Josh had maybe wanted things to shoot at, if only for a little while. I would have felt better, I thought, if the couch were made of flesh and bone. Preferably Billy's.

"I don't know what to do," I said. "If I can't call Aunt Celia, and you won't go up there . . . I don't know how we're gonna make it."

Mom placed her hand on the wall to steady herself and bowed her head. "Just leave me alone, Skylar. I want to be alone."

She turned around and shuffled back into her bedroom.

"Mom—"

The door shut, then I heard the TV turn up. My body slid onto the couch, and I curled into a ball, my eyes shut tight.

Thunder rumbled in the distance, and I heard the first rain-drops fall onto our metal roof with sharp *pings*.

I didn't have another thought for hours, just let the sound of the rain soak into me. At some point I fell asleep, fighting battles in dreams I couldn't remember when I woke up.

chapter fifteen

Rain slid down the glass door, a thick gray honey that muted the drabness of the Paradise courtyard. It was later that night, after midnight, everything outside cloaked in sinewy darkness. Marge was asleep, and the storm was keeping the guests tucked away inside their rooms, so the lobby was silent, save for the occasional burst of thunder and the rain that pummeled the roof with angry fists of water. I looked past my reflection in the glass door, watching as the pool overflowed and the palms thrashed around like crazed dancers.

After months of drought, it was strange to see so much water everywhere, all at once. I wondered if I'd come home from my graveyard shift and see the trailer floating toward Los Angeles. Our piece-of-shit excuse for a home would flood and the used appliances and dollar-store decorations would burst through the door and windows, riding on tiny waves. My bras and my mother's chipped dishes from Goodwill would float merrily down the middle of the highway all the way through the Grapevine, the mountain pass that separated us from LA. I'd collage it—maybe the title would be *The Flood: Part II*. But I knew it was too much to wish that Creek View would be wiped off the face of the earth forever. The other towns needed us: you can't have the light without the dark, right? Maybe our darkness was necessary for other people to see their light.

I went back to tearing up a magazine for Marge's collage, the feel of paper familiar, soothing. Picasso was right when he said, "Art washes away from the soul the dust of everyday life." Just as the rain outside drenched Creek View, my art was washing me clean.

My stomach growled. I ignored it. All I'd had since my meal with Josh the night before was the can of Chef Boyardee in our now-empty pantry. I told myself this was good practice for being a starving artist.

I laid out a fresh piece of the thick poster board I was using as the collage's base on the carpet. I was almost finished with my strawberry field—I'd used all kinds of reds to create the tiny berries. It was like a Seurat—not good like a Seurat, but the sort of thing where if you got really close, the picture wouldn't make sense, but it came into focus with some distance. That was what I hoped, anyway.

There was a burst of thunder, then a crack of lightning. I closed my eyes for a minute, just listening to the rain and the low voices on the radio, a late-night call-in show. Something bright danced across my eyelids, and I opened them up to see headlights sweep across the lobby wall. I put my collage on the battered table in front of the cat pee couch, then went over to the window to see what poor person the weather had brought down our driveway. Through the sheets of rain, I could just make out

Josh's truck. He'd parked as close as he could get to the entrance and when he saw me at the window, he waved. I held the door open for him while he stumbled in from the storm.

"You're soaked," I said.

"Thank you, Captain Obvious."

"Ever heard of an umbrella?"

"Umbrellas are for pussies." Josh shook his body out like a wet dog. "How's the Sky today?"

"Chance of rain."

I didn't want to tell him what had happened, but I didn't want to be fake either—not after our night at the gas station. I walked over to the closet where we kept our towels.

"One of these days, you're going to tell me it's sunny," he said. His voice had gone soft, like when he grabbed my hand by the pool after I'd told him about my mom.

I took out three towels and threw them at him, keeping my eyes away from his. "Maybe. What brings you here in the dead of night?"

I pretended to organize the ancient brochures we had for things to do around the area—tourist traps like vineyard excursions and tractor rides. I needed to give my hands something to do. They kept wanting to touch him.

"Nine and three have issues with the roof, and I was worried they might start leaking with all this crazy rain. No one's in those rooms, right?"

"No. The hippies are still in seven, and there's a couple in two. That family with the minivan is in one."

Their van was at the Mitchells' shop, and they'd been stuck in Creek View for three days.

"Sucks to be them," he said. "My dad ordered the wrong part, and—" He rolled his eyes. "Anyway, we got any buckets around?"

"I'll check the storage closet."

I walked down the hall to where we kept all the cleaning supplies. I wondered what had really brought him out into the storm: the leak in the roof or me? Because I'd tried to think of a million excuses to come to the Paradise during the day, when he was normally here.

When I came back with the buckets, he was looking down at my collage.

"This is awesome. It's Creek View, right?"

I nodded, feeling like someone had just read my diary.

"Yeah. It's sort of a going-away gift for Marge. I'm gonna do the creek next." I pointed to the pile of blue paper I'd been collecting. "It's nothing. I mean, you know, I'm just screwing around. Graveyards are boring as hell."

"Can I see it when you finish?" he asked.

"Sure."

He picked up the buckets. "Thanks for these. Wish me luck!"

"Are you sure you want to—"

He opened the glass door. "Trust me, it'll be a lot less work in the long run."

I watched him hurry across the courtyard. In seconds he was soaked. It was slow going with his leg, and I could tell from his extra-long strides that he was trying to move as fast as he could. Just as Josh made it to the first room, I noticed his keys sitting on the counter.

I grabbed them and walked up to the glass door. He turned around, realizing his mistake, and I held them up. He shook his fist at the sky and started walking back, but I pulled open the door and ran out. I didn't even realize what I was doing until I was halfway across the courtyard. I gasped as the rain hit me. It came down like bullets, and I shrieked, holding my arms above my head to protect my face. I kicked off my flip-flops so that I could run toward Josh more quickly.

"You're insane!" he said, when I got to him. "I was gonna come back."

But he was smiling, and when I handed him the keys, he kept my hand in his for a few beats.

"It didn't seem fair that I got to sit in there all cozy and dry," I said, breathless from my mad dash across the courtyard.

He shook his head and reached out a hand to brush away the strings of wet hair on my face. I felt my body lean into his, like it was tired of asking me for permission first. For a second, I was certain he was going to kiss me. Every cell in my body started fluttering, like I was made of thousands of tiny butterflies. We stood there, balancing on the *maybe* of the moment, until he dropped his hand and backed away.

"I still think you're crazy," he said. "But since you're here, wanna help me?"

I nodded, pushing my disappointment away because it was so stupid, wasn't it, to think he'd want to kiss me—or that I'd *want* him to want to kiss me. I followed him into the first room, holding the buckets while Josh figured out where the leaks were. He would crane his neck up at the ceiling and then gesture for me to hand him a bucket and then we'd wait to hear a drop of water hit the plastic. It wasn't funny, but for some reason, all we could do was laugh as we waited for those hollow-sounding *plop*s. Every time we found another leak, it was like the most hilarious thing in the world, and I didn't care about the not-kiss anymore because I just wanted to laugh with him.

I loved watching Josh laugh. It transformed his whole face. He'd throw back his head, and the sound would come from some deep place inside him, like it'd finally been let out of hiding.

When we'd finished, we stood under the eaves, staring out at the warm light of the lobby.

"Guess there's only one way back," he said.

"Guess so."

But we kept standing there, waiting. For what, I didn't know. Just . . . waiting. The rain slowed up a little; it was still pouring from the sky, but not as hard, and I could hear something underneath the thrash of water against concrete. A soft strumming.

"Hear that?" Josh asked.

"Mm-hmm. The hippies."

It was the couple in room seven, a guy and his girlfriend straight out of 1969. They'd been at the motel for a few days and were often by the pool, playing guitar and singing. Usually Marley or the Beatles. Bob Dylan, that sort of thing.

"He's good." Josh listened closely for a second, then laughed and looked over at me. "Do you know what song this is?"

The rain slowed even more, and I strained my ears to pick out the chords.

" 'Hotel California.' "

The guy's voice was warm, strong, and his girlfriend would occasionally join in, their voices darting around each other, then coming together in sweet harmony.

Josh held out his hand. "May I?"

I saw that hand reaching toward me, and I wanted to take it and not let go, but I couldn't move. I remembered my mom and dad, dancing in the trailer to that Céline Dion song, "Because You Loved Me," their lips always meeting during the chorus. I'd come home to Mom playing it over and over after he died. So I made my hands into fists and gave Josh a throwaway smile.

"I thought you had to be drunk to dance."

"Not in the rain. It evens the playing field."

He took my hand and undid my fist by slowly pulling my fingers away from my palm. Then I let him draw me back out into the storm. My heart beat a steady rhythm against the guitar and the hippies' voices and the rain. I could barely see with the water streaming down my face as Josh pulled me closer to him. He sang along, his voice soft.

"How they dance in the courtyard, sweet summer sweat. Some dance to remember, some dance to forget."

I was keenly aware of how the downpour plastered my clothes to my body, outlining every curve, and how it did the same to him. And it made me feel reckless and scared. His voice in my ear, the rain, his hands on my waist, mine on his chest. How had this become a thing with us, dancing to slow songs?

For maybe the first time in my life I was aware of my lips, like you could take my pulse with them. They wanted skin—*his skin*—against them and, God, I couldn't think. It felt so good to not care about anything, just feeling my bare feet on the concrete, my breath as it struggled down my throat. And warmth. Between my legs and in my belly and everywhere in my head until it was just warmth and need and Josh.

The last note of the song faded, and he tilted my chin up, his face suddenly serious.

This is the moment, I thought.

And I stood there on the knife's edge of us, holding my breath, time expanding so that I felt every drop of rain, every thud of my heart. His lips, so close—

There was a burst of thunder, and Josh jumped, his fingers slipping from my chin. The moment gone. Like a balloon floating up to the sky, unreachable.

I tried to smile, I think. Wanting to cry and glad the rain would hide it if I did. "We should get back in," I said. Whispered. Choked.

I didn't know if he'd heard me. He was staring at the pool, watching the water flow into the planter, drowning the few flowers that had struggled to survive the heat.

"Josh?"

His eyes swept over my face and then he straightened his body and nodded. I didn't wait for him. I just turned and ran back to the lobby.

JOSH

You sure you're ready for this, bro? I flip Blake off. He raises his eyebrows and shakes his head, giving me all kinds of able-bodied attitude, then hikes his arm back and throws the football toward me. I try running, which is surprisingly not too bad, but looking back while I do it—impossible. The football soars past me, and I watch it fall to the grass, then thud around. Pathetic. I haven't sucked this bad at sports since we played those kids in that village where Gomez kissed a goat. And Blake's giving me this embarrassed look and I just tell him, *Let's get shit-faced*, and he says okay and we go through a twelve-pack really fast. I'm drunk-ass drunk, so wasted I can't even walk, I'm like all over the place and I tell him Skylar's hot and he says, *Yeah, she's a great kisser but she only let me touch her boobs.* And I just full on punch him, but I'm so wasted that I kinda nick his shoulder and he's all, *What's that for*, and I say, *Don't touch her*, and he's all, *Holy shit, you're into her*, and I tell him to fuck off and he just keeps shaking his head and saying, *Holy shit.* So I close my eyes and let my body float and I try to feel nothing except now I'm thinking of a girl I can't have because the war won't even let me kiss her, scared of goddamn thunder Jesus Christ and I don't know why I tell Blake this because this is fucking embarrassing to admit but I say, *I haven't been laid in over a year. Isn't that the saddest thing you ever heard?* And he's like, *We need to fix that right fucking now,* and I say, *Hell, no, maybe tomorrow. I'm gonna pass out.* And he's like, *Okay.* And now I'm lying in bed and can't sleep because my leg is starting to do that thing that feels like growing pains except my leg is not fucking there and I'm sorry, I'm sorry. I'm so goddamn sorry. Should've been me, not you.

JULY

chapter sixteen

It was like we'd never danced in the rain or woken up at dawn holding hands in the back of his truck. For the next few days, Josh and I were friendly, like you're supposed to be with your coworker. He'd be fixing a rain gutter or installing a new screen in a room, and I'd wave when I came in, and he'd wave back and then that would be it. I'd read a book or collage, and I'd tell myself it was good he hadn't wanted to kiss me, good things were cooling off between us. I was moving to San Fran, and he was probably staying in the Marines. It wasn't like we would have been anything more than a summer romance. Still, the loss of our easy banter made me realize how much his friendship had started to mean to me. He was the parts of the day where I smiled.

"How many times have you read that page, Skylar?"

I looked up from my book—I hadn't even noticed Marge standing right in front of me. And Marge was not a small woman.

I shrugged my shoulders. "How long have you been here?"

"Awhile." She handed me a Coke while she opened a Diet Dr Pepper. She stuck one of her straws in the can and took a long sip. "So a little birdie told me you were sleeping in your car this morning."

Billy had been over again, and by three A.M., it'd been clear he was spending the night. I'd opted to sleep in my car instead of listen to him and my mother freaking out over a bunch of old CDs he'd brought over. The irony of them belting out Garth Brooks's "Friends in Low Places" was not lost on me.

"Amy," I said.

I thought I'd been so clever, parking behind the hippies' Winnebago.

"Josh."

I took a long sip of my Coke. "Oh."

Marge leaned over the counter and put one of her thick hands on my arm. There was a ring on each finger: costume jewelry that sparkled in the late afternoon sunlight. "Honey, why didn't you just sleep in one of the rooms?"

"I like my car. Besides, it was only for a couple of hours."

I wasn't into airing my family's dirty laundry, and the car was comfortable enough. Whatever. Why did Josh say something to Marge and not to me? If he was so worried about me, why didn't he just—

"What's going on at home?" Marge asked.

"What do you mean?" I frowned. "Did this *little birdie* who happens to be over six feet tell you something?"

She let my annoyance roll right on over her. That was the thing about Marge—she was a rock to Mom's Jell-O.

"Is Billy Easton still coming around your place?"

"Good to know you and Josh sit around and gossip about me like a bunch of old ladies."

Marge rolled her eyes. "Sky, he's just worried about you."

I didn't know how that made me feel, Josh being worried. Relieved, like maybe things weren't so weird between us, after all. Annoyed that he was talking to Marge instead of me.

I could hear the faint sounds of a classic rock station playing on the boom box in the courtyard. Josh was fixing the tiles around the pool. "Hotel California" came on, and was it just my imagination, or did he turn the radio up?

"Sky?"

I blinked. "I'm fine, Marge. Seriously. Mom's just . . . you know. With losing the job she's—"

"I told you to bring her here. We'd figure something out."

I twirled a pencil around. "She's thinking about it."

Mom resented Marge for being there for me when Mom couldn't be, and Marge resented Mom for being Mom.

"Uh-huh."

She reached over the counter to grab a quarter from the till and put it in the candy dispenser that held stale Hot Tamales. "Want one?" she asked, when they came tumbling out.

I shook my head. "I'm gonna eat some real food when I'm off."

All I'd had to eat was a bag of Skittles from the nearly empty vending machine—no home, no breakfast. At least having my Pump and Go money meant I could buy some lunch when I got off work. The owner had agreed to give me an advance, something I never would have asked Marge for. Money was tight enough for her as it was.

Marge chewed on her Hot Tamales for a while, looking at Josh. Then she turned back to me. "You going to watch the fireworks down by the creek tonight?"

It was a Creek View tradition on the Fourth. There was this

abandoned field that everyone would bring their fireworks to—whatever they'd bought illegally in Vegas or whatever. Then they'd hang around and drink beer and set them off.

"I don't think so," I said. "I'll probably hang with my mom. The kids in the neighborhood will have some fireworks."

"You all ready for school?"

The million-dollar question.

"Yeah. My roommate called. Her name's Cynthia. She's from Vermont—seems nice."

But when she'd called me yesterday to introduce herself, the conversation hadn't felt real. Not with everything in limbo. *Stay. Go. Stay. Go. Wait. Wait. Wait.*

Marge's face lit up. "That's great! What's her major?"

"Something with journalism or—" My cell rang, and I held it up. "Sorry. Important. Can I . . . ?"

Marge nodded, and I ran outside.

"Hello?" I made my voice low, like my mom's.

"Hi, is this Denise Evans?" said a woman.

"Yes, it is."

"Hi, Denise. This is Sharon down at the Valley Outlet Center. We got your application, and something in our customer service department just opened up. I wanted to see if we could have you come in for an interview this Thursday, around three?"

"That'd be great. Thank you so much."

"Excellent! We'll see you then."

I did a silent dance. "Thank you. Looking forward to it."

I hung up and clutched the phone to my chest. Now all I had to do was get my mom sober enough to go.

———

"You *what*?" Mom was sitting on the couch, her legs folded, staring at me.

Somehow, this was not the reaction I'd pictured. I'd imagined something between *Really?* and *Hallelujah!*

I bit my lip and repeated what I'd just said. "I filled out the application and set up the interview. You're good to go. They're really excited to meet you."

I'd tell her later that I lied and said she'd graduated from high school. It wasn't like they were going to ask to see her diploma, anyway.

Mom stubbed out her cigarette and stood up. "You have no business filling out applications in *my* name—"

"Mom! I'm just trying to help you. I know it's hard to—"

"I don't care!" She screamed the words, her face suddenly ugly. "I didn't ask for your help, I don't *want* your help." She threw her cigarettes across the room. One of her porcelain angel figurines wobbled as the pack hit the shelf it was sitting on. "Jesus, Sky, you're driving me crazy!"

She pushed past me, stomping toward the fridge.

"Great, Mom. Just go get another wine cooler. I'm sure that'll fix the problem."

She turned around, her eyes narrowed in this hateful way that I'd never seen before. "Get out."

"What?" She had to be joking.

"I said, get out. Just"—she put her hands over her eyes, took a deep breath—"give me a couple hours to clear my head, okay? I don't wanna fight like this."

I crossed my arms and dug my fingers into my ribs to keep from crying. I stared at her for a long moment, then grabbed my keys and my wallet. I made sure to slam the door behind me.

A breeze had picked up outside and a dusty sunset lingered in the sky. I was free for the night, but I didn't know what to do with myself. I sat in my car, taking deep breaths, trying to remember what it felt like to throw a glass bottle. Was she kicking me out for a few hours, or for good? I knew which one Billy would prefer.

Dylan didn't answer when I called—she was probably working. I dialed Chris.

"What you need," he said, "are some seriously good burritos."

"This is your answer to my life crisis?"

Long pause, then, "Just come over."

As soon as I got to his house, his mom sent us to Market to grab some Cokes. On the way there, I told Chris what had happened at home.

He shook his head. "Sounds like she's having a total breakdown."

"Yeah, I *know*. She's like a completely different person."

He pulled into the little parking lot in front of the bodega and shut off the engine. "Okay. Let's take this step by step—"

"Chris, my life is not an equation or a word problem, okay? It sucks to the tenth power—that's all you need to know!"

I was shaking, literally shaking, and I couldn't stop. Didn't people only do that in movies?

"Come here," Chris said, his voice soft.

He reached over and hugged me, and I wasn't going to cry, I wasn't. That wouldn't solve anything. I closed my eyes until the tears retreated down my throat and back into my chest, where they seemed to live these days.

Chris squeezed me, and I squeezed him back before I pulled away. "It's gonna be okay, *chica*. Trust me. You're getting out of here, one way or another. But you need a day off: just one to have fun and chill out. Can we do that?"

I nodded.

"Come on, let's get these Cokes and go back home."

"Okay."

I wanted to argue with him, but the truth was, I needed a day off from the mess that was my life. I stepped out of the truck and slammed the door behind me. I heard a whistle and turned around. Josh and a bunch of people he'd graduated with were standing outside, drinking out of bottles covered with small brown paper bags.

"Garcia! What's up, man?" one of the guys yelled. He was looking at Chris and me with a dirty grin. He must have been the one that whistled.

"David. What up?" Chris walked over to them, and I followed with a reluctant shuffle.

Josh nodded to me but kept talking to some girl that we'd gone to school with. Stacie. Or Stephanie. Something like that. She had big boobs and long red hair. And his finger was hooked into one of the belt loops on her tiny jean shorts. For a second, it was the only thing I could see.

"You guys together now or what?" asked David.

I looked away from Josh and shook my head. "Friends."

"With benefits," said some other guy. He was one of those white guys who tried to look all hip-hop, with a gold chain and baggy shorts that showed off most of his faded boxers. Chris just rolled his eyes at me as if to say, *Morons*.

I said "Shut up" at the same time that Josh said "Don't be a dick." He didn't look at me, and I didn't look at him. The wannabe gangster laughed and gulped his beer.

I couldn't figure out where the whole "with benefits" comment came from until I realized that from where they were standing, it must have looked like Chris and I had been making out in the truck. Shit. Josh probably thought—wait, I didn't care. Did I?

"I'm gonna go inside," I said.

Here I was, worrying about what Chris and I had looked like in the truck when what I really needed to be focusing on was the fact that my mother was losing her mind. And how was I suddenly caring about Creek View sexual politics? I was getting out. This crap shouldn't rattle me. But was I getting out? I crossed over to the sodas and yanked open the door to the refrigerated section, closing my eyes as the cold air blasted me. The bells on the door jingled as someone came inside.

"Hey." Chris grabbed a couple two-liter bottles of Coke, and I shut the door. "Those guys are idiots—just ignore them."

"I thought that's what I was doing," I said, my voice hard.

"You are. I'm just saying, you know, screw them." He rolled his eyes. "You wanna know what they were talking about?"

"Something obnoxious?"

"They went cow tipping last night. *Cow tipping.*"

"That's a new low for the youth of Creek View," I said.

"Dude, I can't get out of here soon enough."

We paid for the Cokes, and I tried not to look like I was in too much of a hurry, but when we got back outside, Josh's truck was gone.

So was the redhead.

JOSH

Her name is Shannon and her skin's like milk with flakes of cinnamon in it and she's pressed up against me and it feels good, I guess, I mean it should, and she whispers in my ear that her parents aren't home and fuck it Skylar's obviously into that Chris dude, I saw them in his sorry excuse for a truck, should have totaled it when I had the chance, so what the hell am I waiting for and I just say, *Okay, cool,* and we get to her house and I'm kissing her like what Skylar said about her and Blake—to forget, like I need a body—and I can't believe he felt her up and what did she do to him, doesn't matter, and I kiss this girl, kiss her hard, bite her lips and her neck and she moans, but she tastes like beer and cigarettes and I bet Skylar tastes sweet, like the powdered sugar on those little white doughnuts and I shouldn't be thinking about Skylar, not when this girl's hand is in my pants and—fuck—it's been so long, but I can't. I want this but I don't want her. I close my eyes and try to relax, *relax, goddammit, relax.* This used to be so easy why isn't it easy and my hands are on her breasts, which feel good, I mean, I'm not fucking gay so they feel really good and I don't deserve Skylar, never will, so I should just go for this because she's going for Chris and this girl says to me, she says to me, *I'll do anything you want.*

And that's it.

My hands fall from her chest and I go, *What did you say?* And she says, *I'll do anything you want,* and I pull her hand out of my pants and back away and almost trip on her shoes that she'd kicked off and I keep saying, *Sorry, sorry,* and I get myself out of her room, her house, and I don't look back because you know what I'm thinking about, don't you? That woman running out of her hut and waving her arms around and screaming, *I'll do anything you want*—how the hell'd she know English?—and we had to take her son anyway because he was killing our guys with his little homemade bombs and the look on her face . . . I drive away fast and I go to my favorite spot off the highway and I sit in my truck until the sky turns black. I keep replaying the whole thing in my head, how I couldn't get it up and what the hell does that mean, isn't there enough wrong with me already? I don't know if I'll ever be able to do this again. Be close to someone. Maybe it's a punishment, I don't know. I don't deserve to be here and I'm a worthless piece of shit so yeah, me not being able to get it up just evens the scales a little bit more. Just a little bit, though. Why did I make it when so many other guys got wasted? And now it's like I lost a leg and gained another fuckin' eye that's letting me see everything in this totally new, crappy light and all this shit that used to make me *me* I either can't do or is so fucking stupid—God, what's the point of me? I just want to go back, man. I want to be on post—I don't care how boring it is. All I need is my gun and the guys and it doesn't matter anymore that everything there is sad and hopeless and dead or dying. It's like that here too.

chapter seventeen

Chris's neighborhood started celebrating the Fourth early. The people up the street were blasting mariachi music, and every now and then, there'd be the whine and fizzle of fireworks from the middle of the street. The air smelled like barbecue and sulfur and the kind of wild abandon you can only have on holidays. It wasn't completely dark yet, but it had finally cooled down enough for us to be outside for extended periods of time. Dylan, Chris, and I were in his backyard lying on the trampoline, which floated on a sea of discarded toys and failed gardening attempts. I was in the middle, wishing I could bottle up the feel of their warmth, a *thereness* I wouldn't have come September. Dylan's long hair was tickling my arm, and every time Chris laughed, his foot would knock into mine. We elbowed and slapped each other, snorted with laughter. It was hard to imagine I could have this with new college friends. Already these moments were few and far between, now that Dylan was a mom.

She looked over at us. "Do you remember when we saw that shooting star?"

"It was awesome," I said.

Chris nodded. "True that."

Sixth grade, Halloween. I was Van Gogh (which nobody got and everyone thought was weird), Dylan was a sexy witch, and Chris was a ninja. We'd been lying on the trampoline, just like we were now, but holding hands because we'd heard a freaky noise in the neighbor's backyard. Then we saw it—the flash, a yellow-whiteness that streaked across the sky like it was trying not to be seen. As if we'd caught angels playing tag.

Now we lay there, older but maybe not wiser, staring up at the sky and watching dusk crawl in for the night shift.

"Haven't seen one since," Dylan said, her voice flat.

I closed my eyes. "Nope."

We lay there, that memory and all the years that followed hovering above us.

Chris sat up. "Speaking of falling stars: did I tell you guys I'm taking an astronomy class next semester? It's gonna be so badass. There's actually a ton of math, which most people don't know—they think it's just stargazing, but there's this whole lab component where we—"

Dylan held up her hand. "Is this going to involve big, scientific words? Because if it is, I'm gonna go pee."

I was tempted to join her. Every time Chris mentioned school, I felt like I was outside the window of a toy shop, looking in at all the stuff I couldn't have.

He stood and started jumping, soft at first, then harder. "What's that? Your bladder's full? You have to *pee*? Wow, you must be really uncomfortable right now."

"Christopher! What the hell?" Dylan yelled. "Grow up. *Jesus.*" But she was smiling as she reached out and tried to grip the side of the trampoline.

Chris laughed and spun in the air as he lifted himself higher and higher. Our bodies jolted off the trampoline's thick net, and I gasped, spreading my arms wide, like Chris could catapult me into the sky. I closed my eyes, for once loving the sweet terror of not knowing where I would land. Floating in the air, crashing back down, Dylan beside me, the net always under me. I gave myself up to the free fall. No rules or boundaries or barriers. The three of us let go and flew.

There was a thunk, barely heard over the squeaking of the springs, as Dylan's oversized purse slipped over the edge of the trampoline. Makeup, loose change, and a few of Sean's pacifiers spilled onto the grass beneath us, breaking the spell.

"My bag!" Dylan shrieked.

"Chill," Chris said. He stopped his jumping and landed on the grass. "*Damn.* You carry this much crap around all the time?"

Dylan looked over at me, and I held up my hands. "You guys leave me out of it."

She scooted over to the edge of the trampoline and swung off. "I gotta pick up Jesse soon, anyway. You guys coming or what?"

Fireworks at the creek. I used to go with my parents when I was little, sitting on my dad's shoulders as the sky exploded all around me. Later, it became an annual thing for Dylan, Chris, and me. It was the one Creek View party I actually liked.

But at one point or another, everyone from town would wind up there—which was exactly why I wouldn't be going tonight.

I shook my head, my good mood gone. "You guys go ahead. I should probably get home to check on my mom." I hoisted myself off the trampoline and slid my feet into my flip-flops.

Dylan grabbed my hand. "She's just gonna be in her room.

Or with Billy. *Ugh.* Come on. I'm an independent mama tonight! I need me some Skylar time."

Which was worse: Josh and the redhead or Mom and Billy? *Decisions, decisions.*

She did a pouty face, and when I sighed, she knew she was winning me over. "Please? You'll feel better, seeing all those pretty lights."

"My dad bought a bunch of sparklers," Chris said. He gave me a semiparental look. "And I distinctly remember you agreeing to one night of fun."

I stared up at the lavender sky, my stomach pinching at the thought of being cooped up in a trailer that smelled like stale cigarettes and old beer. If Mom even let me in.

"I can't believe she kicked me out," I said, the anger flaring up again.

"Dude." Chris put his hands on my shoulders. "One night of fun."

Screw her. I didn't deserve this shit.

"Fine," I muttered. "But this party doesn't really qualify as fun."

Dylan threw her arm around my waist and gave me a vise-like hug. "That's the spirit."

We drove to the creek after we picked up Jesse at the dairy factory where he worked, filling up gallons of milk for eight to twelve hours a day. Chris and I sat in the back of Dylan's car, and as we sped along the highway, I'd catch myself watching the way Jesse looked at Dylan. How he'd grab her hand and kiss it when he thought no one was looking, or the way she'd lean into him when he was talking, like he was the only person in the world. It wasn't like they were perfect—they had epic arguments. Still. It was like I was suddenly aware of this parallel universe made of iridescent bubbles and stardust.

"Disgusting, aren't they?" muttered Chris. This was our bit, giving Dylan and Jesse shit for acting like an old married couple. Chris called it self-preservation.

I laughed, but my heart wasn't in it. "Yeah."

Dylan turned onto a narrow dirt lane bordered by cornfields and parked among the jumble of cars at the edge of a large clearing, her headlights slicing through the sudden darkness. Fields surrounded us on three sides, with the creek at the far end, boxing us in. I could just barely see its inky water, slithering beyond a wall of brush. The only light came from the fireworks people were setting off and a sliver of moon that played hide-and-seek behind a charcoal cloud. Smoke from the fireworks settled over the land like a thick mist. Everything—the moon, the fireworks, the fields—had an otherworldly beauty, and I shivered, greedy for these bits of loveliness the universe was throwing our way tonight.

It was the usual Creek View crowd, and as we got out of the car, people called out to us or raised bottles of beer in greeting. I let Dylan be our official spokesperson and kept my eyes down or unfocused. I wouldn't let myself look for him. If he was with her, making out in his truck or lighting fireworks, then fine. Whatever.

Chris handed me a sparkler. "Ready?"

I nodded and he brought his lighter close to the tip. It lit and sparks began to fly, kissing the night. I twirled, and the sparkler spit light around me in fire-colored swirls. I heard the sound of my laughter, and for a second, I was ten years old again, running around with my dad.

Dylan and Jesse and Chris lit their own sparklers, and we sort of skipped around until they died out. The air filled with pops and screeches, fire and color coming from all directions. It was magical, those sudden bursts of rainbow light. I longed for my razor blade and shimmery paper. Or maybe colored chalk and black cardboard. I wanted to put this down on paper so it wouldn't end.

I caught myself scanning the crowd, and I closed my eyes. Pining away got you stuck in a dark bedroom at the back of a trailer, with a bottle of Prozac and some cheap-ass boxed wine to keep you company. I had friends. A scholarship. A job. I needed to wake the hell up.

Wake. Up.

"Okay, guys, stand back!"

I opened my eyes and watched as Chris set a firecracker on the hard-packed dirt. As soon as he lit it, he darted toward us, like it was about to sting him. The flame sparked, then the firecracker spun on the ground, faster and faster, letting out a high-pitched scream while it shot out hot, bright light. White, yellow, pink. I had to cover my ears, it was so loud.

That's when I saw Josh, walking away from the field. Alone.

He looked pissed off, his face dark and stony except for the shards of light cut into it, sparks from the fireworks. He stumbled over something but kept going, his back rigid.

And suddenly the redhead and him not kissing me in the rain didn't matter—I had to make sure he was okay.

"Be right back," I said to Dylan. I didn't know if she'd heard me, but I took off after him.

"Josh!" I called.

He seemed to slow for a second, then went on, walking faster.

The air filled with the sound of dozens of firecrackers being shot off at once.

Someone grabbed my hand. I turned around.

"Blake, let go—"

He shook his head, his mouth set in a thin line. "He just wants to be alone. Trust me."

Blake let go of my hand, and I looked back at Josh. All I could see was a dark outline walking into the shadows along the creek.

"But—"

"He'll be okay. When he's like this, best thing to do is just let him go off."

"When he's like what?"

Blake shoved his hands in his pockets and shrugged. "Like Josh. The new Josh."

"What happened?"

He threw his hands up. "He said the security here was shit, and we shouldn't be exposed like this, and I was all, 'Dude, it's cool,' and then he just bolted. I tried to follow him, and he told me to fuck off. His words, not mine."

How many Joshes were there? I was starting to lose count.

Blake waved at someone in the darkness, then turned back to me. "Alexis is here. Gotta go, or she'll kill me for talking to a girl that's not her."

He gave me a sheepish smile and backed away, and I knew he was thinking of his party and how clingy he'd gotten after one too many beers.

"See you," he said.

"Yeah."

I waited for him to leave, then headed off in the direction

I'd seen Josh go. It didn't matter what Blake said; it was almost like I didn't have a choice.

It must have been hard for Josh—I had two perfectly fine legs, and even I kept stumbling over roots and rocks and whatever else was on the ground. The clouds had shifted, bathing everything in bright moonlight, but it was still difficult to see more than a few feet ahead of me. The creek was to my right—I could hear it—but the path Josh had taken led away from it, toward the train tracks. I'd almost given up when I saw an opening between two large bushes.

I pushed through, and I was suddenly at the edge of a field beside the train tracks. Josh was leaning against a run-down picket fence, staring at the tracks, his arms crossed, his face hard. I could still hear the firecrackers in the distance.

"Josh."

His head whipped around. "Who's there?" he asked, his voice harsh.

I took a few steps forward. "It's Skylar."

He peered into the darkness, and when he saw me, he looked away. "What are you doing here?"

I couldn't tell if he was angry or annoyed. Definitely not happy to see me.

"I saw you take off and . . ." *And what?*

Following Josh had been an instinct. For weeks, it was like my body was always aware of where he was. But everything about him right then said he didn't want me around. Probably wished I was the redhead.

He turned and placed both hands on the fence, leaning into it.

"Are you okay?" I asked. *Just go. You're the last person he wants to see.*

"I'm fine."

Another firework went off, and he flinched, just slightly. The only reason I noticed was because I was making a point to. The moonlight was bright enough that I could see the tendons in his arms popping out as he gripped the fence.

I leaned against it, close, but not too close. "What's wrong?"

Josh shook his head.

"Can I help? I mean, is there something you need or—"

Another firework went off, and he let out a frustrated grunt and hit his fist against the fence. "I'm so fucking tired of this."

"This?"

He swept his hand over the sky, the fields. Everything. "This."

I should go. Just . . . go. Go. But I couldn't move.

"Why are you here, Sky?" His voice was low, accusatory.

"I don't know," I whispered.

Our eyes met and something flickered in his, but before I could figure out what it was, there was a sudden, loud burst of fireworks—the air exploding with sound and light. It was as if everyone in the clearing had thrown their stash into a pile and lit the whole thing. Fear lashed across Josh's face, just for a second, and he turned away from me, staring out at the dark field on the other side of the fence with the intensity of a German shepherd. I reached out and grabbed his hand.

"It's okay," I murmured.

He looked at me, and I kept my eyes locked on his, and we stood like that, facing each other, my hand gripping his or his gripping mine—I didn't know because I think both of us were terrified at that moment, but for different reasons. When the fireworks finally stopped, he nodded and let go.

"Thanks," he said. He closed his eyes, took a deep breath. "I'm such a fuckin' pussy."

"Right. Because pussies volunteer for the Marines during a war."

He snorted. "There was a signing bonus."

"That is so not why you joined."

Josh turned to me, his eyes searing. "Are you with him?"

It was so unexpected, his question, that all I could do was stand there for a second, stunned.

"With . . . who? What are you talking about?"

But I knew, of course I knew. Was he jealous? Something fluttered in my chest, and I bit back a wild desire to smile.

"Garcia," he said. Market. Chris hugging me in his truck.

"*No*." I stepped closer. Just a few inches between us now.

A muscle in his jaw twitched, and he crossed his arms, gazed up at the sky. In our silence, I could hear the sound of the rain pounding on the Paradise pavement, his voice close to my ear, singing. *Some dance to remember, some dance to forget.*

There was another firework, a red one that bled onto the sky, and he stared at it. I could see its fire reflected in his eyes, like dozens of arteries. Then it was quiet. Neither of us said anything for a bit, and then I couldn't take it anymore. I needed to know.

"That girl outside Market . . . is she, like, part of your group?"

"Not really." He ran his hand along the fence. "She's just this girl I've hung out with a few times."

"Oh." *So this wasn't the first time.* Ouch.

He looked at me and his voice softened. "She's not . . . I mean . . . you know. It's nothing."

Relief. Crazy, ridiculous relief flooded through me. Which meant I needed to leave, just get back to Chris and Dylan as fast as I could because it shouldn't have mattered who he dated. I began edging away, but there was a faint train horn in the distance, and Josh beckoned me closer.

"Come here," he said.

I followed him over to the train tracks. "Is this the part where you tie me to the tracks like in those old cartoons?"

He shook his head. "You have one twisted mind, Evans."

I smiled a little, and he leaned over and reached for my hand. "Check this out."

His skin was warm, and one of his fingers had a Band-Aid wrapped around it. I wanted to know why—like if he'd cut himself or did he have a blister or what? Somehow it mattered.

He put my hand against the metal rail. "Feel that?"

We were only touching for a few seconds, but there was a hum in the pit of my stomach. In the spaces between my ribs. At the tips of my ears.

The metal shivered under my fingers, vibrating from the weight of the train. "Yeah."

The train sounded its horn again, and the vibrations got stronger as the wheels moved closer. Josh looked in the direction it was coming from, his whole body tense.

"This is the part where we move far away," I said, my voice tight.

But we didn't. In the moonlight, I could see the shadows under his eyes, the way he looked ready to spring onto the tracks.

"Josh, you're freaking me out."

Maybe I was panicking, I didn't know, but I hated the way he looked—like he'd gone far away and I wouldn't be able to reach him. Not then, not ever. I grabbed his arm, and he looked at me, confused, like he'd forgotten I was there.

"I used to jump these all the time. Remember, I told you?" he said.

I nodded.

His eyes slid to the tracks. "The key is to be ready. You step back and let the first couple of cars go by, get the rhythm. Spot an open boxcar with your name on it. Getting in or falling on your ass—it all happens in a matter of seconds."

I could feel the train in my chest and thought about how dying on these tracks would be the epitome of a small-town death.

"I like the part where you said we step back. And I hate to break it to you, but you're not jumping this train tonight."

Or ever. What the hell was he thinking?

Josh stood up as the train's headlight came into view. "Give me a little credit, Sky. I'm not gonna try to do it in the dark. Even with two legs, that'd be hard as hell."

I decided to table this discussion for later. Because it was sounding to me like he intended to try it when it wasn't dark—and there was no way that would end well for him.

He put an arm across me as we stepped back, like you do with a passenger when you're driving and you suddenly hit the brakes. The train wasn't that fast—but way too fast to hitch a ride on. It chugged by, a monstrous mass of creaking, rusted metal with open boxcars like dark mouths that swallowed the night as they whipped by.

Josh closed his eyes, turned his face toward the wind the

train had churned up. I watched him, my eyes tracing his jaw, the bridge of his nose, his chin.

His lips.

He almost looked at peace. Almost. I tore my gaze away from him, stared at the train. My body was suddenly this alive, buzzing thing I had no control over anymore. Maybe I was in as much danger of jumping as he was. For a second, it felt like anything could happen. Anything.

The last of the boxcars passed us, leaving a perfect, complete silence. Josh turned to me. "If you could be anywhere in the world right now, where would you be?"

I opened my mouth to say San Francisco or maybe Madrid— somewhere exotic. But what came out was, "Here. Right here."

I looked at him, surprised. He held my eyes for a minute, then looked in the direction the train was going.

"Me too."

Fuck, I thought. Just that—*fuck*.

chapter eighteen

It was Florence Nightingale syndrome—it had to be. That's the only explanation for why I was suddenly obsessed with Josh Mitchell. Like in *A Farewell to Arms*, I was a nurse falling for her patient. Obviously I wasn't Josh's nurse or whatever (insert crude Dylan joke about "playing doctor"), but ever since graduation, I felt like I'd been trying to take care of him. Like inviting him to Leo's or going after him the night of the Fourth. But I was supposed to be with a slightly geeky, yet totally adorable San Franciscan who loved art and wanted to use words like *chiaroscuro* and *proletariat* and *existentialism*. Josh was the past, and all I'd ever cared about was the future. And, anyway, that didn't matter because he was probably going back to his base at the end of the summer, and I was going to school.

Right?

If that night by the train tracks taught me anything, it was that no matter how much you tried to get out of Creek View, it was gonna find a way to get its claws into you. What I'd said— that being by those train tracks with Josh was the only place *in the whole world* that I wanted to be—was the push I needed. I was getting out of Creek View in less than two months, and nothing was going to stop me.

A few days after the Fourth, I put my newest escape plan into action. As soon as my shift ended at the Paradise, I changed into the skirt and silk tank top I'd worn for graduation, then double-checked the documents in the manila folder I'd left on the front seat of my car. Inside was an application for food stamps that had my mother's signature on the bottom (forged), two copies of our recent pay stubs, a copy of our utility bills, and my transcripts. I didn't need the transcripts, but I thought the 4.0 might help me if I ran into trouble at social services.

I pulled onto the highway, my blouse already sticking to my back with sweat. I leaned forward and let the breeze blow over me. Someday, I was going to have a car with air-conditioning. Maybe, I thought, I should make that my life's goal. It seemed manageable.

The sun beat down on me, burning my left arm as I traveled north on the highway. It wasn't busy, just the usual flow of traffic—mostly big rigs and dusty pickups, with a smattering of commuters and travelers. I passed road-tripping families in minivans with bumper stickers like MY KID IS AN HONOR STUDENT AT (FILL IN THE BLANK) or SKI MAMMOTH. I envied the kids in front of me with their feet propped up on the backs of their parents' seats, watching DVDs. I couldn't even imagine a life like that. To me, *they* were the ones in a movie.

For a while I got stuck behind a big rig, and I eased out from behind it, speeding by as quickly as I could. It didn't matter how many of those trucks I saw—they would always make me think of Dad. What if he hadn't had those last few beers before he got in his truck? What if someone had given him a ride home? What if the big rig had stopped for gas instead of driving past Ray's at the same time my dad was pulling out? *Whatifwhatifwhatif?*

My phone rang, and I checked my rearview mirror to make sure there weren't any Highway Patrol dudes sneaking around. I grabbed it out of my cup holder and answered, careful to keep my eyes on the road.

"What's up, lady?" Dylan said.

"I'm on the road, endangering my life by talking on a cell phone."

"I'm guessing that's code for *hurry up*. Where are you going?"

"Long story."

I couldn't bring myself to tell her I was applying for food stamps, even though Dylan and her mom had used them plenty of times. To me, it felt like such a failure. I never thought my mom and I would get that low. I wasn't ready to admit defeat.

"Okay, well, could you please, *please* babysit my little man tonight? Jesse's taking me to Fresno for dinner and a movie."

"Fancy," I said. "What's the occasion?"

She said something, but I couldn't catch it over the wind.

"Huh?"

I pressed the phone hard against my ear.

"Three-year anniversary, remember?"

"Oh! Awesome. Sure, I'll watch Sean. What time?"

"Six? I was thinking maybe—"

My car started making a funny sound, and I groaned. "Sounds good, Dyl. Sorry, I better go. My car sounds like it's trying to cough up a fur ball."

"Yikes. Okay, hurry back, then."

I hung up and finished the rest of the drive listening to a classical CD that never failed to chill me out, trying not to think too much about the sounds my car was making. I wondered what Bach would have thought if he'd looked into the future and seen my sweaty Hicksville self driving my broke-ass car through the middle of nowhere, swaying in my seat to his Concerto in Whatever Minor. I collaged a few unicorns onto the bland scenery, just because, and kept swaying.

An hour later, my exit came up. As I pulled into the social services parking lot, I had to smile because, seriously, how many people roll up to get food stamps after collaging imaginary unicorns? I killed the engine, hoping the acrid, burned-rubber smell that was spiking the air wasn't coming from my car. I looked at my reflection in the rearview mirror and pulled at my hair to get it into something resembling a neat bun, then wiped my sweaty face with a fast-food napkin. The napkin came away coated with grime. I sighed, then grabbed my folder of paperwork and put my hand on the door handle. My fingers hesitated, the folder damp under my palms. *Move*, I told myself. But I couldn't.

People walked in and out of the low building, none of them looking particularly better or worse off than me. Kids shuffled after their parents, a young woman got on her cell phone and immediately started laughing. An old man squinted into the sun, scanning the parking lot for his car. Nothing about the building or the people screamed Welfare, but I couldn't get out. As the minutes ticked by, I watched the tinted glass door, telling myself that after the next person, I was going in. It became a game, only not the fun kind.

Okay, the next time a girl with a ponytail goes in, so do you.
After the overweight dude in the Mazda comes back out—
Once three people wearing any red exit the building—
Was I really gonna do this? Have my mom get food stamps

so I could waltz off to some fancy college while she wasted away in our trailer? I imagined her at the grocery store, having to use those checks that everyone knew were for poor people. They'd stare at her, knowing. Maybe they'd judge her, wonder why their tax dollars had to pay for her milk and chicken breasts. It would be like when I had to get free lunches at school—which, by the way, never felt free because they cost you your pride. They'd give us poor kids these little green tickets, and that's what you handed the lunch lady. You could only use them for certain foods, stand in certain lines. So as soon as you brought that ticket out, everyone knew what you were, who you were. Or they thought they did, which was bad enough.

I let my hand fall from the door and closed my eyes. The sun beat down so hard on the metal roof of my car that I shivered. I made myself concentrate on the exact quality of the heat. On the lines the sweat traveled down my body. Sweat on the backs of my knees, between my thighs, dripping into the creases of my elbows, sliding along my upper lip. I tasted like the ocean. I boiled away, my hopes rising out of me like steam.

I thought of the cool, fresh air of the city I'd always dreamed of living in. The art museums and trolleys and the mysterious fog that blanketed it. I could almost smell the cappuccinos I'd planned to drink in bohemian cafés or hear the indie music in the bookstores I would spend my free time in. I pictured the friends I'd make, my kindred art people, and the dorm room I was supposed to move into. I'd already bought a cute desk lamp, that pretty comforter. A cork board.

I thought of the receipts, stacked neatly on the desk in my bedroom.

It wasn't too late to return all of it.

JOSH

Got an e-mail from Tyler. They lost Gomez yesterday. His daughter would be, what, three or four now, right? Fuck. Teresa must be losing her mind. Every picture I ever saw of him and his wife, she was kissing him, smiling so big. *Fuck.* Guess you two are catching up on old times now, shooting the shit while you look down at the rest of us. This is why I don't check my e-mail too much. Never know what the hell it's gonna say when you open it up. When it all first went down, I couldn't handle the hang-in-there-bro e-mails or the killed-a-hajji-for-you-today ones. Guys asking me how I am, trying to get me to accept Jesus into my heart or just telling me what's up over there and who else got fucked like you and me during the second deployment. But lately I've been reading more, sending more. Tyler said the unit's going on leave in a couple of weeks. Wanted to know if I'd come down to Camp Pendleton to say hi and all that shit. Man, I just . . . it'd be great. And not great. You know. I can hear our voices, talking about home: *I miss walking around barefoot* (Jones). *I miss Starbucks* (Harrison). *I miss sex—that's my Starbucks* (Sharpe, of course—horniest dude on the planet). *I miss Hannah* (you), and we all called you a pussy and you flipped us off. I didn't miss much. I think, more than anything, I missed knowing I had a hell of a good chance of waking up this side of heaven. Tyler said everyone was planning on having a picnic or something and there was gonna be a memorial for the guys that didn't make it this tour. I don't think I can handle that. Tyler probably knew that because at the end of the e-mail he was all, *Dude, it's not your fault.* Semper Fi, *motherfucker. Come on out. We miss you. Time to move on, buddy.* I don't really know what it means to move on, but lately, with Sky, I'm starting to feel like I want to because when I look at her, I don't see you or the war or any of the shit in my head. I just see *her,* and it's like suddenly I can breathe again after holding my breath for so long.

chapter nineteen

I only managed to get ten minutes down the road before white smoke started pouring out from under the hood.

"No. No. Nonononononono!" I yelled.

I kept petting the dashboard as though I could make my car change its mind and suddenly start behaving, but soon I could barely see out the windshield and I had to pull off the road. All there was for miles were fields and orchards and vineyards. Cars sped by as I got out and went over to the hood, dust whipping into my eyes, tangling my hair. The sun was deadweight, bleeding all over me so that I could barely breathe. I popped the hood but couldn't even open it, the metal was so hot.

"Fuck!"

I kicked the front bumper. I kicked it again and again and again, cursing while smoke billowed around the front of the car. I kicked until I was worried I'd broken a toe and then I sank down to the dirt near the passenger door. Tiny pebbles dug into my skin, ripped the cheap fabric of my skirt. I looked down at my feet—my one nice pair of shoes were so scuffed they were no longer my one nice pair of shoes.

I broke. Shards of bone and scraps of skin and *fuck this life*.

I cried harder than when Dad died or Dylan got pregnant. I cried so hard I thought I might crack a rib, those sobs like hurricanes that came up from my stomach. I wanted to punch myself for being such a baby.

Instead, I leaned into the car and grabbed my phone, biting my tongue until the tears stopped. Then I dialed. I hated doing it, but Creek View only had one auto shop. Blake picked up on the first ring.

"Skylar Evans! What's up?"

I wondered if Josh was there and what he thought about me calling Blake. Would it remind him of that ill-advised week I'd had with his brother? It didn't matter. Nothing mattered anymore.

"I need a favor." My throat was raw, and I held the phone away from my ear for a second and coughed.

"I don't do favors for girls who break my heart."

This was typical flirty Blake, nothing new, but I couldn't do the banter thing, not now. My body was shaking, and my brain had gone numb.

"Blake. My car just broke down on the 99, and it's hot as hell, and I'm having a really, *really* bad day, so can you please just send out your tow truck?"

His voice instantly became serious. "Where are you?"

"Like, an hour away. Near the outlet?"

He cursed under his breath. "Hold on." I could hear him talking to someone in the background, a bit of arguing, then, "Josh is on his way home from his doctor in Fresno, so he's coming your way. I'll call and have him pick you up, and I'll get the tow truck out there later. Just make sure you lock up the car when you leave. You okay?"

Josh. God, this day couldn't get any worse. Didn't the universe understand that Josh had made my problem so big I could hardly see the other side of it?

"I'm—I'm fine. Um. Thanks."

"I'm sure you'll find a way to pay me back someday," he said. *Eww.*

"You. Have. A girlfriend."

"That's why I said *someday*, Sky."

"I'm hanging up now."

He started to say something else, but my finger was already shutting him up. The phone off, I chucked it into my bag, then grabbed the old blanket I kept in my trunk. I didn't know when Josh would be showing up, so I trekked over to a tiny stand of trees at the edge of the huge cornfield I'd broken down next to. My clothes were a mess—sweat-stained and dirty—and my face had tracks of mascara running down it. I hardly had any water left in my bottle, and I could already feel a headache coming on. I laid the blanket next to the tree and sat against the trunk, keeping my eyes closed. It was cooler in the shade, but not by much. I tried not to think of the dirt that had dusted over every inch of my skin or the way my silk shirt clung to me. I blocked out the sound of cars passing on the highway, focusing in on the way the hot breeze rustled the cornstalks. I imagined swimming pools and icebergs and cold showers. I fell into a black hole. It was deep and good, and I never wanted to leave it.

"Sky."

I woke with a start, gasping. Josh was standing over me, his mouth turned down. The sun was a little lower.

"Hey. Sorry, I must have . . ."

He reached out a hand, and I hesitated for a second, then took it. He pulled me up in one quick, fluid motion. I wondered if I smelled.

"What the hell are you thinking, sleeping on the side of the road—you're lucky some crazy serial killer didn't come and kidnap you."

His voice was hard, like he was genuinely angry with me.

I shrugged. "Who would want to do that? I look like a bag lady. Plus, I know self-defense."

He frowned again, then reached out a hand and touched my cheek. I stood absolutely still, my entire world whittled down to those few centimeters of skin under his fingers.

"Were you crying?" he asked, his voice soft.

I turned away and reached down to pick up my purse and the blanket.

"Just a little," I admitted. "Tears of frustration, though. Not wimpiness."

"I would never accuse you of wimpiness."

He smiled, and I made the mistake of looking into those eyes. They were epic. Blue blue blue. The storminess from the Fourth was gone, and they were gentle and so what I needed. And didn't need. Needed. God, I didn't know anymore. *Hell.*

He took another look at my face, then gestured to his truck. "Let's go."

I let him help me in and then I pretended to search inside my bag for something while he got in, and the only way I knew he was struggling a bit was a muttered curse. God forbid he take off the huge-ass wheels. I looked back at my car—now that I was working at the gas station, I needed it more than ever. I turned away from it and stared out the windshield.

Josh started the truck and blasted the air conditioner. I leaned back and sighed as arctic air shot out at me.

"Oh my God, that feels so good," I said. My car was already feeling like a bad dream.

He eased back onto the highway, then glanced over at me. "I think we need to get you to Dairy Queen stat."

"Those are the best words I've ever heard."

He gestured to my outfit. "So, this is interesting."

I smoothed my wrinkled, dirty skirt. Total mess.

"Yeah. Can we not talk about it?"

"Sure."

He fiddled with the radio until he got to the classic rock station. The truck filled with an insistent beat and familiar words—an old Rolling Stones song my dad had loved, "Paint It Black."

Josh drummed his fingers on the steering wheel and nodded his head, his lips moving with Mick Jagger's growl.

"You've seen *Full Metal Jacket*, right?" he asked, turning to me.

I shook my head. "Vietnam movies aren't my thing."

"It's not the most accurate movie, but the guys and I used to watch it all the time—the first part's pretty good. I had this friend who used to quote it, did the voices and everything." He was quiet for a minute, and it was like a cloud had passed across his face. So fast that I thought maybe I'd imagined it. "Anyway, it's pretty good for what it is."

"My movie tastes are more boy meets girl, girl falls in love with boy, and everything's happy at the end," I said.

His lips turned up a little. "Okay. But still. It's a classic. Anyway, that song's at the end of it. It's . . . Dairy Queen."

"It's Dairy Queen?"

"No." He laughed and pointed off the side of the road.

"Oh. Right. That was fast."

He swung into the drive-thru, and we ordered Blizzards, trying to goad each other into getting as many flavors as possible. When I tried to pay for us, he swatted my hand away.

"Josh—you rescued me! I'm, like, a damsel in distress. Let me buy you a Blizzard—it's the least I can do."

"Skylar, shut up."

I wanted to be annoyed, but I just laughed. Maybe it was a post-crisis adrenaline rush, where everything's slightly hilarious.

He handed me my Blizzard, and we pulled back onto the road. I took a bite.

"I think if I could only eat one thing for the rest of my life, it'd be this," I said.

He scrunched up his nose. "I don't know about that."

I held up a spoonful for him. "Don't knock it till you've tried it."

He hesitated for just a second, then leaned over and took a bite. I knew it was dumb, but seeing my spoon in his mouth made me so happy. *Damn Florence Nightingale.*

"That's disgusting," he said. "It should be illegal to put Reese's Peanut Butter Cups and mint together."

"Yes, because your combo of pineapple and Snickers is a real winner."

"You know, I'm starting to feel like you'd rather walk home." He changed lanes to get closer to the shoulder.

"Okay, okay." I held out my hands in surrender. "Pineapple and Snickers are a match made in heaven."

He switched back to the fast lane. "That's what I thought."

We drove in silence for a while or turned up songs we liked and talked about how great they were, unless it was one of Josh's heavy metal songs, in which case I pointed out all the ways it was appalling. Sometimes we stared out at the fields as we drove past them, talking about Creek View and whatever popped into our minds.

"Writing poetry?" I teased, pointing to the black leather journal sitting on top of his dashboard that I'd noticed the night he picked me up for Leo's.

Josh took a bite of his Blizzard, shrugged. "Just something my therapist is making me do. God, that sounds so gay. *My therapist.*"

"Are you coming out of the closet right now? Or are you saying all gay people have therapists?"

"Oh, you know what I mean. Don't get all PC on me," he said, lightly shoving my shoulder.

"Well, somebody has to."

He rolled his eyes. "Yeah, okay. It's not gay, it's . . . *bleh.* I don't know. It sucks."

"That's where you were before you picked me up, right? Blake said something about a doctor in Fresno."

He nodded. "Yeah. I go a couple times a week. I have rehab and therapy and . . . just stuff." He cleared his throat.

"So it's shitty, then?" I asked.

"Yeah, pretty much. It's better when I go to San Diego, to the military hospital. There's a dog there."

"A dog?"

I knew about his trips to San Diego, but he'd never told me much about them.

"Yeah. He's a Lab, totally awesome. He chills with us, hangs out when we're talking and stuff. This one dude lost both his arms—his Humvee went over, like, three IEDs. So he pets the dog with his feet." He shook his head. "Guess I'm lucky, huh?"

"You do have nice arms."

He snorted, and I looked out the window, biting back a smile.

"The dog in San Diego . . . he sort of reminds me of this one we had in our regiment—Buddy. He was this black Lab, a bomb dog. A killer in the field, but a total softie when he was off duty. He'd come out with us when we were patrolling, sniffing out IEDs."

I took the cover off my shake and spooned it into my mouth. It was thick and sweet, and I felt like I could eat ten of them. It was so good I almost forgot my whole life had just blown apart.

"It's kind of hard to imagine a dog out there."

"I know, right?"

I thought about the night of the Fourth, the look in his eyes when the fireworks went off.

"So, the therapy is helping? The dog and stuff?" I asked.

"Sort of, yeah. A friend of mine bit it this week, so I was feeling all . . ." He sighed. "He had a little girl. Just sucks, you know?"

"God, yeah." I wouldn't have known unless he'd said something. Sometimes he was a complete mystery. How did he hold it all in? I thought of that little girl, growing up without her dad, and my heart hurt for her.

Josh looked over at me. "Let's talk about something else. Your day's been shitty enough."

"It's okay. I mean, you can talk to me about . . . whatever. Honestly."

"I know." He brushed my arm and smiled. Such a little thing, that act, but it felt huge. Seismic.

I tried to think of something as far away from Afghanistan as possible. "Do you believe there's intelligent life on Mars?"

"You are one weird chick."

"Yeah, but you're thinking about it, aren't you?" I said, grinning. "Alien attacks and all that."

Josh grunted. "Yeah, I am." He tapped his fingers against the steering wheel. "Okay. There has to be intelligent life on Mars. Humans kind of suck at life."

I laughed. "Yes. Please don't let us be the last word in evolution."

"Amen, sister."

I held up the copy of *Shantaram* sitting on the seat between us. It didn't seem like a very Josh book. For one thing, it was, like, a million pages.

"What's the deal with this?"

His eyes slid to the book, then back to the road. "Friend of mine made a list of books for me to read. This one's about an Australian con man in India—it's pretty cool. Did you know Indians do this with their heads when they talk?"

He wiggled his head from side to side, and I laughed.

"What number is it on the list?" I asked.

"Thirty-nine out of a hundred and twenty. I had a lot of time to read in the hospital."

Wow.

"What will you do when you finish all of them? Is he gonna give you another one?"

Josh gripped the wheel, stared straight ahead. The look on his face made me want to take the words back, snatch them out of the air.

"No," he finally said.

Oh.

I wondered if it was the guy he'd told me about that night we threw the bottles. Or someone else—the one who'd given him *Slaughterhouse-Five*. How many friends had he lost?

"Well . . . maybe I can make a list for you—if you want."

He looked at me, surprised. "Yeah?"

"Yeah. I'll start you off with *Green Eggs and Ham*, and we'll work up from there."

"You're just pissed because I read more than you do."

I nodded. "Guilty. Lately all I want to do is work on this collage I'm making for Marge. But I like *Slaughterhouse* so far."

"Nice."

"Was that on the list?"

"Number one."

He cleared his throat a little, and when he glanced at me, I saw that his eyes had clouded over again. "Can I . . . can I tell you something?" he said suddenly. "It's a secret—probably shouldn't even be . . . but I've gotta—I want you to know."

It made me happier than it should have that he trusted me, but the look on his face turned me cold inside.

"Yeah. Whatever it is, I won't tell anyone." I tried to smile. "Cross my heart."

"You know how Marge's son was in the Army?"

"Yeah. He died in Iraq, right?"

"No."

And then Josh told me the truth about Marge's son.

I sat there, stunned, trying to reconcile the image I'd always had of her hero dying in battle with this new one of a severely depressed kid lying in a bloody bathtub.

"—and sometimes she'll look at me like . . . I don't know, Sky, I just . . . it's intense, you know?"

He frowned at the road in front of him.

"Yeah," I said, my voice soft.

I wanted to tear this picture of Marge's son out of my mind, him in that bathtub. I couldn't imagine Josh ever—

"You're not him," I said. Did I sound strong? Certain?

Josh looked at me. Nodded. "Damn straight."

He said that in a case-closed kind of voice, and so I sat there, grieving for Marge and this kid I'd never met and worrying about the one sitting beside me, the mess of it all swirling around my head, dizzying.

More silence, but after a while it was the good kind, like the blanket I had on my bed that was so soft, just touching it made me sleepy.

We passed the Taco Bell where my mom used to work and the gas station where I now spent my weekends. I could see Chris's truck outside, and I imagined him in there with his bright orange shirt, selling candy bars and huge fountain sodas. We'd be home in a few minutes. The thought of seeing Josh's red taillights made me feel unmoored. It was different than the gnawing sadness from the social services parking lot. But it was still there.

He turned into the trailer park. Knowing I wasn't leaving it after all, I felt like I was seeing it for the first time. The chain-link fence surrounding the property, the sagging hulks of metal, the kids hosing one another down because the only pool in town was at the Paradise.

"What a shithole," I murmured.

Josh reached out and grabbed my hand and lightly squeezed before letting go. Suddenly I didn't know which way was up.

"The real question," he said, "is if there *is* intelligent life on Mars, would you rather live there or in Creek View?"

"There," I said automatically.

He nodded his head. "Yep."

chapter twenty

When Josh pulled his truck up to my trailer, Billy's red pickup was in the driveway. He parked behind it.

"Thanks," I said.

He looked at the steering wheel for a second, then turned to me. "What happened today?"

I shook my head and put my hand on the door handle, keeping my back to him. Before I could do anything, Josh shut off the ignition.

"I'm walking you to the door this time," he said.

"It's cool, I can—"

"Nope." He pointed to Billy's truck. "That dude is seriously bad news, Sky."

He was out of the truck before I could say anything else. I sighed and grabbed my bag, then slid out.

As we started up the steps, I turned to look at him before I opened the door. "My mom's not doing so well," I said. "So don't think . . . I mean, she's not usually like this."

"Have you *seen* my family?"

"Yeah, but . . ." I didn't really know what to say except *go home*, and he obviously had no intention of doing that.

"I just want to make sure you're okay," he said.

That look again. The one he'd given me when he'd found me sleeping under the tree.

I nodded and when I opened the door, I could feel the heat of him behind me, lending me courage when I saw the half-empty boxes all over the floor.

They could only mean one thing, those boxes—but where could we possibly go?

"Mom?" I called.

Her bedroom door was shut, and I heard laughter and the thud of a bottle hitting the floor.

"Coming!" Her voice was muffled, but the plywood was thin, and I could hear the clink of Billy's belt as he put it on.

I turned around. "Josh, you'd better—"

And even as his eyes were saying a resolute *no*, the door opened and out walked Billy, shirtless, and my mom, wearing her threadbare bathrobe. My *dad's* bathrobe.

"Hey, baby," she said. Her eyes were a little unfocused, and her smile faded when she saw Josh behind me.

"Hi," she said, her voice flat. She'd never liked the Mitchells. She used to say they were white trash—looked like the shoe was on the other foot now.

"Hello, ma'am. Good to see you."

"Ma'am?" she said, then giggled. *Giggled.*

I felt Josh stiffen behind me. "He's just being polite, Mom."

He'd been the same way with Marge—I figured it was a military thing, because he never used to talk like that. But it was nice, and I was embarrassed for my mom. In all the years of being broke and dealing with her crap, I'd never once been ashamed of her. Until now.

Mom frowned, and Billy shuffled over to the fridge to grab a beer. For a minute, the four of us just stood there, none of us belonging.

In the truck with Josh, I'd almost forgotten my horrible afternoon. But now it all came rushing back, and my bones were heavy with failure.

"Home from the war, huh?" Billy said, cracking open the can. His toenails were too long, all yellowed and broken at the ends. How could my mom share her bed with those feet?

"Yep," was all Josh said. No *sir* for Billy, I noticed.

"That's a real shame about your leg," Mom said. She looked down at Josh's prosthesis and shuddered a little. I wanted to dig my own grave, then throw myself in it. Why had I let him come in?

"Anyway, I was just getting us some Cokes and then we're gonna go over to Dylan's for a bit." I looked at Josh, a question—a desperate plea—in my eyes.

"Yeah," he said, not missing a beat. He checked his watch. "Better hurry. She's probably waiting."

I gave him a grateful smile, then turned back to my mom.

"What's up with the boxes?"

She flushed and looked at Billy. A slow smile spread across his face. "Well . . . Billy's . . ." She coughed and motioned to her bedroom. "Can I talk to you for a second?"

"Um."

I looked back at Josh, and he put a hand on my arm. "It's okay. I'll wait."

I nodded and followed my mom into her dimly lit room. It smelled like sex and booze—I didn't even know what sex smelled like, but, suddenly, I just *knew*. I felt nauseated, like the world had started spinning a little too fast on its axis.

"What's going on, Mom?"

But I knew. Of course I knew.

She smiled, but it wasn't her real smile. It was too bright, and somehow apologetic and defiant at the same time. "Billy's moving in."

I could feel the WHAT THE FUCK look on my face, my jaw dropping in an almost comical way.

"No," I said.

"Baby, he's gonna help us pay the rent and—"

"So, what, you're, like, some prostitute now? He pays rent, and you—"

Her hand flew up, and it was hitting my cheek before I could duck out of the way.

"Don't talk to me like that," she growled.

"I'm sorry," I said, my voice thick. My ear started to ring, and my cheek stung.

And I was. I knew this wasn't her. We weren't that family—the screaming, hitting kind—never had been. This was a drunk, depressed woman, and soon she'd see that this was all a mistake, and how could I have called my own mother a prostitute?

Insane. I was going insane.

"Mom, I can cover the rent. I've got the job at the gas station and—"

"You're going to college. Then what will I do? I'm being realistic, Sky."

I shook my head, which was starting to throb, and lowered

my voice so that Josh couldn't hear us. "I'll stay. I'm staying. We don't need him, Mom."

She grabbed a pack of cigarettes off her bedside table and lit one. I noticed that her hands were shaking the tiniest bit, but I wouldn't help her light it.

"You can't give me everything I need, baby."

I had two choices: sad or angry. I turned around and opened the door, letting it slam against the bedroom wall. In the living room, Josh and Billy were standing close, in each other's faces. I'd opened the door just in time to hear Josh say, "Touch her, and I will personally fuck you up."

They turned to look at me, Josh's eyes immediately settling on my bright red cheek. A muscle twitched near his jaw. I caught his eye and shook my head. It seemed like he'd gotten taller while I was in the bedroom, and his eyes had taken on a hawkish, focused intensity that was more than a little intimidating. I was seeing Josh Mitchell the Marine for the first time. It wasn't hard to imagine him with a gun in his hands.

Billy's oily smile fell on me. "Now, honey—"

"I'm paying the rent now," I said. "And I say you're not moving in."

"That's not your decision to make, Skylar," he said.

I heard my mother come up behind me. "Mom," I said, turning to her. "*Please.*"

She just stood there, a shell of the woman who used to come home with cinnamon twists and soft tacos for us to share while I told her about my day. Finally, she shrugged her shoulders.

"This is for the best," she said. "You'll see."

"How could this possibly be for the best? Mom . . ."

"You'll see," she repeated.

I felt my cell buzz in my pocket, and I knew it was Dylan, who was supposed to go on a date that she really needed and deserved, and who was waiting for me to take care of her son. This situation with my mom wasn't something I could fix in a night—Billy was halfway moved in, and neither of them was sober. Someone had to be the adult here, and as usual, it was going to be me.

"Josh, I'm just gonna grab some stuff—give me a sec?"

He nodded, and I pushed past my mom to my bedroom. I yanked clothes off hangers without looking at them and stuffed them into a bag. Then I put my laptop under my arm because I didn't trust Billy not to hock it. It was a cheap piece of crap that I'd bought after a year of saving, but I bet a pawnshop would give him enough for a few cases of beer. I threw a few things from the bathroom into my bag, then went back into the living room.

"Where are you going?" my mom asked.

"Do you care?"

"*Skylar*." She raised her hands, palms up, like I was being difficult.

I walked to the front door and opened it. The heat of the day had faded, and a slightly cool breeze was tickling the trees that stood behind our trailer and blocked it from the highway. Billy came up to me, his hand out like he wanted a hug or something. Josh stiffened, and I hit Billy's hand back before Josh could make good on the threat I'd overheard. I could handle Billy myself.

"You're not my father. You never will be."

He ran his tongue over his lips and just stared at me, and I couldn't move until Josh came to my side and grabbed the bag out of my hand. He shot Billy a loaded look, then put a hand on my back. "Ready?" he murmured.

No.

I nodded. "Yeah."

I walked out the door, and Josh closed it behind him. I stopped on the last step and just stared ahead of me. Not seeing anything. I gripped the cheap metal handrail as all that resolve I'd shown inside slipped away. *Now what?*

Josh came down and stood in front of me. "Hey," he said, soft.

I shook my head. If I spoke, I'd cry and Billy would hear, and that would mean he'd won. So I stood there. I couldn't move—as if taking that last step would mean I'd never go back.

I looked down at him, and the moment our eyes met, he reached up and pulled me against him.

"You did good," he whispered.

The shock of his body against mine paralyzed me for a second, but then I buried my face in his neck and tightened my arms around him, breathing in his cologne, his Joshness. His breath caught, and he gripped me tighter. The whole day swept through me in one shudder, and he held me, even though the tears that had sneaked out were soaking his shirt.

"It's okay," he whispered. His lips brushed my hair. "I've got you."

I've got you.

My blood racing, his heart pounding against my chest, I lifted my head and pressed my lips against his cheek. It was warm and scruffy, and I wanted to do it again and again, but I didn't. I felt him smile.

"Thanks for having my back," I said.

"Any time."

Then he let go, keeping his arm around my shoulders as he led me across the street to Dylan's. When he handed me my bag, his fingers brushed against mine, and I held them for a second. Glanced at him.

The door swung open, and Dylan looked from me to Josh, her eyes going wide. I let go of his hand, but I could tell she'd seen all she needed to.

"What happened?" she asked.

I could feel Josh beside me, and it felt like he belonged there. "Everything."

chapter
twenty-one

I leaned over the boxes of fresh-picked strawberries at my favorite roadside stand, scanning the speckled skin for any imperfections. Dylan and Chris were farther down the table, looking at some of the vegetables, but all I wanted were the strawberries.

The woman behind the plywood counter had turned her newspaper into a fan, her brown eyes squinting against the sun as she watched the workers in the field beside her. A battery-operated radio played love songs in Spanish, and Chris hummed along. I inhaled the sweet scent of the berries, content.

They were beautiful—lush and red, the same color as Josh's truck. It was hard to believe anything so delicate could grow in this heat, but they loved it. They were part of this place, part of the dusty earth and hazy blue skies of Creek View.

"I'll take this one," I said to the woman behind the table.

"Four dollars." Her accent was heavy, like Chris's dad's.

She grabbed the tray holding three tiny green baskets overflowing with fruit and put them in a used grocery sack while I fished around in my pockets, looking for the ten-dollar bill I'd brought with me.

"Your dad working today?" Dylan asked Chris as she chose her own box.

He nodded. "Yeah, but he's up at the cucumber place. Man, I can't wait until I start making some real money so he doesn't have to do that shit anymore. His back's all jacked up."

"Soon," I said, giving his arm a squeeze.

I grabbed another box of berries to bring to the motel for Marge as a thank-you—she'd been letting me sleep in one of the rooms for the past week. I kept trying to pay her rent, but she always refused. She'd jokingly referred to it as an "employee benefit." At first, I'd felt weird around Marge, knowing about her son. It had been an easy secret for her to keep: he'd killed himself in Ohio, before Marge moved to California and bought the Paradise. I wanted to reach out to her somehow, but there was no way I could make up for what happened to him. And I had to trust that she was dealing. Her kindness, her booming laugh, and the way she took care of me . . . I decided Marge was made of steel. Under that skin was a fortress.

"Those for Marge?" Dylan asked. I nodded.

"I wish you would come stay at my place," Chris said. "I told you, Olivia can sleep on the floor. She'll think it's a sleepover— six-year-olds love that kind of stuff."

"I know, but I just have this thing about Shrek sheets."

Chris snorted. "Whatever."

The truth was, I liked being on my own. I'd thought I'd cry myself to sleep every night, missing Mom and feeling homeless, but the only time I did was when I thought about having to go back and live in the trailer for good.

I slung the bag of strawberries over my arm and held out my hands for Sean so Dylan could pay for her food.

"Hey, which meal plan did you pick for San Fran?" Chris asked.

"Haven't decided," I said. "What do you think about going to Bakersfield to see a movie tonight?"

"Uh, sure. Okay, but wait. I'm seriously concerned about the meal plans at BU—"

"Oh my God, taste these strawberries," Dylan moaned.

"Did you just have an orgasm, like, right here in front of us?" I asked, ignoring Chris's question and pretending to shield Sean from Dylan.

"Oh, yeah," she said.

Sean wriggled in my arms, his eyes on the strawberries. Dylan held a mushy one up to him, and he sucked on it.

"Aw! His first strawberry," she said, her voice tender. Sean beamed, swatting at the bright red juice that covered his face. "Chris, take a picture."

Chris pulled out his phone. "Sean, my man, we are *totally* gonna show this to your first girlfriend," he said.

"No doubt. I'll be humiliating him as much as possible." Dylan leaned down and kissed Sean's face. As he let out a happy shriek, I buried my nose in his fuzzy hair. I loved his baby powder smell—it seemed to make the world right, just for a moment.

"I sort of want to eat him. Is that wrong?" I asked.

Dylan shook her head and reached out to wipe at Sean's face with a tissue. "I want to about ten times a day."

Sean reached for her, whining in a cute kind of way until Dylan scooped him up.

"I'm gonna call Child Protective Services on your ass," Chris said. "Humans aren't supposed to eat their young."

"Yeah, I'll get some kind of citation for giving my kid too many kisses."

I watched her twirl him around, both of them smiling and laughing. Somehow, things had worked out. When she'd first gotten pregnant, we'd all thought it was the end of the world. And I knew there were days when it was hard as hell, but it had turned out, she survived.

"I'm gonna miss this," Chris said, throwing his arm around my shoulders.

I shrugged him off. "Stop saying that. You're depressing me."

It was like every few seconds, Chris was pointing out that we were all going to be apart for pretty much the rest of our lives. It didn't help that I had no freaking clue where I was going to be next week, let alone September.

"Hey, there's always Christmas break. And spring break. And summer. Unless, of course, my professors recognize my brilliance and I get an internship. In which case—"

"Oh, get over yourself," I said.

My voice had a slight edge to it, and I laughed it off and gave him a slight push. Chris didn't seem to notice, just laughed with me.

Be happy for him. It's not his fault.

We squeezed back into his dad's truck, gasping at the hot vinyl and keeping our faces away from the infernal air blowing out of the vents while the faulty air-conditioning kicked in.

"So, there's no chance Asshat's moving out anytime soon?" Chris asked as he pulled onto the highway.

It was the name we'd decided to give Billy.

I shrugged. "I haven't seen my mom since I left."

I needed a break, but I knew we had to talk. I was just still too raw from having her choose Billy over me. It was weird, not seeing her. I wished it didn't feel good, the distance, but it did.

Dylan leaned in from the truck's cramped back seat. "Do you think she's, you know, *in love* with him?"

"God, I hope not." The thought made me queasy. "I think he's taking advantage of the situation. And she's letting him."

"Honestly, I don't know how she can put her tongue in his mouth," Chris said.

"Don't even . . . *ugh*." I covered my face and groaned.

"That's an image I never thought I'd have in my head," Dylan said.

Sean whimpered, and Dylan lifted up his favorite stuffed animal and made it dance for him.

"Asshat's an asshole," she cooed. "Yes, he is."

I grinned and watched her working him up to full-on belly laughs.

"Dude, that's just wrong," Chris said. "You've scarred him for life."

Dylan shook her head. "It's all about the tone of voice."

I tried to pretend this was my life for the next year, living in Creek View or maybe a couple hours away, in Fresno or Bakersfield. Of course, Chris wouldn't be driving because he'd be in Boston, so it would just be Dylan, Sean, and me getting strawberries. I'd be talking about the classes I was taking at a community college in between shifts at the Paradise or some other job. Maybe it wouldn't be so bad. I'd be close enough to Mom to keep an eye on her but not have to deal with Billy on a daily basis. I could go to school, kind of, and I'd be around to help Dylan out with Sean.

No.

God, just the thought of that other Skylar filled me with the kind of hopelessness that makes a person stay in bed all day and do nothing but watch *Judge Judy* and chain-smoke. Except . . .

For just a second, I saw Josh's face, the way he'd looked at me on the steps in front of the trailer—angry, worried, and some other thing I couldn't name. *Wouldn't* name. If he didn't stay in the Marines, he'd be here.

"What are you thinking about?" Dylan asked.

I started guiltily. "Huh?"

"You're smiling like you've got some dirty little secret," she said.

I could feel her staring at me, putting pieces together, replaying that moment on her porch after Josh walked me across the street. I rearranged the boxes of berries on my lap, then looked over at Dylan, my face, I hoped, a blank.

"What?" I said. "I was zoning out."

Dylan's eyes widened. "You're thinking about him, aren't you?"

"Asshat?" Chris asked, confused.

Dylan shook her head. "Chris, you are such an idiot." She leaned over the seat, staring me down with her chocolate brown eyes. "I know that look, Sky. But I've never seen it on *you* before."

I glared at her. "I'm *not* thinking about Josh."

She sat back, smirking. "Who said I was talking about Josh?"

Shit.

"You tricked me!" I said. I tried to slap at her, but she ducked into the corner, laughing.

"You bitch!" she said. "I can't believe you've been holding out on me. Details—*now*."

"Wait, wait, *wait*." Chris slammed his hand on the steering wheel. "Skylar. Tell me, please, for the love God, tell me there's nothing going on between you and Josh Mitchell."

I felt high, jittery, like I was everywhere at once.

"There's nothing going on."

"Yet," said Dylan. "Every time I go to the Paradise, you two are attached at the hip."

You two. Attached. I felt the blood creep up my neck, and I collaged a wall to hide behind. A thick stone one that only archers and big men with swords could get past.

"We just hang out," I said. Dylan raised her eyebrows in a totally lecherous way. "We play chess or read by the pool. Most of the time Marge is with us!"

"Josh does not play chess," Chris said.

"Actually, he does. And he's really good at it," I said, defensive.

Chris pointed to himself. "This is my Not-Convinced face."

"This is my Shut-Up face."

"This is my Oh-My-God-Sky-Is-Getting-It-On-With-Josh-Mitchell face," Dylan said, looking comically scandalized.

I threw up my hands, groaned, played my part. But inside . . . *inside,* I'd turned into something that craved moonlight and whispers and dark corners.

With Josh, it felt inevitable. Only a matter of time. Every second we were together this past week had brought us closer to the promise I'd seen in his eyes the day I moved out: the excuses to touch each other, how close we sat, the long hugs before he went home. But whenever it seemed like Josh might go for it, I chickened out, made up excuses because I couldn't have that mess on top of everything else . . . could I?

Chris glared at me. "Flings endanger the pact."

"Yes, Christopher, I know."

He looked at me for another second, his eyes narrowed. I could see Dylan in the passenger mirror, shaking her head. *Unbelievable*, she mouthed. I set my elbow on the window and covered my lips so that she wouldn't see me smile. It sort of *was* unbelievable. I didn't know how long I could pretend I didn't care about him.

"Five more weeks," Chris murmured, like a mantra.

For you, I wanted to say. The fluttering feeling in my chest died.

Judge Judy. Chain-smoking.

"Yeah," I whispered. "Five more weeks."

"And did your roommate call again? Are you doing that girly thing where you try to coordinate your dorm decorations or—"

"Chris." I gripped the boxes of strawberries, kept my eyes on the road ahead of me.

"—are you just gonna do your own thing? Dude, I hope your roommate has a TV because mine is all—"

"*Chris*," I said, louder.

He looked over at me, shoved his sunglasses farther up his nose. "What?"

"I don't want to talk about it."

"Why?"

"Because I don't know if I'm going, okay? Haven't you been listening to me these past few weeks? *No*." My voice was getting loud, but I couldn't help it. "You haven't. You've been in this perfectly happy I'm-getting-out-*tralala* world, but I'm not *tralala-ing*. At all."

I bit my lip and stared out the window, feeling like an idiot. The whole Josh ambush had turned me into an emotional pinball.

Dylan squeezed my shoulder.

"Sky." Chris reached over and shut off the radio. "Everything's gonna be fine—"

I turned in my seat so that I was facing him. He used to be the only person in the world who got me totally and completely. But not anymore. It felt like he'd already left—more and more often, it seemed like Chris didn't understand me at all.

"You keep saying that, Chris. Every time I try to tell you what's going on, you keep saying, *Don't worry, it'll work out,* blah blah blah. But it's *not* working out, okay? *It's not.* I mean, I live in a motel room."

Chris gripped the steering wheel. "I hate to be the one to break it to you, but your mom's an adult woman. How many times are you just gonna drop everything when she loses her shit?"

I stared at him. "It's only been five years. Her *soul mate* died—that's not something you bounce back from right away," I said.

"And you lost your *dad.*"

"Thank you, Chris. Like I didn't know that," I snapped.

Dylan leaned forward. "Okay, you guys—"

He glanced over at me and shook his head. "I've tried to be cool about your mom, okay? I know it sucks for her and she's been through a lot. But so have you, Sky. And lately, it almost feels like . . . you're looking for an excuse to stay."

I stared at him. "*What?*"

"Not cool, Chris," Dylan said.

He frowned, his voice softer. "I don't know if it's Josh or what, but you need to get the hell out, or I swear to God, you'll end up spending the rest of your life in this shithole, just like all those girls—"

"You mean like me?" Dylan asked, her voice suddenly hard.

"God, Dylan, I'm not saying that," he said, stricken.

"Might as well," she spit. "You know what it feels like, being friends with you guys? Do you have any idea how it sounds when you talk about how crappy this town is and how you'd rather die than end up saddled with a baby, living in a trailer park, broke as hell? Every time you say that, you're describing *my* life. A life I'm actually okay with—I'm sure as hell a lot happier than either of you."

Chris and I sat there in stunned silence. Dylan glared at us, arms crossed, chest heaving.

I felt the sting of her words. Every time I'd ever said anything about people who wanted to stay in Creek View, I'd been talking about her. I'd just never thought about it that way. It always seemed like she'd understood that she was mine and therefore exempt from my disdain of all things Creek View. To me, she wasn't one of *those girls*. And I knew for a fact she was *the* girl for Chris, only he'd never tell her that.

I turned around, forcing myself to look her in the eye.

"Dyl—"

But she cut me off.

"My life is your worst nightmare. I get it."

"No, it's not like that," I said.

She looked out the window. "Forget it."

I opened my mouth, but what the hell could I say? I slumped down in my seat. "I'm sorry," I whispered.

I closed my eyes and listened to the slap of tires on the road and Sean's gurgles. A heavy, suffocating silence settled over us, louder than the shouting match we'd just had. Was this what it meant to grow up, to move on?

JOSH

You play chess? That's the first thing you ever said to me—well, first thing after *Private, you better get that hair into regulation.* We were still in the States, back when I thought I was the shit. You were holding your chess set and I'd been a smart-ass, said something like, *No, sir, I'm no ninety-year-old grandpa,* and you just stared at me with that look you get—all Clint Eastwood and shit, until I said, *No offense, sir.* You laughed. I can't believe I only knew you for a year and a half—how can one person change you in two football seasons? But you did. You didn't give up on me. Told Command I had promise. *Promise.* No one had ever said something like that about me before. And they believed you, let you show me the ropes, teach me what it really means to be a Marine. You were a good soldier, the best, and you cared about all of us, even that little dick, Panelli. I'll never forget how before we went out each day, you'd tell everyone in our squad that we were cocksuckers and we better not die or we'd have to look up from hell and watch you screwing our sisters and wives and even our mothers. So most of us, *most of us,* didn't get dead. Chess and you taking a picture of me reading

Slaughterhouse-Five, telling me I'd need proof someday because nobody in Creek View would ever believe I had actually read a goddamn book, let alone five. Talking about God and why there's evil in the world and bitching because the Steelers won the Super Bowl. Camp Leatherneck, me not missing home at all and you missing it like crazy, always talking about going to college and how when you had leave you were gonna marry Hannah. And you wanted kids, and I said I didn't because people like me, we just end up disappointing one another and I'd probably be like my dad, and you told me I had to get over it, get over my dad and my mom and how screwed up everything is because you said, *Josh, you're gonna have it all. I know it. You're gonna have it all.* And for the first time, I'm almost believing that.

chapter
twenty-two

"Okay, so remember, the queen is the best piece. You gotta guard her with your life."

Josh was pointing to the carved chess piece on the board in front of me, and I nodded, trying to keep all the rules he'd taught me in mind. Playing chess by the pool had become this thing we did every few days, when it was almost twilight and the heat of the day had dwindled to a bearable warmth. It was one of those perfect summer evenings—the sky looked like someone had thrown a can of pink paint onto it, and the crickets were playing their reedy symphony. One of my baskets of strawberries sat between us, washed and still warm from the sun, and if I leaned forward, I could catch a bit of their sweetness in the air. But I couldn't look at them without thinking about everything that had gone down with Chris and Dylan. It'd only been a few hours, but the fact that neither of them had called didn't bode well.

"And she can move in any direction?" I asked, prolonging my inevitable loss. I didn't want him to go home and leave me to wrestle my demons alone.

"Right," he said. "She's your nuclear bomb."

"Uh-huh."

Whichever way I went, he'd be saying "checkmate" within a few moves. My finger hovered above a rook, then a knight. Undecided, I sighed and pushed forward a pawn he'd be able to capture in his next move.

"You okay?" he asked. He put his hand on my knee, for just a second. If I'd been a different Skylar, I'd have put my hand over his.

The pact. The pact.

"Sorry," I said, busying my hands with remaking my ponytail. "Just . . . stuff's on my mind. It's fine."

Everything I was doing was like this chess game—full of second guesses, indecision, waiting.

"You want to talk about it?"

"Not really," I said.

"Fair enough." He looked at where I'd moved my pawn, then sat back, studying the board. "Hmmm."

"Just kill me and get it over with."

"You're not so good at the patience thing."

"And you are?"

"Oh, yeah. In the military, it's all hurry up and wait." He leaned over the board. "Hearts and minds," he murmured. "Hearts and minds."

"Huh?"

"Just this thing they told us overseas. How we were there to win the hearts and minds of the Afghanis. Every day, some commander would say it. Or you'd see it on this sign above the entrance to our camp."

"Are you good at it?" I asked.

"Winning hearts and minds?"

I nodded.

"Don't really know . . ." He looked up at me, his eyes mischievous. "Yet."

I stopped breathing, and he made his move, a blatant murder of one of my rooks.

"Damn. I forgot about him."

"Gotta watch your troops." He leaned back and popped a strawberry into his mouth, stem and all.

"Dude. You're not supposed to eat the green part."

He shrugged. "Nutrients. Trust me, once you've eaten camel balls, you'll eat anything."

"*Eww.* Seriously?"

He laughed. "No, but you totally believed me, didn't you?"

"Jarhead."

"Yep."

"Okay, stop distracting me," I said. "I'm trying to annihilate you."

"Good luck with that."

"You know, I'm only pretending to suck at this. I'm letting you win."

"Oh, yeah? Why's that?"

"I have to pay for your mechanic services *some* way."

As promised, Blake had sent the tow truck out to pick up my car. A few days later, it'd been sitting in the Paradise lot good as new. Josh had not only fixed the radiator, which had been the last straw for the Prizm, he'd also managed to replace or mend several other things. And he wouldn't let me give him a dime.

"Oh, that," he said. "I just put it on your tab."

"I have a tab?"

"Uh-huh. We'll discuss payment at a later date, but I'm thinking homemade chocolate chip cookies, back rubs, that sort of thing."

"Do I look like the kind of girl who makes chocolate chip cookies and gives out free back rubs?"

He held up a finger. "Not free."

"Well, I don't bake. Especially not for boys."

"What about men?"

I shook my head, blushing. "I have the distinct feeling you're trying to rile me up so I'll make a dumb move and hand you this game on a silver platter. True or false?"

"I plead the Fifth."

"Of course you do." I couldn't look at him, not when he smiled at me like that, so I stared at the board, chewing my lip.

Josh cleared his throat. "So, uh. There's this thing tonight. Down by the creek. Just a couple of people, a bonfire. You should check it out."

"Check it out? Like it's an art exhibit or something?"

He rolled his eyes. "You know what I mean. It'd be good for you to . . . have fun."

"I have fun."

He gave me a look like, *Sure you do.* "Well, anyway. I'll be there. If you get bored, call me and I'll come pick you up."

Was he asking me out? I always thought he'd be direct about that kind of thing. The old Josh Mitchell would have grunted, cavemanlike: *You. Me. Creek. Sex.* Or something.

"Thanks. I'll think about it."

I wished I could call Dylan to make sense of it. My heart felt like it was running a marathon—God, could he hear it? I looked up after I made my move, and he smiled at me before turning his attention back to the board.

"You're getting better at this. It's taking me longer to massacre you, anyway." He grimaced as he took my pawn. "Rookie mistake. You could have moved your knight here—" He pointed to a square on the side of the board. "Or you could have—"

A sudden crack pierced the air, a car backfiring on the highway, and Josh froze. Then he stood up, his sudden movement causing the chessboard to topple over and the pieces to scatter. He stood still for a minute that seemed to go on forever. Then he let out a long breath, shook his head a little.

"Fuck," he muttered. He took a few steps toward the pool, his back to me.

I stood up slowly, walking on eggshells. "Josh?"

He didn't turn around, just stared out at the pool with his hands on his hips.

"Hey," I said. I stood in front of him and reached for one of his hands. When our skin made contact, he gripped my fingers, and I shifted closer, careful not to move too suddenly. He looked past me, like there was a slow-motion car crash happening over my shoulder.

"I'm sorry," he whispered.

I shook my head. "Nothing to be sorry about."

He swallowed, his Adam's apple pushing in, then his arms went around me. He smelled like baked bread, the way skin does when it's been out in the sun, and I bunched his T-shirt up in my fists as I held him to me. After a couple minutes, he let go and looked down at the chess pieces scattered all over the patio.

"Shit."

He started to lean down, but I held up my hand. "I'll get them."

"I can do it."

"Josh—"

"Sky. I've got it, okay?" he snapped.

I nodded and stepped back. "Okay. I'll just . . . I'm gonna grab a Coke. Do you want anything?"

"No."

I walked toward the glass door, my eyes smarting as he struggled to reach down for the pieces. I prayed none had fallen into the pool. Knowing him, he'd rip off his leg and dive in after them. I pulled the glass door open with trembling hands.

"Hey, sweet pea." Marge was standing just inside the lobby, her hands tucked into the pockets of one of her tropical-island-themed muumuus. From the look on her face, I could tell she'd been watching the whole thing.

"Hey. He's just—"

"You don't need to explain to me, hon."

I pretended not to notice the long look she was giving me, but when I started to walk past her, she gently grabbed hold of my arm. I had the sudden urge to lean into her thick body and sob, but I just cocked my head to the side and waited.

"You okay?"

I nodded, but my chest felt tight, and nothing, nothing, nothing was making sense anymore.

She frowned. "Just be careful. I'm glad he has you, but you have to look out for yourself, too. You get what I'm saying?"

If only she knew how much he'd been taking on for me. What was I doing for him? Nothing. It wasn't like I could go into Josh's brain and alter his memories. Take the war away. Give him his leg back. I'd never felt so powerless in my life.

"Yeah. Totally. Um. I'm gonna . . ."

I pointed to the front door and walked out, then ducked around the side of the motel, to the orchard surrounding it. I lay on the grass and closed my eyes, collaging against my eyelids. The Golden Gate Bridge. Josh in uniform. My trailer. The angel from the Paradise sign. Strawberries.

I didn't get up until I heard Josh's truck start, then peel out of the driveway.

JOSH

Marge comes up to me and hands me a cold beer before I leave the Paradise for the day, which is cool of her since she probably knows I just made a total ass of myself. I put your chessboard in my bag, and we sit there for a while, just watching the sun set. Don't know where Sky went, and I'm scared I screwed everything up. I'm starting to realize that she's my only real friend in the world right now. I can't lose that. I've tried so hard to play it safe with her, and I thought I was doing okay until I went all wounded warrior on her and . . . *fuck*. Marge says, *Josh*, and I say, *Hmmm?* and she says, *Sky is like a daughter to me, you know that*. And I say, *Yeah*. Then she says, *Be careful with her. She's a tough cookie, but you could hurt her real bad*. And I say, *I would never hurt her*, and I really mean it because this feeling I have for her—man, it's like absolutely nothing I've felt before, which is freaking my shit out, and Marge goes, *She's a good girl*, and I say, *Yeah, I know*. And then she's all, *What does your therapist say about her?* and I have to admit that I haven't talked to him about Sky and she says, *Well, maybe you should*, and I get that what she's really saying is *This isn't such a good idea, you have one leg and your mental evals from the Corps were shit, weren't they?* And I want to tell her I don't give two fucks what anybody thinks, but that's not true so I just say, *Yeah, I hear you, Marge.* She gives me a little hug and says, *I'm not saying it's a bad thing, the two of you. I'm just saying to be careful is all, sweet pea.* And after she leaves, I start thinking about the wives and girlfriends. When I was at Walter Reed and later in the Wounded Warrior Regiment, they'd come and try to help their men, you know, and the dudes would be telling me how hard it is for the relationship and shit, and I start thinking about Sky, like, if this becomes something—which it probably won't because I'm too much of a pussy to make a move (I know, can you believe it?)—I'm just thinking about what I'm asking of her. If we get together. I'd be asking her to, like, deal with my shit. Like what happened today. She doesn't need that in her life; she has enough problems. And I start picturing her trying to help me do stuff because I can't man up or whatever, and everything turns dark and wrong, and I'm back in that shitty place I was in when I first woke up and saw how the hospital sheet lay flat against the bed when there should have been a leg under it. I need your help. I need you here with a six-pack and your goddamn wisdom. This is your territory. What am I supposed to do when I'm bad for the one good thing in my life?

JOSH

You know, I don't even need you to answer that, bro. Marge is
right. I gotta back off.

chapter
twenty-three

My fingers moved over the piles of paper on my bed, like brushes in a can of rainbow paint. I'd spent the past hour tearing up the colors I needed for the next installment of my collage for Marge. Didn't matter that it probably wasn't a going-away gift anymore. I still wanted to finish it. I had about half of it done: the highway snaking through the whole piece, the creek, the strawberry fields. I'd decided to begin working on the orchard behind the Paradise, so I was going through the old magazines from the lobby, tearing out all the brown and green. My hands were sticky with glue, and I hummed along to Sia, playing in the background. I loved taking these pieces and making them part of a whole, giving them a place to belong. More beautiful than when they started.

I pieced together a trunk, branches, leaves. With this collage, I could remake Creek View, transform it into something beautiful and clean. Under my hands, it breathed with new life.

I forced my mind to stay on the collage, giving every bit of my awareness to it. I wanted to pretend for a few hours that it was still May and Mom was fine and I was going to San Francisco and Josh Mitchell was only the memory of a kiss on a cheek. I found my groove and stayed there. It was warm, wombish and a little melancholy, but in a good way. The making pulsed through me, like someone was guiding my hands over the paper.

I didn't hear the knock on my door at first. But soon the tentative taps became purposeful rapping.

"Just a sec!" I called.

I ran into the bathroom and rinsed the glue off my hands. When I opened the door, Dylan was standing there, wearing a miniskirt, a skin-tight tank top, and platform sandals.

"You're getting together with Josh Mitchell tonight," was the first thing she said to me. "I've decided it's the only way to save your shitty summer—you need a hot fling with that sexy one-legged boy. Sex is the ultimate de-stresser."

I looked down at my baggy pajama pants and oversized T-shirt. "I don't think so."

"Well, I do."

Dylan swept past me, and I caught a glimpse of Amy at the reception desk before I shut the door behind me.

I turned off my music and gestured to a chair. "You want to sit?"

Dylan plopped down and crossed her legs. I didn't know what to say after our fight that afternoon. How did you apologize for years of belittling someone? We sat there looking at each other until the silence became unbearable.

"The collage is looking pretty good. The strawberries look real," she said.

"Thanks. I used this metallic red paper I found in an old book."

"Cool."

The seconds ticked by, and the silence was so silent it turned into a high-pitched whine. I grabbed an M&M's ad and started tearing the brown parts out. I set the paper back down and finally looked her in the eye.

"Dyl . . . I'm sorry. I honestly don't know what else I can say. I love you, and I think you're an amazing person, and I've been an asshole."

"Okay."

"That's it?"

"What, you thought I was going to hold a grudge? That's Chris's style."

She was right. That *was* Chris's style. Which explained why Dylan had come over and Chris had not. I'd already tried to call him, but I refused to try more than once.

"There is one teeny, tiny catch, though," she said.

I raised my eyebrows. "What?"

"There's a party tonight by the creek. I have it on good authority that Josh will be there. Ergo, you will be there."

"I know. I'm still not going."

"How do you know about a party?"

"Josh told me." She lit up, and I shook my head. "It's not what you think. It got weird and—"

She held up her hand. "My forgiveness after *years* of insults will only be given to you if you come out with me tonight. Hooking up with Josh is strictly optional, but encouraged."

I shook my head. "This is a seriously complicated situation."

I thought of his chess pieces lying scattered beside the pool, the way he'd suddenly become distant and cagey.

"I won't take no for an answer," Dylan said.

I twisted the long piece of brown paper in my hand into a branch, feeling the paper bend and mold under my fingers. It was too thin, and the glue coating my skin was making it tear. Dylan sat there staring at me, waiting for me to capitulate. I balled up the paper and fell back against the bed with an over-dramatic groan.

She handed me a dress she'd folded into her bag and pointed to the bathroom. "Go put this on."

Josh probably wouldn't be there, I reasoned. He certainly hadn't been in a partying mood a few hours ago. I could just go, stay for a half hour, then come right back.

"Fine." I held the dress out to her. "But I can't wear this."

It was cute, but I knew it would be much shorter than I was comfortable with. And tighter. It was the kind of dress that probably made boys check their pockets to see if they had a condom with them. At least, it was that kind of dress when Dylan was wearing it.

She twirled her foot around. "Just try it on. It won't be as short on you as it is on me."

I sighed and went into the bathroom. I pulled my hair back and started washing my face.

"What's this room called again?" she asked.

"*Viva México*."

Most of the decorations consisted of Frida Kahlo prints. I'd been obsessed with Frida ever since I'd seen Salma Hayek in a movie about her life. I loved how Frida painted her pain. Whatever crap was happening to her, she put it on the canvas and let the colors and lines tell her story.

In addition to the Fridas, I'd pinned up *lotería* cards that Chris had gotten me on a trip visiting relatives in Mexico. Next to a sombrero hanging on a hat rack there was a *Día de los Muertos* piñata in the shape of a dancing skeleton wearing traditional Mexican clothing. There were even maracas on the nightstand.

"Lots of this shit's creepy, Sky. No wonder you're sitting here all by yourself, listening to wrist-slitting music."

"Sia's introspective, not depressing. There's a difference." I had to admit the piñata was a little creepy, especially in the middle of the night when the wind from my open window made it dance around.

"Whatevs," Dylan said. I heard her sigh and flip through one of the old celebrity magazines I was collaging with. I started brushing my teeth, just in case fresh breath ended up being important tonight.

"You know, I'm going to take some classes in September," Dylan said. "Become an X-ray technician. That's legit."

I stuck my head out the door. "Dyl, seriously. I'm sorry. Don't feel like you have to—"

"No, I've been thinking about this for a long time. I mean . . . I don't want to be here my whole life. Plus, Seanie deserves more."

I nodded. "What's Jesse say?"

"He's down. That boy would move to freaking, I don't know, *Russia* with me if I wanted to go."

"It's really cold in Russia."

"Yeah, fuck that."

I left my pajamas in a heap on the linoleum floor and pulled the dress over my head. There was a floor-length mirror behind the door, and I turned around to see how bad the dress was.

"How's it look?" Dylan called.

I want him to see me in this.

"It's okay," I said. I let my hair fall around my shoulders and put on some mascara.

When I came out, Dylan put two fingers in her mouth and whistled. *"Hot!"*

I blushed and slipped on my All Stars to feel a little bit more normal.

"Hate those shoes, but I'll take what I can get," she said.

I pointed to a picture of Frida sitting in a man's suit, her hair short, with a pair of scissors in her hands and hair at her feet.

"This is how I was feeling today," I said. "I'm gonna wear whatever shoes I want."

Dylan looked at it, then back at me. "Tragic much?"

Chris would have gotten it, I thought. Or maybe Josh. Then I felt guilty because this was exactly the thing Dylan had meant, about Chris and me being so down on Creek View people.

She stepped closer to the painting. "Don't do that to your hair."

"I wasn't going to," I mumbled.

"Ready?" she asked.

I took one more look in the mirror. "No."

Dylan grabbed my arm. "Our friendship hangs in the balance. Get your ass out."

I glanced at my collage, then shut the door behind us.

Dylan nudged me in the ribs and nodded toward the group a few feet away from the bonfire. About fifteen people, they all stood close to one another, sizing up who they wanted to take home that night.

"There he is," she whispered.

Josh was in the center of their circle, sitting in the bed of his truck, legs dangling over the tailgate, a bottle of beer in his hand. Each time he took a sip, he held the bottle's neck with his thumb and index finger and tipped the beer into his mouth. I didn't know it was possible to envy a bottle of beer, and I got lost for a moment, watching his lips against the glass. Hypnotized. It was terrifying, how my body had started reacting to him. He was a fix I needed bad.

Dylan laughed her husky I'm-thinking-about-something-naughty laugh. "Wow."

I tore my eyes away from Josh. It was like I'd been deep diving in some fantastic water underworld and now I had to come up for air. "Oh, shut up."

Dylan whipped out her troublemaker red lipstick and swiped it over her lips. "Sky, you better get in on that before one of the Swensons suggests a threesome."

The Swenson twins, notorious sex fiends, who, if memory served correctly, had both slept with Josh on multiple occasions. Possibly at the same time.

"I really wish that the boy I'm in love with hadn't slept with three-quarters of the Creek View population," I said.

I hated the longing I felt. I didn't want this need to be near him. I didn't want to feel murderous every time a girl touched his arm—like one was doing right now.

"Oh my God. *Sky*." Dylan stared at me, incredulous.

"What?" I clutched at my dress, certain there was a big-ass rip in back or something. I pushed against her arm. *"What?"*

"You just said *love*."

"No, I didn't," I said quickly.

The word had tasted sweet, exotic. *Love*. I shivered.

"This is almost as good as losing your virginity!"

"A little louder, Dylan. I'm not sure everyone heard you."

"Oh, come on. You have to admit, this is pretty epic. Especially since it's *Josh Mitchell*."

She kept talking, but I wasn't really paying attention anymore because my eyes had strayed involuntarily to Josh again, and he was staring at me, eyes wide, mouth open. Taking in the dress Dylan had made me wear. I couldn't resist the chance to raise my eyebrows a little and smirk. This was how you played the game, right? Some girl came up to him, holding out a bottle of beer, shoving her breasts in his face. I looked away. This wasn't a game I could play, not even if part of me wanted to.

"Hey, baby," said a soft, male voice.

I turned around, and Jesse was instantly all over Dylan, his hands on her waist, his body pressed against hers. It was kind of amazing that she'd gotten pregnant only once—I'd never seen people more hungry for each other than those two. But instead of being annoyed or mildly disgusted by it like I used to be, I was sort of starting to think it was beautiful.

He whispered something in Dylan's ear, and she threw back her head, laughing hard. "I'm not letting you get away with that," she said.

"Um. I'll let you guys—"

Dylan pulled away from Jesse's lips. "No! We have to get you and Jo—"

I held up my hand. "Jesse doesn't need to know the details."

"Aw, c'mon, Sky. I won't tell nobody." Jesse looked at me for the first time, his eyes comically surprised. "*Damn*, girl. That dress is—" Dylan smacked him on the arm, and he laughed. "Don't freak out on me," he said. "It's just, I've never seen Skylar wear . . . you know. Your kind of clothes."

"Shit," I said, pulling at the hem. "I *told* you, Dylan. It's too short."

She rolled her eyes. "That was sort of the point. You look all *ooh-la-la*. It's *exactly* what you need to be wearing right now."

"Is *ooh-la-la* like Moulin Rouge *ooh-la-la*, or Tate's *ooh-la-la*?" I asked. Tate's was this skeezy strip club about thirty miles up the highway.

"Does it matter?" Dylan said. She squealed as Jesse leaned into her, whispering again.

For a second I heard Josh's voice above the collage of conversations and music pumping from somebody's car stereo, and I pretended to look around so that I could watch him. The guy next to him said something, and Josh laughed. They knocked their beer bottles in a half-assed, manly toast, then drank. It was like nothing had changed—even with one leg, Josh Mitchell would always be a local god.

I'd thought he'd be excited to see me, want to hang out or something, but it was as if I wasn't at the party at all. He wasn't looking at me, seemed much more interested in the girls near his truck. Was this a bad idea, me coming? After what had happened at the Paradise, maybe I was the last person he wanted to see. Here, he could pretend cars backfiring didn't remind him of a war he was still fighting, even though it was thousands of miles away.

"Skylar. You look . . . wow."

Blake. Of course it was Blake.

"Hey."

Dylan, finally aware of my presence again, grabbed me and put an arm around my shoulders.

"She's not here for you, Blake. Back up off."

Blake rolled his eyes. "Down, girl," he said. "I'm not drunk enough to make an ass of myself just yet."

"Since when did you become self-aware?" I asked him.

"I'm always aware of myself," he said. Typical Blake. "So." He clapped his hands and rubbed them together. "I'm helping with drinks—wanna come check out our selection?"

"I don't drink, remember?" I said.

Blake shrugged. "I can work with that."

My options weren't great: be Dylan and Jesse's third wheel or hang out with my ex-fling. I couldn't stand here all night, so my impatience made me choose the greater of two evils.

"Fine, I'll go over there." I turned to Dylan and Jesse. "You guys coming?"

"Um. In a minute." That was Dylan-speak for *I'm going to have a quickie in my boyfriend's back seat.* "If that's okay?"

"You're giving me a ride home, don't forget," I said.

Dylan swatted me on the butt. "Don't do anything I wouldn't do."

I shooed her away. "Get out of here already."

I followed Blake to the table that was set up next to a truck bed full of bottles and ice. I had to keep fighting the urge to pull at the hem of my dress, so I settled for clutching my purse like I was walking through a dark alley.

"So why are you all dressed up?" Blake asked.

His eyes were straying over the dips and curves of my dress, like he was trying to figure out the quickest way to take it off. I wanted *Josh* to look at me like that and—God, I couldn't believe I was thinking this way. It was like some horny Creek View girl had taken over my brain. I'd worn this dress so that Josh would see me—and only me—for the rest of the night.

But it wasn't working.

"I'm not dressed up," I said. "I just . . . It's a party, isn't it?"

I suddenly felt like a seventh grader at her first school dance.

He squeezed my hand. "Yeah. And I'm glad you came."

I pulled my hand away and shook my head. "Alexis: girl-friend. Me: *not* your girlfriend."

He opened his mouth to say whatever Blake-ish thing he was going to say, but we were at the drinks table and this girl named Tina was throwing a bottle around like she was in the cast of *Coyote Ugly*. I didn't know her very well—she'd graduated the year before me—but her mother was the only person on the Paradise "housekeeping" staff, so sometimes we hung out around the pool.

"Hey, Skylar. What'll it be?"

"Um . . ."

"Make her that fruity thing you gave Jessica," Blake said. "Virgin, though." He gave me a playful punch on the shoulder. "You'll like it, I promise."

Tina poured the drink, then Blake handed me the red cup. "To Skylar Evans—because she's finally joining the party."

I raised my cup. "To Blake Mitchell—no, never mind. To me."

"Oh, *burn*," he said.

Someone near the bonfire yelled, "Skylar!"

Not Josh.

It was one of the guys next to him—his friend Brady. I'd gotten to know him a little bit because he'd started coming around the Paradise now that Josh was home. Brady waved me over, but I barely noticed because one of the Swenson twins had her hand on Josh's knee and her lips close to his ear. He smiled, slow and easy. He'd heard Brady call my name, of course he had, but either he was intent on ignoring me or he was more interested in what that Swenson girl was offering him.

What the fuck? There was no way I'd imagined this thing that had been growing between us all summer. Slowly, especially for Josh, but growing.

Just when I'd decided to make some lame excuse and go home, Josh's eyes met mine. I raised my eyebrows, like, *Well, I'm here.* For a minute, it was just the two of us and the smoke from the bonfire and all those little moments at the Paradise, swimming across the distance between us: the way he'd tease me for using so much ketchup with my fries or how he'd call me ma'am, half joking. And how he'd started hugging me when he went home, each hug lasting a little longer than the last until hugging became holding.

"C'mon," Blake said, walking toward Josh's truck.

I looked back to where Dylan and Jesse had gone. I was stuck for a while, unless I wanted to walk back to the Paradise. Three miles wasn't that bad, was it?

"I'll give you a ride home if they ditch you," Blake said. I frowned, thinking about how he'd said that over spring break. "No strings attached, honest." He tipped his bottle against my cup.

"Fine."

To Skylar Evans—because she's finally joining the party.

chapter
twenty-four

"I'm a fuckin' U.S. Marine, that's why!" Josh shouted, red-faced but smiling. "First to fight, the President's Own, you punk."

He kicked at one of the guys nearby. "Whoa, now," the dude said, blocking his crotch. "Watch the junk."

I wasn't sure what we'd missed, but apparently Josh had won some sort of argument and suddenly everyone was doing the hitting-bottles, talking-too-loudly-then-chugging thing. What was I doing here?

"Hey, you," Brady said. He hopped down off his perch next to Josh and wrapped his arms around me.

"Hey . . . Brady."

I gave him an awkward pat on the back and tried to disentangle myself from his too-friendly hug. This was why I never borrowed clothes from Dylan. It was like every guy in the circle was seeing me for the first time. Except Josh. He just said, "Hey," and went back to talking to other people. I couldn't read him. It was like all those afternoons at the Paradise were nothing.

A Swenson girl—I couldn't tell which was which—looked at me with barely disguised hostility.

Brady leaned against the truck. "So, Skylar, we were thinking of heading into Bakersfield for some late-night Denny's. You up for it?"

I shrugged. No. No. And no. "I have to get up early for work tomorrow."

"Yeah, but all you have to do is walk five steps from your room to the desk," Blake said.

For the next half hour, there was talk of a bunch of random crap I couldn't bother to concentrate on. Video games, some football team. For the most part, I stared down at the pink liquid in my cup, swirling it around. Someone started passing a joint. I shook my head when Brady handed it to me.

"Still straightedge, huh?" he said.

"Yep."

Josh was a few inches away, but instead of talking to me, he let that Swenson girl put her hands all over him, and I knew, I just knew, he was going home with her. This wasn't the same Josh who joked with me about Dairy Queen Blizzards or talked about Afghani sunsets. Maybe I'd imagined him. I had probably just felt so sorry for him or for myself that I'd built those moments into something they had never been.

I tried to nod and laugh in all the right places, but pretending had never been my style, so I stood there, waiting for Dylan to show up so I could have her take me home. The bonfire gave the air a cozy smell, and all I wanted to do was find a thick quilt and lie down by the fire and feel good and sorry for myself. My mind collaged one by my feet. My head was starting to pound, and it was hot and cold and loud and silent, and this wasn't me. Not at all. I handed Blake my cup.

"I'll be back in a sec," I said.

"You want me to—"

"No. I just need to grab my sweater out of Dylan's car."

Blake looked like he was going to follow me, but then Brady started talking shit about the Dallas Cowboys and he got distracted.

I didn't look back to see if Josh had noticed me leave, just walked away, in the opposite direction from where Dylan's car was. My feet started taking me to my dad's favorite part of the creek, where the sand was softest and the beach was shaded by tall, leafy trees. It was the place I went to when I felt lost because he'd said that no matter what happened, it would always be ours.

Soon, the party was a distant murmur, the music and laughter already memories. I walked more slowly, feeling close to my dad as I looked up at the familiar bend in the creek and the trees that leaned over it. His spot. I wished he were there right then, to tell me why boys were such jerks. I wanted to ask him if it would always be this hard.

If I were a real Creek View girl, the kind Josh liked, I'd be hammered right now, not thinking about my dead father. Maybe I'd barf in the bushes, then down another beer before going to Denny's and ordering a Moons Over My Hammy and drinking coffee until the sun came up. Maybe I wouldn't even show up for work. I'd just go home and give Mom and Asshat a surly look before passing out on my bed. Then I'd wake up and do the same thing all over again for the rest of the summer so that I never had to think, not once, of how Mom was ruining her life and by extension mine or about Josh or school or anything. I'd just drown myself in booze and boys, like a good little Creek View girl.

"No." I whispered into the night, just to hear myself say it.

I thought about Josh sitting there in the bed of his truck, ignoring me after all those days full of stolen glances and secret smiles. I didn't know how I could have misread all of that. God, I was such a moron, why did I think—

"Skylar!"

Josh.

I stopped, my eyes on the creek. The water was black, threaded with silver moonlight. Away from the party, I could hear the gentle slapping of the water against the bank and the anxious string quartet of crickets in the clumps of bushes that pushed through the earth. A breeze danced around me, and I shivered, clutching at my arms.

I was half naked and just about the stupidest person I'd ever known.

"Sky—what are you doing?"

I wondered how fast he'd had to limp-walk to catch up with me, and for a second I felt bad. Then I remembered how, a few minutes ago, I'd hardly existed.

"Leave me alone, Josh. Just go back to the party." I couldn't look at him, just spoke to the empty space in front of me.

"Look, I . . . I don't want you to be out here alone, okay? People have been drinking, and it's not a good idea for you to—"

I turned, hurling words into the space between us. "Don't you have a Swenson to fuck?"

It was out of my mouth before I even knew I was thinking it, and for a second, we just stared at each other.

"No" was all he said. The word hung in the air, heavy with a million other, longer words.

My fingers clutched at my dress, all my shaking hidden within the folds of the thin fabric. I could feel this thing in me building—anger at myself, him, Dylan, everybody. I was volcanic. And the fire burned up my throat until it filled my eyes. It wanted to burst, burn, destroy. I turned away and focused on the creek, the way it swept by, not caring about our trivial human drama at its bank. I heard Josh step closer, felt the warmth of his body, even though he wasn't touching me. I wanted to lean into him, to jump off this cliff I kept finding myself on whenever I was around him.

But he obviously didn't want that. Had changed his mind, or something.

"Skylar, I—"

I whirled around, practically falling against him. "You *what*, Josh? You're the one who told me to come to this dumbass party!"

"I'm sorry," he whispered. His eyes were shuttered, hiding away so that I couldn't get a read on him.

I didn't want remorse—I wanted a fight.

"What does that even mean, *I'm sorry*?" I snarled. "Are you apologizing for ignoring me or for inviting me in the first place?"

He shrugged, pushing at the loose sand underfoot with the toe of his flip-flop. "I'm sorry for being a dick."

"I think I need a little more specificity, Josh." I was classic pissed-off, hands on my hips, nostrils flared. "I mean, what *I* think is being a dick and what *you* think is being a dick are probably two totally different things."

He looked down at me, those eyes pressing against mine even though we were a good four feet apart.

I couldn't breathe when he looked at me like that. Couldn't think. God, it was so unfair that the first time I really cared about someone it was some screwed-up, womanizing soldier who was probably only being whatever he was with me because he spent all that time in Afghanistan not getting any.

"What did you want me to do?" he said, his voice low. "After what happened at the Paradise and—"

"Josh, that was nothing to be ashamed—"

"My brother was all over you. You're his ex, which makes me an asshole for going after you because he's obviously still into the great, unattainable Skylar Evans and—"

"What the hell's that supposed to mean?"

"C'mon. Ever since you were in junior high you've been on this pedestal, looking down on all of us—"

"You know, I thought you were different, but you're not, are you? You're still a total player, still crazy full of yourself—"

"Right, Skylar. You're right. In fact, why don't we just do it right here? Yeah, I mean, you'll have to be on top because of my *fucking metal leg*, but whatever, let's just—"

"Am I supposed to feel *sorry* for you right now?"

"Sure, why not? You can be like all the other girls around here, wanting to hand out mercy screws like it's their patriotic duty."

"Go to hell."

"Been there."

"That's great, Josh. Play the wounded-soldier card. Bet it works every time."

He shook his head and looked up at the sky, his lips pursed.

The night was wearing thin, and I was already dreading the after—going back to the motel, alone and knowing how badly the whole thing had gone. Wanting his goddamn face out of my head, but it would be the last thing I'd think of before I fell asleep.

"I just don't get you," I whispered. I bit my lip and let my eyes fall to the water trickling by our feet. "I mean, at the Paradise or my mom's house, it seems like you're this whole other . . . and I wore this stupid dress because I thought . . . I thought that you . . ."

My eyes blurred again and I turned my back on him, trying to find some tiny reserve of control. Josh reached out and pulled me toward him, my back against his chest, his forearm resting on my collarbone.

"I'm sorry," he whispered again, his lips touching my hair.

I shivered and pressed closer when I should have been pulling away. It felt like the world was holding its breath.

"I don't know how to do this," he said. "You're so different from the rest. Every time I try, I just keep screwing it up."

He leaned his forehead against the back of my head, and everything in me that was wound up so tight suddenly unraveled.

"I don't know how to do this either."

He sighed, relief and frustration and wanting all mixed up. We stayed like that for a few minutes, his breath against my neck, his heartbeat in my shoulder blade. It was the same creek I'd been going to all my life, but in his arms it took on a magical quality, everything tinged in iridescent silver, the velvety black night encircling us.

He still had his arm around me, and I leaned down and kissed his wrist, letting my lips linger against his salty skin. His fingers tightened around my shoulder, and I smiled as my lips traveled to his thumb, his index finger.

"Sky," he whispered.

My name in his mouth sounded like a warning, but he wasn't letting go, was gripping me harder, and after all these weeks of anxious hope, it was suddenly so easy to just turn my body a few degrees and press my lips against his.

His hands in my hair.

His tongue in my mouth.

My hips against his.

My fingers clutching his shoulders.

Josh saying over and over:

I love you.

I love you.

I love you.

chapter twenty-five

And then: Josh's arm around my waist as he led me away from the creek, everyone staring as we got into the truck, me sitting close to him as he drove to the Paradise, the truck swerving every time he kissed me. Then us laughing between kisses as we tried to open my door, shushing each other, touching and holding and smiling.

I'd finally gotten the key into the lock, but Josh was kissing my neck, and I turned around and let him press me up against the door because I just wanted more more more. He tasted like cinnamon gum, and I loved the way he'd bite my lower lip, like he wanted to eat me up.

"I"—kiss—"have the key"—kiss—"in the"—kiss—"lock."

He just said, "*Mmmm*," and grabbed me around the waist, then turned the key behind my back. The door swung open, and I could smell the incense I'd burned that afternoon, its smoky vanilla scent clinging to the air. I'd imagined this moment so many times. And now it was happening, but it was so much *more*.

His eyes were heavy with want, the lines around them gentle, and when he kissed me again, there was nothing, *nothing* except his lips and hands and the feel of his heart beating underneath my palm. I grabbed his hand to pull him inside, but he stayed in the doorway, watching me.

"How's the Sky today?" he asked, his voice soft. His eyes were focused, like he really needed to know it was okay to do this, here and now.

"Perfect. Not a cloud," I said. "Low seventies with a breeze." His description of heaven, from when we went to Subway together.

He got this look on his face—a peaceful sort of happiness mixed with . . . love. That one look seemed to shatter every defense I'd worked so hard to build around me. I didn't know what was going to happen, was terrified of everything I was feeling, but it was a good terror, the kind you get on those freaky free-fall carnival rides where you know you'll lose your stomach but you don't care because the rush—*the rush*—is what it's all about. Wanting him made me feel completely out of control, like I couldn't even think because I had this overwhelming need to have him. Tonight. I was going to lose my virginity. To Josh Mitchell. *Josh Mitchell.*

He stepped through the door and shut it behind him. And when I kicked off my shoes and moved toward him, I was crossing a line I could never retreat back to. Moonlight filtered in through the sheer curtains covering my window, turning him into soft angles, smudged lines. I ran my hands up his arms, letting the shadows mix us together, like we were already becoming a part of each other.

His fingers brushed the top of my thighs, then slid, ever so gently, under the hem of my dress. "We can do other things," he murmured, "if you want. We don't have to—"

"I want to," I whispered.

He reached up, his palms warm on my cheeks. "Yeah?"

Was I ready?

"Yeah."

He looked at me for a long moment, his fingertips hot against my skin. I smiled up at him, and he leaned down and kissed me, a soft brush of the lips.

The dress was easy to take off—Dylan only bought those kinds of dresses, and Josh had a lot of practice. Even though it was warm in the room, I had goose bumps everywhere, but the places he touched me turned to flames. I pulled Josh toward the bed, but he hesitated, biting his lip and casting a doubtful glance toward it.

"What?" I whispered, suddenly wondering if I was being whorish and had gotten this all wrong.

"It's just . . ."

A flash of—something, I couldn't tell—but then he shook his head and leaned in to me, his lips on my mouth, my eyes, my neck.

I reached up and started unbuttoning his shirt. My fingers skimmed along his dog tags, and I could feel his heart pounding faster and faster.

His lips found my ear, and when I shivered a little at his touch, he laughed, soft and low. I felt clumsy and uncertain, all of my inexperience matched against his countless times of doing this. For a second, I panicked, like I'd swum out to sea and lost sight of the shore. But then I caught his eyes and saw the way he looked at me. Hungry, yes, but tender too.

I've got you.

I ran my fingers along the raised letters on the dog tags that spelled out all the pertinent information the military needed about Josh. But the important stuff—how he watched out for me, how good he was at chess, the way he always hit his knee when he laughed—they weren't the sort of things you could stamp onto a thin piece of metal.

He swallowed as my fingers reached for the last button on his shirt. I slipped it off his shoulders and slid my hands across the bumps and ridges on his chest I'd noticed that first night, when we'd gone swimming—a dozen scars that told a story he'd never shared with me. He watched my fingers slip over his chest, and as I pressed my lips to each scar, he shuddered, gripping my hips. I made my way up his neck and kissed his closed eyes, and he reached behind me and unhooked my bra—it was off in one single movement.

"You are way too good at that," I whispered.

His lips turned up, and he ran his fingers down my back, his eyes following the lines of my body like he was tracing me. I wrapped my arms around his neck and leaned into him, our bare chests pressed together. Our lips met again, each kiss harder, more insistent than the last. My body responded to every touch, and Josh's breath quickened. His hands moved from my back to my chest, and I gasped a little as his fingers brushed up against my breasts, then skimmed the elastic waistband of my underwear. His eyes held mine, and something in them gave me the confidence to reach my hand down between us and touch him. He closed his eyes and moaned softly into my neck.

"You," he whispered, "are way too good at *that*."

"Now we're even."

There were a million thoughts in my head or no thoughts or

maybe just a single overriding one that was telling me *yes*. Yes to Josh. Yes to this. Just *yes*.

His kisses slowed, and he leaned his forehead against mine. I breathed him in.

I was ready.

My hands trembling, I reached for his belt, but he shook his head and pushed my hand away. I looked up, uncertain. Wasn't that what I was supposed to do? Didn't he want that? Maybe he wanted to—

Then I saw his face. Every bit of gentleness had suddenly drained out of it. He looked . . . disgusted? Like he couldn't believe he'd ended up here. He let go of me and backed away, toward the door. We'd never even made it to the bed.

I crossed my arms over my bare chest. I suddenly realized I was naked. "What?"

He shook his head. "It's . . . we just . . . can't."

My heart was twisting, cracking, and my hands were still warm from touching him, and my chin was raw from his stubble, but he was leaning against the door as though he couldn't get far enough away from me.

"Josh."

I barely heard myself say his name; it was a whisper, all broken confusion.

He shook his head, mumbling. I caught the words *mistake, sorry*, but it was like he was on the other side of a door and I was trying to listen in. I couldn't catch everything he was saying, wasn't even sure I wanted to.

I stood there with nothing on but my underwear, watching as he grabbed his shirt from the floor and threw it on. His fingers were trembling as he tried to button it, and he cursed under his breath. I reached for the throw blanket I kept on the end of my bed and wrapped it around me.

"What the hell is going on?" I said.

It didn't make sense. I knew he didn't think this was a mistake—I'd seen how much he'd wanted me. He'd told me he *loved* me!

"If this is about Blake—"

"It's not about Blake."

"Okay, so tell me—"

"Sky."

"We can slow down—"

"It doesn't feel right."

I stared at him. The shimmering bubbles of happiness that had been floating all around me popped one by one, the whole breathlessness of our summer becoming nothing more than old soap on a stained industrial carpet.

"It doesn't feel right," I repeated. Dull, dead.

"No."

Josh gave up on his shirt and threw open the door. He stepped out, into the night that had held so much magic for me just a few minutes ago, then looked back. I turned away before he could see what those few minutes in my room had cost me.

"Sky . . . I'm sorry," he whispered.

I heard the door shut behind me. I practically ran to the bathroom, then sank onto the cool linoleum, gripping the blanket from my bed. My sobs echoed, and I wondered if the guests on either side of me could hear. I turned on the shower and got in, crying as the water rained down, scratching at my skin until I couldn't feel him on me anymore. I stayed like that until the hot water ran out and then for a few minutes longer because my body didn't feel the cold.

Didn't feel anything.

JOSH

Fuck. Fuck Fuck *Fuck*. I don't know what to do. What the hell
should I do? Tell me, fucking just tell me, man. Please. *Please.*
What am I doing? I should go back, just tell Sky I freaked
because since the war I haven't . . . and it's a mess down there
and she's not like the others, she's never—no, I can't. The look
on her face when I said what I said . . . God, I want to go back
but I don't, I leave the Paradise and I go to Market and buy a
bottle of whiskey. Javier doesn't card me because he feels sorry
about my leg, only Jenna Swenson is there too and I feel so
fucked up and she follows me to my car and I don't care anymore about anything because I've lost Skylar and how the hell
could I have done that to her she fucking trusted me I was going
to be her first and now she hates me, I disgust her I know it and
I keep pouring the whiskey down my throat and I forget Jenna's
there and everything's going blurry and warm and dark so dark
fuck I just want to cry or fight someone or—Jenna whispers
what she wants to do in my ear and I say okay because what's
the point of anything and I might as well I don't give a fuck
what Jenna thinks and we've been here before so many times

and we drive out to this field I used to take girls to and, I don't know man, I just . . . I'm not even here. I'm chugging the whiskey and Jenna's on her knees and it feels good, yeah it's amazing but all I can see is Skylar's face and when it's over I pull up my pants and Jenna wipes her mouth and I tell her I'll drive her home. I don't let her kiss me. Even though it's been hours, I can still taste Skylar's lips, sweet just like I thought they'd be. I swear, if God or some angel or whatever came to me right now and said I had two choices: I could have Skylar for, like, the rest of my life, but I'd never get my leg back, or I could have both my legs, but not Skylar, I would seriously choose one leg. But I've got no leg and no Skylar, and I give up. I fucking give up.

chapter
twenty-six

My shift at the gas station was almost over. Chris would be coming in soon, and I was sort of dreading talking to him for the first time since our fight. The whole argument seemed so stupid now. He'd been right about Josh. I still didn't understand what happened the night before, but Chris had seen it coming. I should have listened to him. Everything was upside down now.

The door opened, and the store filled with an electronic *ding-ding-ding-ding*. The Swensons walked in, laughing hysterically about something. When they saw me behind the counter, their jaws dropped a little. Maybe I was imagining that last part.

"Hi," I said.

"Hey," said one of them. I could never remember which was which, but this one had the pointier nose.

I knew everyone had seen Josh and me leaving the party together last night. I remember how stupidly giddy I'd felt when he took my hand and walked me over to his truck, in front of everybody, and helped me inside. He'd kissed my forehead before he shut the door.

The memory gutted me, and I wrapped my arms around my stomach, protective, like the Swensons could somehow know what had happened in my room. But how could they? It was Josh's and my terrible little secret.

I ignored them while they went up and down the aisles looking at all the food like they'd never seen overly processed carbs before. It took me a minute, but I finally realized they were high as kites. This was one of the reasons why working at the motel was the perfect job for me—I only ever saw strangers who were passing through town. I didn't have to interact with my peers or wear oversized, bright orange shirts under fluorescent lighting that made me look like a fat ghost.

"Shut up," one of them whispered.

I looked over to where they were standing by the chips. One of them was covering her mouth with her hand, squirming like she had to pee.

"*Shut. Up,*" the nonsquirmy one said again.

They started giggling, and I rolled my eyes and started restocking the cigarettes. Then I heard one of them say *Josh*. I gripped the pack of American Spirits in my hand.

"So he just took you out there last night and—" More whispering. I heard my name, some shushing noises. I turned around.

Took her out *where*? My body went cold, imagining him leaving the motel, finding that Swenson . . . and . . . *no*. Just *no*. He wouldn't do that. He was a bastard, but he wouldn't . . .

"Jenna, you are *so bad*," said the squirmy one. She looked at me, and I lifted my chin.

"Why don't you just tell me?" I said. "Because you obviously want me to hear."

The pointy-nosed one—Jenna, I guessed—gave me a cat-eats-mouse grin. "I don't really think my sex life is your business."

Sex life. Sex.

It was like walking into a glass door. It's shocking and hurts, and you're the biggest idiot on the planet.

"You're right," I whispered. "Not my business at all."

She'd won. I could tell by the surprised look on her face that she'd expected some kind of nail-scratching girl fight over it. But she could have him.

She laughed. "Obviously."

They turned their backs on me and stumbled over to the freezer. I stared at the counter, weightless.

The door *ding-ding-ding-dinged* again, and I jerked around, half expecting it to be Josh, a sick part of me wanting him to have to deal with both of us at the same time. But it was Chris, looking sheepish as he walked up to the counter.

"Dude, I'm a jerk. I'm sorry I went off like that in the car yesterday."

I opened my mouth, but nothing came out except a slight croak.

"Are you okay?"

I shook my head and bit my tongue as hard as I could. The tears stayed in as Chris made his way around the counter. He looked over at the Swensons and then pushed open the door behind the register marked Employees Only. I followed him inside, barely seeing the shelves of extra candy bars and warm bottles of soda. His brown eyes filled with worry, and I wished, not for the first time, that my heart could love him in a different way. It would have been so easy. So nice.

"What happened?"

I shook my head. "You were right. I'm sorry I screwed up the pact."

My voice broke on the last word, and Chris immediately pulled me into one of his bear hugs. The familiar smell of him made me realize how much I'd pushed him away this summer, and the tears started to fall, hard.

"Did something . . . I mean, did he—" I could hear the panic in his voice, and I shook my head.

"I'm fine. It's just that Josh is . . . Josh," I said into his chest. "I was dumb to think he'd changed."

"Want me to send a couple of my *cholo* cousins over to his house to castrate him?"

I cry-laughed into his chest. "Maybe."

He looked down at my bleary face. "I'm half serious, you know."

"Nothing happened. I mean, nothing worth castration. Besides, he already lost a leg."

Chris snorted. "Don't care. Doesn't give him the right to do whatever he did to you."

How was I going to get through life without Chris and Dylan right there, whenever I needed them?

I stepped away and nodded toward the little window in the door. The twins were still in the back of the store, gazing in awe at the freezer section.

"You mind dealing with them? I just want to go home, and they're wasted."

"Dumbass Swensons," he muttered. "Sure."

"Thanks."

I turned to go, but he held my arm. "Sky. Seriously. Are you okay?"

I shook my head. "No. But I will be. Just another day in Creek View, right?"

"Dude, fuck this place."

"Yeah. For real."

I grabbed my bag and practically ran to my car. My phone buzzed—a text from Dylan.

Hey. I heard something at Ray's about Josh and Jenna Swenson.

My fingers flew across the keyboard, possessed.

I know. Did he have sex with her?
No, but . . . just come over. Can't text this.
That bad?
Yeah.

———————

A blow job.

Was that worse than sex? I couldn't decide. There was something so intimate about it. Or maybe it made him a worse kind of guy, for letting some girl do that to him without . . . unless he . . . oh, God, I couldn't even go there. I'd started to think he left because he was embarrassed about his leg, and maybe that was forgivable on some level, but that hadn't kept him away from Jenna Swenson. To be ditched for someone like her just added to the humiliation.

Chris and Dylan acted like they were on suicide watch, which was both comforting and super obnoxious. Dylan had already promised Jesse she'd go watch one of his pickup basketball games, but she'd insisted that I shouldn't be alone. Chris suggested Leo's, but I was not in a dancing mood. Clearly. Then he suggested *Inception*, which was playing at the drive-in. I agreed to go, but only to avoid being at the Paradise. I needed a break from the constant reminder of Josh.

I sat in the passenger seat of Chris's dad's truck, my legs tucked underneath me, a tub of popcorn and a half-eaten box of Junior Mints lying between us. I loved the drive-in—getting there early with fast food and tons of candy, hanging out with Chris and Dylan in the back of the truck until the movie started. The El Diablo was a ramshackle collection of screens and outbuildings, but it still had a weird kind of magic. It was one of the few things that I knew I'd miss when I was gone. We hadn't been since before graduation; this summer had been too hard with my jobs and dealing with Mom and Dylan taking care of Sean. I already felt nostalgic—who knew if we'd ever be here again, just the three of us?

The movie hadn't started yet, so Chris and I were listening to a mix I'd made him back in freshman year. He was frowning at the dark screen, absently tapping out the rhythm to a Muse song on the steering wheel.

"What's up?" I asked.

He looked over at me, then shook his head. "I was just thinking about how I want to kill that *hijo de puta.*"

I rested my head on his shoulder. "Then you'd go to prison and have to kiss BU good-bye."

"True. Might be worth it, though."

I looked up at him. "Thank you for not saying 'I told you so.'"

He put an arm around me and squeezed my shoulder. "Honestly, I wish he'd proved me wrong. Sucks to see you get treated like this."

"It's my own damn fault."

"Um. *No.* It's not, actually."

I sat up. "I don't mean it's my fault that he did what he did. It's my fault for thinking he wasn't a man-whore, you know?"

"The leg distracted you. Could have happened to anyone."

I thought of that night at the gas station, Josh holding my hand as we waited for the sun to rise. It didn't make sense. *He* didn't make sense.

I covered my face and shook my head. "Subject change?"

"Okay. Um . . . what kind of dream would you have someone architect for you?"

He'd already explained the whole plot of *Inception* to me, since I hadn't seen it before—a group of people who could create custom-made dream worlds that people paid to get into.

"A manless lesbian colony in the Bermuda Triangle."

"You going gay after one boy problem?"

"Two boy problems."

"And what lesson have we learned, young Skywalker?"

Chris gave me his Jedi face, and I threw a piece of popcorn at him. "I've learned," I said, popping a buttery kernel into my mouth, "to avoid anyone with the last name Mitchell."

He nodded sagely. "Yes, you will go far."

The movie started, and we settled back. I didn't really care about Leonardo DiCaprio's problems, couldn't concentrate on anything but the deep ache that had infiltrated my bones, eating away at the marrow. Was this what it had felt like when

Frida Kahlo found out that the love of her life, Diego Rivera, was cheating on her? *With her sister?* If I felt like this over a boy I'd only kissed for one night, I couldn't even imagine the pain. No wonder her paintings were so bleak and violent. I wanted to do something drastic like she did—cut off all my hair, start dressing like a man. But I didn't think I could handle any more changes in my life.

"I'm gonna go to the bathroom," I said.

Chris looked over. "Want me to come with?"

"I think I can handle it on my own."

He rolled his eyes. "I meant, like, walk over there with you. You know, so you don't get attacked or something."

"No, I'm cool. I'll be right back."

"'Kay."

I opened the door and quietly shut it behind me. The lot was full, mostly with teenagers making out in trucks or hanging around, drinking beer. Only a small percentage of people ever actually watched the movie. It was more about the experience— like tailgating, but without the football game.

I weaved through the cars, catching snatches of the film through open windows. Behind me, the screen loomed, giant and glowing. A plane flew overhead, the red lights on the ends of its wings winking at the clouds. I wondered if the people up there could see the movie.

I stuffed my hands into the pockets of my jeans and kept my head down. I didn't know who'd heard about last night—probably everyone, because it was Creek View. It was humiliating, just imagining people talking about how Josh and I left together and then he and Jenna—

My eyes pricked, and I pinched my arm, hard. It was my own stupid fault, falling for someone like Josh.

I passed the little snack bar crowded with people and was almost to the cinder-block restrooms when I heard my name.

"Skylar."

I froze. *Fuck him*, I thought. *Fuck him for going to a movie after what he did.*

I took a breath and kept walking, but I heard him behind me, catching up. "Sky, please. Wait."

I turned around, my breath catching a little when I saw his face. His eyes were red, and there were dark circles under them, like purple bruises. He looked miserable—and drunk.

"I don't want to talk to you, Josh." I could feel the tears try to force themselves up my throat, and I pushed them down.

He swayed a little, and I noticed that he was gripping a bottle of whiskey. "Let me just . . . I've gotta explain to you. I didn't want—"

I stepped up, close to him. I pictured myself, face red, eyes daggers. I had to be strong now; I could fall apart later.

"I'm actually kind of impressed," I said. "Here I was, thinking you cared about me, when you were probably just trying to prove something. Maybe even had a bet going. Like, *Yeah I lost my leg but watch me get the only virgin in Creek View.* And then . . . what? You felt guilty about it? Because we'd become friends or something? I don't even know what we—" My voice started to shake, and I bit off my sentence.

"No. Sky . . . I just freaked, okay? And I wasn't thinking straight, and I wanted to come back, but I was all fucked up—"

"Was that before or after your field trip with Jenna Swenson?"

Josh opened his mouth, closed it again. Something like defeat settled around his eyes. Then he hung his head, like a schoolboy who'd gotten caught.

"Did you tell her you loved her too?" I whispered.

My voice caught, and when he looked up, I had to take a step back because he was so amazingly good at looking like he gave a shit.

"Just let me try to explain. *Please.* Sky, I—"

"You know what the worst part is?" I said, anger trumping hurt. "It's not last night. I don't care that you saw me naked or that we messed around—that sucks, but whatever. It's that a tiny part of me . . . I mean there were moments when I thought about giving up everything I'd ever worked for, just so I could be around you a little longer."

I'd never forgive either of us for that.

He drew a sharp breath, and I couldn't stand to see the pain in his face because if I fell for it again, I wouldn't be able to say what I needed to. I had to be able to look at myself in the mirror again.

I took a breath. "And *that's* why I want you to go fuck yourself."

I turned around and walked into the women's restroom, went into an empty stall, and stuck my fist in my mouth. I bit down hard, tasting sweat and blood and wanting my dad so bad. I wanted him to not be dead so he could be the dad with the shotgun and run Josh out of town and then tell me that it didn't matter that Josh Mitchell had decided he didn't want me the way I wanted him. I leaned my forehead against the cool metal of the stall.

Ten deep breaths.

One prayer: uncertain and desperate.

Five recitations of *FUCK, FUCK, OH GOD, FUCK.*

Two tears.

Then I flushed the toilet because people would be wondering what the hell I'd been doing in the stall for five minutes, opened the door, and walked back to the truck.

"What'd I miss?" I asked Chris.

"Dude's dream is turning into a nightmare."

JOSH

When it's light, I get out of bed. I put lotion on my stump and roll the cotton guard over it, then put it into my prosthesis. I walk across the hall to the bathroom. Piss. Brush my teeth. Throw water on my face. Make sure my hair is regulation, high and tight. Go into the kitchen. My brother's there, and he doesn't know what to say except, *Morning.* And I say, *Morning.* I can feel him watching me, just like the Afghanis used to when we raided their houses or walked through their fields. So many eyes, watching us. Like we're bombs that are about to go off. Sometimes we were. Blake says, *You okay, man? I heard . . . I mean, last night I thought I heard . . .* But he can't say it. Used to be he heard a girl in there, but now it's just me and the fucking spiders in my head. I go, *Yeah, dude, I'm cool,* and he nods, says, *Cool.* Sometimes I drink coffee and eat Entenmann's with him, but if it's been a really bad night, I do like my mom and get a cold beer and go sit on the back porch and stare at the day and wish that fucking IED had killed me. Then I go back in the house, change into something clean, get in my truck, and drive in the middle of the road until I remember that there aren't any IEDs on the side of Highway 99, and so I get back in the right lane, but not before I think maybe I should just stay right there in the middle.

Just to see what happens.

AUGUST

chapter
twenty-seven

This choreographer named Twyla Tharp once said, "Art is the only way to run away without leaving home."

So I ran. As far and as fast as I could.

I decided to redo the collage for Marge, this time making it from Creek View itself. I got rid of the one I'd spent the summer working on. I didn't just throw it out—I burned it. I cried as the flames licked the angel wings, the strawberries, the orchard. Hours and hours of work and love. But I didn't want anything that represented me losing myself. I dragged a flaming log over the part of the collage with the creek—Josh had helped me cut the scraps of blue paper for it. I could still picture him leaning over the table in the lobby, eyes intent on the job. I'd thought it was so cute, how serious he was. The collage was of Creek View, but, to me, he was all over it.

I needed something clean, new. And I wanted to face Creek View head-on, not hide from it or try to make it bearable. The old collage became a pyre, a smoldering end to a part of myself I never wanted to see again.

I borrowed the digital camera Chris's parents had gotten

him as a graduation present and spent my afternoons taking pictures of Creek View: close-ups of the creek's muddy water, the leaves in the orchard behind the Paradise, cows in the fields, an orange sky after the sun had finally gone down, the trailer park. I'd drive the hour to Bakersfield to get prints made up at Walmart. At night, I'd spread out my poster board in the lobby and cut into the photos with my trusty razor blade, rearranging them so that the trees were made up of dozens of little jagged slivers of leaves on glossy photo paper or creating waves in the photographs of the creek, until the water jumped off the page. As my hands moved, I tried to keep my mind still, giving all my attention to the details of the collage. For two weeks, I didn't stop running away.

I'd gone by my mom's place a few times—I started thinking of it that way, as *Mom's place*, instead of home. Billy's truck was often there, but when it wasn't, I'd slip an envelope filled with cash into the mail slot. No note or anything, but she'd know it was from me. We may have been on hiatus from each other, but I wanted to make sure she was eating. I knew we'd have to talk face-to-face eventually, but I wasn't ready. Not with everything else going on. I'd have to check on her soon, though. I felt selfish and guilty being relieved at not having to carry her burdens.

I'd started a nightly ritual of going through every piece of mail I'd ever gotten from San Francisco, trolling the website, e-mailing with my roommate. I created origami sculptures out of my acceptance letter and the pages I'd torn from the booklet they'd sent me. I didn't know if I was preparing to go to San Fran or getting ready to say good-bye to the dream. It was like I couldn't make a decision. I didn't know what I was waiting for.

Mom wasn't going to change anytime soon. And everything with Josh was over. So why couldn't I just go?

Josh and I had gotten really good at avoiding each other. I was only working graveyards now (Amy was ecstatic about my sudden desire to spend the cool Creek View nights holed up in the stuffy Paradise lobby), so the only time I saw him was by sheer accident. He'd look like he was about to say something, and I'd brush past him, into Market or out of Ray's. He didn't come to the gas station on weekends, and Dylan said he must have memorized her shift schedule because he hadn't once come in while she'd been working at Ray's.

"Because he knows I'd give him a piece of my mind," she said, which was true. You don't cross the people Dylan loves.

I saw Jenna Swenson a few times: pumping her gas or in the drive-thru lane at McDonald's. Whenever we saw each other, she'd look away quickly, and once or twice I caught her staring at me. It occured to me that Jenna's heart might be broken too. Maybe she felt just as used up as I did. When it came to Josh, we were both collateral damage.

Still, each time I saw her, I couldn't help but wonder what exactly she had that I didn't. It was stupid, I knew, but I hated the thought of her hands on Josh—of his on her. When these sorts of things came up, I'd retreat into my cave of a room and cut, glue, create.

It was Blake, of all people, who tried to break the silence. I was at the gas station on a Saturday night, flipping through one of the glossy magazines we sold. I'd been there for three hours, and the lights were giving me a headache—that and the piped-in pop music. It was the kind of night when it felt like every stupid song was written for you, and I kept having this ridiculous fantasy that I didn't even want to come true, of Josh walking in and telling me he loved me and somehow managing to sweep me off my feet. But my life had suddenly become a Taylor Swift song: breakups and heartache and other girls. I knew there was nothing he could say that would take me back to the moments before he left my room. And I didn't think he wanted to go back. He obviously hadn't been happy to be there in the first place.

The electronic bell rang, and I looked up. For a second, my heart literally stopped because I thought it was Josh—somehow, I'd seen the eyes first. Those blue-green swirls.

"Blake."

I didn't have a problem with him, not really, but my voice betrayed how very little I wanted to do with his family and, if I was being honest with myself, a little disappointment.

"Hey, Skylar. How's it going?"

I shrugged. "Slow. I'm waiting for all the drunk people to come in."

"What time does that usually happen?"

"Anytime after ten." I closed the magazine and moved over to the register. "You on pump six?"

"Uh, no, actually. I sort of came in here to talk to you." He fiddled with the Giants cap he was wearing and looked everywhere but at me.

"About?"

"You know." He grabbed a bottle of 5-Hour Energy, rolled it around on the counter, tossed it from hand to hand.

"I'm not a mind reader, Blake," I said. I grabbed the bottle out of his hand and put it back on the pyramid display I'd made.

He took off his cap, ran a hand through his hair. "Look. I

don't know what the deal is with you and my brother, but ever since . . . you know, the party at the creek and all, he's—I'm really worried about him."

"Well, then, you should probably give Jenna Swenson a call. I hear she's pretty good at cheering him up."

"Dude, Jenna's a slut, and we both know that. Josh doesn't give a shit about her."

"I'm not really sure why we're having this conversation, but if you think it will impress me that Josh doesn't care about the 'sluts' he uses, it doesn't."

"Okay. Sorry I used that word. I'm just saying that he doesn't . . . Dude, you know this is a really weird conversation to have with you. I mean, we've hooked up, and I have no idea what went down between you and Josh—"

"Nothing happened," I said. Of course everyone probably thought I *slept* with Josh and then got ditched by him so that he could mess around with Jenna Swenson on the same night.

"Whatever. The point is, he isn't the same since 'nothing'—as you say it—happened between you two."

"What do you mean *not the same*?"

Blake frowned for a second, then looked up at me, finally meeting my eyes. "He'd kill me if I told anyone this, but . . . He gets these nightmares. Like, really bad ones. From the war. Every night, Skylar. And when you guys were hanging out a lot, he wasn't getting them. Or at least not like before—I wasn't waking up in the middle of the night because my brother was screaming like he'd just lost his leg."

I looked down at my hands, clasping and unclasping them. No matter what he'd done to me, I'd never have wished that on Josh. It broke my heart. I thought of him by the pool, saying he was a waste of space. How could someone hurt you so bad but you still wanted to hold him and tell him it was going to be okay?

"Look," Blake said. "I'm not trying to make you feel sorry for Josh—he's a Marine and a Mitchell and he can deal. It's just . . . I feel like it's Day One of him being home all over again, and I want my brother back. I want him to be, I don't know, *happy*."

My heart sort of lifted at the brief image that flashed in my head of Josh being lovesick over me, but then I remembered he was a bastard.

"Why are you here, Blake? Because I'm working, and this really isn't the place for an intervention, or whatever it is you're doing."

The door dinged, and a couple of kids came in and headed for the candy aisle. It looked like they were going to take their time.

"Talk to him," Blake said. "Please. He's messed up. I know he's sorry for whatever he did. Josh needs someone like you, okay?"

Someone *like* me or *me*? Because there was a huge difference. Didn't matter anyway—I'd already told him how I felt.

I shook my head. "I'm sorry." And I was—for Blake, for his family. I knew what it was like to see someone you loved suffering. "And I think you've got the wrong idea about me and Josh. I didn't matter to him. Not much, anyway."

The kids finally walked up, each with a candy bar in his hand. Blake moved to the side, and I used my happy everything's-great voice as I reached for their candy.

"Hey, guys." I rang up the bars, careful to keep my focus on the kids, my not-so-subtle message of *go away* to Blake. "Good choices."

The little boy with the five-dollar bill clutched in his hand said, "Thanks."

"Okay, Sky. I'm gonna . . . I guess I'll see you around."

I nodded. "Yep. Night."

When the store was empty again, I buried my head in my hands. I hadn't realized how much Josh had been helping me get through the summer until he wasn't there anymore. I wanted him to ask me how the Sky was. And then I wanted him to make it stop raining.

———————

Chris and Dylan sprawled on the cat pee couch in the Paradise lobby while I kept my post behind the front desk. Chris was leaving in a few days for Boston, and the three of us were trying to spend as much time together as possible. It was nine, the beginning of my graveyard, and we were just finishing up some Blizzards from Dairy Queen. I'd refused to get mint and Reese's Peanut Butter Cups, even though it was my favorite.

"I wonder if they have these in Boston," Chris said. "Did you know they call milkshakes *frappes*?"

"That's weird," Dylan said.

"And they call sprinkles *jimmies*."

"Oh, God. You're going to come back with some weird accent, aren't you?" she said.

"I don't know of any Mexican-Americans with Boston accents. My family would never let me live it down."

"You all packed?" I asked.

He shrugged. "I'll just do it the night before. I mean, it's not like I have that much stuff to bring. It's a tiny-ass dorm room, you know?"

"It's gonna be so cold there," Dylan said. "Like, snow and everything!"

I swallowed the lump in my throat. "You're going to have a blast."

I pictured the deferral forms that were sitting on the little table in my room. I'd already filled them out and checked the little box that said I would not be going to San Francisco University until January or maybe even next fall, but I hadn't been able to mail them yet. I was still waiting for a sign—something from the universe that said, very definitively, "Stay" or "Go."

Chris hesitated for a second, then said, "Have you decided about—"

"Still on the fence." I cut my pictures of the strawberry fields into tiny diamond shapes. They were next on my collage. "Being here with Marge is good, though."

Dylan blew on her toenails and applied a second coat of nail polish. "You do have a sweet deal over here. Well, except for the fact that Josh is still on staff. Why hasn't Marge fired his ass?"

I hadn't told them about Blake's visit. Part of me wanted to protect Josh, even though I knew he didn't deserve it. I wondered if it was a coincidence, his nightmares going away when we were hanging out so much.

"He's a good worker," I said. "Plus, it's not like she knows about . . . that stuff. It doesn't matter. We're on opposite schedules anyway. Plus there's always the chance he'll stay in the Marines. He might be gone in a few weeks."

I hated how it made me miserable, thinking of him going. The only thing worse than having Josh around would have been never seeing him again.

A pair of headlights swept across the window, and I heard the familiar sound of Marge's 1960s VW bug. A minute later, the screen door opened and Marge walked in—with my mother trailing behind her.

"*Mom?*"

"Hey, baby," she said.

Marge motioned for Chris and Dylan to follow her to the pool. "Let's give them a second."

They stood, exchanging a nervous look. When she walked by me, Marge patted my hand. "If we get any customers, just holler."

My mom stood by the door, like she was afraid to come any closer. She was thinner, paler, but she was clean and had dressed in a flowy skirt and beaded tank top I'd always thought she looked nice in.

I slid off my stool and walked across the lobby, not stopping until my arms were around her.

"I missed you so much," I whispered.

She still smelled like Mom. Even the trace of cigarette smoke that clung to her hair felt familiar and nice. She started crying, a silent sob that shook her body. I could feel her tears on my cheeks as I pressed her to me.

"I'm so sorry, Sky," she said in a choked voice. "So, so sorry."

"It's okay. It's all okay now."

She hadn't said anything, but seeing her outside the trailer, showered and dressed—I knew we were going to make it through this. I let go of her and took her hand, guiding her over to the couch.

"You want anything from the vending machine—Coke or water or something?"

She shook her head and patted the spot next to her. It was still warm from Dylan's and Chris's bodies. She ran her hand through my hair and tilted her head to the side as she took me in.

"Are you okay, baby? You look"—she bit her lip—"older."

I couldn't hold the tears in any longer. I let my head fall into her lap and sobbed like I had always wanted to when I was a little girl, after Dad died.

"*Shhhh*," she whispered. "*Shhhh*."

I let her run her fingers through my hair and rub my back. For once, it felt good to be helpless. After a while, I sat up and wiped my eyes.

"Thanks," I whispered.

Her own eyes were wet too. "Look at us," I said, gesturing to our blotchy faces.

"I know. What a pair." She squeezed my hand. "I really am, you know. Sorry."

"I know."

She took a deep breath. "Marge and I have been talking."

"Uh-huh." I didn't comment on how the last time I'd suggested she talk to Marge she'd used the phrase *when pigs fly*.

"I wanted to make sure you'd have someone close by if you needed help with anything."

"Close by? What do you mean?"

She took a breath. "Well . . . Billy has a job offer in Florida—a really good one. His friend is doing this thing with used cars. Fixing them and reselling. He said we could make two thousand a week, easy. Billy will keep an eye out for used cars to buy, and his friend will fix them up nice. I'd be the, I don't know, secretary. Or something."

My whole body went still.

"Florida?"

"We'll be making good money, and I can visit you—"

I stood up. "You're going. With Billy. To *Florida*?"

"Baby, this is a good thing. A real good thing." She smiled and reached her arms out to me, but I backed away.

"How is this a good thing? Mom, it's gonna fall through. Two thousand dollars a week? No way. And what will you do if it doesn't work out?"

And what about me?

She looked at me, eyes wide, bewildered.

"You don't have to do this," I said. "I told you, I can take care of both of us."

"You're going to college," she said, her voice firmer than I'd heard in months. "Someone in this family has to make something of her life, and we both know it's not gonna be me."

I leaned against the counter, letting the universe's—God's?—message sink in. Not sure if I believed it. Was I actually going to San Francisco?

"But . . . Florida? I mean, how will I see you and what am I supposed to do for the summers? The dorms aren't year-round."

"You can stay with Marge in the summers and on your breaks, she said so, or maybe you could come to Florida. We'll figure something out, I promise."

"I don't know, Mom." I stared down at the carpet, feeling like I'd been hit over the head.

"This is a real good opportunity," she said. "Maybe we could even send you some money—help out with your school supplies. Books. Or whatever college kids need."

That would never happen. Someone like Billy didn't just suddenly make a good life for himself.

"What about the drinking?" I didn't want to fight tonight, but I had to know. Everything hinged on it.

"Better," she said.

She stood in front of me and put her hands on my shoulders. "Do you know how proud I am of you? I don't even have my GED, and look at you—scholarships and that working thing . . . what do you call it?"

"Work-study," I said. It was a grant from the school that guaranteed me a job on campus to help with expenses.

"Right," she said. "Work-study." She kissed my forehead. "Everything's gonna be fine. You'll see."

It wasn't, though. It felt like nothing would ever be fine again.

"So, you and Billy are . . . serious?"

Mom looked away from me, toward the glass door that led to the patio. "Baby, Billy is gonna be around for a while, okay?"

Billy. I never would have guessed he'd become the monkey wrench in my life.

"I know you don't like him—hell, I didn't at first. Maybe when you get a little older, you'll understand." She shook her head. "No, I don't want you to understand. I want you to find someone like your daddy, but someone who maybe doesn't drink as much. And I want you to be happy. Billy and I are just two lonely people that need someone. He treats me right and makes me laugh. And right now, that's enough for me."

I thought of Josh and me, how we'd moved closer and closer over the summer. We were like my mom and Billy, maybe. Just two lonely people that needed someone. The ache in the pit of my stomach that I'd begun to associate with Josh heated up. I knew that wasn't true for me—it wasn't just because I was lonely. My feelings were real, whatever they were. But his weren't, and that just plain sucked.

Mom put a hand on my arm. "Sky, look at me."

I did.

"I know you're worried. But I won't have you giving up your dream. Your father would kill me," she added, with a little smile. She put her arms around me. "I love you, Sky. I love you so much."

I hugged her back. "I love you too."

I was going to school and being all but kicked out of Creek View.

So why wasn't I happy?

JOSH

We sit in a circle, young old men. Look into our eyes and you can see the war, how even though we're home we never left. One dude doesn't have arms or legs. Another has PTSD so bad he twitches all the time. Dude next to me just said his wife left him because she couldn't deal with his "war shit"—the nightmares and the piss-poor memory because he hit his head too hard on the roof of a Humvee when a bomb went off. Another said he's tried to kill himself three times. He says he knows he's batshit crazy but he doesn't know what to do about it, and a dude who fought in Fallujah says, *It's okay if you're batshit crazy. As long as you're batshit crazy functional.* One of the older guys bursts out laughing and says he's gonna tell his wife that next time she calls him a psycho. We have contests to see who has to take the most meds—a Marine sergeant wins: forty-three pills a day. One dude shows us the tattoo he got with the names of all his friends who died. It's a long fucking list. We drink bad coffee and smoke too many cigarettes and the room smells like shit because fifteen guys are farting for two hours. Today it's my turn to talk. I tell them how when you laughed, you'd hold your stomach and shake your head and that the last time I saw you laugh was when some kid grabbed his crotch and yelled, "I MICHAEL JACKSON!" Some of the guys crack up and the dude who lost an eye and both his hands says, *I miss those little bastards.* He's smiling, which he doesn't do so much. The therapist says, *Can you tell us about the bomb, Josh?* and I shake my head because not today, I can't. And I just start shaking, shaking and I can't stop and these guys who are all banged up inside and out, they say, *It's cool, bro; you're doing good, man, real good; we got your back, don't sweat it.* And for a second I remember what it feels like to be thousands of miles away from home and fall asleep in a room with a bunch of guys and feel like a family and I don't know which is better: remembering or forgetting.

chapter
twenty-eight

Chris left three days after Mom's visit.

"Soon this'll be you, *chica*," he said as he hugged me.

He pulled away and looked down at me, inspecting my face as if I were on the witness stand. His brown eyes were bright with excitement, and it was only because I'd known him his whole life that I could see the sadness behind them.

"Promise me you're getting on that bus, Sky."

"Nine A.M. on August twenty-seventh," I said. "Don't worry."

Now that I knew I was leaving too, it felt like everything was happening at warp speed. I'd be gone before I knew it.

"I'm gonna miss you," Chris said.

I kicked his shoe, keeping my eyes on the ground. It was weird how it felt like only yesterday that he was helping me with my math homework, using candy to show me how to add and subtract and divide. But the math we were doing today—the him being subtracted from us—wasn't as easy for me to understand.

"How was it saying good-bye to Dylan?" I asked.

He sighed, and it made him sound older. "She's never gonna be mine, you know? I mean, it's not like I thought she ever would be, not after Sean." He shrugged. "Time to move on. Uh, literally."

"Hot little math majors?"

"Oh, yeah."

"Call me when you get there, okay?" I said.

"Yeah. I'll text you a pic of my room."

The heaviness I'd felt ever since my mom told me I could go to school was threatening to push me into the ground. It didn't make sense—I should have felt lighter than air. Instead, it seemed like I was running out of time that I desperately needed. I didn't know what I needed it *for*, though.

Mrs. Garcia stuck her head out of the minivan. "*Mi hijo—vamanos!*"

Chris waved at her and gave me one more hug.

"I love you, *gringa*," he said.

I bit my lip. "I love you too."

He swung his backpack over his shoulder, and as he turned toward the van, I grabbed his hand and squeezed.

"Chris."

I wanted to have the perfect words to tell him how he'd been family, how I wouldn't be who I was without him and how my life was a collage of memories and he was in every one. But the words couldn't get past the lump in my throat, and as his eyes became glassy, I knew that it was okay. He got it.

Chris jogged to the van and jumped inside. Just as they started to drive off, he pulled open the door and yelled, "The pact!"

I laughed and gave him a thumbs-up. Then he slid the door shut, and they were off. I stood alone on the Garcias' front porch, waving long after they'd turned the corner. All his siblings had gone with him to the airport, so the house was quieter than I'd ever seen it. If Dylan had been there with me, we'd have tried to cheer each other up somehow, but she'd said her good-byes that morning, since she had to work the lunch shift at Ray's.

I sat on their steps and stared out at the empty street in front of me, thinking about all the hours I'd spent there dreaming and imagining and playing. After a while, I stood and took a picture of the house for Marge's collage, this time with a disposable camera I'd bought since I'd been borrowing Chris's.

I wanted to call Josh. To share memories I had of Chris and me growing up that Dylan was tired of hearing about. I wanted him to wrap his arms around me, and I wanted to let myself sob about losing my best friend. I wanted the impossible.

I couldn't go back to the Paradise—it was only three in the afternoon, and Josh would be there, repainting one of the rooms or maybe fixing the filter in the pool. I got into my car and headed toward the trailer park. Now that Mom and I had reconnected, I was trying to pop in once a day to say hi, and I didn't want to be alone with this emptiness that was seeping into every part of me until I felt like I was made of concrete.

I spent the afternoon on our busted-ass couch, watching the Syfy channel because Chris loved it and it felt like as good a way as any to say good-bye. Every few minutes I would think of him, wondering at what stage in his journey he was. I pictured him arriving at the Fresno airport, going through security, browsing the magazines in one of the gift shops. I didn't actually know what the inside of an airport looked like, but I'd seen enough movies to make a good guess.

I carried our plates from lunch over to the kitchen sink and threw in the pan I'd used to make grilled cheese. Almost everything was packed in boxes. Mom and Billy were leaving a few days after me.

"I miss him already."

"Yeah, he's a good kid," Mom said. "But you'll see him at Christmas and then you can tell each other all about school and everything."

I washed the dishes, then put them in the draining rack and dried off my hands. I tried not to pay too much attention to the wineglasses in there or the bottles of beer I'd seen in the fridge. If I thought about it too much, I'd be begging her to stay.

"I've gotta get to the Paradise."

Mom pulled her hair out of her ponytail and started braiding it. "No graveyard tonight?"

"Amy wanted to switch, so I'm off at midnight. I'll drop by tomorrow, okay?"

"Sure."

The breeze on the drive to the Paradise felt good, but I was all out of sorts. Luckily, it was a strangely busy night, with a late checkout and then a new guest who insisted that they *had* to be in the *Gilligan's Island* room that had just been vacated. So I got to play maid for twenty minutes, changing the sheets and cleaning up the room.

I checked in the new guest and then spent the rest of my shift walking around in circles, bugging Marge whenever I got so bored I couldn't stand it. I tried to write a to-do list of the things I needed to get done before I left for school, but all I could think about was Chris being on the other side of the country, the wineglasses at Mom's house, and Josh Mitchell being such a disappointment.

When Amy came at midnight, I headed out to the pool, too keyed up to go to bed. I sat down on the lounge chair and leaned back. On the table next to the chair was a half-finished bottle of whiskey. Every now and then, guests left stuff out—suntan lotion, cups, magazines. I picked up the whiskey—Jack Daniels— and inspected the bottle by moonlight. I remembered that Josh had been drinking a bottle of whiskey when I'd seen him at the drive-in.

What was it with this stuff? Dad and his beer, Mom and her wine, Josh and his whiskey. I unscrewed the cap and sniffed it— it smelled like a secret, the kind you held on to for dear life and prayed no one would ever find out.

A plane passed overhead, and I imagined Chris inside it, looking down, even though I knew he was already in Boston. He'd sent me a picture of his room with his hand in the center of the photograph, doing a thumbs-up. I ran my palm along the side of the glass bottle, tracing the grooves with my fingertips.

Chris and Dylan had always been cool with my decision not to drink. They'd understood because of Dad, but that didn't keep either of them from having a good time. Sometimes I'd felt a little jealous or left out when they got a buzz—it was like they were in this warm, fun place that I was always on the out- side of. It was just one more thing that made me feel like I never really belonged.

When Mom drank, she didn't drink to have fun—I knew that. She drank to forget.

I swirled the amber liquid in the bottle, watching it splash up, like a tiny fountain. I closed my eyes, tilted my head back, and took a sip.

Fire.

Hot, hot, gross, burning, God-how-can-people-drink-this-shit fire fire fire.

Warm.

Liquid honey filling the cold places that had gotten bigger and bigger inside of me since Mom went off the deep end, since Josh said, *It doesn't feel right.*

Another sip—disgusting, what am I doing, I should throw this out and—

Rubbery goodness.

I wasn't made of hard, unyielding concrete anymore. It took a little while, but the whiskey broke it up and turned me into warm sand. Creek sand in the sun.

Another sip—really not so bad, kinda nasty at first, but it wasn't long before I was floating and the stars were so amazingly bright, like that night at the gas station.

Fuck Josh Mitchell.

Another sip. Oops, where'd that cap go? Fuck it. Another sip. Another.

I don't need him. Or Chris. Or anyone.

Tears threatened, and I thought of Dad.

Daddy.

Suddenly, more than anything in the world, I wanted to go to the creek. I had to go. Had to be as close to him as possible. We'd scattered his ashes there, and now Mom and I were both ditching him. How could we do that? Maybe, if I went there, I could figure out—whoops! sat up too fast—I could figure out why everything felt wrong.

JoshJoshJosh. I shook my head.

Fuck. Him.

I stood, swaying a little, clutching the bottle in one hand and digging in my pocket for my car keys with the other. The creek. The creek. That was where the answers were.

I left the bottle on the table and stumbled to the back gate. Stubbed my toe on a rock.

"Ouch!"

Damn. That really hurt.

It took me a minute to fit my key into the lock once I'd gotten to my car—duh, wrong key. I started giggling and got inside quick and shut the door before Amy could hear me.

I turned on the car, and it was like a sign from God when the radio started playing this song that Maverick aka Tom Cruise listens to in *Top Gun* with the blond chick he's into. "Sittin' on the Dock of the Bay." In the movie, they're on this porch swing, and he tells her it was a song his dad had listened to a lot, and I'd always loved it because my dad had liked it too. He used to sing it to me at night, like a lullaby, and he'd taught me to whistle by having me practice the whistling part of the song. I turned it up as I backed out and headed toward the highway.

It took me a second to realize my headlights weren't on, but I noticed before I got on the road. The Paradise sign blazed, and the neon angel winked at me. I waved to her, half tempted to flip her off, but I didn't know why. The Paradise had been good to me, even if it had brought Josh into my life. I got on the 99, and somebody honked, and I *did* flip them off, which felt dangerous, like throwing beer bottles at a boarded-up gas station.

I turned the radio up and sang at the top of my lungs. I didn't realize I was crying until I pulled onto the dirt road that led to the creek. When the song ended, I shut off the radio and took a big breath, trying to concentrate on the road in front of me, which was sort of hazy and rolling, like I was driving on water. Empty fields were on either side of me, and there wasn't any moon, so it was pitch-black except for my two yellowish headlights that were zigzagging all over the road.

My cell started to ring, and I grabbed it out of the ashtray I never used, where it was lying on top of change and gum wrappers.

The caller ID said *Josh*.

"What the hell?"

I stared at the phone, my insides turning to jelly, my hand shaking. What did it mean that he was calling me tonight, right now, when everything in me ached to be with him, but *NO*, *no way* was I going to answer.

"Fuck you, Josh. Fuck you!" I yelled at the phone. It kept ringing, and just when I was about to throw it onto the seat next to me, the car suddenly lurched, then dived off the road. I screamed, the phone flying, my hands gripping the wheel. My teeth slammed together, and my forehead hit the steering wheel. The air bag didn't open, but it didn't matter because the car suddenly stopped, the engine making a horrible, grating sound. I looked around me, at the headlights pointing into a wall of earth.

A ditch.

I'd driven into a deep ditch on the side of the road. Everything was close, too close, and I couldn't breathe, and Dad, this was what Dad must have felt like, right when the big rig—

I unbuckled my seat belt and tried to open the door, but it wouldn't budge. I started panicking, feeling like the car was underwater and I was sinking. I had to get out, had to get out before the car blew up or the walls of earth caved in and buried me alive.

I rolled down the window and turned off the ignition, leaving the headlights on. My body shaking, my head pounding, my stomach clenching.

I felt something on my foot and reached down—my cell phone. I shoved it into my pocket.

Spinning. Spinning. *Oh, God, what's happening?*

I gave up hope of ever opening the door and hoisted myself out the window, then reached up to brace my body against the side of the ditch. There was just enough space for me to crawl out. When I got onto the road and looked down, the tears came. There wasn't a house around for miles, and unless there were some couples hooking up by the creek, there wasn't anyone around who could help me. How the hell had I—

Josh.

I whipped the phone out of my pocket and nearly fell over from the effort. I swayed in the middle of the deserted road, looking down at my car. I'd been fine, almost to the creek, about to get some answers from the universe or God or my dad when *he* had to push his way back into my life, calling in the middle of the night. I went to my recent calls and pressed the number on top.

I started screaming into the phone as soon as I heard his hopeful "Sky?"

"You fucking asshole, why the fuck are you calling me? Now my car's in a goddamn *ditch*—"

"Sky, slow down," Josh said, his voice instantly commanding.

"No, I *will not* slow down. Fuck you. You don't get to tell me what to do—"

"*Sky.* Are you hurt?"

"I'm not some soldier you can just order around to do whatever, and I'm not Jenna Swenson who's just gonna suck your—"

"*SKY.* What do you mean your car's in a ditch?" He was yelling over me, his voice frantic.

"Oh, like you care. I'm guessing you're only calling me at one A.M. for one of two reasons: either you're as drunk as I am or—"

"You're *drunk*?"

Now he was really shouting and the whole world was spinning and I had to sit down, only when I tried to sit down, I ended up falling onto my back, which was hilarious and kind of painful.

I started laughing and crying at the same time, and I could hear him start his truck in the background and then there was his voice, his voice I'd been missing so much for days and days and days, pleading with me, begging me, and *SCREW HIM.*

"Where are you? I'm coming. Where are you?"

"I don't need your help. You've done enough, can't you see that? *God!*"

"Okay. I know you're mad, but can you just—"

"If you hadn't called me, I'd already be at the creek with Dad, I mean not *with* Dad, but—"

"The creek? You're at the creek?"

"Yes. I mean . . . no. I don't know, I'm . . . It's none of your business where I am!"

"*You* called *me*! I'm just trying to help. Please—tell me where you are."

"I don't know, I'm . . . it's a ditch. I can't describe a fucking ditch, Josh."

I heard him grunt in frustration, and I hated that my alcohol-poisoned brain thought that was cute. I could imagine the look on his face, how pissed he was, though why he suddenly cared I didn't know.

"Are you hurt? Is anything broken? Are you bleeding? I'm calling 9-1-1—"

"No!" I yelled. "I'm not hurt. I'm pissed. Do you know how much money this is going to cost me? Why did you have to fuck-ing call me—"

"Sky. *Please.* Just stay where you are. I'm close. Are you on the highway or—"

"Don't ever call me again."

I threw the phone at my car, smiling at the satisfying *thunk* of it hitting the roof. I struggled to stand up, then dusted myself off. A wicked rush of vertigo made me lean over, hands on my knees. I closed my eyes, took a breath, and managed to stand. Belatedly, I realized it was a very bad idea to throw my phone into a pitch-black ditch with only my headlights to help me find it.

I looked over the side, surveying the mess I'd made. The car didn't look banged up so much as stuck.

"Dammit."

The tears started again, and I couldn't stop them, and I

wanted my dad and Chris, and *fuck*, I'd been driving drunk, I could have killed someone, and what had I said to Josh? I couldn't remember, just him yelling and me freaking out on him.

"Oh my God. Oh my God. Oh my God," I whispered, hugging my arms.

I heard a roar behind me and jumped as Josh's truck gunned down the dirt road. When he was about six feet from me, he screeched to a halt and jumped down from his truck—faster than I'd ever seen him—and literally *ran* over to me.

"You can run?" I asked, dazed and squinting at his bright headlights.

"Tell me what hurts," he demanded.

His hands roamed over my face and touched the back of my head. It didn't matter how drunk I was—everywhere he touched made me shiver. My skin was a traitor.

He looked into my eyes and held up three fingers. "How many fingers am I holding up?"

"Screw you."

"Dammit, Sky, come on. How many?"

"Three."

"Okay," he said to himself. "Okay, good."

He gently ran his hands along my arms, his fingers pushing into the bones. "Does this hurt?"

I shook my head—bad idea. "Whoa," I said, tilting to the side.

He reached out for me and wrapped his arm around my shoulders. I remembered the feel of his bare chest and how he'd shivered a little when I'd undone the buttons of his shirt. I looked at him now, wearing a faded Marines T-shirt and a pair of basketball shorts. It looked like he hadn't shaved in days, and my fingers reached up, without my permission, to stroke the hair on his cheek. He closed his eyes and swallowed.

"Why did you call me?" I whispered.

His pretty pretty pretty Mitchell eyes opened, then looked away from mine before he said, "I needed . . . I mean, I thought—" He stopped and ran his finger over my forehead, frowning. I winced.

"You've got a big bump here," he said.

"I hit the steering wheel when I went over."

"We've gotta get you to a doctor. You might have a concussion."

I pushed him off me. "Can't. I don't have insurance. I'm fine, it's just a—"

"I have money. I'll pay the—"

"*No,*" I said. "I don't want your money. I don't want—" I clutched at my stomach and shoved my other hand over my mouth. "I think I'm gonna be sick."

I limped-ran over to the ditch and slammed to my knees. Josh was right behind me, and I put out a hand, waving him off.

"Go away, Josh," I said through clenched teeth. I was getting that feeling in the back of my throat, and I knew I was seconds away from throwing up all that whiskey.

I felt his fingers in my hair, gathering it up, and I couldn't wait any longer, couldn't yell at him again. I opened my mouth and retched.

It felt like everything I'd ever consumed in my entire life was coming out of my stomach. I could hear Josh's murmurs, but I didn't know what he was saying. I felt like I was going to die. I couldn't remember ever having been that sick. When it was over, he pulled me to my feet and led me over to the truck. His arm was around my shoulders again, and as he held me to him, I kept stumbling; once I stepped on his fake foot.

"I'm sorry," I whispered, over and over.

"*Shhh*, it's okay," he said.

He gave me some Subway napkins, which made me sad because we'd gone there together. Then he handed me a bottle of water and turned away to call someone while I tried to clean up.

I was leaning against his truck, my eyes closed, when I heard him walk up to me.

"Blake's gonna come out with the tow truck and get the car. I'll take you to Marge and then come back and help him, okay?"

I opened my eyes. "Why'd you call me?" I said again.

He hadn't answered the first time. I didn't know whether it was the alcohol or if I had finally given up lying to myself, but seeing him, being near enough to smell his Old Spice—I loved him. I didn't want to. Had to stop. But I loved him.

"Doesn't matter," he said. He reached past me and opened the door. "Let's get you home."

He picked me up before I could protest, and I grasped at his shoulders, the world spinning wildly. *Please don't let me throw up on him. Please, God, please.*

"I've got you," he said. "Don't worry."

I've got you.

For a second we were cheek to cheek, and I thought of dancing at Leo's and lying in the bed of his truck and how he'd kissed me by the creek.

"Josh," I whispered.

I had to tell him we were like a collage. Pieces that could be put back together in a new way, a better way. If I didn't say it now, I never would.

"Yeah?" His voice was low, rough.

Then I blacked out.

JOSH

Hannah called me. Your Hannah. Said she got my number from one of the guys in the unit. She started crying right away and it made me think of how you said she always cried whenever you guys talked on Skype. And how you'd spend half the time trying to convince her you weren't going to die. You were everything, *everything* to someone, so why the fuck am I still here? Don't even know why I wanted to check around the corner of that fucking hut—did I hear a noise or was I bored? Maybe I wanted to take a piss, I don't know, I don't know, I don't fucking know. And your Hannah. She wanted to know. All of it. Details. And I cried too and she was telling me, telling ME, it was okay and that you loved me and she was so happy we were together when it happened because she said she couldn't have handled the thought of you being alone or with some of the guys that got under your skin. And when I told her . . . when I told her how you'd gotten her a ring she just fucking lost it. Said your mom had seen it in . . . in the stuff the Marines gave her. Your personal effects. And it was so hard, man, it was so hard but I told her your plan and how you were gonna ask her and she got really quiet and it was like, it felt like you were there. In that moment. Were you? Three weeks. Three goddamn weeks and you would have been able to put that ring on her finger. I hung up with Hannah and I didn't even think, just started dialing Sky's number. I needed to hear her voice because everything was getting dark in me and she's the only light I've found since all this shit happened. I just thought, if she would answer, if she would answer, maybe I could, I don't know, just tell her in the right way why I was so messed up. But me calling nearly got her killed and it's like God's saying, *Stay the fuck away from her, Josh.* And I have this, all this stuff inside me—what happened and now Hannah's voice and the dreams and how I hurt Skylar so bad she got drunk and I can't do it anymore. I can't, I can't, I can't, I—

chapter
twenty-nine

Everything hurt. Even my fingernails. The sun was driving stakes into my eyes, and my head . . . oh, God, my head. Picture me in Edvard Munch's *The Scream*, and you'll have the right idea.

"Time to wake up, Sleeping Beauty." Marge pulled open the curtains, and I let out a shriek.

She grabbed the pillow I was trying to put over my eyes. "Nope. Time to join the living."

I heard her walk across the room, then the sound of the shower being turned on. I was pretty sure something had died in my mouth, and my throat was raw, like I'd been screaming or something.

I felt strong arms around me and then I was standing. I forced my eyes open and gave Marge a bleary glare.

"I can't."

She nodded. "Yes, you can. Let's go."

Marge pulled me to the bathroom, then went back out into my bedroom. "I have a hangover cure at the pool, when you're ready. I called in for you at the gas station, but don't even think of going back into that bed."

I grunted and pulled off the clothes I'd been wearing the night before and left them in a dirty pile on the linoleum. The hot shower pounded my skin, and I stood under it for a long time. The night came back to me in flashes: the whiskey bottle, my car in the ditch, someone holding back my hair while I barfed. Who was—

Then I remembered.

"*Fuck*."

I sat down in the bathtub and let the water pummel me. It was too hot, but I wanted it to burn. I deserved it.

How could I have gotten in a car after what had happened to my dad? I could have died. Worse, I could have killed someone else. I stared at my hands, raw and bright red from the hot water. I had no idea who they belonged to.

It took me forty-five minutes to shower, brush my teeth three times, and put on clean clothes. My bones felt like someone had tried to grind them into dust. I never knew you could hit rock bottom so literally.

I pushed on my sunglasses and stepped outside. I had to cover my eyes as I made my way over to the pool—the sun was so blinding. From where it was in the sky, I could tell we were well into the afternoon. I could see Marge between my fingers, sitting at her favorite table with the large umbrella over it.

"Well, sweet pea, you really screwed up, didn't you?" she said.

I'd pieced enough of the night together in my head to know that I had become the world's biggest hypocrite.

"Marge, I—" My voice broke.

She looked at me over her John Lennon sunglasses. "You remember."

"Enough," I whispered.

"Good." Then she patted the chair next to her. "Some people get second chances," she said. "I know you won't waste it."

I wasn't so sure. My judgment had become seriously impaired since I'd graduated high school.

She pushed a glass of thick red juice across the table. "Hangover cure."

"What is it?" I asked.

"V8." She held up a white bag. "And crackers."

I swallowed the bile that was tickling the back of my throat. "I'm good, thanks."

"Sit. Drink. Eat. *Now*."

I groaned as I lowered myself into the chair next to her, then I held the glass up and took a tentative sniff. "Blended brains?" I asked, with a grimace.

Marge glowered, so I plugged my nose and drank. She nodded and handed me two white pills. "Excedrin," she said.

I popped the pills and finished off the juice. She opened the crackers, and I put up a hand to ward them off.

"You'll regret it if you don't," she said.

I couldn't imagine feeling any worse, like *ever*, but I took a cracker and nibbled on it.

"Josh?" I asked.

"He took really good care of you, Sky."

So much of last night was a blur, but bits and pieces were coming back to me. The fear in Josh's eyes when he first saw me, the way he'd picked me up to put me in the truck.

"Did he yell at a doctor?" I asked. I had flashes of the ER and Josh getting in someone's face.

Marge chuckled. "Yeah. They wanted us to wait for over an hour, and he pulled rank, so to speak." She looked over at me and patted my hand. "You don't have to fight it, you know."

I finished the cracker and leaned back in the chair, closing my eyes. "Fight what?"

"It's not every day you get to watch the two people you care most about in the world fall in love."

I moved my head—too quickly—to glare at her. The patio flipped upside down, and I held my stomach, clenching my teeth as the V8 threatened to come back up.

"That's not exactly what's been happening," I said.

"Sky. Give me a little credit. Just because I'm old doesn't mean I'm blind. That's *exactly* what's been happening."

I looked at the freckles on the back of my hands, tried to find constellations in them. "He really hurt me," I said.

"I know." She sighed. "After Josh finished getting your car out of that ditch—"

"Oh, God, the *car*." I'd actually forgotten about it.

"—he told me what happened between the two of you. I'm really sorry about that, sweet pea. You must be pretty cut up about that Swenson girl."

Just hearing her name made me want to go on a rampage. Real violence, maybe with machetes.

I grabbed another cracker and focused on scratching the salt crystals off it while Marge looked at me in a shrinkish kind of way.

"You up for a little walk in the orchard?"

I was up for lying down and dying, but I followed her

through the back gate and into the orchard behind the Paradise. Marge hooked her arm through mine, and we stepped over weeds and tree roots until we got to the neatly raked paths between the trees. The shade protected us from the heat, and for a while we just walked under the small green apples that clung to the branches above us. The sun felt good, for once, and a hot breeze whipped around our ankles and tossed our hair. The Excedrin was kicking in, and I started to feel a little more human.

I tilted my head back and looked at the dusty green leaves dangling above me. I felt like I was in another world, a planet of trees. I drew closer to her as we walked and laid my head on her thick shoulder. Marge rested a hand against my hair for a moment. We kept walking to the sound of her labored breath and hundreds of trees shaking in the wind—all of them whispering, pleading, crying.

"Josh said he told you about my son."

"Yeah." I looked up at her, frowning. "I hope that was okay."

She smiled her sad smile. "Of course, sweet pea. I could only tell the story once, and Josh was the one who needed to hear it. But I'm glad you know."

Marge sighed, and the sound was so lonesome.

"When he came home, Kyle wasn't himself," she said. "I'm guessing Josh isn't always himself, either."

"I don't even know who Josh *is*," I said.

There were three Joshes: the asshole from high school, the gentle, generous guy who wanted to protect me, and the soldier who would forget where he was, staring off into space, lost in a country thousands of miles away. I still had no idea which was the real Josh—or was he all three?

"He doesn't know either." She stopped and faced me. "Have you ever thought that maybe you're helping him figure that out?"

I shook my head. "No. And I don't want to. I can't . . ." My eyes filled, and I turned away.

"You're so young," Marge said. "Both of you. But you have old hearts."

I think I knew what she meant. Still. He'd broken mine.

"Marge, there's no way I could ever trust him. And I don't think he even wants to be with me. He's . . . lonely. Bored, maybe."

But the words sounded hollow, rote. It didn't make sense, how Josh ran from me. What he did with Jenna. But neither did all the good stuff—the way he'd stood up to Billy, how he taught me chess and bought me food because he knew I was hungry.

Marge reached up to run her fingers over one of the apples. "When Kyle left Iraq, it was almost like . . . almost like he was battling with something all the time. Sometimes it won, and sometimes he won. What Josh did to you: well, I think he'll have to explain it himself. But you should give him a chance to do that. I'm not making excuses for him. I just thought you should know what he's up against—and what you're up against."

"Me?"

"Even just being friends is going to be a burden sometimes, hon. But he could sure use a good friend like you right now. As for more than that . . . you'll have to go with your gut. It's not going to be easy."

I looked at the dead grass around our feet, at the haze that made the sky look sleepy. "I'm leaving soon," I said.

"Yes, you are." She leaned against a tree, giving me one of

her soul-searching looks. "But it's not one or the other, sweet pea."

I threw my hands up. "I don't know what to do. About this or about anything. Marge, *I don't know what to do.*"

She put her arm around my shoulder and held me close. Her familiar rosewater scent was comforting, and I breathed it in. "You'll do whatever the right thing is. Except for last night, you always have."

But that was the problem: I didn't know what the right thing was anymore.

JOSH

Every time I close my eyes I see you. The way the ground flies up and how you're in the air, like a giant threw you, with your back against the clouds. That face. Every time I close my eyes I see your face looking down at me. Just for a second. All surprised like someone's playing a fuckin' joke on you. And I feel and I don't feel—everything—all at once and then it's just blood and dirt and people shouting and that kid still holding the soccer ball Marlon gave him and I wonder if he thinks we're gonna take it away now that it isn't a good day anymore. Gomez running around saying *fuckfuckfuck* and me shouting, *Where is he? Where's Nick? Nick! Nick!* And nobody says anything and all I can see is the medic's face and the sky so blue God it's not blue like that at home and the poppies everywhere red red blood and poppies. The reporter's saying, *IED, IED.* No shit it's an IED. Then Gray's above me saying, *Stay with me, Josh. C'mon, soldier, wake the fuck up. Tourniquet,* he yells. *I need a fucking tourniquet,* and then he slaps my cheek. *Stay with me, dammit!* Me screaming, *Nick—my leg—Nick—my leg,* and then the drill sergeant's voice in my head, shouting all the damn time, us running for miles and miles at Camp Pendleton singing, *I don't want no teenage queen / I just want my M14 / If I die in the combat zone / Box me up and ship me home / Pin my medals upon my chest / Tell my mom I've done my best,* and I hold my rifle close to me and I'm not letting it go until someone pries it out of my dead hands and then the helicopter, looking like an alien insect dancing in the sky, and dust everywhere and the Navy corpsman's saying, *We're getting you out,* and someone crying because it's true Marines do cry and then they put me on the stretcher and I can't feel my leg my leg what's wrong with my leg and before I pass out I say, *Morphine give me morphine.*

Doesn't that come from poppies?

chapter thirty

It was late afternoon by the time I decided to look for Josh. I borrowed Marge's car, but since my phone was buried in the ditch, I couldn't call him once I'd started driving. So I went by his house, then Market, and finally down to the creek. No Josh. Panic started to settle in by the time the sun turned orange. I couldn't remember what I'd said to him last night, but I knew none of it was good. And I kept thinking of Marge's son. What if Josh wasn't through the worst part and I'd pushed him over the edge? When was the moment when her son couldn't handle it anymore—what had set him off?

The ironic thing was, I'd kept pushing Josh away in the beginning of the summer because I didn't want this feeling I was having now, this horror that I might lose someone else I loved. There was nothing worse than that: a hurt so bad it feels like someone is ripping off hunks of your soul like it's a loaf of bread.

I pulled into the turnoff for the creek and slowed down at the ditch. The only evidence of my accident was a deep gash in the field my car had crashed into. I touched the tips of my fingers to my forehead—it felt like a golf ball had been surgically inserted under my skin. It must have been a bitch to get my car out of there in the middle of the night. I figured Josh had earned a little bit of the forgiveness I was willing to give him: not just for getting the car, but for how he'd taken care of me. It was hard to admit, but I didn't know what I would have done without Josh last night.

Now I just needed to find him. I idled near the ditch, trying to think of places he might be. My head was pounding: from the hangover, from the fear that I was too late to tell Josh . . . something. I still wasn't sure what I wanted to say. I just knew I needed to find him. Now.

On a whim, I drove toward the field used for fireworks on the Fourth. My hunch paid off—Josh's truck was parked close to the little path that led to the train tracks. *The train tracks.* I could see the look on his face as he watched that train go by, and suddenly I had to get to him, as fast as possible.

Give me a little credit, Sky. I'm not gonna try to do it in the dark.

As if on cue, I heard a train whistle, not too far off. I jumped out of the car and flew through the brush, tripping over roots and slapping away the dry branches that smacked my face. I could hear the train now, chugging along, coming closer. Faster than me.

A train horn blasted the air, and I hurtled forward, screaming Josh's name at the top of my lungs. If he tried to jump, there was no way he would make it. If his prosthesis got caught under him . . .

No.

"Josh!"

I could see the black mass of the train to my right now. I stumbled and fell onto my knees, scraping the skin off.

"Josh!"

He couldn't hear me over the sound of the train. It was going faster than the one we'd seen together, the boxcars flying by in a blur, the wheels sharpening themselves on the tracks, round knives.

I bolted between the final two bushes. Josh was standing close to the tracks, his body in a tense crouch. I could only see the right side of his face—he was completely focused on the train, his eyes following the sides of the boxcars. An open one was just a few cars away. He reached out an arm.

"Josh!"

The open boxcar was coming up. I sprinted across the dirt and launched myself onto his back.

"Whoa!" he yelled.

He tried to swing me around, but lost his balance so that we both tumbled to the ground, hard. He shouted in pain and then clutched at his leg, and I was saying "Sorry! Shit! Sorry!" but in an instant, Josh had me pinned to the ground and was on top of me, his fist drawn back and his other hand pushing painfully against my chest.

I gasped and reached up my hands to protect my face, but then he saw it was me and immediately relaxed.

"Sky?"

I let out a shaky laugh.

"Hey."

We stayed like that for a second or two, the methodic pounding of the train's wheels on the steel tracks keeping time: him leaning over me, me looking up at him. His eyes were bloodshot, and he was covered in dust, his T-shirt ripped around the collar where I'd tried to hold on to him. He looked at me like he hadn't seen me in forever, and I felt his breath on me, hot and familiar. It would be so easy to throw my arms around him and pull him to me. I heard Marge say the word *burden*, saw her dead son in the bathtub. I lay still, my eyes locked on his.

Josh studied my face, then he rolled off me.

We lay in the dust on our backs, staring at each other as the train swept by. Soon the only sound was our breath and the insects that were buzzing around the fields. I sat up and crouched over him. The path from my lips to his wasn't that much distance to cover, but I'd already promised myself that wouldn't happen again. I'd come here to be his friend, that was all.

"Is your leg okay?" I asked.

"Why the hell'd you do that?" he said, ignoring my question.

"I didn't want you to jump the train," I said. "I mean, obviously."

He sat up and rubbed his thigh, but didn't say anything. The train was just a speck on the horizon now with black clouds of smoke trailing behind it. I saw the longing in his eyes as he watched it get farther and farther away.

"Why's it so important to you?" I asked, my voice soft.

He leaned back in the dirt, his hands behind him. His eyes glazed over, and I knew he'd gone somewhere I couldn't follow.

"Josh?"

"I just needed to . . . blow off some steam. I had a lot on my mind."

"Throwing bottles at the gas station wasn't enough for you?"

He half laughed, a bitter exhalation. "Not after Afghanistan."

That pissed me off. Downplaying it like it was a totally acceptable way for him to deal.

"Josh. News flash: you don't have two legs. It sucks, it sucks so bad, and I'm sorry, but you don't. You can't jump trains anymore."

"Thanks, Skylar, I had no idea. I mean, I thought I was walking funny, but—"

"Don't get sarcastic with me, you son of a bitch. How do you think it feels, to go driving all over town worried that someone you lo—just fucking worrying that you're, I don't know, dead or something."

"Well, I'm not. Sorry to disappoint you. I seem to be doing that a lot lately."

"You're such a—"

"Just *stop*, Skylar. *Stop.* You have no idea. No idea what happened, what I did. You have no . . ."

Josh put his head in his hands for a minute. I stayed quiet, just kept my eyes on him, even though I wanted to put my arms around him so badly.

"I killed my best friend, okay?"

His words pushed all the air out of me, all the light from the sky. He looked up, his eyes wet and so lost.

"Your friend with the books," I whispered.

"Nick." He nodded and drew in a ragged breath. "If I hadn't told him . . . Why'd he have to have my back like that? Always covering us—"

His hands gripped his elbows so hard, like he was physically holding himself together, and then he leaned forward and just kept saying *godgodgod* over and over.

I grabbed his arms. "Josh." He didn't seem to know I was there. "*Josh*," I said again, my voice louder.

He looked up. "He was standing right next to me when I stepped on the IED. I saw him fly up, like . . . like he weighed nothing. So light."

He told me everything.

What he saw, how it felt, who was there. He shuddered a little, and I gripped his arms tighter, wanting so badly to stay strong for him but feeling like the world was breaking apart and rearranging itself in new and horrifying ways. I didn't want to go there, to those places he was describing, but I didn't want to be where he wasn't.

"It should have been me," he whispered. "He was so much better. So much *more*."

"No."

"It's my fault. If I'd just—"

"It's not your fault. It's not."

"We're fighting ghosts out there. Gotta be fucking vigilant. Trust me—I screwed up. You don't know."

"I do. You're good. Even though you treated me like shit, I know you're good. So whatever happened out there, it wasn't your fault. It's war, and war is fucked up. But you made it, and now you've got this life."

"What the hell is it good for?" He shrugged me off and ran his hands back over his head. "I'm fucking pointless."

"Feeling sorry for yourself or trying to jump a train isn't gonna bring him back."

His head snapped up, like he had something to say about that, but when I put my hand over his, he relaxed a little. "I know," he whispered, after a minute. He looked at the train tracks. "I just wanted to see if I was still me."

I thought about Marge's son, how he'd slowly fallen apart. The blood in the bathtub. The three Joshes.

"You *are* still you—losing a leg doesn't mean you're an entirely different person." But even as I said the words, I knew that wasn't true. He *had* changed; I just didn't know how to tell him I liked post-Afghanistan Josh better.

He grunted and I took a breath, forcing the words past my mouth. "Have you talked to the Marine Corps about this? I'm sure they could—"

"Sky, just drop it." His voice held a tinge of command in it. It was what I'd come to think of as his Marine voice. "This is my thing and—"

"I can't. I'm sorry, but I don't want to get a phone call in San Francisco telling me you got run over by a train, okay?"

"I'm not gonna get run over by a train." He smiled, but it looked painted on—a red slash on his face. "Seems like these days you'd *want* that, anyway."

"That's not even funny."

I stood and he moved to get up too, so I held out my hand, but he waved it off. "I've got it."

I let my hand drop and looked up at the sky, anything to avoid being an audience. But I could tell from his labored breathing that he was struggling, so I grabbed his arm. He tried to shake me off, but I held tighter.

"Why do you have to be so goddamn stubborn all the time?" I snapped.

"*Me?* Are you serious right now?"

I knew he was thinking about last night and how I wouldn't tell him where I was or what had happened.

"Just let me help you up."

Josh looked at my hand, like he wanted to push it away . . . *again* . . . just like that night, but he finally gave a slight nod, and I pulled him up while he pushed against the ground with his other hand.

I knew the fall had cost him when he didn't straighten up right away but rested his hands on his knees and took a few breaths instead. He wanted to be the perfect stoic soldier, all *oorah* and stuff. I had to tuck my hand behind my back because I wanted so badly to run my fingers through his hair. It was the longest it had been all summer.

Friends, I kept chanting to myself. *Friends*.

"Thanks," he muttered.

"Sure."

I looked at the tracks. I'd be going in that same direction in just a few weeks.

I took a deep breath: dust, smoke, manure. No matter where I went, this place would be with me. It had seeped into my bones. I knew it'd never let me go, and I suddenly found myself not wanting it to. I was part of Creek View just as much as it was part of me. But I could see the next few weeks, months, years spread out before us. I'd find my arty boy, and Josh would find a Creek View girl or, if he stayed in the Marines, some tanned, blond girl from San Diego. Maybe we'd see each other when I came home to visit Dylan and Marge. I'd think of him whenever I saw a man in uniform. I'd wonder, forever, what would have happened if he hadn't freaked out that night. If there had been more than those few kisses.

Josh straightened up, the pain only showing in the grimace he made and how tightly he clutched his hips.

"Anyway," I said, "I just came to tell you . . . thanks for last night—for, uh, taking care of me and the car, and I'll pay you guys, whatever it costs. You have no idea how mortified I am. Well, maybe you do, I don't know. Anyway, I hope we can somehow be . . . friends."

"Friends," he said, his voice dull.

I wanted him to hold my hand, just like he'd done in this spot a little over a month ago. I wished I had the guts to tell him I didn't want to be anywhere else but with him, right here, right now. I'd been so brave that night.

I cleared my throat and looked out over the fields. The sun was transforming them into warm tangerine rivers that rippled and splashed in the breeze. I could imagine Monet painting them, getting the quality of light just perfect, like his bales of hay.

"Yeah," I said. "I'd really like that. I'm leaving in a couple weeks, and I don't want to go with everything being . . . weird."

He turned around and started to walk toward the truck, but I noticed the slight limp, the way he favored his left side.

"Josh?"

"Yeah," he said, not looking back. "Friends. Cool."

His voice was this frozen, robotic thing, and I was so tired of wanting things I couldn't have. I didn't realize I was crying until I felt a tear drop off my chin and then a sob broke out of me, and I slapped my hands over my mouth to keep everything in, but this avalanche of emotion was straining against my fingers, trying to get out.

Josh stopped, his shoulders tense. Then he turned around, his face stony, but his eyes . . . *his eyes.*

"What do you want me to say?"

"Anything!" I was shouting, but I didn't care. "Cool?" I said, mimicking him. "I mean . . . what . . . why can't you . . ."

I trailed off and just stood there, watching him watch me. Wondering what he thought of me, now that he'd seen me at my very worst. Wondering what *I* thought of me.

Josh walked up to me, every step pushing me farther away from the girl I'd been at the beginning of the summer and closer to this present, unknown Skylar. He put his hands on my shoulders, and I leaned into that sudden, unexpected touch.

"I fucked up," he said. "So bad. And I don't know how else to say I'm sorry." He let his hands drop. "But I don't want to be your friend, Sky."

I blinked. How many times was I going to read this guy totally wrong? Marge had led me to believe that he felt everything I did. That he . . .

It didn't matter. I'd be leaving soon. I was trying to be forgiving, nice, or . . . but I had Dylan and Chris, and who cared, so whatever. We didn't need to be friends.

"Fine," I said. "Great. Have a nice life."

I started to walk past him, but he grabbed my arm and turned me around. "You can be really stupid sometimes, you know that?"

I shook him off. "What the hell's that supposed to mean?"

"I'm fucking crazy about you!"

I stood there, not breathing, not even thinking, really. I just let those words wash over all those cut-up, bruised places inside me.

"But—"

"That night in your room. I left because . . . because I didn't know how to do . . . to do any of that stuff. I mean, the way I am now. And I didn't want you to think—it's like how could you possibly want—"

"Josh, you lost your leg, not your—"

I stopped, blushing all the way to the tips of my ears. Josh looked at me for a second, then threw back his head and laughed. Then he wrapped his arms around me and pulled me close to him.

"You're amazing, you know that?" he murmured.

I shook my head, scared to say anything. It was too easy to tip the balance between us. I didn't know why I hadn't realized it before: he'd left because he thought I wouldn't want him. That *I* would change my mind. Of course that was why he'd freaked out. And even though I had so much to be angry with him about, all I could concentrate on was the fact that I was in his arms.

I breathed him in. God, he smelled good. Whatever combination of things made a man smell like a man.

"I'm such an idiot," I said. "I should have known that's why you—"

"You're not an idiot. How could you know? I didn't say anything and . . ." I felt his heart start beating faster. "What happened . . . after. That wasn't me. I mean, it *was* me, but I just felt so . . . I wasn't there, Sky."

He pulled away and looked down at me. "I can't even explain why I let her get in the truck. It was like . . . like I was watching myself. But I couldn't do anything. And I was drunk, and—it had nothing to do with you."

"But that's the problem, Josh." I stepped away from him and scratched at the tears on my cheeks. "I mean, not to be graphic or whatever, but that should have been *us*. I know I don't have, like, any experience, but I wanted to . . . to do everything with you and then you went off with her and it felt like . . . it made me feel worthless. It made me stop trusting myself."

He looked down for a minute, and it was as if there was this huge mountain between us, and I hated that after everything we'd been through this summer, we'd have to admit that it was impossible. *We* were impossible.

"One chance. That's all I want," he said.

I shook my head. "I'm just freaked that if I say, okay, yes, I forgive you, that the war and everything will be like this Get Out of Jail Free card, like you can just wave it around and say you were having a bad day or—"

"I won't."

He stepped closer to me, his eyes full of a hopeful kind of terror. I could feel the weight of that terror, pressing against me. I gazed out at the empty field behind the tracks. Despite the heat, the constant drought, and the unforgiving earth, things were growing. From seeds to stalks of corn taller than me, they pushed through the earth and survived. I decided that if I came from a place where miracles like that occurred on a daily basis, then why couldn't they happen to me?

"If you ever do this to me again, Josh, I'm gone. Like really, really gone."

He nodded and held out a callused hand. "I know. But I won't. I swear to God, I won't."

I was like a painter standing in front of a canvas, paint dripping off the brush, knowing that whatever I put on it, I wouldn't be able to take back. I had to be ready.

I pushed his hand away.

Then I leaned across the space between us and pressed my lips against his. He gasped a little, surprised, but then his hands were in my hair and his lips were all over me—my cheeks, my nose, my neck, my ears, back to my lips, my eyes, and—very gently—my bruised forehead. I wrapped my arms around his neck, and he half lifted me off the ground, and we were laughing, and crying, and kissing.

He tasted like hope and healing. He tasted like the future.

chapter
thirty-one

The first stars were coming out when we left the train tracks. Josh leaned me up against his truck, and these kisses were soft and gentle. Like we had all the time in the world. Then he pulled away a little and took a closer look at my forehead.

"How's the head?"

I shrugged. "It'll be okay."

"You scared the shit out of me last night," he said.

"I know." I still hadn't had time to process the whole thing yet. I couldn't believe I'd gotten into a car drunk off my ass. I couldn't believe I'd been *drunk off my ass.* "God, Josh. It's like I was possessed or something."

I understood now what Josh had said about the night he left me, how he'd felt like he'd been watching himself but couldn't do anything.

He looked down at me. "What happened?"

"I just felt . . . I don't know. Chris left, and my mom's leaving, so I guess I can go to school, but I wasn't happy about that. I was all mixed up, and the bottle was there, and I just thought,

Screw it. Everyone else gets to drown their sorrows. And then you called, and . . . and I realized *why* I felt so crappy in the first place. Why I wasn't happy about going." His eyes got sad, and I kissed him. "But I'm okay now. And I'm never drinking again. I mean it this time."

"Yeah, I'm gonna go ahead and support that decision," he said. "Especially because I'm not exactly stoked about you going to San Fran and having some other dude help you in the middle of the night."

"Jealous already?" I teased. But just the mention of San Francisco threw me back into orbit. The very last thing I wanted to do was leave Josh now that we had finally gotten together.

"Maybe a little." He looked down. "A lot?"

"I'll just make sure to tell them about a certain Marine I know."

"You'd better."

My stomach growled, and we laughed.

"You want to get some dinner?" he asked.

"I guess it'd be a bad idea to pass out on you again." I traced his jaw because I wanted to, and now I could. "How 'bout I go to the Paradise and take a shower and then you come over whenever you're ready, and we'll get some food and . . . just . . . I don't know. Be together."

"I like your plan."

It took another ten minutes for us to get to our separate vehicles, so by the time I got back to the Paradise with Marge's car, it was dark.

Marge was sitting by the pool when I came in. She looked up at me, eyebrows arched. I couldn't keep the smile off my face.

"I'm guessing it went well?"

I nodded. "Yeah." I crossed the patio and gave her a hug. "Thanks," I whispered.

"Well, I love both of you to death, you know that, sweet pea." She patted me on the back, and I broke away.

I was halfway to my room when I turned back around. "Marge?"

"Uh-huh?"

"It's gonna be hard. I mean, he's . . . we'll need help sometimes. I think."

She nodded. "You know where I am."

I went into my room, leaning against the door after I shut it. I was still sore from the accident, hungover, and tired. This was the happiest I'd been in forever. I opened the little drawer beside the bed and put away the box I'd purchased at Market on my way home. Just in case. I blushed, seeing it there on top of the Gideons Bible that was in all the rooms.

I could almost hear Chris shouting all the way from Boston: *The pact! The pact!*

———

Dylan was pissed about all of it. I knew this was the first of many lectures I'd be hearing from her.

"I know," I said on the phone, for the hundredth time. She'd been on me about drunk driving for the past forty-five minutes, and because I'd lost my cell phone in a ditch, I was stuck next to the night table with the room phone.

"It's just . . . you could have died. Like, *died*."

"Dyl—I know, okay?" I deserved every word of this, but Josh was going to be there any minute.

"And you're getting back with Josh? Just like that?" I heard the snap on her end of the line.

"We were never together in the first place," I pointed out.

"The whole Jenna Swenson thing was, what, an accident? Like her mouth just fell on his—"

"Look, it's not like I'm okay with it. But I have to give him the, I don't know, the benefit of the doubt on this."

I thought of what Marge had said in the orchard, about going with my gut.

"So you're just gonna go to San Fran and hope he doesn't turn back to his usual horn-dog ways while you're busting your ass at school."

There was only one explanation I could give. And giving it was like jumping off a building with my eyes wide open. I took a breath. Jumped.

"I love him."

There was a long pause on the other end of the line. A very long pause.

"All right," she finally said. "But I'm warning you right now that the next time I see him, Josh Mitchell and I are having some words."

I didn't envy him that conversation, but he deserved it, and I was thankful to have someone like Dylan in my corner.

"Fair enough."

"And I'm gonna be your eyes and ears while you're gone. You have to promise me that if he messes around on you again, that's it. I don't care what shit went down in the war—that doesn't give Josh an excuse to ruin your life."

I nodded, even though she couldn't see me. "My thoughts exactly."

"Okay," she said.

"Thanks, Dyl."

"Yeah, well, just be careful, okay? It's not like I can go to Walmart and buy a new Skylar if this one breaks."

"I know."

"And you're the one who has to tell Chris about all this craziness. I, for one, don't need him yelling in my ear for an hour. So have fun with that."

I groaned. "I never thought I'd say this, but I'm sort of glad he's in Boston at the moment."

"Uh-huh. Gotta go, Sean's getting antsy. Let's drive to Bakersfield tomorrow and get some civilization, aka fancy coffee drinks."

"Sounds good."

"I love you, Sky. Even if you're *totally insane* for getting with Josh."

I laughed. "Love you too."

I lay down on the bed and closed my eyes. I still had to get dressed, but I just needed a minute to settle down after my conversation with Dylan. She'd gone all mama bear on me, and I was tired after so much explaining and apologizing. My body sank into the mattress, and I was asleep in seconds.

It took me a while to realize that the knocking on the door wasn't part of my dream. I opened my eyes. Another knock.

"Shit."

I swung my legs over the bed and stumbled to the door. When I opened it, Josh was standing in the doorway, holding a tray with drinks and a bag from McDonald's. He'd shaved and smelled all kinds of good. I was wearing a ratty old pair of cotton shorts and my gym shirt from our high school, but at least I'd managed to shower.

"I fell asleep," I said. It was a greeting and apology in one.

"I figured. I tried calling the room, but there was no answer. I hope this is okay."

I grabbed the drink tray and set it on the table, suddenly shy. "It's perfect."

He stepped inside, both of us, I think, keenly aware that this room did not hold good memories.

"We can eat by the pool if you want," Josh said.

He put the food down and let the messenger bag he'd brought with him slip to the floor, never taking his eyes off me.

"Or . . . I brought my laptop and some DVDs. We could just hang out and—or we could go, I don't know, wherever you want."

"Because there's so much to do in Creek View," I said.

"True." He stuck his hands in his back pockets. "Your call."

"Let's stay here," I said.

He swallowed. "Okay. Cool."

I pulled my hair into a messy bun, then reached across him and shut the door. "I think it's like taking off a Band-Aid," I said.

"What is?"

"Us. In this room. We just have to . . ."

"Rip it off?"

I nodded.

"Right. Yeah." He took a step toward me, then said, "Close your eyes."

I closed them. It was like Christmas morning, but way, way better.

I felt his lips on my neck, then his hands on either side of my waist, his thumbs grazing the skin under my shirt. My eyes still closed, I slid my hands up his arms until they were around his neck, then his lips finally reached mine, our mouths opening, his hand slipping up the back of my shirt, fingertips trailing along my spine. I pressed myself closer to him and felt him react to that, which made me smile.

"Busted," he whispered.

"Uh-huh." I leaned back and smirked a little. "I think the Band-Aid is ripped off."

He cleared his throat. "Yeah. I think we, uh . . . yeah."

"Dinner?"

He leaned in and kissed me, just once. Then he sighed and nodded. "Yeah, guess we better eat before it gets cold."

He set up the laptop while I got the food together, then he held up a DVD case. "I brought a few others, but this reminded me of the summer before I left."

Top Gun. Of course.

"Good choice. Bed or table?" I asked, gesturing at the food.

"Bed," he said immediately.

I laughed. It was exactly what I would have expected Josh Mitchell to say, but after our first failed attempt at this, I wasn't sure of anything.

We talked a little, me filling him in on Mom, him telling me about a new dog they'd gotten at the military hospital in San Diego. I sat on the side of the bed closest to the door, so I'd be on Josh's right side. I'd never been as aware of his prosthesis as I was now, with maybe the first couple of times I saw him as the only exceptions. For a lot of the summer, I'd pretty much forgotten about it. I wondered if he could sense it. He walked around to the other side of the bed and sat down, kicking off the tennis shoe on his good leg.

Josh sighed when he leaned back on the pillows. "I can see why you passed out," he said. "How much sleep did you get last night? Er, this morning."

"I have no idea. And Marge was waking me up every two hours because of all the concussion stuff."

"You know, I had a pretty bad head injury after the bomb. They call it TBI—tramautic brain injury. Lot of guys have it. You gotta be careful with that, Sky." He squeezed my hand. "Like, don't go jumping on people's backs."

I smiled. "The CAT scan was fine, I'm not worried. And I feel way better—no headache or anything. What about you? Any sleep after last night?"

"Four hours? I don't know. I crashed after I got back from the shop—no pun intended."

I rolled my eyes. "Wanna bet on who falls asleep during the movie first?"

"Five bucks says it's you."

"You're on." I pointed to the bedside table, where our drinks were. "Now, hand me the caffeine."

chapter
thirty-two

Josh won the bet.

Even though snuggling up to him after we were done eating was making my heart race, I still managed to fall asleep by the time Goose's wife came to visit. The room was almost completely dark, except for the light seeping in from the patio and the glare of the computer screen. The darkness, Josh's warmth, and the sounds of my favorite movie all conspired to lull me into a light, dreamy sleep.

"Sky." Josh's voice, soft and low in my ear.

"*Hmm?*"

"You owe me five dollars."

I opened my eyes. "Damn. Did you fall asleep at all?"

"Yeah, but you were out first." He brushed my lips with his, which took away every bit of tiredness I felt. "It's, like, two in the morning. I'm gonna let you sleep, okay? I'll see you tomorrow."

I tightened my hold on him. "You can sleep here." Heart beating, palms starting to sweat a little. "If you want."

He leaned toward me and the tips of our noses touched. An Eskimo kiss. "Are you sure?"

I nodded. "Yeah."

"Okay."

He sat up and closed the laptop, put it on the floor next to him, then pulled his shirt over his head. He took off his dog tags and set them on the bedside table. Then we just looked at each other for the longest second in the history of seconds.

"Come here," he whispered.

I reached for him, and he pulled me onto his lap, my knees aligning with his hipbones. I closed my eyes for a second and thought of all the things that had brought us together: a kiss on the cheek, a bomb, my mom leaving the till on the counter at Taco Bell. So random, and yet being here made perfect sense.

"Tell me what you're thinking," he said.

I opened my eyes. "When you use that voice, I feel like I have to salute you."

"That sounds a little kinky."

"My thoughts exactly."

"*Sky.*"

In my name, I heard everything I was feeling inside—the want, the uncertainty, the overriding fear and bone-crushing happiness.

"I love you," I whispered against his lips. "That's what I'm thinking."

"Yeah?" Those eyes, looking at me like I'm medicine.

"Yeah."

This kiss was different from all the others we'd had. It was hungry, and full of heat, but limitless. Like we both finally knew we could have as much as we wanted. I could barely breathe, especially when his hands left my face and found their way up my shirt. I pulled it over my head, and Josh's lips followed the line of my bra until he'd taken it off and thrown it on the floor.

"Now what?" I whispered.

"This is going to get tricky." He cleared his throat. "I'm not really sure how . . ."

I moved my hand behind me and rested it on his prosthesis. "Maybe we should start here."

Something like panic crossed his face, and I pressed my cheek against his and whispered in his ear. "We can stop, if you want."

He shook his head and slid his hands down my arms. "I don't want to."

I smiled, and he reached up to pull the rubber band from my hair so that it fell in waves around my shoulders.

"I've been wanting to do that all night." He slid his fingers through my hair. "Beautiful."

I slipped off his lap and stood up, pulling him with me. Then I reached for his belt buckle, hesitating for a second, remembering how he'd pushed me away. He tilted my chin up.

"I'm not going anywhere," he said. His voice was just above a whisper, rough and low.

I'd never taken someone else's pants off before, so I was clumsy and he had to help me, which made us laugh.

"If we end up crashing onto the bed, just pretend it's really romantic," he said, kicking them off his good leg.

"I don't have to pretend."

He reached down and pushed a button on his prosthesis, releasing the airtight cylinder around his stump. "Mind if I use you for balance?" he asked.

"It'll cost you."

He grinned. "Hope so."

He held on to my shoulder as he took it off and then leaned it against the wall, balancing on his right leg. He gave me another uncertain look, and I kissed his hand where it still rested on my shoulder. He sighed and let go of me and sat on the bed as he rolled what looked like a few big socks off of his stump. It was thinner than I'd expected—he was so muscular and thick everywhere else. The stump itself was rounded off, like it'd been sculpted, and in the morning I would see how the skin at the bottom was scarred and red. But it was a part of him, a part of this guy I'd known all my life who had managed to make me fall in love with him in a matter of weeks.

He ran his hand over the stump, then he looked up at me, his face resigned, like he expected me to be horrified.

"You're not freaking out."

I shook my head. "I only freak out when you ditch me."

He looked like he wanted to say more, but whatever he'd intended to say died on his lips the moment I stepped out of my shorts. He moved to the edge of the bed and pressed his lips against my stomach, set his hands on my waist. I ran my hands through his hair, down to the *Semper Fidelis* tattoo between his shoulder blades. His fingers slipped below the elastic on my underwear, and I became this fluttering thing, so light I thought he'd have to keep holding on to me so that I didn't float right out of the room. His eyes stayed on mine as he pulled down my underwear, and I think I started shaking because he took my hands and kissed them and asked if we should stop, and I just shook my head and let him pull me down onto the bed so that we were on our sides, facing each other.

I put my hand on his thigh, and he tensed for just a second. Then he wrapped his arms around me and closed his eyes, holding on tighter as my fingers slid down his stump. It was strange, seeing it, touching it. But now that I knew what had happened and how he could have been the one who died instead of Nick, all I could feel was grateful. That he was alive. That he came home. That we had found each other.

"Does it hurt?" I asked.

He shook his head, his eyes still closed.

"Hey. Look at me."

He looked.

"The Josh I grew up around, with two legs and an ego that couldn't fit through the door? I didn't love him. I didn't even always *like* him." One corner of his mouth turned up. "This is who you are. The real you." I rested my forehead against his. "And I want you so fucking bad."

"Wow." He leaned back a little. "You sure you've never done this before?"

"Shut up."

Then it was just breath and touching and his eyes never leaving mine and his voice whispering beautiful things I never would have believed a Mitchell could say. We laughed as we tried to figure out how to do this together.

"A one-legged Marine and a virgin walk into a bar," Josh whispered.

"You are *not* telling jokes about this," I said, laughing into his shoulder.

There was some pain, which Dylan had told me would happen. It really wasn't so bad—it beat driving into a ditch, anyway. Josh asked me if I was okay about ten times.

"I'm fine—now stop asking me. That's an order." I tried to look stern, and he cracked up.

"Yes, ma'am."

Then there was that floating feeling again, only way more intense, and Josh's Van Gogh eyes on me the whole time, and I knew I'd never be able to collage this, not in a million years.

I didn't know there were so many ways to say *I love you*.

The best part was falling asleep in his arms and knowing he'd be there when I woke up. For the first time in Creek View, I felt like I was home.

JOSH

Last night with Sky was like my first firefight, when I didn't know shit and I thought, *That's it, I'm dead, I'm fucking dead,* but then when the shooting stopped and I realized it was over and I was alive and had all my body parts, it was the greatest feeling in the world. I wanted it again and again. I wanted it to never stop. Man, I'm turning into such a pussy, aren't I? I just didn't know it could be like that. You were always trying to tell me that I was missing out on the real thing, but I just thought you were whipped. Now I know. Last night was the first night since you died that I didn't have a nightmare. No waking up, looking for my rifle. No boy with the soccer ball. No visions of you staring down at me, with blood all over you. Just long, deep sleep, the feel of her warm body in my arms, the sound of her breath as she lay on my chest. Truth is, I scared myself yesterday—scared her too. Don't know why I felt like I had to jump that train. I just needed something, a rush or—life and death. That's what I needed. Life and death, standing right next to each other. That's what it was over there for us, right? It made everything matter, even though it sucked balls. Taking a piss was even important. Like that time I went to the outhouse and one of those fuckers sent a mortar over the wall and after I realized I wasn't dead, I just lay down on the ground laughing. But I can't do that anymore—laugh at death or beg it to let us switch places. I need to figure out why I got to live. I don't know who made that IED, who buried it in the ground so I'd step on it. I'll never know. I used to think it was his fault you died, whoever put that thing under the dirt, but more and more I wonder if it's just a circle, where everyone's guilty, everyone has blood on their hands. End of the day, it just feels wrong that the world is happening and you're not in it. Feels wrong that we're not out there together right now, talking about our girls, playing chess. Feels wrong that I might not have gotten Skylar if none of this had happened. Like I had to trade you for her. I'm scared shitless, man. Because if I'm really gonna do this, really live my life, I've gotta leave you behind. I can hear your voice right now, even though you're not here. I know exactly what you'd say: *Good luck. Shoot straight. Don't get dead.*

chapter
thirty-three

The composer Stephen Sondheim said, "Art, in itself, is an attempt to bring order out of chaos." As I ran my hand over the finished collage, I decided that he was right. The mess of my life, of Creek View, of the summer, had been transformed into something beautiful.

Marge's collage wasn't just a bunch of cut-up photographs I'd arranged on poster boards. Somehow, between the night of the Mitchells' party and the moment I saw Josh's leg—*really* saw it—the collage had turned into a love letter to Creek View. Inexplicably, through the act of photographing, cutting, arranging, and gluing, I'd begun to see my hometown as a place of possibility. Of desire. Of different and unexpected kinds of love. It was as if by really looking at the world around me, I could finally see myself.

I felt like God. I wanted to say, "It is good."

The highway: it was where Dad had died, but it would also take me away from here so that I could follow my dreams.

The Paradise: the sign itself was an uncut photograph so that it looked like a beacon within the explosion of photo shards. It was whole, the heart of everything.

The strawberry fields and the trailer park, Chris's house and the creek.

The train tracks and the field where we'd lit firecrackers on the Fourth.

Market and the old gas station, which always went together in my mind after that night when I was hungry and I waited for the sunrise in the back of Josh's truck.

The orchard where Marge told me about her son, the endless sky, and the sun blazing like fire.

I smiled as I sifted through eighteen years' worth of memories. True, there were a lot of bad ones. But I was starting to realize that they had all brought me to this moment, as if my sorrows and joys had conspired to birth me.

"That's badass, Sky," Dylan said. She was looking over my shoulder while she bounced Sean on her hip.

"Thanks. I hope she likes it."

"She's gonna love the shit out of it." Sean reached out, but she pulled him away. "Don't drool on Auntie Sky's art."

"Can you grab one side, and I'll get the other?" I asked.

Dylan nodded, and we maneuvered all four feet of it out of my room and across the patio and into the lobby. Marge was sitting at reception, waiting for Amy to come in and take the graveyard shift.

"Is that what I think it is?" she asked, looking up. She had a stack of new tabloids sitting next to her and a can of Diet Dr Pepper, with one of her colorful straws poking out of the top.

"A decoration for the lobby," I said.

We held it up so Marge could see it from a distance. It took her a second to figure out what it was, but when she did, she covered her mouth and her eyes filled.

"Sky. It's . . . wow."

I blushed, and Dylan helped me set it on the table.

Marge stood up, and I wrapped my arms around her. "I wanted to say thank you, and this was the only way I knew how," I whispered. "I don't know what I would have done without you, Marge. I really mean that."

She gave me one of her bear hugs while big, fat tears soaked my shirt.

"Right back at you." She sniffed and hugged me even tighter. "I'm gonna miss the hell out of you, sweet pea."

"You too," I said. I pulled back. "But I'll be visiting all the time."

"Don't get your hopes up, Marge. You know she'll be off somewhere with Josh. We'll be lucky to eat a meal with her," Dylan said.

Marge laughed. "Don't I know it."

"Whatever."

I rolled my eyes, but I knew she was right. Two weeks together, and already Josh and I were saying words that, not long ago, would have freaked me out: words like *always*. My life was being planned in sentences that started with *we* instead of *I*, yet it felt like the most natural transition in the world.

A dog barked outside, and Sean squealed.

"I'm gonna check his water," I said. "Be right back."

I ran out to the side of the motel, where I'd chained the present I'd gotten for Josh early that morning. He looked exactly like the bomb dog Josh had described his unit having in Afghanistan—a black Labrador retriever.

"Hey, boy," I said.

He jumped up and barked again, tail wagging. I checked his water and scratched him behind the ears, and he licked my cheek.

Perfect. He was exactly what Josh needed.

I heard Josh's truck roar up the driveway, and I took the Lab off the chain and held on to his leash. He was strong, practically dragging me toward the sound of the truck. Josh parked next to my car, and I waited for him to get out. His radio was crazy loud, as usual. Audioslave pounded out his open windows, and he was singing along, totally oblivious. I felt like I was seeing what he was like when he was in Afghanistan with his buddies. It made me sad that he wouldn't see most of them ever again and that it would take years for me to piece together a picture of what the war had been like. But we had time.

He caught me watching, and I laughed at his pretend grimace.

"Don't quit your day job," I shouted. He did some air guitar, thrashing his head around, and I laughed. God, I was going to miss him.

He turned off the truck, and the Lab barked, like he somehow already knew he and Josh belonged together. Josh leaned across the cab and looked down.

"What have you got there?" he asked.

"Come find out."

I waited to let go of the leash until Josh came around the truck.

"Go get him," I whispered to the Lab. He bounded up to Josh, tail going nuts. Josh's face broke open with this wide grin I hadn't seen since before he deployed, and he knelt and let the

Lab sniff him and lick his fingers. He was laughing and letting the dog jump all over him—it was the happiest I'd ever seen Josh.

"He likes you," I said.

Josh looked up at me. "Did I tell you about Buddy—the bomb dog my unit had?"

I nodded. "Uh-huh."

"Looks just like him." He ran his hands down the Lab's flanks, talking quietly to him.

"Did one of the guests bring him?" he asked.

"Nope." I walked over to him and put the leash in his hand. "I thought you might need some company while I'm gone this semester."

He looked at me, confusion turning to sudden understanding. "You're serious."

"As a heart attack," I said, using my favorite Marge-ism. I couldn't control the goofy smile on my face. "I remembered what you said—about Buddy and the therapy dogs. I didn't expect to find a black Lab when I went to the shelter in Bakersfield, but he was there, looking up at me like, *Can we go home already?*"

Josh gazed down at his dog, then at me. "Unbelievable," he said. "You know that? You're fucking unbelievable."

Then he was kissing me, and the dog was barking, and Dylan was catcalling, and it was so great and so awful at the same time because I didn't want to leave him or Dylan or Marge or Mom or this dog who had already wormed his way into my heart.

I checked the time on the new cell phone I'd gotten to replace the one that had been destroyed in the ditch. "I better go," I said. "See you tonight?"

He brushed my lips with his. "Can't wait."

We hardly spent any time apart, nights included. I blushed at the thought of what those two words—*can't wait*—promised.

Josh wrapped his arms around me in a quick hug. "You gonna be okay over there?"

I nodded. "Yeah. Mom said Billy would be out all day, so I think it'll be good."

"Okay." He looked like he was going to kiss me again, but pulled away when we heard Dylan's voice.

"*Hello!* Some of us want to see her before she goes," she said.

Josh sighed. "Fine, but I get her back by seven."

"Eight," Dylan said, a hand on her hip.

"Seven thirty."

"Fucking jarhead." She gave him a grudging smile. "Fine. Seven thirty. But only because it's my little man's bedtime."

She whirled around and went back into the Paradise with Marge laughing behind her. This was the nature of Dylan and Josh's relationship—aggressive joking around. It took her a few days to look at the whole Jenna Swenson thing in the way I'd decided to look at it, but I think it made her feel better to inform him that if he ever pulled, and I quote, any shit like that again, Dylan would personally castrate him with a rusted butcher knife.

"I'm going to pretend that I wasn't just auctioned off like a cow," I said to Josh once Dylan and Marge were back inside.

"It's more like child custody than an auction," he said.

"And now you've reduced me to a six-year-old. Sexy."

He kissed my mock frown, the kind of kiss that made me really disappointed when he pulled away. "Bet you're glad I got that extra half hour now, huh? Just think of the possibilities."

I shoved his shoulder. "Dumbass."

"I love you," he said, somehow playful and serious at the same time.

This could be my life, I thought. Wake up next to Josh, do my own thing, know I'll see him later, then fall asleep and do it all over again the next day.

I kissed him—otherwise I'd tell him to start unpacking the car because I wasn't going after all. He'd insisted on driving me to San Francisco, even though we both knew it'd be harder to say good-bye once we got there. It would be so easy . . .

The Lab whined and butted his head against us, and I pulled away. It felt like we were already saying good-bye.

"Go play with your dog."

Josh gave me a little salute. "Yes, ma'am."

When I turned around, he slapped my ass, then laughed at my pretend scowl and pointed at himself with an innocent shrug. "Jarhead. What did you expect?"

I rolled my eyes and left him to do whatever stuff Marge needed before we left for San Francisco in the morning.

When I went back inside, Marge was back at the desk and I could hear Dylan at the end of the hall, changing Sean's diaper in the bathroom.

Marge gave me a long look. "You did it, you know."

"What?"

"The right thing."

I looked out the window, at Josh wrestling with the dog. It was horrible, just imagining what I'd be feeling right now if I hadn't gone looking for Josh at the train tracks. No matter what hell we'd have to go through in the future with everything life would throw at us, it was worth it. I knew it was.

"Yeah," I said. "I guess I did."

I put my arm around her shoulder. "I know Josh will never be . . . I mean, no one can replace your son. But you're family to him. And to me. I hope you know that, Marge."

She held on to my hand and nodded. "I do, sweet pea."

Together, we looked at the collage lying on the table. Josh would put it up for her later that day, I was sure, and then there'd always be a little part of me at the Paradise. It was bittersweet, the idea of the collage being there when I wasn't. I was finally putting down roots, just when I was getting ready to leave.

JOSH

It's been almost a year since we walked onto that field. But I won't let that be my last memory of you. Instead, this is what I see: It's the first real day of spring and we're patrolling on foot and the mountains surround us, giant and snowcapped, and you turn around in a circle with this huge fuckin' smile on your face and you shout, *Look at this beautiful world!* And then I take the picture that's sitting on my desk right now. That's what I'm gonna think of from now on, every day, when I see that smile on your face. *Look at this beautiful world.*

Ma'a salama, brother. See you on the other side.

chapter
thirty-four

Dylan dropped me off at the trailer, after making me promise I'd come to her house for some ice cream and, as she put it, "lady time" before I went back to the Paradise. The car my mom and I shared was in the driveway, newly fixed by Blake and Josh. She was using it until she left, and then Josh was going to drive it up for me if I wanted it at school.

For a minute, I just stood outside, staring at the faded paint and the dry grass. I'd spent my entire life in that trailer, with the exception of the last month at the Paradise, but I knew my separation was complete when I realized that I was a visitor now and would probably be one wherever my mom lived, for the rest of my life. I tried to imagine another family moving in. It hurt.

I remembered sitting on the front steps with my dad, looking at the stars, or running through the sprinklers with Dylan and Chris from June to October. I'd had my first kiss in front of the rusted barbecue—Aaron Fisher, eighth grade. I smiled, thinking about the pumpkins my mom and I used to carve and then line up in a row leading to our door on Halloween or the Christmas lights

Dad would string up. I thought of all the summer evenings I'd spent sitting in the chairs under the trees beside the trailer, reading books that helped me escape Creek View, at least for a little while. Magical kingdoms, Russian love triangles, and the March sisters couldn't have been further away from the trailer park.

I heard the clank of pots inside—the kitchen window was open, and Mom must have been washing dishes. I walked up the stairs and, for the first time in my life, knocked on the door. I heard her turn down the TV and then the door was open.

My mom beamed. "Sky!"

She wrapped me in a hug, still smelling like her apple-scented shampoo. I breathed her in, missing her even though my arms were around her. She sat me down at the kitchen table and fluttered about—was I thirsty? Hungry?

While Mom got me a glass of water, I looked around. She'd cleaned. I could smell the Windex and Pine-Sol, but I wasn't sure if it was just for my benefit or if she and Billy were actually capable of playing house together. Even though nearly everything was boxed up, there were a few things that announced Billy's presence—a leather La-Z-Boy, man-sized work boots by the door, a toolbox.

Seeing Billy's things in the house, as if they belonged there—and I supposed they did, now—made it seem like Dad was finally and truly gone. It was another change the summer had brought to my life, a gradual letting go of the need to remember him all the time, to strain for his presence. I didn't know if that was Josh or just growing up.

Mom seemed to know what I was thinking. "You know, I still love your dad," she said.

I nodded. "Yeah, I know." I thought about the thrill I got

from seeing Josh's clothes strung about my room or his tooth-brush standing in the plastic cup by my sink, leaning against mine. I wondered if Mom felt that way about Billy.

"Are you happy?" I asked.

She made little circles with her finger on the tabletop, a soft smile playing on her face.

"I am." She reached out and grabbed my hand. "I know I put you through hell, and I'm real sorry about that. I never wanted things to be . . . the way they got."

I held her hand in both of my own. "I know."

Mom laughed her smoker's laugh. "Seems like you've got yourself a boyfriend too." She pointed to my neck. "Those his dog tags?"

I fingered the thin metal chain under my shirt and nodded. He'd given them to me the night before, placing them over my neck. Other than Nick's chess set and Vonnegut book I was pretty sure they were Josh's most prized possession.

"Hon," she continued, "if you don't mind me asking . . . isn't it sort of hard being with a guy like that?"

I tried not to bristle at the "like that"—it sucked how every-one wanted to give Josh labels instead of just accepting him as he was.

"No," I said. "He's just . . . Josh. You know?"

I wasn't being entirely honest, but I had begun to guard Josh's privacy even more than my own. I wasn't going to tell her about the nightmares he still sometimes got—although he told me he'd been having them a lot less since we got together. And I didn't want to get into how I'd had to find ways to adjust to the days when he just needed to be alone or how he'd get depressed or really pissed off about his leg or something that reminded him of Nick. Sometimes I felt like I had to walk on eggshells around him, but usually I just tried to be real and blunt and loving. That worked most of the time. He did the same for me.

Mom gave me a long look. "He's the real deal for you, huh?"

"Oh, yeah."

She nodded, her eyes softening. "I felt that way about your dad. It's a good sign."

For the next few hours we talked, pulling out our memories like forgotten photo albums. It felt good to be with her and to see her sober and herself again. The blank look was gone from her face, and her eyes were clear and alive. It was more than I'd hoped for, and whatever I thought about Billy, I was thankful he seemed to be taking care of her. It was hard to admit, but I was happier now than I'd been in a long time. Years. I hadn't realized just how much I'd taken on with my mom until I backed away. It felt good to worry about myself for once.

The sun went down, and the shadows began to yawn and stretch across the thin carpet. My last night in Creek View had begun. I couldn't eat much of the dinner Mom tried to give me—I was too wound up about everything. I remembered Chris being like that on his last night too. I'd been frustrated that he was so distracted, but now I understood. It was a lot to process. Getting what you've always wanted, after wanting it for so long that the wanting was imprinted on your very being—it was too much.

By the time I got back to the Paradise, my eyes were puffy and red from saying good-bye to my mom and Dylan. I was exhausted, but anxious to see Josh and milk as much time as I could out of the hours that remained for us. I walked in through the back gate and was halfway to my room when I saw him standing on top of the flat roof that covered the bank of guest rooms. His back was to me, and he was looking over the orchard, his arms crossed, toward the mountains that towered over the valley. It was still a little light outside, the sky a purplish gray, but there was already a sliver of moon and a handful of stars. A warm breeze made music out of the leaves in the orchard and—so faint I almost thought I'd imagined it—a train whistle blew.

I walked to the ladder Josh had propped up against the building and climbed it slowly, one hand over the other. The wind muffled my ascent so that when I got to the top, he still hadn't turned around. For a moment I just stood there, watching him. It was easy to imagine he was a general surveying a conquered land. Back straight, legs spread slightly apart, he looked down on the flat fields, the winding creek, and over the highway that was an endless black river slicing through all of it. The red and white lights from the cars sparkled in a friendly sort of way, giving us conspiratorial winks as they passed by. He stood over it all, watching. Waiting.

I walked over and slipped my arms around him so that my hands rested on his chest, my head between his shoulder blades. I felt his heartbeat in the palm of my hand, strong and steady. He put his hands over mine and we stood there for a long time, gazing out at the land that had tried—and failed—to conquer us.

Up there, I could see how Creek View had finally taken its proper place within the geography of us. It wasn't quicksand or an insurmountable mountain, and it wasn't Afghanistan, with its poppy fields and bombs. It was just a place—a part of me, a part of Josh, yes, but not big enough to define us. Not small enough to forget about. Together, it would be easy to map out new territory.

A little bit closer to the stars, anything seemed possible.

Author's Note

By the end of April 2014, there were over two thousand U.S. military deaths in Afghanistan and nearly twenty thousand service members were wounded in action.[1] In 2012 alone, there were more suicides in the military than deaths in combat, and most of those suicides were young men between eighteen and twenty-four years old.[2] As of writing this, more than half of the 2.6 million veterans of the wars in Afghanistan and Iraq struggle with physical or mental health problems related to their service.[3] The VA continues to be underfunded, and many veterans fail to receive the quality care they need.

Though I've borrowed from many, many sources, Josh is, first and foremost, a creation of my own. However, despite being a fictional character, the challenges he faces are very real, as were the experiences he recounts as a Marine in Afghanistan. Any mistakes I've made here regarding the military or the war in Afghanistan are mine alone.

For further research, I recommend the following: David Finkel's excellent books *The Good Soldiers* and *Thank You for Your Service* should be required reading for, well, everyone. I

---

1   U.S. Department of Defense
2   NPR.org
3   *Washington Post*/Kaiser Family Foundation

also recommend *Outside the Wire: American Soldiers' Voices from Afghanistan*, edited by Christine Dumaine Leche, which is a collection of essays written by soldiers during their combat tours. I am deeply indebted to everyone who participated in and worked on the absolutely phenomenal NPR series about the "Darkhorse" Marine battalion—in fact, all of NPR's journalism regarding wounded warriors, veterans' issues, and the wars in Iraq and Afghanistan is top-notch. You would do well to delve into their archives.

I would be remiss if I didn't mention the other victims of this war: the men, women, and children of Afghanistan. Simply put: theirs isn't the story I'm telling. But it *is* a story I want to hear and a very worthy one—a necessary one. Trent Reedy's critically acclaimed YA novel, *Words in the Dust*, is a good place to start. Learn more about his incredible experiences as a soldier in Afghanistan that inspired the novel, as well as the work he is doing on behalf of women and children there, at trentreedy.com.

I have done my job here if *I'll Meet You There* helps you, in some way, to not forget the Joshes in your community. Please join me in supporting them by giving to the Wounded Warrior Project (woundedwarriorproject.org). This is a wonderful organization that is doing great work on behalf of men and women like Josh Mitchell and their families. Why do we need to do more than read or write a book? David Finkel says it best in *Thank You for Your Service*: "The truth of war is that it's always about loving the guy next to you, the truth of the after-war is that you're on your own."

Readers: We are the soldiers of the after-war. Fight on.

Acknowledgments

And now for some epic acknowledgments. If this were an Oscar speech, I'd totally be talking over the time-to-shut-up music.

Why did I write this book? And how the hell did I learn to curse so damn well? I come from a military family: both my parents were Marines and I grew up tracing the faded lines of my grandfather's Marine Corps tattoo. Though I never served, I like to think I have a little *oorah* in my blood. While the Army is well represented in my family, I've always been a bit obsessed with the Marines. Their culture is fascinating, and, let's be honest, they have the best uniforms (dress blues win hands down every time—ladies, you know what I'm talking about). You don't have to agree with everything about military culture or the politics/acts of war to appreciate these men and women. I myself struggle with many aspects of what we do and why we do it. But getting to know the Marines and Soldiers who helped with this book and delving deeper into my own family history have opened my eyes to a world I'd shut myself off from for a long time. This is the power of fiction: more than anything, it was Josh Mitchell who made my heart bigger than I thought it could be; as Skylar fell in love with him, so did I. And love changes you, doesn't it?

One of my earliest memories of my father is seeing him off the day he left to fight in the Persian Gulf. We had a yellow ribbon around the tree in our front yard, and near the end of the war I caught him on CNN, sleeping on a bench in Kuwait (true story). That war was quick (for us) and seemed painless. But then my dad came home. He was only thirty-one, but he'd lost most of his hair, his teeth, his weight, and his hearing. He drank too much. Started doing drugs. He was sad. It took a long time for people to figure out what Gulf War Illness and PTSD were. Back then, we didn't know how to talk about that. You were a Marine: you could take it. Right? It took me most of my life to realize that there were war wounds that didn't bleed. I wrote *I'll Meet You There* for my dad and for every wounded warrior I've talked to or read about or heard telling their story. I wrote it because when the Marine Honor Guard played taps at my grandfather's funeral and handed my grandmother an American flag it was sad, and awful, and beautiful. I wrote it because young adults are being recruited for the military while they're still in high school and they need to know what war really is and what it means to serve. I also wrote *I'll Meet You There* for the Skylars of the world, the poor kids who count their pennies and have to grow up faster than they should. To all the Chrises and Skys and Dylans of the world I say this: it gets better. Love is medicine and dreams are oxygen.

So this is the part where I thank people. It took a village to write this book. First, to the Marines and Soldiers who shared their experiences with me: it was an honor to hear your stories and I will be forever changed and humbled by them. Your generosity and openness about your service and such a difficult topic as PTSD is what allowed this book to be what it is. Ryan D. Cooper, USMC: I feel like you and Josh would be buddies. You were with me on this from the word *go*, and I have you to thank the most for helping me get into Josh's head and for knowing everything from how to get blood off of boots to how many guys are in a squad. Seriously, you rock. Big hug to my BFF from elementary school, Kristin Grantis, for putting us in touch. To Cpl. Frederickson D. E. (Ret.) 3rd Force Reconnaissance: it takes a real badass of a Marine to be willing to read a love story and critique it so well. Thank you for "batshit crazy functional" and other choice phrases, as well as for everything you shared with me about your journey. Talking to you helped me understand the challenges of adjusting to civilian life—once a Marine, always a Marine, right? CW2 Thomas Henderson, Instructor Pilot (U.S. Army): thank you for giving me an idea of what it's like for a medevac pilot in Afghanistan and for not being weirded out by my very personal questions. Your descriptions of Afghanistan, the people, and what it was like coming home were gorgeous. Thanks to Timme Jacobs for putting us in touch. Kevin Hanrahan: wow. First, let me tell the world how awesome you are. World, meet Kevin Hanrahan: he was a company commander in Iraq and was the Deputy Provost Marshal for U.S. forces in Afghanistan. While in Afghanistan, he played a huge role in spearheading the increased use of dogs there and lobbied the Army to adopt an innovative and lifesaving explosive-detecting dog program. He has served three combat tours and was awarded two Bronze Stars and an Army Commendation Medal for Valor. This all makes me question my life choices. Kevin, thank you for sharing your passion about military dogs (I'll take them all, please) and your personal story about life once you got home—your continued work on behalf of military dogs and their soldiers is inspiring and SO IMPORTANT.

Now, for my family. My uncle, CW3 Michael J. Edwards (former Marine and currently U.S. Army), for sharing stories of your (three!) deployments to Iraq. My aunt, Wendy Edwards, Army Wife Extraordinaire and civilian who worked for the Marines as a Family Readiness Officer and Readiness and Deployment Trainer: thank you a million times over for answering all my questions about military leave, medical facilities, how IEDs work, and all manner of other random questions. PFC Daniel J. Edwards, my cousin who recently served at Camp Leatherneck in Kandahar Province, Afghanistan: proud of you, cuz. Sgt. Carrie Fry (U.S. Army), for Pashto assistance and sharing stories of your deployment in Afghanistan, and Sgt. Stephen Fry (U.S. Army), for that hilarious reaction to finding out both my parents had been Marines.

This book wouldn't exist at all, or at least not as you've read it, if it weren't for Shari Becker, Leslie Caulfield, and Jennifer Ann Mann. You gals saw Josh before I ever did. You saw my heart and held it up for me and told me I wasn't allowed to look away, even though I was scared as hell. I will be forever grateful. Extra thanks to David Fulk, for early input on the manuscript. To my agent, Brenda Bowen: here we are again. Thank you for your astute reads and for reminding me to stay in the writing cave. My editor, Kate Farrell: thank you for wanting to bring this story into the world and for being so enthusiastic about my work. To everyone at Macmillan/Holt, especially Ksenia Winnicki, Stephanie McKinley, and Samantha Mandel: I'm so glad you have Josh's and Sky's backs. Amy (A.S.) King: you are boss and so were all your notes. Thanks for being a kickass adviser on this, my creative thesis—shots of Jameson for all! I was so happy to have you with me at the finish line for my MFA, reminding me it was okay to ditch the learn'd astronomers of our world from time to time. Rita Williams-Garcia: your wisdom on my first draft was invaluable and set me up for the most satisfying writing journey I've had to date. Amanda (A.M.) Jenkins: giving you a bear hug right now for bringing out the jarhead poet in me like no one could. Patricia Lee Gauch: thank you for telling me to meet my own high standards, for teaching me about ecstatic moments, and for early comments on the manuscript. Kathryn Gaglione: for so much, but especially for getting me in touch with Drew, taking me to Arlington on Memorial Day, and understanding why I was WAY TOO EXCITED to go on a tour of the Marine Corps

Museum. You are a gem of a friend. Sarah Roberts: kindred spirit and endless support. Missy Wilmarth: say hi to the Navy SEALs for me (blowing kisses optional) and give a big hug to Jared Wilmarth, PS2 (U.S. Navy).

All my friends and family: there are so many of you who have supported me in these crazy past couple of years. Some of you fielded specific questions, offered encouragement, listened to me vent, beta-read, or did any number of things—thank you. My Twitter, blogger, Goodreads, and YA reader community: you make getting up to work every morning a joy. Thank you for your support and enthusiasm. Wesley Hughes, the "Amp4Life" (amp4life.blogspot.com): thank you for your amazing videos on life as an amputee. Your generosity is astounding and you helped me SO MUCH. This is what the Internet is for. My Allies: when shit goes down, I want you by my side—we make one intimidating army. Thank you for being my literary gun buddies. Group hug for the entire Vermont College of Fine Arts community, my home away from home and second family.

To my husband, Zach—*I've got you.* Thanks for being my wingman. This book broke my heart again and again, but you were always there to put it back together (TS&TM&EO). My mom, for showing me early on that girls can play too. You taught me to hold my head high and never stop fighting, which is why I'm here today, getting to Live My What. My dad, for winning the war inside and for teaching me cadences (and how to curse like a true Devil Dog). Thank you for sharing your story with me—I know it wasn't always easy to go back there. And, of course, my grandfather Dan Weeks, proud jarhead and first-rate Papa. I miss you every day. You were the epitome of *Semper Fidelis.*

To the men and women who serve, or have served, in the U.S. armed forces, and to the families of those who have been killed in combat or died as a result of PTSD-related injuries: each word of this book is a token of my gratitude for your service and an effort to honor those who have been lost. I'd like to take an extra moment of silence for the two former students at my high school, Clovis High, who died in combat: Spc. Thomas J. Mayberry (U.S. Army), who was killed in Afghanistan when he was only twenty-one, and Sgt. Steven M. Packer (U.S. Army), who was killed in Iraq. He was twenty-three years old.

Finally, to the Joshes out there: I wish you sleep without nightmares, laughter every day, cold beer on warm summer nights, and love—so much love.